T[illegible]e at

Shingle Cove

Also by Elise Darcy

The Living Apart Together series

Living Apart Together

It Takes 2 to Tango

Dear John

Love on the Rooftop

Standalone books

Lola & The Man

A Mallorcan Affair

The Villa in Sicily

We'll Meet Again

The Sunrise Coast series

New Beginnings at the Harbour Inn

The Secret of the Summerhouse

The Cottage by the Sea

The Guest House at Shingle Cove

The Houseboat by the Quay

Return to Willow Tree Cottage

The Bookshop of Memories

The Beach House

A Summer to Remember

The Guest House at Shingle Cove

A Novel

ELISE DARCY

Penny Lane Press

ISBN 978-1-913147-13-6

There are secrets in all families, you know. —**Jane Austen**

1

'What do you think, Dad?'

'Well, I will have to talk it over with your mother.'

Alice raised her eyebrows, wondering what was going on as she headed to the front door and picked up a letter the postman had put through the letterbox. She glanced into the lounge as she passed by. Jeffrey was standing with his back to the door talking to their daughter, Freya. She cast her gaze down at the letter. It was from another estate agent vying for their custom. No sooner had they instructed an estate agent to sell their home than all the local agencies had got wind of it. Alice stopped a few paces from the lounge and stared at the letter, thinking of a recent conversation she'd had with her only child.

'Why can't I be like you?' Freya had said.

'Because everything, including marriage, involves work, and you've never really wanted to work a day in your life,' she'd replied.

She rolled her eyes at the memory. She'd regretted what she'd said the moment it came out of her mouth. It wasn't true. Much to Alice and her husband's surprise, Freya had followed in her mother's footsteps and taken a degree in archaeology and anthropology. She'd continued beyond either Alice or her husband's qualifications and earned herself a master's degree. She was now doing a research thesis on the Middle East for a PhD. What Alice had meant by that comment about being workshy was that Freya still hadn't got a full-time job, and she was in her mid-twenties. She had volunteered at the Museum of Archaeology and Anthropology in Cambridge while doing her thesis, but she wasn't interested in a teaching position.

'Then what are you interested in?' Alice had barked at her one day. The expectation was that with her qualifications she would go into teaching.

'I don't know. I want to do something exciting like go on archaeological digs in the Middle East and have adventures and make discoveries,' Freya had replied.

Alice remembered thinking that Freya hadn't changed. She sounded like a nine-year-old. But then again, Alice recalled being where Freya was now, imagining she'd be on an archaeological dig in Egypt, unearthing something amazing, like an undiscovered Egyptian tomb. What she'd found instead was a fellow teacher, her husband Jeffrey, and a job teaching classical civilisation at the local high school. It was awful to diminish people's dreams, but she wondered when Freya would realise that at some point she'd have to get her head out of the clouds and find an ordinary job like everyone else.

Alice sighed. She'd thought Freya had turned a corner when she'd met Theo, a newly qualified solicitor working at a law firm in London. He'd been on a stag do in Cambridge with a friend, the groom-to-be who lived in the town, when he'd bumped into Freya in the street. He'd been drunk. It hadn't been the most auspicious start, but the next time they'd met had been at his best friend's wedding. It had turned out that Cambridge was a small world for Freya and Theo; they had a mutual acquaintance – the bride-to-be. And so, like all good romances, their relationship had started at a wedding. It wasn't long before they'd moved into a flat together and Freya had found a job. It was only part-time, but it meant she could continue her studies and they could save for their own wedding.

Then disaster had struck. Theo had been made redundant, their savings had run out, and they'd had to give up their flat. With his parents living hundreds of miles away in Spain, and the bills mounting up, the only option had been to move in with Freya's mum and dad two months ago. Now, Alice felt railroaded into a decision that was not of her choosing – selling the family home to give her daughter and future son-in-law that all-important deposit to get on the property ladder once they both had full-time jobs.

But then again, how could she say no? Their house in Cambridge, which they'd purchased over thirty years earlier, soon after they'd both qualified in teaching, was now worth a lot of money, even though they hadn't updated it in years. After a splurge in the eighties, the kitchen, bathroom, and their old furniture were now very dated. The problem for Alice was that things were moving at a pace she hadn't imagined when they'd marketed the house just a month earlier.

Secretly, she had been hoping they wouldn't get a buyer. It had shocked her when an offer had appeared on the table within a day of their first viewing. Had they put the property on the market priced too low? That had been her first thought. But the estate agent had reassured her that if there was lots of interest, then a potential bidding war was possible. Alice didn't like the thought of a bidding war. It sounded very cut-throat – not at all how they had bought the house. She remembered that they'd had two viewings with a lovely family member whose mother had passed away. It had all been very laid back. They had put in an offer a week after their second viewing, having mulled over all the pros and cons. The offer had been accepted, and the process had begun. No bidding wars, or gazumping, or investors to compete with. Just a family home being sold to a young couple starting out in life, looking forward to their future and raising a family in the house.

Jeffrey was hoping to get enough money out of the house sale to give their daughter a good leg-up on to the property ladder. Alice didn't disagree. But she was wondering what they would get out of the sale. Where would they live? And how much money would they set aside from the sale for a new home and their retirement? They were only sixty, and they had always known that they had the house to fall back on and sell to fund their retirement plans, although she'd always hoped it wouldn't come to that – and she hadn't thought they'd be funding their daughter in their lifetimes.

Alice smiled at Theo, who was emerging from the kitchen eating a slice of toast. At least that was one bright spot on the horizon. 'Job interview?' She looked him up and down. Alice was so used to seeing her daughter's fiancé in jogging pants and a t-shirt that she did a double-take. Theo was wearing a suit jacket and tie.

He nodded. 'Yeah, I'm hoping this is the one.'

Her smile faded. Unfortunately, she'd heard that one before. A newly qualified solicitor, he'd been made redundant from his first job as the firm restructured. It was a case of first in, first out.

His small redundancy payout had kept them going, along with Freya's wage from her new part-time job at the museum where she had previously volunteered.

'Good luck.'

Theo finished his slice of toast and Marmite as he walked upstairs. He still had jogging bottoms on, but the interviewers wouldn't know that. The first round wasn't being done face to face, but online. Alice shook her head. How things had changed. In her day, when she had first started out at work, she recalled going along to just one formal interview for a position.

Alice glanced at the briefcase by the door and frowned. Some people might imagine there were legal papers in that case. She knew better. Theo volunteered for a charity, doing pro bono work. It was something he was passionate about. He often said that if he won the lottery, that was what he'd do full-time – use his legal knowledge for the benefit of others without worrying about a wage. In between his pro bono work, which she knew he enjoyed, Theo fancied himself as a writer. Alice shook her head as she watched him walk up the stairs. She thought he should consign that dream to a point in the future, even to retirement, when he could afford to spend time writing.

Alice could speak from experience – not hers, but Jeffrey's. Her husband had dreamed of being a novelist before he settled down and faced reality; very few writers made any money, let alone earned a full-time wage from their endeavours. The trouble was that the news always highlighted the rare exceptions who hit the big leagues with their break-out novel. Alice knew it was her husband who encouraged Theo's interest in writing – Jeffrey's teaching career had been in creative writing.

Alice had recently retired from teaching after her subject,

classical civilisation, had all but disappeared from the curriculum, along with the dwindling number of secondary school students who wanted to study it. When she was still teaching, her hobbies in her spare time had been her pets and painting. She had always left work at the school gate.

Her dream to pursue a career in archaeology had been left behind completely. With few lecturing positions available, and a reluctance on her part to commit to further study once she and Jeffrey had bought their house (even though she'd known back then that she wouldn't get a position at a university without at least a master's degree), she'd taken a teaching post as a stopgap. It had turned into anything but. She had fallen into teaching in a secondary school, and that had been where she'd stayed, although it wasn't something she'd naturally enjoyed.

Her husband's career had been another story. He had desperately wanted to be a writer. He'd had a book of short stories published, but that was it. In an argument years earlier, when he was struggling with his first novel and coming to the realisation that it would never happen, she'd thrown the old saying at him, 'Those who can't, teach.' He wasn't cut out to be a novelist.

Teaching creative writing had therefore seemed especially apt in her husband's circumstances. It had started out as a temporary job. In the end, it had become a career he loved, with a little bit of regret thrown in that he would never be a writer of the material he taught. Jeffrey still taught creative writing part-time at a local further education college, and he'd been the first to encourage their daughter's boyfriend to write when he'd got to know Theo and realised he was a kindred spirit.

Alice wished Jeffrey hadn't planted an impossible dream in

Theo's head. She stared wistfully up the stairs, thinking about Freya. To get a mortgage, the young couple were reliant on Theo getting his foot back in the legal door. Her daughter wasn't getting a full-time job any time soon. Unlike Alice, Freya was pursuing her dream of becoming an archaeologist. From BA to MA, she was now registered for an MPhil in Archaeology at Cambridge, with the intention of progressing on to complete a PhD.

But she didn't want to be a lecturer. Teaching wasn't for her, which was why she worked at the Museum of Archaeology and Anthropology. Cataloguing artefacts, Freya dreamed of her big break, joining an Egyptian dig and visiting the Bibliotheca Alexandrina in Alexandria by the Mediterranean Sea. The new library had been built in homage to the Library of Alexandria that had been, until it was lost to antiquity, one of the largest libraries in the ancient world.

Alice turned from the lounge door, the estate agent's letter still in her hand, thoughts of Theo getting through the first round of interviews for the new position interrupted by the sound of Jeffrey still chatting to their daughter in the lounge. She recalled that first conversation over putting the house on the market. She'd been stunned by the suggestion at first, after they had worked all their lives for the house. It was all going to go to Freya in the end anyway. Why did Alice and Jeffrey have to turn their lives upside down now? She knew why. If Theo and Freya wanted to stay living in Cambridge, they needed a hefty deposit. The Bank of Mum and Dad had savings, but nowhere near enough to help them on the property ladder – unless they sold the house. Freya and her partner had been on track saving for a deposit, then along with Theo being made redundant, there had been a housing boom and prices had shot up way beyond their reach. They'd need more deposit money. And to top the situation off, as soon as the young couple's landlord had found out that Theo had lost his job, he had given them notice to quit because he'd wanted to sell up. And here they all were.

They had a lot riding on this sale; they'd had an offer accepted on a little cottage in Grantchester, a village walkable distance from Cambridge. There was also a lot riding on Theo getting another job, and more importantly, Alice agreeing to go through with selling the house.

Alice sighed. Freya and Jeffrey were talking about the property market yet again. They'd marketed the house just before Theo had lost his job. Unfortunately, even if Theo secured another position – and soon, so their mortgage offer wasn't withdrawn – getting a buyer so quickly on their own property in Cambridge would not do Freya and Theo any favours if Alice and Jeffrey didn't find a new place that suited them to buy. After so many years of living in the same property, finding another house to call home was going to be difficult, especially for Alice.

Although she'd thought she wanted her own space back when they all moved in, the fact was that she was enjoying living together with her family. She'd miss Theo, and she'd miss Freya walking in after a day at the museum, telling her all about her day, the new artefacts the museum had acquired, and how her PhD was going. Alice had even borrowed some of her daughter's books for her own course that she was starting, and had been enjoying chatting about their shared interest. It reminded her of when Freya used to live at home before she moved out.

Alice had never expected that Freya would have the same love of archaeology that she did. She couldn't talk to Jeffrey about it as she could talk to Freya. Of course, Jeffrey would listen, but she could tell he was only being polite. He wasn't all that interested, although he did like the sound of a trip to The Valley of the Kings in Egypt when he retired.

When Alice saw Theo and Freya together, cuddled up on the sofa, or getting ready for a date night at the theatre or cinema or a club, it reminded her of a time gone by – the time just before she and Jeffrey had bought this house, when they had gone on holiday to that guest house. The time before Freya arrived on the scene. 'You know, it doesn't sound a bad idea. We could get a little rental, travel, maybe even go on that round-the-world cruise I've had my eye on, or a road trip in a campervan.'

Alice stopped in her tracks as she passed the lounge door, her thoughts interrupted. *Run that by me again*, she felt like saying when she overheard her husband. She frowned. Had Freya suggested to Jeffrey that if they couldn't find something they wanted to buy, and put a chain together, then the solution was to sell up anyway and go into rented?

2

'That's settled then,' she heard Jeffrey say.

Settled? She stared at the door. Did he really think they were going to move into rented accommodation? Alice shook her head. When it came to their daughter, he was always the biggest soft touch.

Alice thrust the letter from the agent into her pocket and walked into the kitchen.

'Oh, Mum, I didn't realise you were up.'

She stared at Freya. Why did her daughter think she would still be in bed at nine o'clock in the morning? Maybe because she was retired. And she had been avoiding Freya since the house had gone on the market, feeling absurdly childish, as though it were Freya's fault. Which it was. In a way. But as Jeffrey had pointed out, why wait until they were six feet under to help their daughter out? Why not now?

Freya tucked a strand of her brown hair behind her ear. Alice couldn't decide whether it was the way she dressed, younger than her years, or her small, slight frame, but Freya, in her blue dungarees, checked shirt and Doc Marten boots didn't look in her mid-twenties, but in her late teens.

Freya cast her dark eyes over at her mother. 'I'm not sure this job is going to work out for Theo.'

'Really?' Alice was surprised. 'He didn't say anything to me. In fact, he seemed very upbeat this morning.'

'I just got this feeling. It's all about networking, y'know. We went along to the Christmas office party of the firm where he'd been made redundant. He thought it would be a good way to network, which is how he got this interview.'

Alice and Jeffrey exchanged a glance, reading in each other's expressions the same thought. Neither of them were sure what this had to do with his interview.

Freya frowned. 'I asked him what was going on but, typical Theo, he said he didn't want to talk about it. I did say I hoped it didn't have anything to do with those silly DNA kits that were handed out by the executive of the American company who was at the party. And before you ask, yes, it was the company he is having the interview with this morning.'

Alice turned to look at her husband. He'd gone as white as a sheet. Alice turned to look at Freya. 'What was that about a DNA testing kit?' Alice asked, hoping her nonchalant tone didn't betray her.

'Oh, it's all the rage in America to give these kits as presents. Just not Theo's thing. So, I reckon they're going to ask, and he probably won't lie and say we're going to use ours.'

Alice heard her husband breathe an audible sigh of relief. He said, 'I'm sure that won't affect his chances of getting the job.'

'Yeah, you're probably right. I suppose I'm just being paranoid that things won't go our way and he won't get another job just when we need it.'

Alice knew she was referring to buying their own place.

'Anyway, about selling the house. I know you haven't found anything you like yet …'

Alice frowned. It wasn't for want of looking. The trouble was that after living in their house for so long, it was going to be a wrench to leave. Besides, it wasn't as though she'd had a lot of time to get her head around the thought of moving, let alone putting the house on the market and going through with it. Now she felt under immense pressure to find somewhere.

Their buyers, a couple with a young family, were after moving in soon, so they could get the children settled into the local primary school. Alice was surprised it had sold so quickly. She was aware the house needed updating, but the young couple were looking for a home in Cambridge so they could settle down and raise their family, and they were happy to put their own stamp on the place. Alice liked that the house had been sold to a family rather than investors. However, it still didn't change the way she felt; it was all proceeding too fast.

'Look, Dad and I had an idea …' Freya said, looking at Alice sheepishly.

Alice had already overheard their idea about letting the sale go through and moving into rented. She caught Jeffrey throwing her a sheepish look, too. 'I overheard what you two were talking about. I am not moving into rental accommodation.' Alice had nothing against renting. It was the thought that they might never find something of their own that was the problem. That she might never find another house that she felt in her heart she could call home. She didn't want to settle in a rented house with the possibility that after six months, they would have to move again.

'Mum, be reasonable …'

Alice thought she was being very reasonable, agreeing to selling up in the first place. Jeffrey had persuaded her they should downsize, as he would be retiring soon too and it would help their finances. She could see the positives, at first – until she discovered there was nothing on the market she was interested in. She didn't even know where they would live. They could downsize and stay in Cambridge, but from what she'd seen, that might mean buying a flat, and after years of living in a house, Alice wasn't sure that was what she wanted. A change of location was looking more likely. But Alice loved Cambridge and didn't know where else in the country she would enjoy spending her retirement.

Alice thought of their buyers. That was another issue. They were a lovely couple. How could she possibly pull out of the sale now and take the house off the market? She wished she'd not been there when they viewed. She could tell they were besotted with the place.

She looked from Jeffrey to Freya. 'I don't want to have this conversation right now,' she said, walking to the door.

'But Mum, you've got to have it at some point.'

Alice walked out of the kitchen and across the hall of their double-fronted home to the lounge, almost tripping over one of the boxes in the hall. 'For goodness' sake!'

Jeffrey appeared at the door. 'Everything all right?'

She cast a black look in his direction. As soon as they'd put the house on the market, he had started packing, focusing on moving day even though they had nowhere to go.

Alice walked into the lounge. Wherever she looked and wherever she turned, she felt she was tripping over boxes. The prospect of moving into rented accommodation didn't feel right either. Everyone else was getting what they wanted out of the sale, even her husband.

Jeffrey followed her into the lounge, but quickly retreated to his study next door when she didn't answer his question. Of course everything wasn't all right, but she had a pang of guilt for making this difficult for him. The situation with Freya and Theo all living under one roof wasn't his fault. *He's just too quick to consider what's good for them and not for us*, thought Alice.

She knew he hadn't had a good year, and that this was what he needed too. He'd never brought up moving just so that he could take early retirement – but Freya had given him a reason to make that decision. She knew he wanted to leave teaching, perhaps finish that novel he'd started decades earlier, but they needed the money from his job until he retired. Releasing money from the house would mean he could stop work straight away.

They'd had the conversation. Jeffrey was no longer enjoying his job. A hefty chunk of his time now involved working on a laptop from home, teaching online. To save money, streamline courses and make them more accessible, the college had branched out into distance learning. He was finding the whole experience stressful. Jeffrey didn't like working on computers, although Alice reminded him that it was what he'd have to do if he wanted to write. Unless he was planning to crank out a novel on an old-fashioned typewriter.

In her heart, although she wouldn't tell him and burst his retirement dream. He might like the idea of being an author – but the reality was that he just wasn't the type to sit on his own for hours writing. Or doing anything, for that matter, that didn't involve meeting people face to face.

Jeffrey was a people person through and through. He missed

the face-to-face interaction with his students and the banter with his colleagues at work when his job had shifted online. He'd become withdrawn, agitated, unhappy. Mild depression, the doctor had said, brought on by stress. It wasn't uncommon with big changes in life, and that included his work life. But she had pointed out that even online he could see his students, chat to them. In time, perhaps he'd master the new system. She worried that he'd regret his decision to leave teaching altogether.

Alice sighed. Despite her doubts, he knew there was no going back. For her husband's health, and her daughter's and Theo's future, the house had to go.

3

Alice felt the sudden urge to run away from it all. Just the other day, she and Jeffrey had ended up having their first full-on row for as long as she could remember. It had been over his zealous packing.

Alice looked around the room, which, apart from the furniture, was now devoid of their personal effects. He'd even packed away the lamps and pictures. It was ridiculous. Their lounge didn't feel like their lounge any more without the personal mementos and the familiar framed photographs.

'I don't want to be here right now,' Alice whispered to herself. And in that moment, an idea formulated in her mind. She rushed out of the room and into the study, taking Jeffrey by surprise when she tapped him on the shoulder. He was sitting at his desk, his back to her, headphones on, preparing another online course. He took his headphones off and turned around in his swivel chair.

Alice said, 'I've got an idea.'

He smiled. 'I'm all ears. Is this about moving?'

'Well, sort of.'

'Okay, fire away.'

'How about we go away for a few days, maybe a week? We could book into a nice hotel, recharge our batteries.' *Get away from all this*, she thought. She frowned at her husband, who was already shaking his head.

'I know you don't break up for the February half-term until the day after tomorrow.' Alice knew the college holiday dates. 'You could take your work away with you. We could book something with Wi-Fi. That's the advantage of working online.'

He was still shaking his head. 'That's not it, Alice.'

She frowned at him. 'So, what's the problem?'

He rolled his eyes. 'There's still a lot to do.'

She grimaced. 'You're not talking about packing up the house, are you?'

'Well, of course. What else?'

Before she had a chance to say anything else, he added, 'I wrote a list and a schedule of where we need to be in two weeks' time.'

He sounded so nonchalant, as though he was planning a student lesson, not packing up their lives. 'You mean you're packing up more stuff?'

'Well, our buyers said they want to be in as soon as possible. They want their children to start their new school at least a couple of weeks before the end of term.'

'You mean before Easter? That's less than two months away!'

'That's what I mean. You can see where we've got to get our skates on.'

'So, what about us? Where will we spend Easter?'

'Well, it looks like we will be Freya and Theo's houseguests. Assuming, of course, he gets this job and their mortgage offer still stands.'

'You are joking. We didn't discuss this.' She halted, realising she'd obviously not overheard the full conversation between Jeffrey and their daughter. 'Oh, I get it.' It felt as though they'd been plotting behind her back.

'Look, if it takes us a bit longer to find a place, or a suitable rental, Freya is more than happy to put us up for a bit.'

'I bet she is,' scoffed Alice, thinking of Freya settling into her new home, the one that would come from the proceeds of her own house sale. 'I don't want to go into rented accommodation.'

'Oh, Alice, it won't be forever. Besides, if we get our skates on and keep looking, perhaps we will find our own place to buy.'

She wished he'd stop using that term, *get our skates on*. It was getting on her nerves.

'Now, you can see why we haven't got the time for a holiday. I've still got the loft to sort out. Besides, if any paperwork comes through from the solicitor, we both need to be around to sign it, otherwise it could hold up the sale.'

Alice couldn't care less about holding the sale up.

'And we wouldn't want Freya's house purchase to fall through, would we?'

She wanted to see Freya settled and happy. She looked at Jeffrey. 'No, of course I wouldn't want their sale to fall through.'

'Well, there you go. So, if we get our skates on, and get packed up, we can relax.'

Alice rolled her eyes, but she could see his point. He was right: if they packed everything up, they wouldn't have anything much to do if they suddenly exchanged contracts. Alice looked at the stack of empty flat-pack boxes that Jeffrey had spent an afternoon assembling. She walked over and picked up as many as she could carry. So far, she hadn't packed a single box.

Jeffrey watched her. 'What are you doing?'

She sighed. There was no good railing against the inevitable. 'I'll make a start in the loft.' Alice caught the surprised look on his face. She knew why. It was the first time she'd offered to help.

'Oh, that would be grand. I've just got some more lessons plans to get done, then I'll join you. We could do a trip down memory lane, while we're at it.'

Alice thought of all the stuff up there. Years of stored memorabilia and paraphernalia, half of which she couldn't even remember. She couldn't decide whether a trip down memory lane was a good idea or not.

She turned on her heel and walked out of the study, taking the narrow flight of stairs up to the first floor of their Victorian terraced home. On the landing, she put the boxes down and reached up, pulling a cord. The loft hatch opened and metal steps unfolded, giving easy access to their boarded loft. They no longer had to climb up there on step ladders like they had done for many years before they'd had the steps installed.

Alice flicked on a light switch. Fortunately, along with the metal stairs, they'd also had a light installed. The sixty-watt bulb was bright enough to illuminate the stairs without switching on the hall light. Alice took the boxes up to the loft and retreated back down the stairs, making her way to the ground floor to grab her warm winter coat, which was hanging on a hook by the front door. She'd forgotten how cold it could be in the loft in the winter.

As she headed back up into the loft space, Alice could see her breath like a little cloud. 'God, it's cold up here.' She hadn't thought to grab her scarf, gloves and hat too. She glanced around, her eyes alighting on a large trunk in the centre of the floor, surrounded by various overflowing boxes, a chest of drawers with an attached mirror – no doubt full of stuff too – and a long mirror she'd forgotten all about. Alice took the empty packing boxes over to the trunk and knelt in front of it. She opened the lid and clapped her hands. On the top of a pile of clothes was a red scarf, hat and gloves set, brand new and unworn; they were still in a cellophane wrapper. She vaguely remembered that someone had bought her the set for Christmas one year. It had been a nice thought, but red really wasn't her colour.

Alice didn't care about the colour now. She unwrapped them from their packaging. The material, chenille, was soft and luxurious. She draped the scarf around her neck, slipped the bobble hat on her head. She didn't want to think about what her hair would look like when she removed the hat. It reminded her she was due for a haircut and a colour. Her short, softly layered style was a warm chestnut colour, not far from the colour her hair had naturally been before it had turned grey a decade earlier. She knew her style framed her round face and full cheeks nicely and complemented her freckles.

She stood up and walked over to the long mirror, staring at her reflection. She was surprised to find that despite her misgivings, the red bobble hat actually suited her. Her gaze dropped to her face, and she studied the fine lines around her brown eyes. She touched her jowls. She no longer had the taut, smooth complexion of a young woman, but she knew she still looked younger than her sixty years. She shook her head gently, wondering where the years had gone.

She turned away from the mirror and crouched down by the trunk once more, picking up the gloves and slipping them on, trying to recall who had bought the set for her. She didn't have a large family; both her and her husband's parents had passed away. She didn't have any siblings. Her husband had a brother in Australia whom they barely saw. He and his family hadn't been back to England for years. Jeffrey had always wanted to fly over there and visit his brother, but it would be an expensive trip, and the years had just rolled on until he accepted it wasn't something they'd do until he retired. Alice supposed that was one positive thing about selling the house. They could finally make that trip.

Alice guessed it was probably Freya who had bought the scarf, hat, and gloves set. It wouldn't have been her best friend, Jane, who was another retired teacher. Alice and Jane went way, way back – back, in fact, to the happiest time in their lives, when they were all in their early twenties and on holiday on the Suffolk Coast.

Jane was also the only one who knew Alice and Jeffrey's secret.

4

Alice's thoughts turned to the blasted DNA kits that Theo and Freya had been given at the Christmas party. She really didn't want to think about that. Instead, she turned her thoughts to her best friend. She would have loved to speak to Jane about her house move. Unfortunately, at this time of year Jane and her husband always took a three-week holiday to Thailand for some winter sun. They'd been doing it for years, even when their two children were small. They could do it because once they'd had their children, Jane had only done supply work in schools. This gave them the flexibility to take the children with them to the Far East in February. They'd had to take the kids out of school, but it was in the days before it was frowned upon and parents were fined for doing this.

Jane had been gone for two weeks already. Alice smiled at the thought that she'd be back in a week. She couldn't wait. Jane already knew about her house move, but Alice wanted to chat about it anyway.

She turned her attention to the task at hand and thought she'd start by sorting the contents of the trunk out. She reached for one of the empty boxes and pulled it towards her, wondering why it was suddenly feeling heavy when she'd hadn't filled it yet. She turned to look inside, and a furry head popped up, meowing at her loudly.

'Oh, crumbs!' exclaimed Alice in surprise. 'What are you doing up here?' She knew very well what Marley was doing there. He'd followed her into the loft. She didn't know why she was acting all surprised. On the rare occasions she ventured up there, he always followed. In fact, he'd follow anyone up there, given half a chance.

Alice lifted him out. He was a cross between a moggy and a long-haired Maine Coon. His long hair always stood on end as though he'd plugged a paw into an electric socket and given himself a shock. She held him up. 'You gave me a bit of a fright, do you know that?' She smiled at him. He was one of those cats that seemed to look permanently grumpy, as though he'd got out of the wrong side of the bed every morning. He scrambled out of her hands and dived back into the box.

'All right, you have that one and I'll use this one,' she said, reaching for the other box. She watched him for a moment, settling down in the bottom of the box for a nap. He was three years old; she'd got him as a kitten from a rescue centre as a present to herself when she'd decided on early retirement last year. She'd made the decision to retire when she'd realised that her job search was futile. There were no classical civilisation teaching jobs out there. Jeffrey had suggested that she could do some classes in I.T. and teach that instead. Alice hadn't been interested. She hadn't even really been that interested in getting another pet. She'd only popped to the rescue centre with Jane, who had been looking to rehome a dog. Alice hadn't expected to walk home with a rescue pet herself – and a cat, at that.

'I thought you were a dog person,' she recalled Jane commenting. 'And how is Hester going to react to the new addition?'

As if on cue, Alice heard a low, guttural woof coming from the bottom of the stairs. She got up and walked over to the loft hatch. Hester woofed excitedly when she saw her.

She smiled at the beagle. 'What are you doing down there?' She'd thought Hester was asleep in her favourite spot on the sofa in the lounge. The dog sat down, her big brown eyes looking up at Alice. She wagged her tail and woofed.

Alice shook her head. 'You're not allowed to come up here too,' she said as Hester put her two front paws on the bottom step.

'No!' Alice admonished her dog.

Hester whined.

'Hester – bed!'

Hester took her front paws off the step and slunk away, head bowed.

Alice stared after Hester until the dog disappeared. She heard her familiar *thump, thump, thump* as she ran down the stairs. Hester was Alice's pet too. She wasn't a young dog; she was now twelve years old. Jeffrey had bought her for Freya, who had been asking for a puppy since she was seven years old. The problem was that by the time Jeffrey bought Hester, Freya was thirteen years old and not all that interested in the new addition to the family. She was too interested in music, makeup and boys – although for the first few weeks, Freya showered the cute puppy with attention and was rewarded with a wagging tail and Hester following her wherever she went.

Alice recalled the other reason Jeffrey had chosen that moment to get Freya a puppy. She had been going through a tough time in her new secondary school. Freya, unlike her close circle of friends, had been given a coveted place in the local grammar school. While her friends were walking to their local comprehensive, she was being bused thirty minutes away to the 'posh' school, as her friends called it, on the other side of town, out in a magnificent country setting. But things had not all been plain sailing when she first started; she had been the odd one out in having to fit in and make new friends.

It was only a few months after getting the puppy, though, that Freya had turned a corner. She had made friends and settled down at her new school. She spent less and less time with Hester until one day Alice realised she spent more time with the dog than any other family member – walking her, feeding her, taking her to the vet. Alice had realised that Hester was, in fact, now her dog. She probably always had been.

Marley interrupted Alice's thoughts by jumping around in the box, chasing his tail. Alice turned to the trunk and starting sorting through old clothes. She was surprised that some weren't old at all, just items no longer in fashion. She vaguely remembered having a clear-out the previous year. Perhaps they were bound for the charity shop and Jeffrey had put them up there by mistake. Now she wondered why she'd thought of getting rid of them. They might be the fashion from last year, or most likely the year before, but the clothes were actually nice, well-made and in pleasing muted colours she could imagine wearing again.

She liked the cords. There were several pairs in brown, grey and pale blue, with jumpers to match, along with checked cotton shirts that made up the sets. She looked at the jumpers and felt like putting one on. It was still freezing up there; the warmth of the centrally heated house below was not wafting up through the loft hatch as she had expected. In fact, she realised that if she didn't close the loft hatch, the cold air up there would waft downstairs.

Alice reached over and pulled a cord. She watched the metal steps fold up and the loft hatch click shut. She could get down at any time by releasing the cord. Alice turned to the trunk and found Marley nestled in the clothes, making himself comfortable. 'Hey!' She picked him up and got a loud, disgruntled meow and a swipe at her hand with his claws.

'We'll have none of that!' Alice said, putting him back in his box. She picked up one of the cosy, soft woollen jumpers. It was little wonder Marley had been making himself comfortable in them. There were several of them folded in a neat pile of varying autumnal colours – rust red, brown, leaf green and beige. She got off her knees and held one up in front of the mirror to determine if it would still fit, although she knew she didn't really need to. Her weight had fluctuated very little since she'd retired. When she had been a teacher, it had been a different ballgame. She had always been snacking and picking at things at home and at work. Her weight had ballooned. She had always known the cause; she had been bored and unhappy in her job.

Now, after being retired for the past year, she had been happy – until the family had got it in their heads to sell the house. Alice had been renewing a deep-seated interest she'd had since she did her degree – archaeology. She'd been visiting museums in London and Cambridge and had started to think about doing an MA; something she wished she'd pursued years earlier, after completing her degree. But she'd met Jeffrey instead, a teacher five years older than her, and had immediately started teacher-training. Her goal had been to buy a family home and have children. Alice stared wistfully off into space. If it hadn't been for Freya coming along …

She cut that thought off; the thought that she might have returned to education to study for a PhD and then become an archaeologist. But that dream had not materialised. The fact was that Freya *had* come along, and Alice didn't regret it one bit.

She smiled at her reflection. The jumper was lovely. However, it was a bit on the snug side; she wondered whether the previous year, before she'd retired, she had perhaps asked Jeffrey to consign these clothes to a spot in the loft and had then forgotten all about them.

She got the pile of jumpers out of the trunk and wondered what she was going to do with them. She was about to put them in one of the cardboard packing boxes when her eyes alighted on some old suitcases. Jeffrey had inherited them from his parents along with some odd pieces of furniture, a standard lamp, and various old, framed pictures, all of which he'd stashed in the loft.

Jeffrey wasn't a hoarder, but he found it difficult to let go of anything that had some sentimental value, which was the reason the loft was full to the rafters and he'd left it until last to have a clear-out. They couldn't take all this stuff with them to another place. As much as she liked a good few pieces of the furniture, and even the pictures, they were meant to be downsizing. Where would it all go?

She walked over to the suitcases, which were sitting on top of another trunk. There were three; small, medium and large. Made of leather, they were rectangular and boxy with old-fashioned buckles rather than zips. There were worn stickers of bygone destinations that were no longer legible. Jeffrey's parents had begun travelling when package holidays had started back in the fifties. At the time, going to Greece or Spain was considered both fashionable and exotic.

Alice smiled. She could just make out one of the stickers – *Costa Del Sol.* She took the medium-sized suitcase down and sneezed. She had brought a duster with her. She placed the case on the floor by the trunk, dusted the top, and unbuckled the straps. She opened the case, lifting the heavy lid up and over. It hit the wooden floor with a thud. She sat back in surprise. The case wasn't empty. Inside was one of her sketches. She recognised it immediately. She hadn't sketched for years. When she'd retired, she'd thought that was what she'd do – rekindle another hobby she'd enjoyed years and years earlier.

She carefully lifted out the sketch, which she'd completed on canvas. It was lying on crepe paper. She thought Jeffrey must have found it lying around in the loft and put it away in the suitcase so that it didn't get damaged – although she might well have just taken these old cases to the tip without bothering to check inside. Alice stared at the canvas. She imagined her idea was to use colour and paint on the canvas, using the sketch as a template for the painting.

Alice recalled where she'd completed the sketch, years earlier, when she and Jeffrey were newlyweds. She recalled her surroundings vividly. She'd been standing on the beach with an easel. Instead of looking out to sea with the beach and sea view, and a fishing boat, or two, bobbing on the water on the horizon, she'd turned inland to face the house where they were staying. It was on a beautiful, unspoilt stretch of Suffolk coastline just a two-hour drive from London. It was a red-brick detached Victorian house, at the end of a street that led to a shingle cove, and it was the most picturesque place she'd ever stayed.

She remembered what she'd been thinking at the time; that she had captured a wonderful likeness of the house. She had been intending to use vibrant pastel watercolours and paint the guest house that sat almost on the beach. But her painting was going to reinterpret what the old place might have looked like in its heyday, before it had ended up with peeling paint, rotting windows and shutters hanging from rusty hinges.

She stared at the sketch, an idea formulating in her mind.

5

Alice glanced at Marley, who was sitting in the open suitcase. He meowed at her. She shook her head at him. Marley had found something far better than an old cardboard box. She rolled her eyes at him as he played with the crepe paper left in the bottom, tearing it to shreds before chasing the pieces around the bottom of the case.

She left him to his fun and turned to take the larger case down from on top of the trunk, wondering if there was anything inside. It was empty. She placed it on the floor by the trunk and turned her attention back to the sketch, wondering if she'd ever finish it. She stood it up on the chest of drawers against the mirror so she could stand back and take it in.

Alice sighed as she turned from the sketch, thinking back to those carefree days before Freya. She frowned as she walked over to the trunk with the medium-sized suitcase still on top. She started filling the suitcase with jumpers, some smart woollen skirts she'd forgotten about, a tweed jacket – green but rather nice – and a pair of fur-lined boots. They must have been in fashion a few years earlier. Not that Alice was into buying something just because it was fashionable. She picked up the corduroy trousers, and decided, in the spirit of saving money, to see if she could still fit into those too.

She was just holding them up to see if she could find the size label when she heard voices down below.

'You can see how that would be a problem, don't you?'

Alice frowned. That was Theo's voice.

'Theo, I'm sure my dad will find a suitable rental. You're worrying out of hand.'

Alice lowered the trousers. That was Freya.

'I'm not worrying out of hand.'

Alice moved closer to the loft hatch. By the sound of their voices, they'd been walking up the stairs on the way to their bedroom and had stopped right below the loft hatch.

'You're right, Freya, your dad will find a rental, but will it allow pets? I don't think he's thought of that – do you?'

Alice stared at the loft hatch. *What were they saying?*

'Yes, I don't expect they've rented for years,' Theo added. 'It won't be easy finding one that allows pets.'

It had never crossed Alice's mind that her pets would be a problem.

'*A* pet?' Freya snorted. 'Do I need to remind you? Mum hasn't just got one pet – she's got three!'

'I'm sure Percy would be no trouble,' Theo said.

'Are you joking with me right now?' Freya's voice had gone up an octave.

'Okay, look, if our purchase goes through—'

'Did you just say *if*?'

'Calm down. I meant *when*, we could look after the pets until—'

'No.'

'Oh, come on Freya, it's the least we could do. After all, they are selling their house to buy you one. They don't have to, you know.'

Alice stared at the loft hatch.

'Just because they're your parents, they don't owe you anything.'

'It's not that. Of course, I'd have them to stay. It's just …'

'It's just … what?'

'This is their home? What if … well, what if Mum and Dad can't find a suitable place and the pets have to ... go?'

'Go?'

'Be re-homed.'

Re-homed? Alice looked crossly at the loft hatch. That possibility had never entered her head.

'There is an answer to that,' said Theo.

'Which is …?'

'Well, they could stay with us … permanently.'

We're selling my home, Alice thought. *You're not taking my pets too!*

'Oh, Theo, that's a lovely thought. And I know how attached you are to them, but …'

'But … what?'

'Well, what if we want to go travelling?'

Alice sat waiting to hear what they said next.

'I take it you're not talking about a two-week holiday abroad?'

Alice could hear Theo's tone change.

'Well, what if I need to go on an archaeological dig somewhere?'

'You mean to Egypt.'

'Yes.'

'Oh, we're not back to that again. When do you think that's

going to happen? And besides, even if it did, I'm not exactly going to drop everything and go with you – am I?'

Alice didn't hear Freya respond. She'd heard them having words since they'd come to live there. Alice knew Theo just wanted Freya to settle down and stick with her part-time job at the museum. The problem was, she knew her daughter. She was meant to be getting married, settling down. But how much was this house-buying business what Freya really wanted?

The sound of Marley jumping out of the box stalled the conversation about her pets that Alice wished she hadn't heard.

'What was that?' Theo asked. 'It's coming from the loft.'

Alice reached for Marley, chasing a bit of crepe paper along the floor, and scooped him up.

'I expect it's a rodent or something up there.'

Or something, thought Alice, looking at Marley's grumpy cat face.

'So, aside from whatever travelling you think you're going to do …'

Alice got the vibe that, like her, Theo thought Freya's talk of archaeological digs abroad in far-flung places was a pipe dream. 'So, do you think we could still take the pets in?' he said. 'You could have a word with your dad and suggest it.' Theo was back to talking about Alice's pets again.

Alice sat there frowning as their voices faded and a door shut down the hall. She gave Marley a kiss and put him down on the floor, rustling the crepe paper. Paws pounced on the paper. 'I tell you what, Marley, I'll let go of this house, but I am not re-homing you or Hester – or Percy.'

Alice was about to open the loft hatch when she heard a bedroom door open. She listened as Freya and Theo walked out of the bedroom. 'I've got to leave for work, Theo, but I want to have a word with Dad first.'

'Fine,' Theo replied.

She waited a few moments before pulling the cord and watched the loft hatch open and the stairs unfold. Alice looked at the suitcase full of clothes, then at the other two suitcases. A quick glance through the chest of drawers, and the discovery of more items of clothing – and shoes – made her pause before climbing down the stairs. She filled the other two cases with various garments, nearly shutting Marley inside one when he nestled in the clothes when she wasn't looking.

Alice shut the cases. She would donate some of the clothes to a local charity, along with the suitcases. But she needed help to get them down from the loft.

6

Alice turned towards the loft hatch and made her way down the steps. She stepped off the bottom rung and called out softly, 'Marley!'

He was standing at the hatch, his grumpy face looking down at her.

'Come down now. I'm not coming up to get you.' Alice decided that they could bring the suitcases down when Jeffrey sorted through the loft. She wanted to close the loft hatch. As usual, Marley wasn't playing ball. His head disappeared. Alice frowned. 'Just great.' She made her way downstairs, wondering if Jeffrey was still in his study. If she was going up there to fetch the cat, they might as well bring the cases down between them.

She walked past the lounge and kitchen to the study. The door was ajar. As she neared, she could hear voices. 'If you think she's going to rehome those pets …'

'I think you need to talk to her, Dad. I mean what landlord is going to entertain *three* pets?'

Alice halted a few paces from the door.

'What exactly do you expect me to say? That's she's got to get rid of them?'

'Not all of them. Perhaps two?' Freya suggested.

Alice stared at the door with a black look. What had happened to them looking after all three of them?

'Maybe keep Hester because she's old and well, she's a dog. I think maybe landlords won't mind dogs.'

Alice shook her head. Jeffrey wouldn't ask her to choose, surely? Besides, there was no way she was getting rid of her pets. Jeffrey knew that.

'Look, I'll ask your mother. Who knows what we'll end up buying. It might be a flat with no garden, not suitable for a dog.'

'Or a high rise,' Freya interjected. 'Then she couldn't take Marley.'

Alice's mouth dropped open. She couldn't believe he'd suggested—

'Perhaps now is the time to declutter everything in our lives – even the animals.'

'She could keep Percy. He could live anywhere.'

Oh, thanks a bunch, thought Alice, listening to them making decisions about her pets. She knew what this was about; despite Theo's keenness to take the animals in – she knew how attached he was – in the back of her mind, Freya was thinking about what would happen if her job took her abroad. Theo might go too if he got a job that had offices around the world. Right now, Alice didn't want this conversation. In fact, she wasn't even going to entertain bringing it up.

She started to back away from the door and bumped straight into Theo. Had had his back to her, and was closing the kitchen door with his foot.

'Oh, sorry Mrs B. Didn't see you there.'

She turned around to discover that he had another plate of

toast in one hand and a cup of coffee in the other. 'How did the interview go?'

He looked at his watch. 'It's not for another hour. Just going upstairs to start work.' Theo had recently secured a position working in insurance, but he was still applying for better paid positions in legal firms. The trouble was, he often worked remotely from home. *Her home.*

She caught Theo glancing toward Jeffrey's study and followed his gaze. When she looked back at him, he was staring at her sheepishly. 'Well, er, I'd better crack on.'

She stepped forward. 'Can you do something for me in a minute, Theo?'

'Of course, sure, anything.'

She smiled at him. He'd been the only dissenting voice in the plan to get rid of her precious pets. 'Why don't you have your toast and coffee first?'

He returned her smile. 'You know where to find me.'

She frowned at his back as he walked up the stairs, then retreated to the kitchen. Hester was asleep by the Aga. She knelt down and stroked the dog's soft ears. 'How would you like a little holiday?'

Hester woofed.

Alice put a finger to her lips in a shushing motion. 'We have to keep it quiet.' She got out her mobile phone and Googled a local taxi company. *This is stupid*, she thought. *I have no idea where I can go with three pets.* She realised that perhaps Freya had a point.

Alice cast that dreadful thought to one side. None of her pets were young. This was their home, or wherever *she* was. It was bad enough that she felt she was being turfed out of her own house, without them losing their home, and their owner, too.

Alice walked up the stairs and knocked on the bedroom door at the end of the hall.

'Come!'

Alice rolled her eyes and walked inside. It had been the spare bedroom until Theo had taken it over and turned it into another home office. She cast her gaze over the modern corner desk, state-of-the-art black leather office chair and desktop computer with two screens. His set-up looked like something out of a NASA control room.

'Can you help me down with something from the loft?'

'The loft?'

She looked at him. He was staring at her as though she'd just asked him to go with her to Timbuktu.

'Oh, okay,' he replied. 'I have to warn you, though, I'm not good with heights.'

'The foldaway stairs are perfectly stable, I can assure you.' She knew that wasn't the point, but she needed his help. 'Besides, you won't have to get in the loft. I just need to hand something down.'

He polished off his toast as they talked. Standing up, he wiped sticky fingers down his tracksuit bottoms and followed her out of the door.

Alice pulled the cord. She could hear raised voices downstairs and guessed that Jeffrey and Freya were still in a heated debate about what they were doing with her pets.

Just as she was thinking of the animals, Alice heard Marley meowing from deep inside the loft.

Theo heard the cat, too. 'How did he get up there?'

'I was sorting through some stuff for the house move. It's some suitcases I need you to help me bring down.'

'Sure thing, Mrs B.'

Alice looked at him. She wished he wouldn't call her that. It sounded very … American, like she was in a sitcom.

'Do you want me to help get the cat?'

'Ah, no, I've got that covered.' She turned to the airing cupboard on the landing, opened the door and found the cat carrier on the floor beneath the shelves full of towels. The reason they stored it there was so they could get the cat down from the loft whenever they ventured up there and he followed.

Alice walked up the steps with the carrier under her arm, pushing it through the hatch before she got up there herself. She turned around. Theo was halfway up the steps. 'If I pass you these, do you think you can manage?' She pulled one of the cases towards her. They weren't heavy. She guessed why. The cases were quite shallow compared to modern suitcases, so a lot less clothing fitted inside.

Theo nodded, holding out a hand for one of the cases.

Alice slid the case forward through the hatch and kept hold of the end until Theo said, 'I've got it!'

Two more cases and a cat in a carrier later, Alice was about to exit the loft when she caught sight of the sketch propped up on the dresser. Shingle Cove – that was where the property was located. It wasn't a place she could forget in a hurry.

'Are you alright up there, Mrs B?'

Alice rolled her eyes. 'Yes, I'm coming.' She left the sketch where it was and was moving towards the hatch when she heard a meow.

'Drat!' Theo exclaimed from the bottom of the steps. He called out. 'I let the cat out and didn't expect him to scoot back up!'

Marley's head popped up. Before Alice could grab him, he darted between her legs and made off towards the spot where the old suitcases had been.

Alice rolled her eyes again. It was her fault for not telling Theo that Marley had to be kept in the cat carrier until the loft hatch was closed, otherwise he'd be back up like a shot. And here he was, causing mischief again. She walked over to see what had grabbed his attention. He was trying to get a lid off a box with his paw.

It looked like a shoebox had fallen behind the cases. She hadn't noticed it when she'd shifted the cases, as she'd been too busy packing them with clothes from the trunk. She didn't remember there having been a shoebox in the loft, but then there was lots of stuff, and she hadn't been up there in an age. In fact, when she thought about it, Jeffrey always appeared to discourage her from going up there. He always said it was because he didn't want her to do herself an injury going up and down the steps.

She picked up the box. 'What have we here?' It was an old Adidas shoe box. She recalled that Adidas had been the make of the first pair of trainers her husband had bought years earlier, when they were first married, intending to start jogging. He never had gone jogging. *This can't be the same box, surely*, she thought, opening it. An inquisitive cat nose peered inside.

'Oh.' Alice stared at the contents in surprise. The box contained envelopes addressed to her husband. The envelopes contained cards – and not just any old cards; they were birthday cards and Christmas cards. She opened one. Then another. And another. Some were addressed to Jeffrey, others to Jeffrey and Freya. *What the hell?*

'Mrs B?'

'I'll be right there,' Alice snapped, annoyed by the interruption. She returned her attention to the shoebox and the cards inside. Picking them out one by one, she realised they were all from a woman called Wendy. 'Wendy?' Alice looked at Marley. 'Who the hell is Wendy? And how does she know my husband?'

She'd never seen any of these birthday or Christmas cards before. And she was sure Freya hadn't either; she would have said something. Some cards dated back years; she could tell by the yellowed envelopes that some were from when Freya was little. There were also some empty envelopes, which suggested to Alice that this woman called Wendy had also written Jeffrey some personal letters.

How long had this been going on? If Wendy was just a friend from years earlier, before she and Jeffrey had met – a friend that Jeffrey had kept in touch with – why hide the cards? Why even keep them?

Alice was even more surprised to discover that one envelope still contained a letter addressed to her husband.

Frustratingly, the handwritten note had faded so much over time it wasn't legible, but what she did discern was that the letter had been written on headed paper from that guest house; the one she had sketched all those years ago – the address hadn't faded. Alice looked at her cat.

Marley's grumpy face looked up at her as if to say, *What are you looking at me for?*

Alice walked over to the open loft hatch. 'I need that cat carrier.'

'Sure, Mrs B.'

'And will you stop calling me Mrs B. It's Alice.'

'Sure thing, Mrs … er, Alice.'

Theo handed up the cat carrier.

Marley played his usual catch-me-if-you-can, hide-and-seek, game as soon as he spotted the cat carrier.

After Marley had given her the run-around for five minutes, Alice cornered him and whisked him into the carrier. Handing it down to Theo, she switched off the light and exited the loft with the shoebox tucked under her arm, intent on confronting her husband over what she'd discovered in the loft.

'So, where would you like me to put the cases and the cat?' He looked towards her bedroom.

'Outside.'

Theo did a double-take. 'Excuse me?'

'In the porch.'

'The cat too?'

Alice nodded. 'The cat too.' She had two more things to fetch, but first she needed to pack an overnight bag with some smalls and toiletries; things the cases didn't contain. Then she was going to confront Jeffrey and find out who Wendy was, and then she was going on a little trip – on her own. *Well, not quite*, she thought when she saw Hester the beagle run into the room. 'Hello, you. I thought you were asleep in the kitchen?'

Hester woofed once.

Alice smiled at her. *Woof* for no, *woof, woof* for yes. It was astounding, but it was as though Hester understood every word.

Once Alice had packed her overnight bag, she carried it downstairs with the shoebox of cards and envelopes tucked under her arm. She passed the front door and saw the suitcases stacked outside in the porch. She could hear Marley meowing. As she approached the study, she half-expected to find Jeffrey and Freya still talking about them going into rented accommodation and what they would do about the pets. That was why her pets were coming with her on her trip. She would not put it past them to rehome the animals while she was gone. She couldn't imagine Jeffrey doing that, but then again, Freya could be very persuasive when she put her mind to it.

'Jeffrey has gone out.'

Alice whirled around at the sound of Theo's voice. She glanced in his study. One wall was full of books – some were on creative writing, but most of the space was taken up by his collection of favourite books. She stared at the bookshelves, recalling Jeffrey once saying that writers need to read. She also recalled asking, 'Don't writers have to put pen to paper or fingers to typewriters and actually write too?' He had known it was a subtle dig at that unwritten novel he had still been intent on writing.

She turned around to look at Theo. 'Where did he go?'

'They went to the estate agents.'

Alice frowned at him. 'What – *our* estate agents?' By that, she meant the agents that were selling their house.

Theo pursed his lips. 'I believe so. From what Freya told me while you were up in the loft, it sounds as though a place has come on the market around Cambridge, smaller than this, but the estate agent rang to say if you were interested, to get in as quick as possible for a viewing before the place is advertised.'

Alice creased her brow. 'Why didn't he ask me to go with him?' She noted those pursed lips again, as if Theo was hiding something.

Alice folded her arms, waiting for an explanation.

Theo avoided eye contact. 'Well … er … the truth is, Jeffrey said that every house you viewed together, you had already made up your mind before you walked through the door.'

'Made up my mind about what?'

Theo shuffled nervously from one foot to another. 'Well, it was as if you'd decided that you wouldn't like it. Because it wasn't Melrose Place.'

Alice stared at him. 'What's wrong with Melrose Place?'

'Well, nothing, but he thinks you are comparing every street and house to where you live.'

'I like it here,' said Alice indignantly. 'What's wrong with liking where you live?'

'Nothing – unless you like it so much that unless something smaller comes up in the same street, you are just not going to find what you're looking for.'

She stared at him. That sounded just like something Freya would say. Although she would not admit that he had a point. She did like her home so much that she couldn't imagine living anywhere else in Cambridge. *Then look somewhere else,* a little voice in her head said.

She brushed that thought aside. She had looked in Grantchester, where Theo and Freya were buying, but properties seemed to come up so rarely there. That was why Theo and Freya were so keen on Alice and Jeffrey's sale not falling through – but the couple whose offer they had accepted had already sold up and gone into rented accommodation. Everyone knew that the only way the sale would fall through was if Alice and Jeffrey withdrew the house from the market.

Alice frowned. 'So, Freya went with him?'

She knew by Theo's expression that she had.

'Um right, well, I've got some work to do,' he muttered.

Alice watched him sidle out of the door. Her eyes dropped

to the box in her hands. She walked over to her husband's desk, put the box down and picked up a pen from his neatly arranged stationery organiser. She scribbled a quick note, looked around for an envelope, couldn't find one, and so folded the paper over. She stalked out of the room but couldn't decide where to leave it. What if it went missing – what if it was picked up and tossed in the bin? She shook her head; that wouldn't do at all. She went upstairs and knocked on Theo's door. She walked straight in, not waiting for a reply.

'Ah, Mrs B – everything all right?'

All right? Alice glared at him. She'd nearly tripped over a box on her way along the hall. Her home was being dismantled around her.

'Mrs B?'

Alice stared at the note, lost in thought. She looked up and frowned, remembering what she'd knocked on his door for. 'Can you give this to Jeffrey?'

'Er … sure.'

Alice guessed he was probably thinking, *Why couldn't she give it to him herself?* Although he didn't ask.

He took the note, and she watched him put it on his desk. 'Good. Right. Well, I'll see you later.'

'You're going out, Mrs B?'

'Yes.'

'Oh, okay.'

Alice glanced at the note on his desk before leaving the room and shutting the door behind her. She paused in her bedroom for the novel on the bedside table before heading down the stairs. She put her coat on and phoned for a taxi before calling out, 'Hester!'

Her dog trotted out from the kitchen. Alice smiled at her. 'Good girl! Fancy going on a holiday to the coast? One woof for no, two woofs for yes.'

Woof, woof.

Alice grinned. 'Well, aren't you a dog after my own heart?' She took the lead hanging from the row of coat hooks by the door and attached it to Hester's collar. Her pets would need food, but she couldn't take that with her too. She opened the front door, walked out into the porch and looked at Marley's grumpy face. He was sitting in the cat carrier on top of the suitcases. 'I know you don't like it in there, but I'm not leaving you here.'

Thinking of leaving her pets, Alice said, 'Oh, my!' She'd almost forgotten Percy. As a cab pulled up outside the house, she rushed back inside, down the hall, and into the lounge.

A moment later, she was back in the porch, holding a birdcage.

'Nice bird,' commented the taxi driver as he approached. 'Last time I saw a parrot was in the zoo. He's very colourful.'

Yep, thought Alice, *Percy is colourful, and so is his language.* She willed Percy to keep his beak shut and not offend the driver. She'd had the presence of mind to grab a cotton tea towel from the kitchen on her way out of the door. She pushed the birdcage across the back seat of the cab, over to the left, then got in and threw the tea towel over it. She sat down in the middle seat and got Hester to sit on her lap. The taxi driver put the cat carrier in on her right and shut the door before putting her bags in the boot. She could hear Marley hissing at Hester. It didn't help that the silly beagle kept sniffing the top of the carrier.

Alice gently moved Hester's muzzle. 'When will you ever learn? You'll end up with a sore nose if he scratches you.' Hester had already been nine years old when Alice had brought Marley home. Hester had accepted the new addition to the family, trying her best to make friends. Unfortunately, Marley hadn't wanted to, and that was the way it had remained. She glanced at Marely, who was hissing at Hester. Alice knew what the problem was. Marley was stuck in a cage and Hester was not – although Marley had been ever so grumpy and out of sorts lately anyway. 'Stop that, Marley,' Alice admonished him. She grabbed the tea towel from Percy's cage and threw it over the cat carrier.

Percy squawked, 'Fat bald man.'

Alice caught the bald taxi driver glancing at her in the rear-view mirror. 'What was that?'

'Oh, nothing, just the silly bird talking gibberish!'

Alice averted her gaze, throwing the parrot a black look. Percy was older than Hester. He'd learnt a lot of his early vocabulary from their then young daughter, who had spoken her mind at every opportunity. Percy had retained the rude, choice words and always managed to repeat them at just the wrong moment, as though he wasn't just parroting, but knew exactly what they meant. It was like he was doing his best to offend people and embarrass her. She threw the tea towel over his cage again. She was beginning to wonder if she should have left Percy at home. She felt mean for thinking that perhaps it wouldn't be a bad thing if Percy was re-homed. The thought had crossed her mind every time he was rude.

Half an hour later, she wondered whether, with hindsight, it was ridiculous to take them all with her. But she wasn't turning back. She looked at her handbag, wondering when Jeffrey would get home, get her note, and ring her up to explain himself regarding Wendy – and ask where she was off to. No doubt

Theo would fill him in about the suitcases that were now missing from where he had put them in the front porch. And it wouldn't be long before they'd notice that the pets were missing too.

7

'Don't worry, I'll Google it.' The taxi driver had pulled over when he realised his fare didn't have the full address. He needed the postcode for the Satnav. 'The Guest House at Shingle Cove?'

'That's the one,' said Alice, feeling quite foolish that she'd phoned for a taxi and left without even checking the guest house still existed. She shook her head. She'd been so consumed with thoughts of the letters addressed to her husband, and so annoyed that he wasn't around for her to confront him, that she'd just left without thinking about the practicalities. She had visions of the taxi driver turning around and driving his dotty passenger home.

'Ah, here we are.'

Alice looked over his shoulder at the photo on the phone. 'Oh, my god – that's it! That's the guest house!' She was actually quite shocked that the property looked just the same, although she could tell it had been updated and modernised. And it was *still* a guest house. But did they have vacancies? She hadn't even checked. And how long would she be staying? Forever, if she found out that Jeffrey had had an affair.

'Ah, here we are – oh!' the taxi driver exclaimed.

'Aren't there any vacancies?'

'There are vacancies. Not surprising this time of year.'

Alice glanced out of the window. The people walking past were wearing thick coats, gloves, hats and scarves to protect against the wind. It was February. She knew the taxi driver meant it wasn't a traditional time of year to get away within the UK.

As if reading her thoughts, he turned round in his seat and replied. 'People are hunkering down, unless they're getting away to somewhere warm.'

She caught his far-off expression, and imagined he'd much rather be on a beach – somewhere hot and exotic rather than here in Britain, in the cold and damp.

For Alice, this wasn't just about getting away. It was about unfinished business. Someone had sent those letters and cards to Jeffrey. Did someone else know what they had done at the guest house all those years earlier? A little voice in her head said, *Is it wise, returning to the scene of the crime, so to speak?*

Alice realised the taxi driver was not preparing to pull away. 'Is there a problem?' She looked at him. 'Can't you find the directions on your Satnav?'

He shook his head. 'It's not that. You do realise this guest house is in Suffolk?'

'I do, yes.'

'But that's a two-hour drive away.'

Alice knew that. What she hadn't stopped to consider, in her rush to get away, was the cost of a taxi from Cambridge to East Anglia. Did the taxi driver even have the time to take her there?

'Can you take me there or not?' she asked, surprising herself. She was not one to be ostentatious and take a cab anywhere if she could walk. *What the hell*, she thought. It wasn't as though she could take all her pets on the train. Besides, when was the last time she'd spent any money on herself or on what she wanted to do or where she wanted to go? Every decision had been a joint one – or had it? She frowned when she thought of the house sale. Still, it made a change to go out on a limb and do something for herself on the spur of the moment. She had her own pension, her own money.

'Yes, I can take you there, but it won't be cheap.'

'I don't care.' Alice sat back in her seat and folded her arms, throwing the taxi driver her teacher look, as she called it, which said she meant business. 'Well, what are we waiting for? Let's go.'

'Fair enough. Don't you want to know the cost?'

Alice decided that she would really rather not, in case she bottled out and told him to take her home instead. 'It's fine. I trust you.'

'I've flicked on the meter.'

'Good.'

The taxi driver threw her a last glance in his rear-view mirror, as if giving her one last opportunity to back out of her trip. Alice raised her eyebrows at him as if to say, *what are you waiting for?*

He shrugged, flicked his indicator and set off.

'May I have that number of the guest house?'

'Of course.' The driver handed his phone to her over his shoulder. 'I kept it up.'

Alice leaned forward in her seat and took the phone, ready to copy the number into her own phone.

That was when she discovered that it wasn't in her handbag or her coat pocket. 'Oh, blast, I've left my phone at home.'

The taxi driver glanced in his mirror. 'Do you want me to turn around and go back?'

'No, it's fine.' It wasn't, but she couldn't turn back now. Besides, it looked as though there were plenty of vacancies, so there wouldn't be a problem if she didn't book ahead. At least she hoped not.

'Use my phone if you want to make a reservation,' the taxi driver said.

'Do you mind?' Alice replied.

'Not at all. Go right ahead. You wouldn't want to travel all that way and discover you can't get booked in, or they are closed this time of year.'

'Good idea.' Although the website said they had vacancies, that didn't mean they were taking bookings.

Alice caught him staring at her. He looked away, as though embarrassed. She could feel her cheeks growing hot. When was the last time she'd caught the attention of a man that wasn't her husband? She raised her eyebrows. *It was at the guest house.* She didn't want to think about that. It made her wonder if this trip was going to turn out to be a bad idea.

'So, have you been to this guest house before?'

Alice frowned. There it was again. It was as though the driver had a sixth sense. Then again, he met all sorts of people throughout his working day. It was probably no surprise that he could guess a thing or two about his passengers.

Alice leaned forward in her seat, not feeling inclined to get into a conversation about the guest house. 'Do you mind putting on the radio?'

'Ah, I can do one better!'

She watched him lean across to the glove compartment, open it, and get out a disc.

Moments later, they were listening to Frank Sinatra belting

out a romantic song. Alice wasn't a fan, but then again, the music was quite soothing, and Marley had stopped hissing at Hester, so that was a plus. Whether it had anything to do with the music, she had no idea. Alice stroked the top of Hester's head. 'Are you sure you don't mind me using your phone?'

'Of course not.' The taxi driver lowered the volume for her to make a call.

'Ah, hello. I want to book a room please.' She waited with bated breath, hoping they were open out of season. 'When did I want to book for? Tonight.' She heard the woman tapping on a keyboard.

A moment later, the young woman asked her if her stay would just be for the one night.

'Ah.' Alice hadn't planned ahead.

'We're not busy this time of year. There are always vacancies, so if you only want to book for a night ...'

Alice wasn't about to up and leave the next morning. 'May I book for three nights, and then take it from there?'

'Of course. So, I'll book you in for a long weekend. What name, please?'

Alice hesitated. She had the impulse to give a false name. But it sounded as though the guest house had changed hands. Besides, no one would remember her from decades earlier. 'Alice Beaumont.' She got out her bank card to make the reservation.

'I'm arriving by taxi in a couple of hours.'

The taxi driver said, 'What about your pets?'

'Oh, crumbs, I almost forgot …' Alice recalled that the guest house had accepted pets. But that was years earlier. It wasn't surprising that the guest house had changed hands in the intervening time. But did they still accept pets?'

The young lady heard the taxi driver. 'Yes, we do. It's what attracts a lot of our guests who bring their dogs.'

'That's wonderful.' Alice breathed a sigh of relief until her eyes roved over to Marley and Percy. 'The thing is …'

'So, we will see you at six. Will you be dining in?'

'Oh – yes.' Alice recalled the remoteness of the guest house. Tucked away at the end of a single street of cottages that led down to a sheltered shingle cove. It felt remote, although it wasn't far from the Victorian seaside resorts of Southwold and Aldeburgh. However, without a car, she'd need to call a taxi to take her to one of the towns. And she knew she had her pets to consider, so she wouldn't have the opportunity to go out for an evening meal even if she wanted to.

Besides it wasn't Alice's intention to venture far from the guest house. She didn't want to visit the bustling little seaside towns; she just wanted a few days on her own to take walks along the beach and perhaps resume a hobby she hadn't pursued for years – sketching and painting.

Alice was about to mention the other guests whom she'd brought with her – her two other pets – when she heard a click on the other end of the line. She'd been cut off.

'So, they have vacancies?' the taxi driver asked.

Alice replied, 'Yes.' She handed back his phone. 'Thanks.' She sat back in her seat, hoping there wouldn't be a problem when she arrived with her dog, her grumpy cat, and her rude parakeet.

8

Jeffrey walked into his study and immediately spotted the shoebox on his desk. 'Where did this come from?'

'What?' Freya asked.

Jeffrey whirled around. He hadn't realised that Freya had followed him into his study. Jeffrey had been talking to himself. He stood in front of his desk, the box hidden behind his back, and said nonchalantly, 'Ah, Freya, I didn't realise you were there. Just talking to myself.'

Freya frowned. 'You never talk to yourself.'

'Well, there's a first time for everything,' he said, eyeing her nervously, hoping she hadn't spotted the box.

Freya shrugged. 'So, what did you think of the flat?'

He frowned. The flat was the last thing on his mind. 'Have you seen your mother?'

'No, I've just walked into the house, remember?' She rolled her eyes. 'Do you want me to find her? Is it about the flat? I knew you liked it.'

It wasn't about the flat, and no, Jeffrey didn't like it. In fact, although he had been perfectly civil to the estate agent and had agreed with her when she'd gushed about the place because stupidly he didn't want to hurt her feelings, he realised he'd given his daughter the wrong impression. Unfortunately, just like his wife, he was beginning to wonder if they'd ever find anything that suited them.

He looked at Freya. She was staring back at him. 'MUM!' she shouted out.

Jeffrey winced, wishing she wouldn't do that. He fingered the box behind his back. He would much rather have a private conversation with Alice. Besides, in a house this size, you couldn't just call for someone and they'd come running.

'Theo!'

Freya's partner appeared at the door. 'Oh, you're back. I heard you calling for your mum. She's gone out.'

Jeffrey looked at Theo, thinking that he must have been in the kitchen next door getting another snack. Although Jeffrey was relieved that Freya's partner had secured another job after his redundancy, the problem was that he was working from home, their home, and he was eating a great deal.

'Did she say where?' Jeffrey asked, still fingering the box behind him, wondering where Alice had found it. He knew he'd put it somewhere 'safe' years earlier, but while they had been packing the house up he hadn't been able to think where. And now she'd found it. Or come across it by chance.

'No, she didn't say where she was going. She was up in the loft and—'

Jeffrey slapped his forehead. Of course, that was it!

'What was she doing up there?' Freya asked. 'She never goes up there.'

'I think she was packing stuff up?'

Jeffrey rolled his eyes, recalling that she'd offered to go up there and do some packing, and he'd stupidly agreed. He frowned. How was he to know she'd come across the box? It was his own fault; he knew he should have tossed it and its contents years earlier.

'So, she didn't say anything before she left?' Freya asked.

Theo shrugged. 'No, she didn't, although …' he looked at them both sheepishly as he stepped forward. 'She said to give you this.' Theo extended an arm at Jeffrey, proffering the handwritten note in his hand.

Jeffrey took the folded piece of paper. 'What's this?'

Theo shrugged. 'Before she left in a taxi—'

'A taxi?' repeated Freya, looking at Theo. 'She left in a taxi?'

He shrugged again. 'How do I know? Although it was a bit … odd.'

Freya cocked her head to one side. 'Odd – how?'

'Well, it looked to me like Mrs B was going on a little holiday?'

Jeffrey looked up as he unfolded the note. 'What on earth makes you think that?'

'The suitcases.'

'Suitcases?'

'She asked me to help her carry them downstairs and leave them in the porch. I notice they're gone, so I presume they went with her.'

Jeff and Freya looked at him, stunned.

'Oh, and I think she took her pets.'

'What?!'

Theo turned to Freya. 'Do you think she overheard …?'

'Shut up, Theo.'

Jeffrey looked at them both. 'Overheard what?'

Freya bit her lower lip. 'I was sort of having a conversation upstairs about maybe that you might have difficulty finding a rental with … well … pets.'

Jeffrey sighed. 'So, you suggested she should get rid of them?'

'Well, not in so many words, but we were talking about them …'

Jeffrey was still standing in front of his desk with the box behind him.

Theo said, 'We were having that conversation standing upstairs in the hall. I think she might have been up there and heard every word.'

'Oh no!' exclaimed Freya. 'Do you think that's why she's gone?'

Jeffrey was thinking about the box. He wanted to think that it was the reason, and that her leaving had nothing to do with what she'd discovered in the loft, but he doubted it. 'Look, she did suggest she wanted to get away for a few days. I kind of poo-pooed that idea.' He wished he hadn't. He'd have liked a break, too. 'Let's see what she's put in the note. She's probably gone to stay with Jane.'

Theo glanced at Jeffrey. 'Who's Jane?'

'Her best friend,' said Freya. 'But, Dad, she's on holiday in Thailand at the moment – don't you remember? It's her sixtieth, and she's on a cruise. Somehow I don't think Mum's flying to Thailand to join her.'

They both knew Alice wasn't fond of flying.

Jeffrey nodded and held up the note. 'Well, at least she left a note to tell us where …' Jeffrey was already skim-reading the note. 'Ah.'

'What is it?' Freya asked.

Jeffrey quickly folded the note and shoved it in his trouser pocket. 'She said she wanted to get away for a few days.'

Freya frowned. 'Is that it?'

Jeffrey looked at her sheepishly and nodded, although that wasn't quite it.

'She didn't say where she was going?'

He shook his head. 'No.'

Theo chipped in, 'Well, she obviously isn't flying anywhere with three pets.'

Jeffrey nodded. 'That's true.'

Freya grimaced. She turned to her father. 'That's not very helpful. You're meant to be exchanging contracts soon. Did she say how long she'd be gone?'

Jeffrey shook his head.

Freya got out her mobile. 'Well, let's find out. And while we're at it, I want to know where she is!'

So did Jeffrey.

Theo glanced at the plate of sandwiches in his hand. 'I know it's not lunchtime, but I felt a bit peckish.'

Jeffrey remained expressionless. His future son-in-law was always peckish. It was a shame he didn't offer to do any grocery shopping. To be fair, he did contribute to the food bill, but that was all Alice and Jeffrey got out of the two of them.

There was a buzzing noise that sounded like someone had received a text. Jeffrey looked at his phone. Theo and Freya looked at theirs too.

Freya said, 'It's coming from the kitchen.' She returned a moment later, carrying another mobile phone. She held it up. 'Oh, no. She's forgotten her phone!'

Or she left it behind on purpose, thought Jeffrey. It seemed possible, given the content of the note.

Freya slipped the phone into the back pocket of her jeans and said, 'Now how are we going to find her?'

'We're not,' said Jeffrey, sighing heavily.

Freya looked at her dad. 'So, we wait?'

'I imagine she'll only be gone for the weekend.' At least, that was what he hoped.

'And if she's not …?'

All three of them fell silent until Jeffrey said, 'Look, I've got papers to mark. I suggest you all go back to whatever it is you were doing. There's nothing to worry about.' Jeffrey was doing his best to sound upbeat, even though that wasn't how he was feeling – far from it. What he wanted was for everyone to vacate his study so that he could sit down, re-read the note, and look in that box to find out exactly what she'd discovered.

'I've got to get to work,' said Freya.

'Yeah, me too,' added Theo, picking up a cheese and pickle sandwich off his plate as he sidled out of the room first.

Freya hesitated. 'Is everything all right, Dad?'

'How do you mean?' Jeffrey frowned. It was a rather stupid answer to a stupid question. How could everything be all right when she'd backed her mother into a corner regarding selling the house? Was it what Alice really wanted? Now, he wasn't so sure. And now there was the box she'd discovered in the loft.

'I meant, is everything all right between the two of you? It's just, it's not like Mum to … you know, go off like this.'

No, it isn't like her, thought Jeffrey. In all the years they'd been married, she'd never done something like this, apart from that time at the guest house on the Suffolk Coast, before they had

Freya. They'd stayed there for their second wedding anniversary, but they'd had a row, and then she'd stalked off and hadn't come back until the early hours. He'd had no idea where she'd been. They had never talked about it. Or more to the point, *she* had never talked about it. She'd reappeared very early the next morning, creeping into bed next to him, perhaps under the illusion he wouldn't notice she'd been gone practically the entire night. They had never spoken a word about it, either at the time or in the years since.

Of course there was that other time they'd stayed there, and they'd had an almighty falling-out and she'd left altogether and returned home without him. Jeffrey didn't want to think about that. If Alice ever found out what had happened that night at the guest house when she was gone …

Jeffrey inwardly groaned. He had no idea if everything was all right, not after what Alice had found. But then Freya would know nothing about that. He smiled. 'Of course everything is all right, sweetheart.'

Freya threw him a dubious look.

'Look, everything's fine. Now please let me do some work.' He motioned at the door for her to leave.

Freya paused at the door. 'You would tell me, wouldn't you, if … well, if you guys were not okay?'

Jeffrey nodded, crossed his fingers behind his back, and said, 'Of course.'

As soon as Freya had closed the door to his study, and he'd heard the front door bang shut, he walked behind his desk, sat down in the faux leather swivel chair and pulled the box towards him. He didn't have to open it to know what was inside. He did so anyway, just to remind himself of what a fool he'd been by keeping it. He listened for the sound of footsteps outside his study. Satisfied that no one was going to come in, he took off the lid and peered inside. There were letters, birthday cards, and Christmas cards going back years. He sat back in his chair and wiped his sweaty forehead. 'God, I bet she has looked through these. Why else would she have dumped them on my desk?'

'God!' he exclaimed again, putting the lid back on the box.

9

'Here, let me help you with those,' said the taxi driver.

The taxi had arrived on the cobbled driveway outside the guest house. Alice didn't recall there having been a cobbled driveway when she was last there. It looked new, as though it had been laid recently. She was standing outside the car, holding on to Hester's lead as the taxi driver lifted her cases out of the boot. She cast her gaze up Shingle Street. The street itself hadn't changed. The neat red-brick terraced cottages looked the same, although Alice imagined some must have changed hands over the years.

Apart from at the guest house, there was only street parking. All the cottages had little front gardens. The taxi had weaved down the centre of the narrow road between the parked cars. The street sloped gently down to the last house – the guest house – before the tarmacadam road ended in a cul de sac. From there, a path led to the sheltered cove where a planked walkway stretched out on to the shingle beach.

There were no facilities, cafés or public toilets, just a very picturesque Suffolk cove that wouldn't have looked out of place in Devon or Cornwall – except Alice knew that if it had been in

Cornwall, it wouldn't have remained undiscovered for long. Her last visit, years and years earlier, had been in the school summer holidays, but even in the height of the summer season, she had been pleasantly surprised to find that it was almost deserted. It was as though Shingle Street had its own private beach. Facilities and activities for children could be found further up the coast in the large resorts like Lowestoft and Great Yarmouth, with their big attractions such as amusement arcades and fairground rides.

Then there were the quieter, smaller and more sedate old Victorian seaside resorts of Southwold and Aldeburgh, which Alice had visited in the past, with their teashops, their fish and chip shops, and even their independent cinemas so that visitors could catch a movie if the weather was inclement. And then there were places like this. She imagined that, apart from the residents of Shingle Street, few ventured to this secluded cove.

Alice turned to the guest house. She recalled when she had first set eyes on the place. If her and her husband's jobs and lives hadn't been in Cambridge, where they'd already settled into their new house, she would have loved to live here instead – although back then she hadn't envied the young woman who had taken on the rundown property. It had needed a lot of work. She smiled at the double-fronted detached red-brick Victorian house, with old-fashioned leaded windows, a gabled roof, and ivy creeping up the outside walls. The property had clearly been updated and modernised over the years.

The taxi driver left her cases in the porch. Alice thanked him and gave him cash, and a tip for being so helpful. They'd made a brief stop at a petrol service station on the way so Alice could withdraw enough cash to pay for the journey and the tip. He'd even put the cat carrier with its hissy occupant on top of the suitcases. He offered her his card in case she wanted to call him for her return journey. Alice took the card. Even though she'd booked in for three nights, now she was there, she felt like staying for a week.

The taxi driver looked at the guest house. 'Do you want me to hang around in case?'

Alice frowned. 'In case …?' She caught his eyes roving to Hester, and then Percy.

Alice followed his gaze. He'd overheard her conversation with the receptionist. She knew what he was thinking; would there be a problem with her pets?

Alice hoped there wasn't. But if there was, she'd just have to do the unthinkable and book them into a local kennel and cattery. Percy would have to stay, though. He would be no trouble, as long as they didn't mind him being left in her room.

Alice shook her head, hoping there wasn't a problem. 'They said they accepted pets.'

'Okay, well, I'll be going then.'

The taxi driver reversed out of the driveway as Alice walked up to the front door. She looked at Hester, then glanced at Marley, wondering if she should have asked the taxi driver to hang around. But it was too late now. She took a deep breath and rang the doorbell, thinking about the young couple who owned the guest house when she was last there. Would she recognise them, over twenty-five years later, if they were still running the guest house? Would they recognise her? Thinking about what had happened when she was last there, Alice hoped not. It made her wonder, considering her history with this place, whether she should have returned.

Alice was looking at the taxi driver's card, thinking that maybe it was a mistake. If she rang him now, it wasn't too late for him to turn around and come back and pick her up – he was probably just turning into the main road. She wished she'd never been up in the loft and set eyes on that sketch of the guest house – although it wasn't the sketch itself but the box of letters she'd discovered that was on her mind. She hadn't spent an awful lot of time going through them. She wished she had. Perhaps there would have been a letter amongst the old birthday and Christmas cards that may have shed some light on who this woman was and how she knew Alice's husband.

Her first thought on discovering the letters had been that Jeffrey had had an affair, or was still having one. But what if it was just a friend, a work colleague? Alice frowned. Then why had she never seen those cards and letters, and why were they hidden in the one place in the house she rarely ever ventured? What she had gleaned was that the correspondence dated back years, to around the time they were last in Suffolk. Was that just a coincidence? Alice stood at the front door of the guest house, wondering if the answer lay inside.

10

The front door opened. 'Can I help you?'

It wasn't a young woman – the receptionist she'd spoken to on the phone – who answered the door, but a large fellow with dark, curly hair and a greying beard beneath a jolly smile. He was wearing jeans and a thick jumper.

'I have a room reservation. My name is Mrs Beaumont.'

'I'm Gerald. Come in, come in. I don't normally do this sort of thing. I leave the running of the guest house to my wife.' He reached for the cases.

Marley chose that moment to hiss at Gerald.

'Marley!' Alice exclaimed, wondering when Gerald was going to tell her that she could only bring one well-behaved dog.

Gerald chuckled. 'Marley. What a great name for a cat.'

'Sorry about that, he's not normally …' Alice trailed off in the middle of her outright lie. He *was* usually grumpy, and hissy if something wasn't to his liking, which included most things lately.

Gerald turned to the cat. 'Now, don't let my beard worry you. I am really a big softie.' He picked up the cat carrier and the suitcase.

She noticed he had said nothing about Percy, as though it was quite normal for someone to turn up with a hissy cat, a dog and a parrot.

Alice let out a sigh of relief as she stepped through the doorway. It didn't look as though the pets would be a problem.

As they stepped into the wide square hallway, Alice couldn't help but admire the polished, warm mahogany panelling that reached halfway up the walls and the pretty delicate flowered wallpaper above. It was so different from what she remembered. She was sure the panelling had been painted cream and the walls an austere white.

'Wow,' she said to Gerald as she approached the little reception desk, 'this looks so different to when I was here before.' She silently berated herself for letting that slip. She had planned not to mention her visit years earlier.

Gerald looked at her. 'Sorry, I don't remember you.' He must have gleaned from her expression that she didn't recognise him either, because he added, 'I've changed somewhat over the years.' He patted his ample stomach. 'I'm a fisherman, so I don't always get to meet the guests. It must have been some time ago that you stayed here. We did this place up years ago.'

Alice smiled. 'I'm afraid it was a very long time ago, soon after I got married. We came here the first time for our honeymoon.'

Gerald's face dropped. 'Oh, I'm so sorry.'

'Oh, you don't have to apologise. The place was lovely back then, even though it needed updating.'

'Um, I was talking about your husband.'

Alice looked at him bewildered until she realised he must have thought she was there on her own because she was either widowed or divorced. 'We're in the process of moving house, so I left my husband to the packing. I wanted to get away for a bit, have a break. On my own.'

'Ah, I see.'

Alice frowned. She could tell by his expression he still didn't understand why she'd booked her break alone.

Percy broke the awkward silence. *'Liar, liar, pants on fire!'*

'Percy!' Alice apologised. 'My daughter, when she was small, taught Percy some naughty words.' He has a rather long memory, and a penchant for coming out with them just at the wrong moment.' Alice could feel her face flushing red in embarrassment.

Gerald burst out laughing. 'Don't apologise! Dear me, you've got your hands full, though.' His gaze shifted from Percy to Marley. 'And who's this fella down here?'

Hester furiously wagged her tail as Gerald knelt down and gave her a stroke.

'That's Hester.' Alice smiled at her dog. At least she could rely on Hester to be the sweet-natured dog she was.

'That's an unusual name for a dog. I like it, though.'

'Yes, my daughter who loves archaeology named her after a famous American archaeologist – Hester Davis.'

Alice heard a woman's voice behind them. 'Sorry I wasn't around when you arrived. Just had to spend a penny.'

She thought the voice sounded familiar. She guessed it was the young lady she had spoken to over the phone when she made the booking.

Gerald walked over to the reception desk. 'Ah, this is Emily.'

Alice followed. She did a double-take. Was Emily Gerald's wife? She was so young. Gerald was old enough to be her—

'This is my daughter. She's helping us out for a bit while she looks for work in her chosen profession. We're so proud. She qualified as a vet.'

Alice smiled at the young woman, whom she guessed was around Freya's age.

'Dad, do stop. You tell everyone who arrives. I'm sure our guests are not interested that I'm a vet.'

'I don't know about that,' said Alice smiling at the young blonde woman, who with her slim build and green eyes didn't take after Gerald at all. 'I've brought a menagerie with me, as you can see. Always handy to have a vet on call. Although I do hope I won't need your services.'

Emily's face lit up when she saw Alice's pets.

Gerald put the cat carrier on the reception desk.

Marley hissed at her.

'My, aren't you a grumpy!' exclaimed Emily, smiling at Marley.

Alice sighed. 'That's Marley.'

'Has he always been like this?'

'Every time I put him in the cat carrier.' Alice thought about it. 'Actually, I'd say he's been out of sorts for the last few weeks.' It occurred to Alice that with everything going on with the house move, she really hadn't been paying that much attention. Now she was worried. Perhaps she should have taken him for a check-up at the vet's.

Emily stood up and leaned across the desk to look at him.

'Oh, I wouldn't get too close in case a paw comes through the cage and swipes you. He's been known to do that.'

Despite the warning, Emily leaned forward just as Marley let out a huge yawn. 'Ah, I think I see what's making your cat so grumpy.'

Alice looked at her anxiously. 'Is something wrong?'

'I think your cat has a bit of tooth decay.'

'Oh,' Alice said in surprise. 'Really?'

Emily nodded. 'I'd have to take a closer look, but I'm sure that's it.'

'Can you do anything for him?'

'No, I'm afraid I can't without a position at a practice, but I can recommend a vet locally, unless you'd prefer to wait until you return home and see your own vet?'

Alice shook her head. Although she wasn't quite sure when she would be home, that wasn't the point. She was sure she'd missed her pet's annual check-up because of the move.

Would you be able to book me an appointment? I will take him straight away as soon as one is free. Would you be able to arrange a taxi too?'

Emily shook her head. 'Don't be silly. I'll take you both in my car.'

'Oh, you are too kind, Emily.'

She smiled.

Alice returned her smile. She didn't want it to appear that she was taking advantage, but she did say, 'You wouldn't give Percy and Hester the once-over – would you? They seem okay, but just in case …?'

Emily looked at the beautiful parrot in the cage. 'Is that Hester or Percy?' she asked.

Percy flapped his wings and squawked, 'Per-cy. Per-cy.'

Emily laughed. 'Well, that answers that question, little bird.'

'Litt-le bird.'

'Gosh, aren't you a clever bird?'

'Cle-ver bird!'

Alice frowned at her clever little bird, willing him not to say anything else. This is how it always started off; Percy would impress new friends, who would coo over his beautiful red, blue, green and yellow feathers, and then he would spoil it by repeating rude words. Alice had decided long ago that her parrot was like a little child; it was almost as though he understood that the words were very naughty and shouldn't be used and said them on purpose just to get a rise out of her.

'And this is Hester.' Alice glanced at her dog, who was sitting by her feet. She was keen to move the focus of attention away from Percy.

Emily walked around the desk. 'Ah, aren't you the cutest thing?'

Hester was immediately on her feet, tail wagging furiously, pulling on her lead to run over and meet her new friend.

Emily knelt down as Hester darted towards her. In between plenty of fusses, Emily had a look in her mouth, her eyes, had a feel around her abdomen, lifted her floppy ears, and pronounced, 'Well, aren't you a picture of health.'

Alice let out a sigh of relief.

Scratching behind her ears, Emily looked up at Alice. 'She is perfectly fine. What is she, ten?'

'Twelve, actually.'

'Well, she's very sprightly for her age.'

'And Percy?'

'Any change in behaviour or eating habits?'

Alice shook her head. 'Nope, still talkative, not off his food or anything like that.'

Emily nodded. 'Good.' She got off her knees.

Hester attempted to follow her around the desk. Her lead stopped her forward momentum.

'Only your cat needs a visit.' She glanced at Hester, who had her two front paws reaching up at the desk, wanting more attention from the nice lady.

'Oh, sorry. Hester – down!'

'It's all right. But you may have to bring Hester with you to see the vet. She might not get on being left alone here without you.'

'Unless she was with you.' Alice shook her head. 'Oh, silly me, you were going to drive me there.'

'Hold on. Let me phone the vet's office and see when they have an appointment free. If they can fit you in at short notice today, I've still got some things to do here this afternoon, but Gerald could take you – if that's okay, Dad?'

'Of course it is. I have a rare day off work today. And it's Friday, so it's a nice long weekend too.'

Alice turned to him. 'Oh, I wouldn't want you to go to all this trouble on my account, on your day off.'

Gerald, a jovial sort, shook his head. 'Not at all. I don't mind.'

'Probably better that way,' added Emily. 'I think he'd make a mess of things if he was left in charge.' She smiled affectionately at her dad. 'My mum is in town doing some shopping for the evening meal.'

'It's your mum who runs the guest house, isn't it?'

Emily nodded. 'That's right.' She reached for the phone, then paused. 'Why don't you get settled into your room? We have tea and coffee making facilities. Then you can unpack and have a cuppa while I phone the vet. I doubt they'll have an appointment this afternoon, but I'll let you know.'

Alice breathed a sigh. 'Sounds perfect, thank you.' She was in need of a drink and was looking forward to seeing her room. As

Emily came round the desk with a key to hand to her, Alice eyed the phone. She ought to contact Jeffrey and Freya and tell them where she was.

Emily noticed their new guest wavering. 'I can make that call now if you like?'

Alice shook her head. 'No, it's fine. Please show me to my room.'

Emily picked up a pen. 'First, would you mind signing the guest book?' Emily opened a leather-bound book and pushed it along the desk towards her. There was a line for each guest to put their name, address, contact phone number and arrival date.

Alice picked up the pen. Her hand hovered over the empty line beneath the name of another guest – Joss Harper. She knew it was very rude of her, but she couldn't help it; she read his details. In the address line, he'd written, *No fixed abode*. There was no mobile phone number given. But it was the arrival date that surprised her the most. According to the entry, he'd been there for weeks. It was no wonder he'd put *No fixed abode*, as though he was homeless. She supposed that after that length of stay, the guest house was his home for the time being.

She thought of the room rate she was paying. It certainly wasn't cheap. Perhaps he had a discount because of the length of his stay? She hoped so. Even so, he would have been better off renting a cottage. She wondered what was keeping him there.

'Mrs Beaumont?'

'Oh, sorry – yes.' She glanced at Emily and wondered if Joss was a young man, and the reason he had stayed so long was staring her in the face, quite literally – the young, pretty, blonde Emily. 'My mind wandered there for a minute,' Alice added.

There was something else on her mind as she made her entry

in the old-fashioned ledger. What if this was how it had always been done? What if they had kept the old ledgers from past years? Alice was thinking about the contents of that shoebox and the woman who had been communicating with her husband. It seemed a stretch, on the one hand, but if she could get a look at the past ledgers, if they still had them, from when they were there last – would her name be registered?

Alice swallowed. She and Jeffrey had rarely spent a night apart, but for two occasions in the guest house, over twenty-five years earlier. She didn't want to think about that. It wasn't something he'd ever brought up – where she'd disappeared to for most of the night on one of those occasions. But now she was wondering why he had never mentioned it. Did he have something to hide too? And did it have something to do with a woman called Wendy?

'Mrs Beaumont?'

'Oh, sorry.' Alice apologised again, realising she had been standing there, pen still in her hand after filling out her details, just staring at the page.

'Is everything all right?'

'Yes, yes. Of course.' She handed the pen and ledger back to Emily. Nothing had been quite right since that night decades earlier, in this guest house.

'Are you sure?'

'This is old-fashioned.' She pointed at the ledger. 'Is that something you've always done?'

'What – the ledger?'

Alice nodded.

'Oh yes, for as long as I can remember.' Emily pointed at the cabinet behind her. It had glass-fronted doors. Alice saw one shelf filled with bound books. So, they *had* kept the old ledgers. She wasn't sure whether Emily would let her take a look, but thought it was worth asking. The problem was, what would she say? *I'm looking for someone who stayed here decades earlier*? Thinking about it, she couldn't imagine they would give out the personal details of their guests.

Emily called out, 'Dad! Can you come and help with the cases?'

Gerald appeared with a tea towel in his hand. He wiped his wet hands, flipped it over his shoulder, and walked over. Picking up a suitcase in each hand, he commented, 'My, these are out of the ark.'

'Dad!'

'Oh, sorry. No offence.'

Alice smiled. 'None taken! I found them in the loft.' She didn't know what else to add – that she'd thrown some old clothes in them and decided on the spur of the moment to walk out?

'Well, I like them,' commented Gerald. 'Stickers and all! Ah, the golden age of travel with the dawn of the package holiday. I bet these are worth something.'

Alice nodded. Although she wasn't that bothered, she was pleased at the thought that when she passed them on to a charity shop, some money would go to a worthwhile cause.

She followed him up the stairs, holding the key in one hand along with Hester's lead and carrying Percy's cage in the other.

A sudden high-pitched kitty cry stopped everyone in their tracks.

Alice winced at the sound. 'Oh, crumbs, I forgot Marley.'

'It's all right, I'll fetch him.' Emily picked up the cat carrier.

'Ooh, did we forget you?' she said in a soppy voice, as she rounded the desk and headed for the stairs.

Marley cried again.

'Now don't you worry,' said Emily, following behind. 'I know this is a strange house, but you'll soon settle in.'

Alice sighed. She doubted it. She realised she'd been so intent on getting away and taking her pets with her that she just hadn't thought it through. Cats didn't like to be taken away from their home, the environment they were used to. She imagined that Marley would not like this one bit.

'And once you've seen the vet, you're going to feel a whole lot better.'

Alice brightened. Now, that was true. He might even be a different cat. *Here's hoping*, she thought when she heard Marley hissing as Gerald opened the door to her room.

'Oh, this is lovely. Absolutely lovely.'

Gerald put the suitcases on the patchwork quilt covering the double bed and paused to look around the spacious top floor room with its two cottage windows in the eaves. The room was painted white, with a beamed ceiling and matching rattan furniture. The wooden floors and rugs gave it a homely, rustic feel. Alice liked it – a lot. She didn't recall having stayed in this room years earlier. Maybe the attic had not been converted at that point.

'This used to be my older sister's room,' Emily said. 'She's moved out now – well, years ago.'

Gerald smiled. 'Yes, she certainly had the room with the best view. I know you couldn't wait for her to move out so you could have this room.'

It sounded to Alice as though there was an age gap. That

explained why Gerald was an older parent. And why, being the eldest, Emily's sister had had the best bedroom.

'Yeah – but that didn't happen.'

Although Alice saw that Emily was smiling, it sounded as though the bedroom had become another guest bedroom instead of passing to her, which probably hadn't gone down well. But then, glancing around the spacious, airy room, with the expensive room rate, she imagined it was one of the best bedrooms in the house.

Gerald just smiled at his daughter. He clapped his hands together. 'Now, if there isn't anything else, I promised your mother I would start preparing the evening meal.'

'But I thought Mum was doing that when she got in with the shopping?'

'She had some extra bits and bobs to collect, so she asked if I'd make a start and keep an eye on it.'

'Oh.'

Alice glanced at Emily, realising that if there was an appointment available with the vet that afternoon, Gerald wouldn't be able to take her either. She watched him walk out of the room and close the door.

Emily shrugged. 'Don't worry, we'll sort something out,' she said. 'Won't we, sweetie?' she said to the cat.

Alice looked at Marley, who was staring out of his cat carrier at the room beyond. He turned his back on them.

'Oh, don't be like that,' said Emily. 'You're going to enjoy your little holiday, especially once you've been to see the vet.'

As if he understood every word, Marley turned his head, looking back at her and hissed.

'Marley!' Alice admonished him.

Emily stood up. 'Don't worry, he'll feel better soon. Now, about your room key. Can I just show you the lock? It's a bit fiddly.'

Alice joined her at the door and handed her the key.

'My half-brother used to have the room along the hall.'

'You've got a half-brother?'

'Yes, sorry, don't know why I said that. Mum lost her first husband when my half-brother and sister were very young, then she remarried, and had me.'

'So, you're the baby of the family.'

Emily's smile faded somewhat. 'Yeah.'

'They've done a grand job of doing it up. I remember when it was in its original state. I don't think the top floor was even habitable.'

Alice put Percy's bird cage down on the dressing table so that he had a lovely view of the cove. She glanced at Hester, who was running around the room, sniffing the carpet. She imagined, even though she could detect no doggy smells in the room herself, that Hester could still smell the pets who had been there before her.

'You've stayed here before?'

Once again, Alice berated herself for letting that slip. 'Oh, it was years and years ago. Decades, in fact. Your parents have done a wonderful job doing it up since they took the place over.'

Emily put the room key on the dressing table under the bay window with views down to the cove. 'Perhaps Mum will remember you.'

Alice whirled around. She wasn't so sure that was what she wanted to hear. Would she also remember what had gone on there all those years ago?

'Well, I'll leave you to settle in,' said Emily, walking over to the door.

Alice frowned at Emily's back, a feeling settled over her once more that going there had been a bad idea.

Hester followed her new friend.

Emily noticed. She knelt down. 'Oh, aren't you a sweetie? But you can't come with me. I've got work to do.'

Alice caught her frowning. She imagined that Emily would much rather be working in her chosen profession as a vet than on reception in a guest house. Even if it was a lovely guest house.

'That reminds me,' said Emily, standing up. 'I must call the vet. I'll let you know when the next appointment is.'

Alice nodded and glanced at Marley. She wasn't going to let him out of his carrier just yet, in case she had the good fortune to get an appointment. Alice didn't fancy another game of cat and mouse to get him in the cat carrier. Once was enough for one day.

Emily closed the door behind her, and Hester stood looking at the door.

'Hester – come here!'

She turned around at the sound of Alice's voice and ran over. 'Good girl! Who's a good girl?' Alice smiled. Before she had got Hester, she had always wondered at the people she heard speaking to their dogs in babyish tones, even having whole conversations with them. She'd hear them say things like, 'No, don't go in there, you'll get all muddy,' as if the dogs understood every word. Alice had never thought she would turn into one of those people until she got Hester as a puppy and had immediately started to baby her terribly. That hadn't changed.

Hester ran over, got a fuss, and then stood up on her hind

legs, front paws on the bed, and poked her nose into Marley's cage.

Marley hissed at her.

'How many times have I told you not to do that?' Alice rolled her eyes as she picked up the cat carrier and popped it on top of the chest of drawers on the other side of the room, where Hester couldn't reach it or the tetchy cat inside. The last thing Alice needed was two vet bills, one of which would be avoidable if Hester just stayed out of Marley's way.

11

When Alice had first got Marley, she imagined that with Hester being the big softie that she was, her new kitten would snuggle up to Hester and they'd be best pals. It wasn't her dog's fault, for try as she might, the kitten was aloof, independent, and not interested in making friends. Any thought of cute photos of her two beloved pets together was consigned to what Alice referred to as *Warehouse 13*.

Alice smiled at the euphemism. There had been a television programme called *Warehouse 13* that she had enjoyed watching with Freya when she was a child. It was all about a huge warehouse full of unusual artefacts. They weren't ancient artefacts, but things with unusual, even otherworldly, powers. They were kept a secret, never to see the light of day. It was how Alice sometimes felt about her life; all the things she'd imagined she would do left in a warehouse of dreams, never to be seen again.

Alice walked over to the window and looked out at the view of the cove, the water glistening as the sun set out of sight behind the hotel. She was thinking of the last time she had been there – the night she had disappeared. What if she had never come back? What if she had taken another path? She'd had that opportunity. A once-in-a-lifetime opportunity brought on by circumstance. Instead, she had gone back to her husband, and Freya had come along. And their life had finally seemed to come together, but for one thing – something that had haunted her all these years.

Alice tried to brush that thought aside, and along with it the young man she'd met that night right there at the guest house.

She closed her eyes and willed herself to think about something else.

A knock at the door saved Alice from going down that rabbit hole and thinking about the consequences of that night; about the fallout that would occur if ever the truth came out. *What am I doing here?* a little voice in her head said, and not for the first time. *This could prove to be the biggest mistake of your life.* But something was compelling her to stay.

Someone knocked at the door again. This time Hester barked. Alice rushed forward, glaring at her dog. 'Shush, for goodness' sake!' she hissed. As much as she was wondering if this trip was a mistake, she would rather not get booted out of the guest house tonight because of her barky dog. Hester wasn't normally vocal. But her dog was in a strange house. In fact, she was doing very well, considering she'd never stayed anywhere but at home. They had a lovely neighbour who always popped in and house-sat when they went away to a place where they couldn't take Hester. They couldn't take Percy or Marley with them anywhere, so their neighbour always looked after the two of them.

As Alice approached the door, she felt a lump in her throat at the thought of moving out of their house in Cambridge for good and losing those good neighbours she had known for years.

Although over time the number of original owners had dwindled; they had died or become ill or downsized so that in her street there was just them and their one next-door neighbour left out of all those who had been there when they moved in. The others were young couples or growing families, who were lovely, but a bit more of the sense of community had been lost with every old neighbour who went. Alice longed for that sense of community once more. But where would she find it?

She opened the door to find Emily with a young man she hadn't seen before. 'Hi. The local vet's office managed to get you fitted into their last appointment in half an hour.'

'That's fantastic.'

'Yes, but the thing is my dad can't take you, and I've got another guest who is turning up soon, so …'

'That's okay, Emily.' Alice smiled. 'I don't mind getting there by taxi if you know a local taxi firm.'

'That won't be necessary. Joss, here, has offered to take you. He's staying at the guest house too.'

Alice shifted her gaze to the young man with the blonde tousled hair, fading tan, and many leather bands on his wrists. So, this was the only other guest besides herself. She hadn't been surprised there were few guests this time of year, but what had surprised her was how long their other guest had been with them.

She noticed that he was wearing cropped trousers and a t-shirt. He looked completely out of place, as though he had just stepped off Bondi Beach in Australia or was on a surfing holiday in Newquay. He looked quite young, and a bit too much like a hippy drop-out to be able to live in a guest house with a daily room rate that wasn't cheap.

Her attention shifted to Emily. She imagined he wasn't giving an older lady with a hissy cat a lift in his car out of the goodness of his heart. She saw him glance at Emily, smiling. The look on his face said it all – he'd do anything for her.

Alice said, 'I'll fetch Marley.' She looked at Hester.

'It's all right, she can stay here with me.'

As if she understood every word, Hester wagged her tail and ran over to Emily.

Joss offered to take the cat carrier while Alice locked the door. She followed Joss, Emily and Hester down two flights of stairs to the homely reception.

They were just heading towards the front door when it opened and a lady walked in carrying two shopping bags.

'Oh Mum, you're back,' exclaimed Emily. 'This is Alice, our new guest who checked in this afternoon while you were out. She's just popping to the vet with her pet. I booked a last-minute appointment.'

Alice recognised Emily's mum immediately. She had aged, as Alice would have expected, but she still had the same hairstyle, a short blonde bob, although Alice guessed she must now have a colour when she visited the hairdresser. The cut framed her round face and full cheeks. She had the same green eyes and slim figure as her youngest daughter.

Alice could feel her cheeks blushing at the thought she might be recognised in return. But the woman was so busy carrying in the shopping bags that she barely glanced Alice's way to begin with.

'Here, let me take those,' Gerald said, appearing from one of the doors off the hallway. He relieved his wife of the bags. She turned around to face Alice. 'Welcome to our little guest house.'

Alice noted there was no sign of recognition in her

expression. She sighed in relief, wondering why she would think the guest house owner would recognise her after all these years. She must have had many guests in that time. *But very few guests whom she had caught sneaking out of another guest's room.*

Alice willed herself not to think about that.

'Our new guest has been here before – haven't you, Alice?'

Alice was just heading for the door. She could hear a car engine revving up outside. Joss had gone ahead to put Marley in the car. She whirled around, wishing Emily hadn't said that.

Emily's mum stepped forward, scrutinising her.

'You have?'

'Oh, it was years ago,' Alice said, with a flick of the hand.

'It's amazing because she remembers the place before you did it up, so it must have been around the time you first bought it,' said Emily. 'I couldn't imagine you had that many guests back then.'

'No, I didn't. By rights we should have waited until the place had some more work done to it, but we wanted to see if people were interested in staying in this area. I recall we had mostly young backpackers, students, and …' she paused, eyeing Alice intently, '… a couple who were on their honeymoon.'

Alice looked away.

'You shouldn't be here!'

'Mum!' Emily exclaimed, as surprised as Alice was by her mother's tone. *Although perhaps her reaction shouldn't surprise me*, thought Alice. There were some things she wouldn't have wanted to see going on under her roof, potentially giving her guest house a bad name. It was a long time in the past, but she must have remembered what she had seen.

Emily's mum flounced off with Emily following close

behind. She heard her say, 'Mum, that's no way to speak to one of our guests, especially a returner. What's got into you?'

Alice didn't hear Emily's mum's response. She did hear Gerald in the kitchen. 'Why are you two arguing?' he asked.

Alice skulked out of the house. She'd just closed the front door behind her, wishing it was a taxi waiting for her and she was leaving that night, when the front door opened. It was Emily. 'God, I am so sorry.'

Alice stared at her. She expected Emily's mum wasn't sorry. She went wide-eyed when she saw the older woman approach, her demeanour apologetic. 'Look, you being here, well it just took me by surprise, that's all.'

'Me too,' said Alice, catching Emily looking from Alice to her mum, her expression one of bemusement.

'What are you doing back here, anyway?'

Emily rolled her big blue eyes at her mother. 'Mum …'

'I'm just asking. It's been so many years since …'

'To be honest, I don't know.' She cut Emily's mum off mid-sentence. Her eyes flicked to Emily before she cast her gaze at Emily's mum. Their eyes locked in silent understanding; this should be a private conversation.

She turned to her daughter. 'Emily, can you go and help Dad with the dinner? I'll be there in a moment.'

Emily lingered in the hallway, the look on her face suggesting she'd much rather stay and find out what was going on.

12

As soon as her mum walked into the kitchen, the first words out of Emily's mouth were, 'Who is Freya?'

She caught her mum glance past her at Gerald, who was standing at the kitchen sink. When she realised her mum wasn't going to answer her question, she turned around and asked him the same thing.

Unbeknown to them, she'd overheard a snippet of a conversation when she'd left them at the door. She'd walked as slowly as she could down the hallway – not so slowly that it looked like a dawdle, but slowly enough to overhear something before she walked into the kitchen. It was a question that her mother had asked Alice: 'Is it about Freya?'

She had heard their new guest heave a heavy sigh and say in a hushed voice, 'I didn't think you'd remember.'

'How could I forget?' her mum had replied.

Now Emily wanted to know who Freya was.

'She's Alice's daughter. We were going to write to each other over the years but lost touch. I was just being polite and asking after her only child.'

'Oh, really.' Emily folded her arms. That had not been what

it sounded like to her. She looked at her mum, who turned her back and started unpacking the shopping bags. Emily glanced at her father. He too, turned around and started unloading the dishwasher. Emily bit her lip. 'Fine.'

❖

'Emily …' said Gerald as she flounced out of the kitchen.

Emily's mum sighed. 'Just leave her be. You know what she gets like when she thinks we're keeping secrets from her.'

'But we are keeping secrets.'

She frowned at her husband. 'Oh, and what would you have me do? Just turn around and say that—'

Gerald held up his hands, obviously forestalling what he knew she was going to say. 'Okay, all right. Let's just drop this – shall we? To be honest, I'm surprised you recognised her.'

'I didn't. It's not like I saw her again, unlike her husband, who I met up with every year in the beginning …'

Gerald held his fingers to his lips in a shushing motion.

She rolled her eyes. 'Relax. Alice has gone out with Joss, something about taking her pet to see the vet.'

'She still doesn't know – does she, do you think?'

'Unless something happened, and she's come here because she suspects something …' She trailed off.

Gerald nodded. 'Do you think we did the right thing all those years ago?'

She threw the bag of apples she had in her hands down on the worktop. 'For goodness' sake, Gerald. How many times have we had this conversation?'

He bobbed his head up and down. 'I know, I know. But over the years, it's played on my mind.'

She sighed. 'I know. Mine too. But it wasn't just our decision, was it? The three of us were in it together. You, me – and Jeffrey.'

'Why do you think he's not here?'

'I don't know. Perhaps he's dead.'

'No, Emily said she's not a widow. Do you think she found out about …?'

She slowly shook her head from side to side. 'No, I don't think that was it.'

'Then what, Wendy?'

She frowned at him. 'How many times have I told you not to call me that?'

'But it's your name.'

'Yes, but you know I go by my middle name. Anthea sounds much more refined and …'

'Posh.'

'Yes, you know I think every little detail just gives an impression. And your name is one of the most important details.'

'Maybe I should change my name too.' Gerald was trying to think of a suitably posh gentleman's name. 'How about Sebastian?'

'Oh, don't be so silly, Gerald.' She frowned at him. 'But seriously, even Emily doesn't slip up.'

'That's because she calls you Mum.'

'And you normally call me, *my love*.'

'Sorry, my love,' he said, walking towards her and putting his hands around her waist.

She smiled at him.

'Apology accepted.'

His hand moved down her thigh. 'Really, Gerald! We've got dinner to prepare for our guests.'

Gerald let out a sigh. 'I don't know about you, but I've got used to having the house practically to ourselves these past couple of months. I've never known it to be so quiet during the winter months.'

'I'm not surprised the house has been empty, with all the wet and windy weather we've been having lately. People would most likely rather go abroad than be stuck inside a hotel room watching the rain lashing the windowpane.'

'We've got Joss, though.' Gerald commented. 'But Joss has been here so long, he's beginning to feel like part of the furniture – or the family.'

'Don't say that. He's not staying.'

'Of course he isn't. He won't want to stay in a guest house forever. But I do think there's someone, keeping him here.'

'Don't say that either.'

'Why not? He's a nice sort.'

'The trouble with you, Gerald, is you just see the good in people. Everyone is a nice sort – in your book.' She turned around to continue unpacking the shopping bags.

'Yes, it's true he does keep his cards close to his chest.'

'His cards close to his chest?' Anthea scoffed. 'I'll say! We know nothing about him.'

Gerald frowned at his wife. 'I do know this – he has the means to pay our room rates, which aren't cheap. And he's in love with Emily.'

'No, he isn't.'

'Yes, he is.'

Anthea glared at him.

Gerald sighed. 'I know what you're thinking – he's not good enough.'

'That's right.'

'But none of her past boyfriends have been good enough in your eyes. Sometimes I think you're afraid of past mistakes being repeated.' Gerald knew the moment the words were out of his mouth that he'd said something he'd regret. Even so, he added, 'She's not your little sister.'

'No, she's my daughter, and that's even more reason for me to look out for her and make sure she doesn't fall into the arms of Mr Wrong. Besides, he's too old for her.'

'He's only in his early thirties.'

'That's still an age gap.'

'You always said Emily had an old head on her shoulders.'

Anthea heaved a sigh and returned to unpacking the shopping. 'I don't want to talk about it.'

'Perhaps that's the problem.'

She whirled around. 'Oh, so you think it would be a good idea if I went to see somebody and talk about my feelings over what I did to my sister?'

'That's a funny turn of phrase. I thought you did it *for* your sister.'

'For her own good. But was it what *she* wanted?'

'Maybe, maybe not,' Gerald replied.

❖

Emily was standing behind the kitchen door, trying to remind herself she wasn't that little girl anymore – the one trying to listen in on her parents and older siblings, feeling left out that she had to go to bed early while they all sat downstairs, talking and laughing, watching TV long after she'd gone to bed. Or rather, after they thought she'd gone to bed. She had always felt left out, being the baby of the family, the little one. She raised her eyes when she heard her dad suggest that Joss was in love with her, as though it was that obvious. It wasn't obvious to Emily. Although he was doing her a favour, taking Alice and Marley to see the vet, if he loved her, he had a strange way of showing it. He wasn't exactly falling at her feet or going out of his way to impress her, asking her out on a date, taking her to dinner or buying her flowers. In fact, she'd be surprised if he was interested in her at all.

Although he came across as easy-going and affable, there were times she caught his pained expression when he thought she wasn't looking. It was as though something significant had happened in his past – or perhaps some*one* had happened. Whatever her dad thought he saw, she didn't feel Joss was in the market for a relationship – not yet, anyway. She wished he was, even though there was an age gap; that didn't bother her. In fact, she preferred it. She didn't want some young gun who still wanted to go to nightclubs and discos or – God forbid – raves. Emily wanted maturity. Sometime in the future she wanted to get married and settle down. She wasn't ready for a family yet. Her career as a vet hadn't even got off the ground. Perhaps when it had, she'd be ready. But she sensed Joss wasn't ready, either.

Emily glanced at Hester, who was standing by her legs, looking up at her, probably wondering what they were doing standing behind the kitchen door.

She was about to go when she overheard her dad saying something about her mum's sister. Emily had never met her. According to family gossip, she was the black sheep of the family. Her aunt had met an American and had emigrated to the US. Her mum and sister were estranged, and had been for years. It meant, to Emily's regret, that the two families had never got together. She didn't even know if she had American cousins, let alone their names or where they lived in the US.

At the mention of the aunt she'd never met, Emily desperately wanted to listen in and find out more, but Hester chose that moment to stand up and scamper off. Emily sighed and followed her. The guest house was a large house. The last thing she wanted was for Alice to arrive back to discover Emily couldn't find her dog.

As she tiptoed away from the door, she couldn't help thinking about her aunt in America. It had occurred to her before now to put her DNA up on one of these sites and see if she had a match with someone from America, a cousin over there perhaps. In fact, hearing mention of her aunt had piqued her interest once more.

Emily had heard of AncestryDNA and other websites of this nature. She had asked when she was younger about her aunt in America. She would have loved to visit and get to know her family over there. It was so exciting. Her mum did not share her sentiments. She wouldn't talk about them, let alone consider visiting, so Emily had set the ball rolling to find them herself. It hadn't taken long to join the site. She was still waiting to see if there was a match.

13

Freya stood in the vault, deep in the bowels of the university museum, staring at her clipboard. She was meant to be cataloguing some artefacts in storage and putting some new acquisitions on display upstairs, but she had something on her mind.

The sound of her mobile phone interrupted her thoughts. She pulled it out of her back pocket. 'Hi, Theo. Date night. Sounds like a plan.' Freya smiled. Friday was always date night. They didn't do anything extravagant. They usually ordered a Chinese or a pizza, or Theo cooked, which was a special treat. Sometimes they went to the cinema, but mostly they had a movie night in.

It was bit awkward doing that sort of thing, though, now they had moved out of their rental apartment and were living with her parents. Cuddling up with Theo on the sofa, with a takeaway spread out on the coffee table, was not something she'd do again in a hurry. Her mum and dad had said they had no objections, and although Freya had offered to buy them takeaway too, they'd said they wouldn't hear of it. She couldn't forget her mum's sideways glances at the takeaway and what they were watching on the television, though – the latest *Avengers* movie. The film hadn't been Freya's choice. It had been Theo's turn to choose, but she'd enjoyed it nonetheless. Her parents had not.

That was when she realised that although she loved her parents dearly, and wasn't unhappy about having to leave the bland, modern boxy rental apartment in a development on the outskirts of Cambridge, she had to acknowledge that this wasn't working. But she only had a part-time job, and Theo was still applying for better paid positions. Their choices were very limited. However, during a heart-to-heart with her dad, he had come up with an idea that had surprised her. She was even more surprised that her mum had gone along with it. If it had been her own house, Freya doubted she would be able to bring herself to sell – but then she didn't have kids, and she knew had no idea about the sacrifices parents would make for their children.

She thought again about her parents' lovely old Victorian semi in its leafy Cambridge Street and the short cycle ride along the towpath of the River Cam to get to Cambridge city centre and the colleges.

'I don't see the appeal,' Theo had said when she had raved about her childhood home before he first set eyes on it. 'I mean, it's old.'

'But it's got character,' she'd said.

He hadn't commented. She realised Theo liked brand spanking new, even if that was a house on a development with no greenery and no pleasant walks by a canal, just concrete and cars – although he had conceded that they were lucky to be able to move back in with her parents. And now her parents were selling up to give them a leg-up on the property ladder.

Freya knew that Theo's parents would have done no such

thing. They had sold up and moved to Spain when he was in the middle of his A-Levels, with no thought as to how he'd finish another year of college. They hadn't been prepared to wait another year so that he could finish college and go to university. He'd spent the second year mostly sofa-surfing and sometimes sleeping rough. Then he'd spent a summer working in a summer camp in America before starting university and moving into halls of residence. He'd always said that if it wasn't for his education and some wonderful college lecturers who had pointed him in the right direction he didn't know where he might have ended up; sleeping rough on the streets, and a life of crime, perhaps.

Losing his job and depending on Freya's family did not sit well with Theo. But he'd settled in rather well – too well. In between searching for jobs, he'd continued doing pro bono work, helping others. It was what he'd always wanted to do, which explained why he'd turned down well-paid jobs in the city in favour of joining a small local firm in Cambridge that specialised in family law.

Freya knew it was what he was interested in. Unfortunately, the small firm had been taken over by a larger one and he had been made redundant. He had received a small redundancy payment, and had thought he'd just walk into another job in a law firm. That hadn't happened. He'd walked into a remote working call-centre job instead. *At least it's something*, thought Freya. She frowned at the thought of the study he'd set up in one of the spare bedrooms. Although Theo found the insurance job mundane, she knew he wasn't missing the commute into the centre of Cambridge. It gave him more time to write his novel. After railing against moving in with her parents, he now seemed far more settled in her family home that she did.

'I'm looking forward to date night. I'll leave work on time, I promise.' Freya smiled. 'The dean has asked to see me. I bet it's about the secondment,' she said excitedly.

Theo was silent. She wasn't surprised. He was not happy about the secondment, and hadn't been from the beginning. It was, however, the first genuine interest he'd shown in her career, even though it had been negative. Freya rolled her eyes, thinking about how she didn't have a career yet, as he often reminded her.

He'd never shown the slightest bit of interest in the past. She could see his eyes glaze over whenever she talked about it. But when he'd found out she'd applied for a secondment that would take her abroad, to the famous library in Alexandria, Egypt, it had been another story. He hadn't been interested in the secondment itself; only in the fact that it meant she'd be away for three months. He hadn't wanted her to go.

Rather than being supportive over her being given the opportunity of a lifetime, he had become sulky and moody, and it had created tensions. She had seen nothing wrong with applying for it without discussing it first. She'd assumed he'd be happy for her. It was the first time they had rowed about anything.

Freya frowned when she thought about it. She was supportive of whatever career decisions he made. She'd told him that. So why couldn't he be supportive of her? He'd shot back that his career didn't take him to the back of beyond, to other countries – to the Middle East, of all places.

Freya had been especially defensive over that comment. Growing up, she'd been surrounded by books on archaeology and anthropology on the Middle East – her mother had kept all her books after doing her degree, and they'd come in handy when Freya had followed in her mother's footsteps, taking the same degree. It was Freya's passion – that and riding horses.

Neither of her parents were horsey types, but Freya had fallen in love with riding as a child.

'Freya, are you still there?'

She frowned and looked at her watch. She'd only been standing there a minute or two with all this going through her mind, but she was keen to get off the phone. It wouldn't take her long to walk to her boss's office upstairs, but she didn't want to be late.

'Look, I'd better go. Wish me luck.'

He didn't. 'I'll see you later, then.'

Freya rolled her eyes and ended the call. She expected he'd be over the moon if she didn't get it. *Well, that's not going to happen*, thought Freya. Nobody else had applied for the secondment. It was, as the saying went, in the bag. There was just the formality of getting things organised with the library at Alexandria. She was so excited. She loved that she was following in her mum's footsteps – kind of. She didn't intend to teach, but like her mum, she'd had a passion for archaeology since high school.

For some reason, her thoughts drifted to her secondary school years, and the discovery that there were few children in her school who had no siblings. She recalled asking her mum why she was an only child.

Her mum just told her that there was a saying, *God laughs when you make plans.* Freya didn't understand what she meant by that, but she recalled her mum's response: that life doesn't always turn out the way you expect.

Freya was finding that out now. She was thinking of Theo. Perhaps it would have been easier if she'd met someone more in tune with her passion for archaeology. But that hadn't happened.

'Penny for your thoughts?'

She jumped at the sound of Jolene's voice behind her. 'When did you get back?' Freya asked, running into the arms of her best friend.

'Today! I was going to text you, but I thought I'd surprise you instead.'

'It's the best surprise!' exclaimed Freya, hugging her best friend tight. She'd missed her. She stood back and took in her long blonde hair, perfectly straight white teeth, freckles and piercing blue eyes.

They'd known each other since they were sixteen, when Jolene had joined her riding school in Cambridge. They both had a lot in common. Both were children of teachers, both loved horses, and both had a passion for archaeology and anthropology. If Jolene had been a boy, or Freya had been gay, her best friend would have been the perfect partner. Freya knew from the off that Jolene wasn't into boys – never had been. That didn't matter, although Jolene had once got very drunk and tried to make a pass at her. Jolene didn't remember, and Freya chose not to tell her. She didn't want things to be awkward between them and ruin their friendship. Jolene was American. Her mother had secured a position at Cambridge University, so they had made the move from Arkansas, where she had taught at the University of Central Arkansas. It had been a temporary post for one year, but her parents had fallen in love with Cambridge and had made it their home. Jolene's father had found work at the university too.

Jolene and Freya hadn't gone to the same school; Jolene's parents sent her to a private school. The best thing about that was that when they got together at weekends at the riding school, they always had so much to talk about. But Freya recalled how much they missed each other during the school week. Freya still missed Jolene when she returned to America to visit friends and family she'd left behind.

Soon after they'd become friends, Freya had met Jolene's parents and they'd invited her to go with them to spend the summer in America. Freya was sixteen, and it was the most exciting thing to happen to her in her whole life. But her parents had point-blank refused. She'd had a carefree, liberal upbringing. It had never crossed her mind at the time that they'd say no. She recalled that they'd had a very heated row about it. She'd told them that she was sixteen; she could do what she wanted. Or so she'd thought. It was the first ever time they'd had a real falling-out, a proper slamming-doors row about something. They'd told her that while she lived under their roof, she was not going with her friend to America for the summer. It wasn't even a discussion; she was going with her parents to France, as usual.

She'd made that holiday hell. Freya cringed when she thought about it. It made her wonder if her two middle-aged parents rued the day they'd had a child late in life. Looking back on it now, she imagined they hadn't been ready for their only child to spread her wings, fly the nest, and leave the two of them behind.

'So, did you get it?' Jolene asked, bouncing from one foot to the other.

Freya had thought Jolene would apply for the secondment too, but she'd said she wasn't bothered. Jolene was single just then, and as she was also pursuing a PhD, Freya knew there was no reason for her not to go abroad. Freya had a feeling Jolene had not applied so that Freya wouldn't face any competition.

'Why the frown?' Jolene continued. 'Don't tell me they withdrew it – or something?'

'Oh, no, nothing like that. But I just got off the phone with Theo.'

'Ah.' The look on Jolene's face as she nodded said it all. 'He's still not keen on you going?'

Freya shook her head. 'I think he's rather hoping I don't get it.'

Jolene nodded in agreement. 'The thing is, though, it's only three months. Perhaps you'll get it out of your system.'

They both stared at each other and shared a knowing smile. There would be no getting it out of her system. Freya loved her job. She wanted to be a museum curator. That was her dream, but more than that, she wanted to go to Alexandria, visit the library and the Alexandria National Museum and learn how the curators in the world-famous museum catalogued their precious inventory. She'd read about their vast collection of artefacts – almost two thousand. If she had the opportunity, she wanted to visit the museum in Cairo too.

'I'm on my way up to the dean now – she's called me to her office.'

'I'd say it's in the bag, wouldn't you?'

Freya put her clipboard down on the long wooden table in the middle of the room. 'I hope so.' She thought it boded well. She was meant to be getting an email confirmation. The fact that she'd been summoned to the dean's office made it seem more official. She imagined there would be paperwork to complete, things to sign to set up a visitor pass or visas, or whatever was required for her trip. She looked at her watch. 'God, I'm so excited!'

Jolene laughed. 'I bet you are. Why don't you head off and I'll finish up here?'

She glanced at her clipboard and frowned. 'Sorry, there's so much to do. We were supposed to get some extra help down here, but no one has materialised. There was talk of an intern for a few weeks over the summer, but that didn't happen.'

Jolene nodded. 'I remember. Now it's February already and still they haven't found anyone.' The university had been loaned a collection of artefacts for a special exhibition in the museum. It was extra work they could all do without, so they desperately needed another pair of hands.

It was quite wonderful that an eminent Egyptian professor from Alexandria, who must have had some ties to the university, had thought of their museum when he'd sent the artefacts over to England. Unfortunately, the timing hadn't been great. Freya, although only part-time, knew they couldn't really afford to lose her while she was on secondment. They would not only have to find someone to replace her, but yet another person to help with the workload.

Freya's expression darkened. 'I thought there would have been no shortage of applicants.'

'Yes, but then it's not like the university has advertised the position.'

'Oh, really?'

'Strange isn't it?' said Jolene.

'I'll say.'

'I only found out because I saw someone take down a poster in the student union, and they said the position was no longer available.'

Freya frowned. 'That's odd.' They both shook their heads and glanced around the cavernous, warehouse-like room, taking in the crates of artefacts that had travelled all the way from

Egypt and were still waiting to be unpacked. It would take a lot of work to get them all catalogued and put on display. Despite knowing she was needed there, Freya still wanted to go on the secondment.

Freya looked at the time. 'Well, I'm off now.' She handed Jolene the clipboard with the list of the inventory. 'I'll be back soon to help out.' Freya had no idea how long she'd be. She imagined the dean would run through her itinerary, working out what flights she'd need to book and where she'd stay in Alexandria – although she knew the university there had student accommodation. It was all too exciting.

Freya took the hairband out of her long brown hair, nipped into the ladies' toilets outside in the hall, and ran a brush through her hair before she made her way upstairs. She felt as though she was going for an interview. She knew she wasn't, but she still wanted to look her best. She glanced at her reflection, checking her mascara and eyeliner hadn't smudged around her large chocolate-brown eyes. A dab of lipstick and a little blusher was all she needed. Like Jolene, she had freckles, but they didn't show as much, as she didn't have her best friend's fair complexion. Freya had always tanned easily, and when she was younger and had spent her summers in France, she had always come back looking as though she'd been somewhere hotter, like the Far East.

Freya smiled. 'That'll do.' She put her hairbrush back in her bag, wishing she'd worn something other than her dungarees, a t-shirt, and a black hoodie. Her outfit was comfortable and practical for her work down in the basement of the museum, but if she'd known she would be called to the dean's office today, she would have chosen something different.

Almost immediately after stepping out of the ladies' toilets,

Freya was back again, putting her hair up with the hairband, thinking that with her outfit she'd look a bit more professional if she put her hair up. She pursed her lips. She'd had an idea, but she'd have to be quick.

'What are we doing?' Jolene said a moment later, after Freya had returned and dragged her back into the toilets. 'Look, I need to borrow your outfit.'

Jolene looked at her. 'What outfit?'

Freya looked at her friend. Jolene was taller than her, and slimmer, but it might just work.

'Wait – you want to wear this?' Jolene gestured at her clothes.

A few moments later, they'd changed into each other's outfits, and Freya was standing in front of the mirror, smiling at Jolene, who was standing behind her. The dungarees were too short for her long legs, and the hoodie was hanging off her slender frame.

Freya turned around. 'What do you think?' Jolene had been wearing office-style grey trousers and a pretty white shirt with delicate grey and yellow flowers. It wasn't an outfit that Jolene would wear while cataloguing artefacts, but she wasn't meant to be doing that today. She'd been volunteering upstairs at reception.

Jolene was looking her up and down.

'What is it?' Freya asked. She'd had to hitch the trousers up a little too high to stop them dragging on the floor and had needed to roll the sleeves up on the shirt. 'This isn't going to work,' she said glumly as she slipped on the flat black shoes. They were a size too big, but were the one part of the outfit she could get away with. She could tell by the way Jolene stood that her trainers were pinching Jolene's toes.

Jolene said, 'The outfit looks fine, more than fine, it's just …'

'Just what?'

'Your hair. I think you should wear it down.' Jolene walked over to where Freya was standing in front of the mirror and carefully took out the hairband, unfurling her long hair.

'I've got a hairbrush.'

'Here, let me.' Jolene brushed her hair and handed the hairbrush back. She put her hands on her shoulders.

'What is it?' Freya asked, seeing her expression in the mirror.

'You look so beautiful.' Jolene dropped her gaze.

Freya turned around, looked at her for a long moment, then stepped forward and gave her a kiss on the cheek. 'You are the best – you know that?'

She smiled. 'I know.'

They linked arms and walked out of the bathroom.

Jolene unlinked her arm. 'Now, go get that secondment.'

Freya smiled. 'Will do!'

14

Freya knocked politely on the door before stepping into the dean's office. She was so excited that her secondment was about to be confirmed that her stomach was doing somersaults. She would *actually* be going to Egypt to work in Alexandria. It was a dream come true.

'Ah, Freya. Come in, come in.'

Freya smiled at the dean, her brows knitting when she saw that she wasn't the only one who had been summoned to her office. She glanced at the young man already seated in front of the dean. Was she late? That wouldn't make a good impression. And what was he doing there, anyway? Did she have competition for the coveted place? She felt her face growing red at the thought that she'd got it wrong and wasn't the only one who'd applied for the position. She hadn't prepared for the possibility that the dean might have a shortlist and be choosing between them.

'Freya, I'd like you to meet Tarek.'

Tarek turned in his chair and stared at her.

She saw him looking her up and down with what felt almost like disdain. *What's his problem?* she wondered.

'He's come all the way from Alexandria.'

'Alexandria!' Freya grinned. She hadn't expected this. They had sent someone to greet her and accompany her back to Egypt. She stepped forward as he rose from his chair. He was tall, with a dark olive complexion, soft brown eyes, and what she thought to be an old-fashioned seventies-style haircut. Her heart pounded in her chest as he took her hand. For some reason, Jolene came to mind and what she'd said when she was drunk; that her heart skipped a beat whenever she looked at her friend. Freya wondered why that remark had come to mind as she looked at her new acquaintance from Alexandria. And was she mistaken, or was he holding her hand a little longer than necessary? The look on his face as he stared at her was the same expression she'd seen on Jolene's face a moment earlier.

The dean coughed into the awkward silence.

'Right, well now I've made the introductions. Freya, I've selected you to show him the ropes.'

Freya nodded enthusiastically. 'Oh, I see. I'm showing him around here before we return to Alexandria.'

'We?' He looked at her, then at the dean.

Freya added. 'When I start my secondment.'

The Dean said, 'You did get my email – didn't you?'

Freya looked at her blankly.

The dean cast her gaze down at her laptop, tapped a few keys and frowned. 'Oh, bother. It failed to send. It's still in my outbox.' She looked up at Freya. 'Well, that explains why we are talking at cross purposes. Tarek has been seconded *here* for three months.'

'Okay,' Freya was thinking on her feet. Three months, that could work. Then she'd fly back with him to Alexandria. 'So, the secondment has been shifted back three months?'

The dean shook her head. 'Ah, I see the confusion. I'm afraid there is no secondment, well not from here to there. Alexandria has come to us instead!'

Freya looked at her, aghast. 'I'm sorry – what?'

The dean cast her gaze to the newest member of her team.

Freya looked his way too. He shifted in his seat.

'I'm sorry, I still don't understand …'

'Tarek has been seconded to us rather than us sending someone—' she looked pointedly at Freya, '—over to Egypt. It works out very well, considering the amount of work we have to do with the new artefacts on temporary loan.' She smiled.

Well it doesn't work for me, Freya thought. *Not. At. All.* She could feel her stomach twisting into a knot of frustration, the like of which she hadn't felt since her parents had refused to let her spend the summer with Jolene and her family at their summer house in America. *Why is life so unfair?* thought Freya, *and so full of disappointments?*

But not for everyone. She eyed the new intern coolly. Although, surprisingly, it didn't seem as though he was jumping for joy at being there. She'd be over the moon if she were in his shoes. But his sullen expression said he wasn't happy – not at all.

That annoyed her even more. He didn't appreciate how lucky he was to get this break and visit another country. She felt foolish for shaking his hand so enthusiastically, greeting him so warmly. He was a horrible, horrible young man. Although, of course, he wasn't. He was tall and handsome with large brown eyes that were staring right at her.

She looked away, wishing he wasn't so good-looking. Damn him.

'It's a good thing too that Tarek here accompanied our new

temporary acquisitions all the way from Alexandria. Aren't we lucky?'

Lucky? Right now, that was the last thing she was feeling.

The dean continued, 'We are also very fortunate to have the son of the head of Alexandria's museum, no less, working with us over the next few weeks.'

Freya shot Tarek a look. So that was how he had wangled the position. It was nepotism – pure and simple. And that was how her secondment had gone straight out of the window.

'Besides, even if the secondment was still up for grabs,' the dean said, 'we couldn't have let you go.'

'Why not?' Freya threw back before she'd censored what came out of her mouth. She sounded like a petulant child who'd been denied a bag of sweeties before teatime.

The dean stood up. 'Because we need our brightest and best to show Tarek how we do things here, and that's you. I need you to work with Tarek to set up the temporary exhibition.'

'What? I thought I was setting up the exhibition in the museum?'

'Yes, you'll be helping Tarek.'

'*Helping Tarek*?'

Tarek stood.

'I'm going to leave you in Freya's capable hands,' said the dean as she walked to the door and opened it. Freya bit her lower lip before she said something she'd regret. She gave Tarek a black look instead.

As if sensing something, he turned around and eyed her coolly. 'So, where's the vault?' he said in almost perfect cut-glass English.

Freya would rather have stormed out at that point and told

him to get lost, but the dean was standing at the doorway, about to close the door behind them. She could hear every word. She commented, 'Well, you two are going to get on like a house of fire.'

Don't bank on it, thought Freya, turning on her heel and walking out down the corridor to the wooden staircase that led to the basement. She could hear his footsteps following behind her. It was bad enough that she had lost her secondment, but the fact that his father had got him this position added insult to injury.

She expected he didn't have the first clue what he was doing. What were his qualifications? Was he even interested in all this, or had his father pushed him into it, and he'd felt duty-bound to follow in his footsteps? She expected he'd come on a little jolly to see some of England, then faff about in a museum for a bit because that was the deal, then go home and tick that little trip off his to-do list. She glanced over her shoulder at the good-looking guy. *Stop thinking that and remember he stole your secondment.* Besides, he wasn't her type. *What is my type?* She thought. A guy she'd gone out with in sixth form, and then Theo, whom she'd met at a wedding, made up the sum total of her relationships. *So what?* she thought defensively, wondering why she was even thinking about that. People went out in sixth form, and they met life partners at weddings – it wasn't unheard of.

'Where are we going?' Tarek demanded, rudely interrupting her thoughts.

'We're going to the archives in the basement – where do you think?' she barked back. They walked on in silence, Freya wondering what she was going to tell Jolene when she returned with their newest recruit. At least Jolene wouldn't remark on how cute he was.

15

'Well?' Jolene ran up to her as soon as she walked into the room. 'When do you go?' She was just asking this when, out of the corner of her eye, she saw a tall, young man walk in. 'Hey!' she exclaimed, shouting in Freya's ear, but directing her loud voice at the stranger. 'Unless you've got a pass, you're not meant to be here. The museum is upstairs.'

Freya rolled her eyes in his direction. 'He's with me.'

'I'm Tarek.'

'Tarek?' Jolene shook her head and then raised her eyebrows. 'Oh, they filled the position after all. We got that extra pair of hands.'

Freya heaved a sigh. 'Yes, and no.' She glowered at him. 'Meet the guy who has been *seconded* …' Freya emphasised that word, 'to us.'

Jolene frowned. 'I don't get it.'

'It's simple. Instead of me going over there to show him the ropes, the mountain has come to Mohammed.' She turned to Tarek. 'No offence.' Freya was aware it probably wasn't the done thing to use that old turn of phrase, but just then she didn't care. Quite the contrary; she hoped he did take offence.

He frowned at her and walked over to where the crates were stacked.

'So, there's no secondment to Alexandria?' Jolene whispered.

Freya shook her head, feeling tears welling up in her eyes. 'And to make matters worse …' She threw him a furtive glance as she lowered her voice to barely a whisper and told Jolene who Tarek's father was, 'I think he only got the opportunity to come here because his father is head of the museum in Alexandria.'

Jolene put an arm around her shoulders. 'I am so sorry, Freya. Look, I know this won't make up for it, but come with me to America when I visit next. I know what you're going to say; it's never the right time. But let's just do it, even if your boyfriend can't come – *especially* if he can't come.'

Freya looked at her.

She grinned.

Freya knew it would be more fun if it was just the two of them – and she knew she'd love to meet Jolene's large extended family. She smiled.

'Is that a yes?'

'Oh, yes.' Her smile faded when she caught sight of Tarek heading towards her. She whispered to Jolene, 'Duty calls, I'm afraid. I have been tasked with showing him how we do things.'

Jolene whispered, 'Lucky you.'

Freya didn't detect sarcasm in her friend's voice. She looked at Jolene in surprise.

Jolene shrugged. 'What? I can't know a pretty face when I see one just because I don't fancy guys?'

Freya rolled her eyes. 'May I remind you that I'm with Theo.'

'Yes, I know. The wonderful Theo with whom you still haven't set a date.'

'I'm only in my mid-twenties.'

'What's that got to do with anything? He asked you, didn't he? You said yes. You're engaged. How old were your parents when they married?'

'Um, in their early thirties, I think.'

'Well, there you go.'

'What's that got to do with anything?' Freya looked at her quizzically. 'In any case, what is your point?'

'I think you are delaying taking that final step.'

'I don't know what you mean.'

Jolene gave her a look as if to say, *This is me you're talking to. You can't bullshit your best friend.* 'Perhaps you haven't found Mr Right.'

Freya shook her head. She knew what this was about. As far as her best friend was concerned, no man would be Mr Right for her.

Talking of Mr Right, her phone buzzed with a text message. She knew it would be from Theo again. She reached for her back pocket where she kept her mobile phone and remembered she'd changed into Jolene's outfit.

Jolene held up her phone. She grinned. 'I think this is yours.'

Freya glanced at her dungarees. 'Shall we change back?'

'Nah, it's okay. Might as well stay in these. We can bring the clothes in tomorrow.'

Freya took her phone, read the text message, and frowned.

'What's the matter?'

Freya sighed. 'I asked Theo to let me know if Mum phoned home.'

Jolene raised her eyebrows. 'Is something the matter?'

Freya lowered her voice. 'Mum walked out.'

'You're joking – really?'

She knew that sounded a bit melodramatic. 'Well, yes and no. I don't think she wants to move. I think the whole house move thing was getting on top of her, to be honest.'

'But weren't they doing it to help you on the housing ladder?'

'Yes. But I think she overheard us talking about re-homing her pets. They were considering whether to go into a rental flat if they can't find anything before exchanging contracts on the sale of their house. It can be difficult in rented if you've got pets. I'm not surprised she wants a break. It's just a bit concerning that she left her mobile at home.'

'She left her mobile?'

Freya nodded.

'Sounds to me as though she doesn't want to be contacted.'

'I don't know, maybe. It was on the kitchen table, so I have a feeling she put it down and forgot to pick it up on the way out.'

'I'm sure she'll be in touch when she realises.'

She probably won't be in touch with me, Freya thought. *I'm the one who was talking about her having to let go of her pets.* She frowned. What a stupid, stupid thing to say. Especially as she loved those animals herself; she'd grown up with them. They were family.

Freya explained what she'd heard second-hand from Theo about her mum's sudden departure.

'So she just packed some cases, took the pets, got in a taxi and left?'

Freya frowned. 'I wasn't there, but yeah, that kind of sums it up. 'She left a note for my dad.'

'What did it say?'

Freya's frown deepened. 'You know, I'm not sure.' Now she really thought about it, her dad hadn't read the note out loud.

Freya felt a knot in her stomach at the thought that there was something going on she didn't know about – something not good. It made her wonder what her mum going off like that was really all about.

16

'So, how was he?' asked Emily as soon as they stepped into the hallway of the guest house.

Alice smiled. 'It was just as you thought. Poor mite has tooth decay, so he must have had toothache.'

Emily smiled. 'Antibiotics?'

'Yes, there was an infection too.'

'Ah, I thought that might be the case.'

At least it was only one tooth. Alice would need to take Marley back to her own vet when she returned home in case he needed further treatment. The appointment with the vet had cost quite a bit – not that she begrudged paying for the treatment, but it was something she hadn't budgeted for when she had turned up at the hotel. In fact, she hadn't budgeted for anything. She had the card to the joint savings account she had with Jeffrey, and that was where her trip was going to be paid from. Unless Jeffrey froze the bank account.

Could he do that? Alice didn't want to think about that either. She knew she should phone and tell him where she was but didn't feel like doing it that day. She'd save that little pleasure for the morning.

'And how was the taxi service?' Emily asked, smiling as Joss walked over and joined them.

Alice turned to Joss. 'The taxi was splendid.' *As was the driver*, she thought. There had been no awkward silences on the car journey; something Alice couldn't abide. They had chatted about the beautiful Suffolk Coast and the family-run guest house. She had talked a little of herself and the impending sale of her house, although she noticed the conversation never touched on why he was there. She suspected that Joss wasn't ready to share his story – just yet.

He had talked about Emily and her family, though, which didn't surprise Alice, considering his obvious affection for Emily. She hadn't let on that she knew how long he'd been staying at the guest house. He'd mentioned that Emily's mum had bought the place soon after losing her first husband, intent on running it as a bed-and-breakfast even though she had two young children. Emily had come along when she'd met and married Gerald.

'Alice?' Emily called as she was making her way up the stairs with the cat carrier.

She turned on the stairs. 'Yes?'

'Will you be still dining in with us this evening?'

Alice nodded. She glanced at the phone on the reception desk, feeling guilty that she still hadn't phoned Jeffrey or Freya and let them know where she was and that she was okay. But she had left that note for Theo to give to Jeffrey. Although she hadn't specified where she'd gone for a break, she had taken the pets, which meant they'd soon realise she hadn't flown abroad or anything like that.

She would have loved to stay with her best friend for a few days, but unless she was prepared to ditch her pets and fly thousands of miles to the Far East, where Jane was on holiday in Thailand, which was out of the question, here she was. Besides, she wouldn't want to intrude on Jane's holiday, even if she was desperate to see her. That left – among the dwindling possibilities of where Jeffrey might think she had gone – her mother's house.

Alice shuddered at the thought. She wouldn't go there. Jeffrey knew that. They'd hardly spoken in twenty-five years, apart from acknowledging each other at her father's funeral seven years earlier. There had been a very awkward conversation with the then teenage Freya, who had rarely seen her maternal grandparents. She had wanted to know the reason they were estranged.

Alice had always expected that Freya would pass them on the street, and one time she had, shortly before her grandfather passed away. Alice only knew about this because Freya had returned home from her shopping trip to Cambridge with her school friends and burst into tears. She'd made the mistake of approaching them. They'd told her to stop harassing them, telling her they didn't know who she was even though they knew very well that she was their grandchild. She didn't know why that episode had come to mind. She'd rather it hadn't. She'd rather it had never happened. Especially when Freya had discovered she'd been lying to her all those years. She'd told Freya that her maternal grandparents lived miles away when, in fact, they had lived down the road – minutes from their house by car, or a fifteen-minute walk – in the lovely village of Grantchester, a very picturesque little place where tourists, writers and artists flocked; a country setting but virtually on their doorstep. Freya could have walked or cycled to see them most weekends.

'Here, let me help you up with that,' offered Joss, noticing that Alice had stopped halfway up the stairs. However, her brief rest stop wasn't to do with carrying the cat carrier. The house reminded her of where she'd grown up – the three-storey Victorian property in Grantchester with large bay windows and a little turret in the roof. However, there was one difference; it hadn't had the sea views or the sound of the waves gently lapping up the shingle beach, or the cries of seagulls outside the windows.

Losing her parents was the price Alice had paid to have Freya; she just wished she'd never told them her secret. Alice recalled feeling bitterly disappointed that they were not open-minded and remained stuck in the Victorian era, believing appearances were everything, as though their neighbours and friends would find out the shameful truth.

Alice had told them once that it was their loss, the decision to have no involvement with Freya. But their choice not to be part of her life wasn't about Freya herself, but about Alice and the decision they'd said she'd live to regret.

'The truth will out,' her mother had told her once when she'd confided to her what she'd done. She'd thought her mother, of all people, would be understanding. She had been under the illusion that she could do no wrong in her mother's eyes. However, their relationship had quickly soured after that, although they'd remained on good terms with Jeffrey.

Alice frowned, thinking of those envelopes and card with her husband's name on. It might turn out that he was no angel either. She still wanted to get to the bottom of whether he'd had an affair.

'Alice?'

'Oh, yes – right. He *is* a little heavy.'

'Do you want me to call for my dad to help?'

On the stairs, standing behind Alice, Joss glanced over his shoulder at Emily. 'No, don't worry, I've got this.'

At the top of the stairs, Alice turned to her left and walked along the corridor, Joss following. 'My room is along here too,' he commented. When she stopped outside the door, he added, 'Hey, we're next-door neighbours.'

Alice smiled at him. Her smile faded when she realised who Joss reminded her of – her husband when he was young.

Alice opened the door, turned around and said on the spur of the moment, 'Will you have dinner with me?' She frowned when she realised what that sounded like; asking a young man to have dinner with her.

'I'm sorry, that's really kind of you but—'

She shook her head. 'Don't be sorry. I know it's a bit weird, an older woman asking you to dinner. I just thought, if we are both dining alone, why sit at separate tables? Sorry, didn't want you to get the wrong impression.' The colour rose in her cheeks, making her feel even more embarrassed.

Joss grinned, shaking his head. 'I wasn't turning you down because I thought you were, well, hitting on me, as the Americans like to say. Raincheck until tomorrow evening?'

Alice smiled. 'Of course. Going anywhere special this evening?' What she really wanted to ask was, *Who is the lucky lady?* She hoped it was Emily.

'I'm going out with Emily.'

'That's wonderful. You make a lovely couple,' Alice blurted.

Joss frowned. 'No, it's not a dinner date.' His tone of voice hinted at his disappointment that it wasn't. 'After she's finished work, I've asked her to come with me to Cobblers Yard.'

'Cobblers Yard? Is that in Southwold?' Anybody who ventured to the Suffolk Coast was bound to discover the coastal town with its year-round bunting hanging across the streets, its pretty little shop fronts, its grand old hotels, Adnams Brewery, and the wonderful Victorian pier. Alice had half a mind to ask if she could go with them, but she didn't want to intrude. Who knew where it might lead, the two of them going out together, even if it wasn't a proper a date? It might well turn into one.

'Ah, no, it's not Southwold – it's further down the road in Aldeburgh.'

Alice knew why she'd assumed it was Southwold. It was closer. But she'd also visited Aldeburgh in the past, a long time ago. She recalled the pebbly beach with the fishermen's huts selling fresh fish caught that day, and the promenade fronting the beach with pretty pastel-coloured villas on the sea front. Although familiar with the town, she commented, 'I've never heard of Cobblers Yard.'

'Ah, I'm not surprised. It's easy to pass it by and not realise it's there. There's a narrow pathway between the shops that leads into a cobbled yard with a small group of shops with old-fashioned shop fronts.'

He reeled them off. 'There's a music shop, charity shop, The Potting Shed that sells flowers. The lady who runs it does landscape work. I help her out doing odd jobs. Then there's the antique shop which has changed hands, the arts and crafts shop, and the bookshop. There aren't many shops, but it's worth stopping by just to see the old-fashioned store fronts.'

Alice would do more than that. 'I'd like to stop by the arts and crafts shop.' Joss had just reminded her that she wanted to try her hand at painting again. 'And I wouldn't mind popping to a bookshop to get a novel.'

'I'm afraid the bookshop isn't open. Hasn't been for years.'

'Oh, that's a shame.'

'And the arts and crafts shop has closed too.'

Alice sighed. It was a sign of the times. Shops closing on the high street because people preferred to shop online.

'That's what I'm taking Emily to see – the arts and crafts shop.'

Alice frowned. 'But I thought you said—'

'Yes, it's closed down now, but I thought it would make a rather good premises for a vet's practice.'

'She's thinking of opening her own practice?'

'Well, no, at least not yet. I'm trying to persuade her. It might be a good idea.'

'Ah.' Alice stared at him. 'Does she know where you're taking her this evening?'

'No, it's a surprise.'

Alice inwardly sighed. Men. Why could they be so obtuse sometimes? She'd seen the way Emily looked at Joss. She expected Emily was in for a surprise alright, when she found out it wasn't a date.

Alice turned around and put the key in the lock.

Joss looked at the cat carrier in his arms. 'Do you want me to bring this inside for you?'

Marley chose that moment to hiss at Joss.

Alice turned around and frowned at her cat. 'I thought you were feeling better?' Clearly, the visit to the vet hadn't put him in a good mood. She looked at Joss. 'I'll take it from here.'

He handed her the cat carrier. 'Thanks for the lift, Joss.'

She'd thought it would be awkward going a distance in the car with a stranger, a young man with whom she'd thought she'd have nothing in common. She'd wondered what they would talk about. But they talked about a great deal – or rather, she had. She had told him about the house move and how she felt her family had railroaded her into it, and that she'd done something incredibly selfish and just packed her bags and walked out for a few days.

'Am I a bad person?' she'd asked him. What she had discovered about Joss was that he was a good listener. It had made her wonder what it was he had done for a living before he appeared to have dropped out.

She remembered that Joss had smiled at that comment. 'No, that doesn't make you a bad person – not at all. I can empathise.' He didn't elaborate, but Alice had caught a look on his face as he turned to go; there was an air of melancholy about him, as though something had happened in his life to throw him off course.

Alice wasn't a stranger to that scenario. Something had happened right there in the guest house a quarter of a century earlier. Considering the events that had taken place that night years earlier, she was still trying to fathom what had possessed her to return. Was she really trying to find out if her husband had met a woman called Wendy there in the past? If that were the case, then shouldn't she be at home right then, confronting him?

'What do you think of the idea?' Joss had been about to step into his room next door, but he paused to ask the question, interrupting her thoughts.

Alice turned to him. 'You mean about the vet's practice?'

He nodded.

'Considering how far we had to drive to the nearest one, I think it's an excellent idea.' What she didn't think was a good idea was Joss taking Emily out that evening just to show her a shop. 'You know what a grand idea would be?'

'What?'

'Having a meal afterwards.'

Joss shook his head at that suggestion. 'I expect she's having dinner with her mum and dad before she leaves, so she won't want to change her plans.'

'Don't be so sure,' said Alice before closing the door.

17

There was a knock on Emily's door.

She rolled her eyes. She was trying to get ready. 'What?' she snapped as she walked over and opened the door.

'Dinner's ready, sweetheart.' He looked at her. 'Well, don't you look a picture? Bit overdressed for dinner, though.'

Emily sighed. 'Sorry, Dad, I should have said. I'm not having dinner with you guys this evening.' And that was the problem with living at home. She'd got used to doing her own thing, away at university when she was studying veterinary medicine. She hadn't had to tell anyone where she was going, what she was doing, and who she was doing it with. As the baby of the family, she had always felt her parents were overprotective. And although she had an older stepsister, there was too much of an age gap for them to be close, like some of her friends' sisters were.

She was envious of her friends who'd go partying or go to the beach together, even hook up with boys, while their parents did their own thing. She had always envied Abigail and Luke, who had seemed to have so much more freedom than her to go off together while she was too young and stuck with her parents.

Emily silently berated herself for going down that rabbit

hole. That was all in the past. And she was lucky to be able to return home for a bit and help out with the business, earning some money while she applied for veterinary positions. The problem was, she just wasn't getting a look-in with any of her applications. Not that there were many positions to apply for, but they all wanted at least some experience.

Being newly qualified, she was increasingly feeling in the same catch-22 as most graduates – she needed a job to get experience. But how would she get that experience if she couldn't even get her foot in the door? She was becoming disillusioned with the whole application process and getting turned down even before the interview stage. So this evening was just what she needed, a night out – a date. She just didn't want to tell her parents all about it.

'I'll let your mother know you won't be having dinner then.'

She went to close the door.

'Going out on a date?'

Emily sighed. 'Yes, Dad.'

'Anyone I know?'

And there it was. She knew her dad only meant well, but this was awkward, especially as it was with one of the guests. 'It's Joss.' But her dad's reaction surprised her.

'Well, that's wonderful. I hope you have a lovely time.'

'Oh, right! Thanks, Dad.'

He turned to go.

'Oh, Dad …'

He turned back. 'Yes, sweetheart?'

'Do you mind, er, not telling Mum?'

He raised his eyebrows. 'About Joss?'

Emily nodded.

'If that's what you want, sweetheart.'

Emily smiled. The thing with her dad was that he always took her side. Even so, she felt she owed him an explanation. 'Look, the thing is, I get the impression mum doesn't much like him. It's the age gap – isn't it?' Emily guessed that Joss was in his early to mid-thirties. If he was mid-thirties, then he was ten years older than her. She didn't care about that. But she would bet her mum did.

Gerald said, 'It's not that she doesn't like him. I think it's just that she doesn't know anything much about him.'

Emily had been down this road before. That was why it would be so nice moving out and living somewhere else. Why did she have to explain herself, or get her parents' (or rather her mum's) permission to date someone? So what if they knew little about Joss?

Emily had been counting on the fact that her mum would be having dinner when she stole out of the house and wouldn't put two and two together if Joss didn't eat at the guest house that evening. It wouldn't be unusual for Joss not to dine in. He didn't always. Sometimes he ordered a takeaway to be delivered, or went and got one himself, spending the evening in his room with his laptop. Was he working online? She'd never asked. She knew he'd done some odd jobs, landscaping work for her sister Abigail's best friend Lili, who worked at The Potting Shed in Aldeburgh. He'd been living with his uncle for a bit in Southwold, and then had moved to the guest house at her sister's suggestion. That was three months earlier. He'd become a bit of a fixture, helping her dad with odd jobs around the house. With a place that size, there was always some maintenance work to be done, or gardening.

Emily didn't understand her mum's objection to Joss. He

wouldn't take any payment for his time, and wouldn't accept a discounted room rate either, insisting he continued paying the full rate. With the guest house normally empty at that time of year, the fact that Joss had stayed for so long, and in one of the most expensive rooms on the top floor with views over the cove, it was little wonder that her dad enjoyed having him around. But it wasn't about the money. Joss was another guy to chat with while they were doing stuff together around the house or weeding the garden – although she noticed Gerald did all the talking. Typical Dad.

Emily walked over and looked at her reflection in the long mirror. It had been a while since she'd worn her little black number. The dress still fitted, thank goodness – being at home, and a bit bored, she'd started snacking in between meals. She'd straightened her long blonde hair, something she rarely bothered with while working at home all day. And she'd dug out her heels from the back of the wardrobe. It was times like these she would have liked a girlfriend – or two – to chat to and tell them excitedly that she had a date. Perhaps it was her own fault for not keeping in touch with her university friends. She had kept in touch through Facebook and WhatsApp. But they were all living in different parts of the country; there didn't seem to be a right time to get together.

The messages between them on social media were dwindling as they moved on into new lives after university. Emily had heard that one had married, a couple were engaged, and one of their cohort had taken a year out after qualifying to go travelling and see the world.

She was the only one out of the small circle of friends on her course who had moved back home. It made her feel a failure.

Perhaps that was why she was messaging them less and less, avoiding finding out how their lives were moving on.

It was the same with old school friends. Some of them had left Suffolk. But she hadn't kept in touch with any of them. Emily had spent a lot of her time after school helping at the guest house. She'd got good money from her parents for doing so, but it had been at the expense of spending time with her friends. And she hadn't been popular at school. Emily was thinking about the times her friends had had house parties when their parents were away, or sleepovers at weekends or on their birthdays.

Unfortunately for Emily, her invitations had dwindled when it became apparent there would be no return invites. She knew some of her friends would have loved a sleepover or a house party at her big old house on the cove. But it was not to be. The house she grew up in wasn't like her friends' houses. Emily's home was a business. It meant her parents didn't go on holiday or spend any weekends away, so a house party was out of the question. The guest house never closed; not even for Christmas. And because of paying guests, a load of giggling teenagers having a sleepover in her room was out of the question.

Emily didn't think phoning her older stepsister was a good idea. Although they'd patched things up – Abigail had apologised over the fact that she'd spent years being unkind to Emily because she'd grown up with her own dad, while Abigail's own father had died.

But there was one person she could call with her news.

18

'Clarissa, it's Emily.'

'Hey.'

Emily could hear Clarissa's dog barking in the background, and children's argumentative voices too. 'Oh, I've caught you at a bad time.'

'There's never a good time,' quipped Clarissa.

Emily smiled. They had some things in common; they'd both moved back in with their parents – in Clarissa's case, with her dad – and they both lived in Shingle Street. But that was where the similarities ended. Clarissa was younger than Emily by six months, and yet she had responsibilities. She was a divorced young mother of two.

'It's not like you to phone – what's up? Everything okay?'

Emily never phoned. If she wanted to speak to her friend, all she had to do was walk out of the guest house and halfway up the street and call on her.

Clarissa had grown up in London, where she'd met her husband. When they'd split up, Clarissa and the children had moved temporarily to Suffolk, to where her parents had retired. She was living with her dad in her parents' cottage on Shingle Street. Nine months after she had moved in, it was looking a lot less like a temporary arrangement.

Emily thought it sad that Clarissa's parents' retirement dream of living in a cottage on the Suffolk Coast has been shattered when Clarissa's mum was diagnosed with early onset dementia and had needed to move into a care home. But at least Clarissa's dad wasn't on his own now. Emily didn't know how they did it, but they were all living in her dad's small three-bedroomed terraced cottage. Clarissa's children had to share a room. It wasn't ideal, but she'd told Emily that her plan was to find her own place to rent when she'd sorted out a job.

'So, what's up?' Clarissa asked again.

'I'm going out on a date.'

'Oh, Em! That's amazing. Who with?'

'Seriously?' Emily said jokingly.

'Ah, with the mysterious Joss.'

'Yep.'

'So, he asked you out? Or did you finally ask him out, like you've been saying you would?'

'No, he asked me. Said he's got something to show me.' Emily rolled her eyes at Clarissa's crude remark. 'Clarissa – I swear you've got sex on the brain.'

'Well, that's because I ain't getting any.'

Emily laughed, but she knew that underneath the light-hearted banter, Clarissa wanted to meet someone. Since she'd broken up with her husband, she'd tried dating apps, but the problem was that with two kids and a dog, and without her own place, it did not surprise Emily when Clarissa told her that most young guys ran a mile. There were some older, middle-aged guys who appeared quite pleasant, but Clarissa wasn't looking for someone to take care of her and her children. 'I can take care of myself, thank you very much,' she'd said.

'So, do you want me to find out about Joss? I have my sources …'

Emily smiled. 'No, thank you – for the umpteenth time.' How many times had Clarissa asked her that since she'd made the mistake of telling her friend some weeks earlier that she fancied the guy staying at the guest house?

'How's the journalism course going, by the way?' Emily asked, changing the subject. Clarissa had been doing an evening course in journalism while she juggled caring for two children and a large pet dog with working in a part-time temping job, typing articles up for a local newspaper based in Lowestoft.

'I finished it. Passed with distinction.'

'Oh, Clarissa. Well done. We must go out and celebrate.'

'I got a job too.'

'As a journalist?'

'A reporter.'

Emily felt guilty that she'd only touched base with Clarissa because she'd had some news of her own. What with helping at the guest house and sending off applications to get a position at a veterinary practice, she hadn't seen Clarissa for some time. In fact, now she thought about it, it had been unusual not bumping into her sometimes on her evening jog up and down the beach.

'I should have let you know sooner, I know. But in between the kids, and the course and my job, and looking for a new place to live … well, things have been hectic.'

Emily frowned. She wasn't the only one who'd been super-busy. But hearing what Clarissa had to contend with just made her feel even more guilty for not finding the time to check in with her. After all, she was only looking for a job; she wasn't faced with all the other things that Clarissa had on her plate.

'Besides, I wanted it to be a surprise,' Clarissa added.

'You wanted what to be a surprise?'

'I got a job with the same newspaper I've been temping with, so I'm having a week off work while they sort out the paperwork for my official start in my new position as a news reporter.'

'So, you'll no longer be temping there?'

'Nope, it's permanent, and I won't be typing up other people's articles. I'll be the one *writing* local news stories.'

Her friend didn't sound as happy as she could be over her new position. Emily knew why. The key word was *local.* Clarissa had aspirations. She wanted to return to London and work in what she called the big leagues. For the BBC or for a large, national newspaper.

'It's a foot in the door, Clarissa. Who knows where it will lead? Perhaps you'll break some big story and it will get their attention.'

'What – around here in sleepy Suffolk?'

Emily bit her lower lip. Her friend had a point. 'Well, maybe not. But you never know …' She trailed off. 'It's a nice surprise though, to hear you've got a position in journalism. It's what you've worked hard for.'

'Ah, but that's not the surprise. My ex is having the kids in the February half-term …'

'That's next week,' Emily commented.

'Yep, so they're going to stay with him in London. He's picking them up tomorrow. That's what all the commotion is in the background; they're excited, getting their bags packed to go on an adventure.'

Emily pursed her lips. She bet Clarissa didn't feel the same way about their little adventure with their dad.

Clarissa lowered her voice. 'This makes me sound like a bad parent, but I can't wait for them to go.'

'Really?' Emily said in surprise.

'Oh, yes. God knows, I could do with a break to recharge my batteries before I start my new job.'

'It sounds as though it's come at the right time.' Emily was no stranger to Clarissa's rants over the fact that her ex never seemed to find the time to have the children, even for a weekend, to give her a break. 'We could get together sometime next week and have a catch-up.'

Clarissa was silent down the phone, which wasn't like her. Emily said, 'Unless you've got other plans, like you're going away – or something?'

'Or something,' Clarissa said, giggling down the phone.

'What are you up to?'

'So, your mum didn't tell you?'

'Tell me what?'

'Oh good. So she can keep a secret.'

Emily frowned at that word, *secret*. 'What's going on?'

'I'm going away too. Having a little holiday. A bit of me-time.'

'I'm glad to hear it.' Emily meant it. She knew her friend had to work doubly hard being a single parent.

'But you haven't heard the best bit. I was going to keep it as a surprise, but as you're going out this evening, and who knows when you'll be back, I just can't wait to tell you.'

'You're going to America.'

'What makes you say that?' Clarissa sounded taken aback.

'Well, isn't it somewhere you always wanted to go?' Emily felt a pang of jealousy. She wished her mum and her aunt, who lived in America, weren't estranged. Perhaps she had cousins her age and would have gone to America for holidays.

'Yes, that's still on my bucket list. But no, I haven't got the money for anything like that. I'm taking a break closer to home, *very* close to home. In fact …' she paused, 'I'm staying at a lovely little guest house on Shingle Cove.'

Emily blinked. 'No way! You're coming to stay with us?'

'Yep, I've got a room booked for the week, full board, nice room up the top with the views.'

'But that's … that's …'

'Crazy – I know. Donut is coming with me to give my dad a break. He'll have the cottage to himself with no responsibilities – even the dog. Few hotels allow pets, you know.'

'Oh, I wasn't going to say *crazy*. It's fantastic.' Emily grinned. She suddenly had the most stupendous idea. 'Now *this* is going to sound crazy …' She winced as she asked, 'Can we have a slumber party?'

'You mean like kids do?'

'Yeah. It sounds dumb, doesn't it?'

'Not at all. As long as I can bring a bottle – and I don't mean juice.'

Emily grinned, thinking of all those years when she was a teenager and couldn't have a single friend stay over, or have a slumber party for her birthday because they would have disturbed the guests. She confided all this to Clarissa.

'Well, we are going to make up for that, girl.'

Emily's grin faltered. Would Clarissa be loud, get drunk, and disturb the other guests? Then again, there was only Alice and Joss. Joss wouldn't care. As for Alice; she seemed nice, open-minded, and young at heart. Perhaps she'd invite her too. Not Joss, though. This would be girls only.

'When are you coming?' Emily asked eagerly.

'The kids are off first thing in the morning, so once I've packed, I'll be with you.'

'Great! I'm so excited.'

'Me too. Honestly, I can't remember the last time I had some time to myself without watching the clock or grabbing some moments after bedtime when I'm so dog-tired I just fall asleep.'

Emily blurted, 'I hope you don't get bored.'

'I don't think that's going to happen. I'm looking forward to meeting the other guests.'

'Oh, there's only Joss, and a lady called Alice here at the moment.' Thinking of Joss, Emily was hoping she could make it out of the front door without her mum finding out who she was going out with. She didn't fancy the third degree about where she was going, or the possibility that Joss might overhear raised voices if she found out that that Emily was going out with him. Thinking of which, she said, 'Clarissa, will you do me a favour? When you turn up tomorrow, if my mum asks, which I know she will, can you say I was at yours this evening?'

'Sure – why?'

'I don't want my mum to find out about me and Joss at the moment. I know she doesn't like him. I imagine it's the age gap, and she's said we don't know anything about him.'

'Well, I for one like him already.'

'Why? You haven't met him.'

'Yes, but we have something in common already – you, my dear friend. I'm can't wait to meet him – and the other guest. Perhaps I'll find out a thing or two about them.'

Emily rolled her eyes when something occurred to her. 'I hope you're not staying here to write an article about the guest house – or more to the point, the guests.'

'Whatever gave you that idea?' said Clarissa innocently.

Emily shook her head from side to side. 'Clarissa …'

'Cross my heart – unless something really interesting came to light.'

'Came to light?'

'Oh, I don't know. If I found out something about one of the guests that I thought would make a good story.'

'Clarissa, you can't go writing a news article about one of the guests.'

'No, of course not. You're right. I wouldn't do that.'

Emily wasn't sure she believed her. Clarissa told her she was looking for a news story. A big break that might catapult her into the big leagues. However, the idea didn't trouble Emily. Clarissa could nose around all she wanted, but Emily couldn't imagine there was anything remotely newsworthy about their current guests.

19

'That's so kind of you, Gerald.'

'Not at all. Where shall I put it?'

'On the dressing table, if you wouldn't mind.' Alice stood by the door watching Gerald walk into her bedroom carrying a large tray. 'I hope I haven't inconvenienced you by deciding at the last minute that I'd rather eat dinner in my room than downstairs.'

'Not at all,' Gerald said again, his ears still burning; his wife was singing a different tune. They'd had words. Gerald didn't see the problem. It just meant taking Alice's meal up two flights of stairs. He got the feeling there was more to it than that, though. 'What's the problem?' he'd asked.

'You know what the problem is – her being here. I want her to leave.' Anthea had put her hands on her hips. 'Do you know what she's doing back here after all these years?'

Gerald had pursed his lips, thinking, *how the hell would I know?* He'd said, 'Look, probably like us, she's had … well, I wouldn't say misgivings, but I bet it's played on her mind all these years.'

'Played on her mind?' Anthea had scoffed. 'That's one way of putting it.'

'Did you recognise me, Gerald?'

The question snapped him back to the present.

Alice stared at him. She wasn't surprised that Anthea hadn't brought the tray up herself. She imagined she wanted her gone.

'We have so many guests come and go over the years that, to be honest, no, I didn't. Sorry.' Just because he didn't recognise her, it didn't mean he didn't remember her, though. How could he not?

He avoided eye contact. 'Well, if that's all, I'd, er, better go, there's … um … lots to do.' Gerald hot-footed it to the door. He lingered a moment, staring at her.

Their eyes locked, neither wanting to talk about what had happened at the guest house all those years earlier.

He left and shut the door.

Alice turned to the dinner on the tray. She'd lost her appetite. At least her pets had eaten. She'd bought some pet food at the vet's surgery, and Gerald had kindly provided dog and cat bowls.

Alice had remembered to buy a litter tray, cat litter, and some plastic bags, and had set it all up in the spacious en suite bathroom. She'd opened the window, letting in the cool sea breeze, so that it wouldn't smell in there. She'd introduced Marley to the cat litter tray. He hadn't used one since he was a kitten. 'Well, you're just going to have to get used to it again, for a few days,' she'd said to him when he looked at her and meowed his disapproval.

Hester and Marley had eaten in her room. Gerald had taken the dishes away when they'd finished. Fortunately, they both ate dry food, so her bedroom didn't whiff of either cat or dog food.

Thinking of food, Alice glanced at her meal. Lasagne and salad with garlic bread, and a slice of cake for pudding with a large pot of tea brewing. Alice put the lid back on the meal, still not feeling hungry. She picked up the teapot, poured herself a cup of tea, and went to stand by the window. It was pitch dark outside. The security light suddenly came on down below.

She glanced down at the parking area outside the guest house just in time to see Joss walking to the car, followed by Emily. She was wearing a figure-hugging black dress, heels, and a smartly tailored coat. Emily looked as though she was going out on a date. Her so-called date did not. Joss had changed into jeans, a jumper and a jacket, but not smart-casual by the looks of it.

Alice sighed and shook her head. 'Oh, dear.' she was wondering what Emily was going to say when she found out they were not going out to a nice restaurant.

❖

'I feel a bit overdressed. Am I overdressed?' The moment Emily set eyes on Joss in his ripped jeans and a baggy jumper that looked as though it needed a wash, she knew she'd made a huge gaffe. This wasn't a date.

'We're not going for dinner, are we?' she said flatly.

So, where are we going? she wondered. She hesitated when he opened the car door. *You know nothing about him,* a little voice in her head said.

'I was going to show you something.'

'What?'

'I wanted it to be a surprise.'

'Well, this is a surprise, all right,' Emily threw back.

❖

Alice watched Emily storm back into the guest house. She expected that the poor girl had been so embarrassed when she'd discovered that it wasn't a date as she had assumed.

Alice heard the front door bang from two floors up. Alice stared at Joss, his surprised face illuminated by the security light as he stared at the house. He threw his arms in the air, then turned around and slammed the car door shut. He too stormed back into the guest house. She wondered if he would try to talk to Emily.

Alice turned from the window when she heard the creak of stairs on the floor below, and footsteps gathering pace along the carpeted corridor. She heard Joss call out, 'Emily!' before a door slammed somewhere. A moment later, there was the sound of someone coming up the stairs to her floor and stomping along the corridor past her door.

Hester stood up in the basket Gerald had provided and ran over to the door. She woofed.

'Hester!' Alice called out in a hushed voice. 'Come here!'

Hester turned from the door and looked at her.

'It's okay. Come here, girl,' she called in a soothing voice.

Hester ran over for a reassuring fuss. Then she jumped up, her front paws on the bed.

'No, leave Marley alone.'

Marley, who was curled up on the duvet and appeared to be asleep, swiped Hester with his paw, just missing her nose.

'Oh, Hester. When will you learn that Marley will not play with you? You will never be pals.'

Hester stood there looking at Marley, wagging her tail, as the cat stood up, stretched, then turned her back to Hester and settled down into a furball, eyes closing.

'There, you see.'

Hester took her paws down from the bed and padded over to her basket, where she settled down and fell asleep.

'Never. Be. Pals.'

Alice rolled her eyes toward Percy, who was in his cage on the sideboard. She had learnt long ago not to answer back, otherwise she'd hear him retort all night. The trouble with Percy was that once he started, getting him to shut his beak was impossible, and there would be no getting away from him in a guest house room.

Alice shook her head. It had been a stupid, spur-of-the-moment decision to bring them all. She was sure that Freya hadn't really meant it when she'd talked about getting rid of her pets. Her daughter had been stressed about the move, about getting her own place, about the thought that it might fall through. *Freya must be aware that the only spanner in the works is me*, thought Alice. *Not my pets.*

She suspected that Freya realised she didn't want to sell up. She wasn't the only one who loved their house. Alice knew Freya loved her childhood home and really didn't want her parents to sell up, either. She'd overheard her talking to Jeffrey, asking if there was another way, and offering to look for another rental and move out. He wouldn't hear of it. He was always putting Freya first. And now here Alice was, running away like a sulky teenager. She knew it wasn't a grown-up thing to do, to run away from problems rather than confront them.

Alice sighed. In the morning she'd phone Jeffrey. She frowned at the thought. He'd want to know where she was. He would offer to come and pick her up. She didn't want him to know she was there, at the guest house. 'Damn, why did I forget my phone?' she said aloud. She knew it would have been easier to text than to get into a conversation.

She glanced at her dinner, which was getting cold, poured

herself another cup of tea and took the slice of cake. She sat in bed with her novel, popped her glasses on and started to read to take her mind off the next morning and that phone call.

She suddenly felt something on her lap. Alice lowered the book and found Marley curling up contentedly on her legs. She stroked the top of his head and was rewarded with the loudest purr. 'Hey, someone is feeling better.'

Alice was pleased that she'd brought Marley, otherwise it would most likely have been weeks until his next check-up with the vet. She thought of Emily, and of what a shame it was that she couldn't find a job as a vet. Her talent was going to waste. She lowered her book further when she had an idea. Perhaps she could show Emily the premises Joss had in mind for a new vet practice in Aldeburgh? She'd love to see Cobblers Yard, and Joss had explained how to find it. Then perhaps Emily might forgive Joss for not taking her out on a date. She hoped so. Alice was feeling guilty that she hadn't spoken her mind and encouraged Joss to book an evening meal for after his surprise.

Alice smiled, determined to get those two back on speaking terms.

20

'Dad – have you heard from Mum?' Freya walked into the kitchen, expecting him to be there, preparing the breakfast.

He wasn't there.

Freya was surprised – and she had always thought that hell would freeze over before her dad did something that surprised her. As far as she was concerned, he was the biggest creature of habit ever to walk the planet.

Freya frowned at her rather unkind thought. But she was taken aback that he wasn't there, asking her what she wanted; he always asked, even though it was the same answer every time – toast and Marmite.

She pursed her lips. 'Am I turning into my dad?' she asked the empty kitchen. Or more to the point – had she been like him all along? Freya was a creature of habit, too. She didn't like change – although at the same time, she wanted that secondment abroad more than anything; that was an anomaly.

It had been a big thing for a creature of habit such as Freya to move out of the only home she'd ever known and in with her boyfriend, into a modern flat on a soulless development on the outskirts of Cambridge. She recalled confiding in Jolene her thoughts when she'd first moved in with Theo, who'd suggested that perhaps the problem wasn't the flat but who she was moving in with. Freya had dismissed that notion. She was in love. They were meant to be together – weren't they?

Freya stared around the old kitchen with its eighties-style light oak door fronts that had been there since before she was born. Now she was back home again, she was having a hard time with thought of her parents selling her childhood home. She didn't want that. In fact, what she wanted was to find her mum and tell her not to go through with it.

She fingered her mum's phone on the kitchen counter where she'd left it. She had either forgotten to pick it up on her way out or had left it behind on purpose – Freya couldn't decide which. What a shame, either way, because she'd read about websites where you could track a phone to find the location. Her thoughts drifted back to her parents selling up. Why couldn't she and Theo figure something out that didn't involve selling her parents' home? In fact, why were they so intent on buying a place together right now? She couldn't even remember how it had all started.

'Oh, yes.' Freya remembered now. He'd proposed. She stared into space, wondering what sort of girlfriend she was that she'd forgotten his awkward proposal on bended knee in the local pub. It had been so embarrassing. She winced when she remembered her reply. It hadn't been very romantic. 'For god's sake, yes, just get up. I'm *so* embarrassed.'

She knew why she'd been so tetchy. It wasn't the fairy tale proposal she'd been expecting. She'd imagined it happening during a romantic sunset on a beach, like in a movie, not in their local pub surrounded by people staring at them.

Freya sighed and walked over to the kettle. She frowned. It

was stone cold. Her dad hadn't even filled it up with water and switched it on. *What the hell?* Freya didn't know why she was acting like this. When she had lived with Theo, just the two of them in the flat, she had always been the first up to make their morning coffee.

Freya filled the old kettle and flicked the switch. She was just reaching up to the cabinet above her for two mugs when she thought she heard her dad. She was about to call out when something told her he might be on the phone. She couldn't hear what he was saying, but it sounded as though he was having a conversation in his study. Freya glanced at the clock on the wall. Who would he be speaking to at seven in the morning, at the weekend? She hadn't heard the phone ring, but then she'd been upstairs in the bathroom at the back of the house.

Mum! Freya forgot her tea in an instant and rushed towards the door, smiling at the thought that whatever had gone on yesterday, she'd phoned first thing this morning to let them know everything was okay. But was it? Freya hurried out of the kitchen, hoping she'd get a chance to speak to her mum before she rang off. She was nearing the study when she overheard her dad say, 'No, I don't know where she is, Wendy.'

Freya came to an abrupt halt outside the study door. Dad wasn't talking to Mum. She frowned. *Who's Wendy?*

An old floorboard in the hall creaked beneath her feet. Freya froze, and heard her dad say, 'Are you serious?' There was a long pause. 'Look, I've got to get off the phone.' Another pause. 'Yes, I realise you didn't have to phone me and let me know, but …' His voice sounded taut. 'I just need to get off the phone before someone overhears this conversation. Of course I'm talking about Freya – who else?'

Freya backed away from the door and ran into the lounge, where there was another phone extension. She picked up the receiver, wishing she'd thought of doing this a moment earlier. It was terribly rude to listen in on someone else's conversation, and it was most definitely not something she'd do in ordinary circumstances. But life had just become far from ordinary in her mum and dad's normally mundane, very ordinary household.

She'd just put the receiver to her ear when she heard a click and the line went dead. She was about to put the receiver back on its cradle when she heard the study door open. Her dad walked past the open lounge. If he'd glanced in, he would have seen his daughter standing there in her pyjamas, the phone in her hand.

Freya stood there frozen, her eyes wide, watching him take the stairs two at a time until he disappeared out of sight. She felt like calling out, *Who was that on the phone?* She heard the familiar squeak of the door as he walked into the bathroom at the top of the stairs. The moment was lost.

What had she overheard him say? *I just need to get off the phone before someone overhears this conversation … Of course I'm talking about Freya.* Had her dad had an affair? Had her mum found out? Was that why she had upped and left so suddenly? Freya shook her head. Her dad, having an affair? 'What a silly thought,' she said under her breath. Even so, there must be a reason he was worried she'd overhear the conversation.

Freya looked at the phone. There was an obvious way to find out who her dad had been talking to. She picked up the phone and dialled one four seven one, hoping the service would give her the last number and it hadn't been withheld so she could speak to this woman called Wendy and find out exactly what was going on. Freya hesitated when the computerised voice on the end of the line reeled off the number of the last caller, ending with the option to press one to return the call. Freya hung up.

'What's going on?'

Freya jumped at the sound of Theo's voice. She didn't hear him walk down the stairs. He must have been on the way to the kitchen when he'd noticed her in the lounge. 'What do you mean?' Freya said defensively, feeling like a small child caught doing something she wasn't supposed to.

He scratched his head. His mop of blonde hair was sticking out. Like her, he was still in his pyjamas. He yawned. 'I thought you were making me a cup of coffee?'

'Yes, I was.' She didn't feel inclined to tell him about the conversation she'd just overheard between her dad and some woman called Wendy.

Theo stared at her. 'Is the kettle switched on?'

'Er, no.'

'So, what have you been doing all this time?'

Freya glared at him. 'What is with you?' She felt like she was getting the third degree.

'What do you mean – what is with *me*? What's with *you* this morning?'

'Nothing!' Freya stalked over. She had her mum's mobile phone in her hand.

He noticed the phone. 'Did you just call someone?'

'For god's sake Theo, what's with all the questions?'

'Well, did you?'

'So what if I did?' Freya shot back, annoyed with all the questions. She knew what this was about; it was written all over Theo's face as he scrutinised her – he thought she was keeping something from him. He followed her into the kitchen.

She got two mugs out of the kitchen cupboards, and a large jar of coffee.

'You were speaking to that guy, weren't you?'

Freya flicked the kettle on and turned around to face him. 'What guy?'

'The new guy at your work, at the museum.'

'Oh, for heaven's sake.' Freya frowned, realising she sounded just like her mum. Was he jealous of a colleague? And how did he even know about the new guy?

'Are you talking about Tarek?'

'Oh, so now you're on first name terms.'

'What's that supposed to mean? Of course we know each other's first names. We work together. How do you know about him, anyway?'

'I thought I'd surprise you with lunch.'

Freya shrugged. 'So, why didn't you?' He'd done it before. He knew what time she had her lunch break, so he'd walk into town, buy a couple of sandwiches or filled baguettes, grab a couple of coffees to go, and surprise her at the museum entrance when she walked out.

'I saw you with him.'

Freya stared at him. So, he'd turned up to surprise her with lunch, and seen them together. 'I didn't see you.'

'I'd just walked round the corner when I saw you walking down the steps of the museum with him. I … I followed you.'

'You followed me?' She said in surprise. 'They asked me to take him to lunch. He's just arrived and I'm showing him the ropes. It's not like I wanted to.'

'Didn't you?'

Freya folded her arms and looked at him for a long moment.

'Oh, my god. Do you think I … we …?' Freya burst out laughing.

Theo frowned. 'What's so funny?'

'Didn't you listen to anything I said last night?' She'd told him all about the meeting with the dean and about her disappointment that she wouldn't get to go to Alexandria and that Tarek had joined them instead.

The look on Theo's face suggested he hadn't been listening the previous night. She stared at him. She knew why he hadn't taken in what she'd said. After she'd told him the secondment was no longer happening, he hadn't been interested in listening to anything else about her job. She knew Theo didn't want her to go.

'Oh, I kind of saw him and jumped to conclusions. Sorry. I know you're fascinated with the Middle East.'

'So, you thought I'd be interested in him just because he's from the Middle East?' She burst out laughing. 'Really, Theo, that is dumb.'

He smiled. 'Yes, it is rather, isn't it? I mean, he is kind of good-looking. He's got a sort of Omar Sharif thing going on there. That's what got me worried. But wouldn't it be boring, you two talking shop all day and night?' He laughed.

Freya pursed her lips and turned around to fill two mugs with boiling water. Despite having taken an immediate dislike to Tarek, for obvious reasons, lunch hadn't been as awkward as she'd thought it would be.

Spending the previous day with Tarek and finding out about his life back in Alexandria had made her want to go there even more – but it had made a refreshing change from Theo and his football, his job applications, and the house move. Of course, Freya wasn't about to tell Theo that. She rather fancied taking

Tarek on a walking tour of Cambridge during one of their lunch breaks the next week. She wasn't going to tell Theo that either – the fact that she was looking forward to it.

'So, what did you guys do at lunchtime, anyway?'

Freya was just pouring the coffee and about to tell him, hoping she wouldn't sound too enthusiastic, when her phone rang, surprising her. No one phoned her mobile much anymore; it was mostly texting and WhatsApp, unless it was a wrong number – or her mum. Freya grabbed her phone from the worktop and answered it without even checking the number. 'Mum?'

21

'Freya, it's me, Jolene.'

'Oh, hi.' She glanced at Theo who was mouthing, *Who is it?*

Freya mouthed back, *Jolene.*

Theo nodded and walked over to finish making the coffee.

'Is everything okay, Jolene?' Freya asked, wondering why she'd called so early on a Saturday morning.

'Oh, did I wake you?'

'No, I was up just making coffee.'

'Great. Fancy some overtime?'

Freya would never say no to some extra money, especially working in a job she loved. 'When?'

'Today.'

'What – like now today?'

'Uh-huh. Did you check your emails?'

Freya shook her head. 'No.'

'The curator asked if we could come in. The email was sent yesterday.'

'I wasn't on the computer. I was busy working with Tarek.' Freya caught Theo glancing over his shoulder at her and frowning.

'Yes, I noticed that.'

'What do you mean?' Freya walked out of the kitchen, across the hall and into the lounge, listening to Jolene's reply.

'You two seem to be getting quite friendly, going out to lunch together.'

'That's because the dean asked me to show him the ropes.'

'If you say so.'

Freya let out an exasperated sigh. 'About this overtime,' she said, changing the subject, 'is that all day today?'

'Yep. The others are coming in at nine. They are closing the museum for the day.'

Freya didn't work at the museum on a Saturday, even though it was normally open to the public at the weekend.

Freya was still frowning. 'The women who work there didn't tell me about the overtime.' Why was she acting all surprised? They were civil to her face, but she could tell they didn't want her there – new, young blood stirring things up, thinking up new ideas and a fresh approach to the displays.

'Will you be there, Jolene?'

'Oh, yes. And Tarek too.'

'I'm not interested in whether he's there or not.'

'If you say so.'

Freya ignored the remark, although she did say, 'I enjoyed lunch with Tarek,' forgetting to lower her voice. There were no secrets between best friends. *But perhaps sometimes there were between partners.* She glanced through the open doorway to the hall just as Theo passed by. His timing was impeccable. He threw her a scowl that said he'd overheard.

Freya hastily added, 'Of course I still hate him for stealing my secondment.'

Jolene said, 'Of course you do,' with an amused inflection in her voice.

'So, why are they asking us to come in?'

Theo stopped in the doorway. He looked at her in surprise. 'Are you going into work today?'

Freya glanced at him and held up a finger, waiting for Jolene's reply.

'There's a new display we are setting up.'

Freya repeated what Jolene had just said for Theo's benefit.

Theo frowned. 'Why can't it wait until Monday?'

'I could do with the money, Theo.' He couldn't argue with that. But his expression as he turned from the doorway said he still wasn't happy about it.

'Is that Theo?' Jolene asked. 'How does he feel about you working with the very handsome Tarek?'

Freya shifted nervously from one foot to the other. 'What do *you* think?' Aware her response sounded rude, she apologised. 'Sorry.'

'No need to apologise. You like him, I get it.'

'I don't! That's ridiculous.'

'Is it? You enjoyed lunch together.'

'So what? It was only lunch.'

'But who knows where that might lead? It could be the start of something, y'know.'

Freya wanted to change the subject. It wasn't going to be the start of anything – how could it be? She was engaged to Theo.

As if reading her mind, Jolene added, 'Some of the best relationships are with those we meet in unexpected circumstances. Think *Brief Encounter*, the old movie where they first meet at a train station.'

'I've never watched it.'

'Well, maybe you should.'

'Do they end up together – the couple?'

'No.'

Freya brightened. 'Well, in that case, I'll watch it.' She didn't admit that there might be a tiny grain of truth in what her best friend was saying. They'd only just met, but every time she thought of Tarek, she felt a flutter in her tummy. What was that? Freya decided she would rather not think about it – or him.

She changed the subject. 'I think my dad is having an affair.'

'You've got to be joking. Did he tell you that?'

Freya glanced at the phone she'd been holding a few minutes ago, hoping to overhear her dad's conversation. She could feel her face growing hot at the thought. 'No.'

'Then how …?'

'I overheard him speaking to a woman on the phone this morning. Somebody called Wendy.'

Jolene went quiet. 'I don't think you should jump to conclusions.'

Freya lowered her voice and repeated what she'd heard her dad say on the phone.

'Or maybe you should,' quipped Jolene, when her best friend had finished. 'Your parents don't seem the type.'

Jolene had met Freya's parents at a rather awkward dinner, when it had turned out they were both under the impression that Freya had brought Jolene home to meet them because Jolene was her girlfriend. Jolene had thought it was hilarious; Freya not so much. She didn't have anything against being gay, and it had been nice for Jolene to come round to her house for a change, but she had been taken aback that her parents had made that mistake; as though they didn't really know her. Perhaps she didn't know her parents quite as well as she thought she did, either. Freya wished she hadn't mentioned what she'd overheard that morning.

'I'll get ready now and make it into work by nine,' she said.

'Great. I'll see you there, and you can tell me more about that phone call.'

Freya sighed as she ended the call. She shouldn't have brought it up. She slipped the phone in the pocket of her pyjamas and eyed the house phone. She listened for a moment. Her dad was still upstairs. She could faintly hear the shower running in the bathroom. If she didn't do it now, she might not get another chance.

Freya picked up the receiver, punched in four digits, and listened once again to the details of the last call from a woman called Wendy. She entered the number on her mobile phone. When she had finished, she replaced the handset and stood there biting a fingernail, staring at the phone number. She didn't recognise the area code.

She walked out of the lounge and crossed the hallway into the kitchen, spotting the cup of coffee that Theo had left for her on the kitchen counter. She took it over to the table by the window, her bed socks sliding on the smooth tiled floor. Her parents' house had draughty wooden sash windows. For years they'd planned to install secondary glazing, but had never got around to it. Freya didn't mind. She loved the old red-brick double-fronted house, with its ivy creeping up one side of the doorframe. It was set back from the road with a small front garden bordered by a low red-brick wall. In the middle of the small patch of grass was a cherry tree. In the summer, it provided welcome shade from the sun coming into the kitchen in the afternoon. In the spring, the tree had beautiful pale pink blossoms.

She stared out of the window at the bare branches, wishing things could go back to the way they had been. *Perhaps the buyers will pull out*, she thought hopefully. She didn't want to return to live in an apartment on the outskirts of Cambridge; the cottage they were buying in Grantchester, although small, was just perfect. But even so, it came at a price – her parents selling up.

Freya picked up her cup of coffee and stared at the phone number. Who had called her dad? Who was the woman called Wendy?

Freya took a deep breath, put her coffee down and tapped the phone icon to dial the number.

'The Guest House at Shingle Cove. How may I help?'

Freya's eyes went wide. 'Oh, er …' She had not expected to hear a young woman's voice. 'Are you the hotel in Weymouth?' Freya was thinking on her feet, plucking something out of thin air. *And how do you know my dad?* she felt like asking. But something held her back.

'I'm afraid not. We're on the Suffolk Coast, near Dunwich. I think you have the wrong guest house.'

Freya hurriedly thanked her, said goodbye, and hung up. A horrible thought occurred to her; was this why her dad was so enthusiastic about selling up? Maybe it wasn't about helping his only child to get on the property ladder. Were her mum and dad splitting up? Was her dad intending to set up home with this person called Wendy, and had her mum found out? Freya bit her lower lip, wondering what to do. She was staring at her phone when a text came through. It was Jolene checking she was still going in to work.

Freya texted back. She was definitely going in, but she had something else on her mind other than the new display or Tarek – Freya wanted Jolene's advice. If her mum wasn't back in a day or two, Freya was thinking should she take a few days off work, go to the guest house herself, confront this Wendy and tell her to stay away from her dad.

22

'Is everything all right, Freya?'

Consumed by thoughts of the phone call and the woman called Wendy, Freya rounded on Tarek, annoyed by the question. He didn't know a thing about what she'd overheard at home that morning, and she wasn't about to tell him. Why was he asking her such a stupid question? It wasn't like it was written on her face: *I just found out my dad's having an affair.*

'Of course everything's fine – why wouldn't it be?'

'Ahem, well, you just put a Mayan artefact in an Egyptian display case.'

'Don't be ridiculous. Why would I do something like that?'

Tarek reached into the display case and lifted out the little figurine she'd just placed in there. He handed it to her. 'I don't know – you tell me.'

Freya's eyes went wide. It wasn't her fault that somehow a Mayan artefact had found its way into the storage box. But she should have noticed. She thrust it back in his hand. 'I need to speak to Jolene.' She stalked over to where Jolene was busy reorganising a shelving unit. She was on her knees, shirt sleeves rolled up, using an electric screwdriver.

Freya stopped in front of her.

Jolene looked up. She switched off the screwdriver. 'Is everything all right, Freya?'

Freya sighed, wishing people would stop asking her that. She shook her head, *no*. 'I can't get this morning out of my mind,' she whispered.

'That phone call you overheard?'

'Yes.'

Jolene put the screwdriver down. 'How about we take a break?'

A break? Freya didn't feel she'd done anything productive enough this morning to warrant one.

Jolene stood up and took her hand. 'Come on, let's get a cup of coffee.'

'But—'

'No buts.'

Freya cast her eyes toward her colleagues, who were throwing disapproving glances their way. Jolene noticed too. 'Never mind them. We're doing overtime today. We can take a break when we like.'

Freya followed her out of the gallery containing the Egyptian exhibits and down the stairs to the entrance hall, where there were some wooden benches and a coffee machine. Jolene had come prepared. She always had spare change for the machine. 'Now, what will it be?'

'A cappuccino, please.'

'Coming right up!'

Freya took a seat on a bench while her friend put a two-pound coin in the machine. A few minutes later, she joined her on the bench with two paper cups of coffee. 'Here.'

'Thanks.' Freya took the frothy cup of coffee.

'Why don't you confront your dad about the phone conversation you overheard?'

Freya turned to her. 'The thing is, I still can't believe it's true – my dad having an affair. I mean – how? When? It's not like he ever had the opportunity to …' She paused.

'Freya – what is it?'

'When I was young, Dad and I would have our own special time, where we'd go off on a little adventure together. Sometimes we'd go into London, just the two of us. He'd take me to Hamleys, and we'd stop at this café and meet one of his friends, a woman. She had a daughter around my age.'

'A girl around your age?'

Freya nodded. 'We'd play together in the park while they chatted.'

'Didn't you ever ask who this friend of his was?'

'I don't think so. Why would I?'

'Do you remember her name?'

Freya's eyes went wide. 'Oh. My. God.'

'What is it?'

'Her name was Wendy.'

Jolene stared at her. 'You have got to be kidding. How can you be sure?'

'I haven't thought about those days out in so long. We stopped seeing her when I was around ten. But I remembered her name because I was really into reading Peter Pan at one point, and it must have stuck in my mind that she had the name from the book.'

'You liked Peter Pan?'

'Don't laugh. What is weird is that I have this memory of a

bedroom with bookshelves full of children's books, among them Peter Pan.'

'Your bedroom growing up?'

'No, it wasn't. This room had prints on the wall of the characters from the book.'

'A dream then?'

'Yes, I imagine it was.' Freya didn't know why she'd got on to that. She thought perhaps it was somewhere they had stayed on holiday when she was a child.

'You know what this means, don't you, Freya?'

'Of course I do. I think he was having an affair with this Wendy – but that was years ago.'

Jolene nodded. 'They're not having an affair now.'

She felt a sense of utter relief sweep over her. 'Maybe mum just came across some old correspondence between them, or something, and found out about the affair all these years later.' Freya frowned. 'That's still not good news, is it?'

Jolene shook her head.

'At least the young woman who answered the phone at the guest house isn't Wendy, though.' *So, my dad isn't having a belated mid-life crisis and going after a younger woman*, thought Freya.

'What young woman?'

'Oh, I didn't tell you. I rang the number. A young woman answered, said it was The Guest House at Shingle Cove.'

'Ah, probably just a receptionist.' Jolene said.

'I've got to find my mum and convince her that it was all in the past, a long time ago, and it's over,' Freya said, moving to get out of her seat, as though she was planning to go and find her mum straight away, even though she had no clue where she was.

Jolene leaned across and grabbed her arm. 'But is it?'

Freya looked at her.

'Why was this Wendy phoning your dad now?'

Freya shrugged. She had no idea.

'Wait a minute!' The look on Jolene's face said something had just occurred to her.

'What is it?' Freya asked, resuming her seat. 'What are you thinking?'

'Did you just say that you met this friend of your dad's several times a year, and she had a daughter?'

Freya shrugged. 'Yeah – so?'

'Was she there every single time?'

Freya thought about it. 'Yes she was.'

'And you went to the park and played together?'

'Yes.'

Jolene stared at her.

'What?'

Jolene bit her fingernail.

Freya leaned forward in her seat. 'What?'

'Look, if the affair ended years ago, why were they still in touch, still meeting up?'

Freya shrugged again. 'How do I know? Perhaps they remained friends after they realised what they'd done was wrong, and my dad was still in love with my mum.' Then Freya had a rather lovely thought. Maybe she'd misread all of it. 'Perhaps they knew each other, and she was his girlfriend before my dad met my mum. In which case, Mum walked out thinking Dad had had an affair, when it wasn't true.' That made sense. Her dad wouldn't have an affair – he just wouldn't.

Freya noticed that Jolene was still uncharacteristically quiet. She frowned at her. 'Just tell me what's on your mind.'

'You're not going to like it.' Jolene gulped down her coffee, screwed up the paper cup and tossed it in the bin. 'Don't you think it's odd that this lady, Wendy, brought her daughter along too?'

Freya shook her head. 'Not really. It meant they could have a chat while we played together.'

'I guess. But what if there was another explanation?'

'Like what?' Freya was getting annoyed that Jolene wasn't just getting to the point.

'What if your dad wasn't meeting up to see Wendy, but … well, Wendy's daughter?'

'I don't get what you mean?'

Jolene sighed. 'Really? Do I have to spell it out, Freya?'

Freya sat back in her seat, surprised. 'Why are you speaking to me like that?'

'Look, I'm sorry.' Jolene pursed her lips. 'I was rather hoping you might cotton on to the possibility rather than me having to say it. I don't want to hurt your feelings.'

'Just say what's on your mind, for goodness' sake.'

'Okay,' Jolene said slowly. 'This is only a thought, but what if your dad and Wendy had an affair, and Wendy's daughter is …'

Freya's mouth dropped open. 'Oh, my god.'

Jolene nodded. 'It makes sense, doesn't it? It is possible she is your half-sister. And I bet your mum doesn't know.'

Freya sat back in her seat, stunned.

'Sorry,' Jolene said in a hushed voice.

They both fell silent.

Finally, Jolene broke the silence. 'What are you going to do?'

23

Alice stretched her arms and yawned. It was early on Saturday morning, and she had woken up with a start. Nothing had disturbed her, apart from bad dreams.

She glanced at the clock on the bedside cabinet. It was still early. Despite closing her eyes again, sleep eluded her. It didn't help that Hester, who had retreated to her basket the previous night, jumped up, front paws on the bed, and licked her face.

'Urrgh, Hester!' Alice sat up. Sad brown beagle eyes looked at her. Alice sighed. She could never be cross with her dog for long. 'Oh, I didn't mean to tell you off.'

Hester took the change in her tone for an invitation to join her in bed. She jumped up on the bed and gave Alice more doggy kisses as she sat up. 'Okay, all right. I'm getting up.'

She gently pushed Hester to one side and got out of bed, reaching for the cardigan she'd left on an easy chair by the window and slipping it on over her pyjamas. She opened the curtains, thinking of home. She knew she really ought to phone her family that morning.

Thinking of contacting them, Alice's gaze shifted from the window to the dressing table in front of her and the pad of writing paper with the words *The Guest House at Shingle Cove* printed at the top. It was identical to the notepaper that someone called Wendy had used to write a letter to Jeffrey all those years earlier. A letter that sounded as though they were breaking things off. Alice decided to write a letter to Jeffrey using the notepaper. The trouble was that it would give the game away as to where she'd gone. But she couldn't resist. She was about to sit down at the dressing table when she glanced at Hester. Before she did anything else she needed to take her dog out. She didn't want her to have an accident in the bedroom.

❖

'Oh, my goodness, it's cold out there,' Alice said under her breath as she closed the door to her bedroom and took off her coat. Hester came scampering in after her and made a beeline for the bed. It was early and Alice had counted on nobody being up and about as she stole through the house with her coat over her nightwear. Fortunately, Hester had been quick doing her business in the garden, appearing as keen as Alice to get back inside into the warmth.

'Now, where was I?' said Alice to herself as she slipped her cosy cardigan back on. Her eyes roved to the headed paper on the dressing table. 'Oh, yes. I was going to write a letter.' She took a seat. There was a little stack of envelopes too, in a cream colour, just like the one she'd found in the loft. Alice sat there, her pen hovering over the notepaper, thinking of a woman called Wendy whom she'd never heard of before she found that letter.

Alice jumped when her cat appeared on the desk. 'Oh, Marley! You gave me a fright!' She watched Marley examine the notepaper. Then he decided to nibble the end of her pen.

'Hey.' She held the end of the pen in the air, thinking it was out of his reach. Marley proved her wrong, standing on his hind legs, paws making a grab for the pen.

'You're playful this morning,' commented Alice, thinking that it had been some time since she'd seen the playful side of her cat. She knew she had Emily to thank for that. And Joss, who had given her a lift to see the vet.

Alice twirled the pen absently, letting Marley enjoy the game while she thought about Emily and Joss. She still felt responsible for the way things had turned out.

Alice shook her head. *Young love.* She remembered it like it was yesterday.

Marley caught the end of the pen between his paws, and nibbled on it, reminding her what she was intending to do. 'Stop that now,' Alice said, moving the pen. She picked Marley up and put him on the floor. He meowed in disapproval and immediately jumped back up on the desk.

Hester, who had been snoozing on the bed, jumped down and came running up to the desk to see what was going on. She woofed.

'No, you're not missing anything Hester. The game is over.'

Realising she wouldn't be left in peace to write her letter, Alice walked over to the food bowls laid on a mat in the corner of the room and put a couple of scoops of dried cat and dog food into two bowls – one for Hester, the other for Marley. She put Hester's down first. When she was finished wolfing down the food, Alice said, 'Bed!' She pointed at the basket.

Ears down, sad puppy dog eyes staring at Alice as though she'd been told off, Hester padded over and flopped down on the cushion in the basket, adding a little whine just to make Alice feel guilty. 'Good girl.' Alice patted her head. 'Stay!' Hester did as she was told, as usual, giving Alice a chance to put Marley's food down without Hester stealing it.

Marley sat on the bed, watching her. He licked his paw and started cleaning his fur.

'Here you are, Marley. It's breakfast time.'

Marley sat for a long moment, staring at his food bowl.

Alice wasn't surprised. This was her cat's modus operandi. In fact, she imagined it was the same with most cats. Marley would do things in his own good time. There was no ordering him around, like Hester. Telling him what to do fell on deaf cat ears, although he could hear her very well.

Alice resumed her seat, glancing at Hester, who was dozing once more.

She heard a dull thud and glanced over her shoulder. Marley had jumped off the bed and was eating his breakfast. She smiled and turned in her seat, her brow creasing in a frown, having second thoughts about writing a letter to Jeffrey. But she'd made up her mind.

'Now, where is that pen?'

Alice searched the desk, then the floor around the desk, and even got out of her seat, pulling the chair out to see if it had dropped on the wooden flooring where she'd been sitting. The pen, as far as Alice could see, had vanished.

She sat down and scratched her chin. 'Pens just don't vanish into thin air!' She glanced at Hester, who was fast asleep and oblivious to the search. Alice raised her eyebrows and turned around in her seat, just in time to see a furry tail disappear under her bed. 'Marley!'

24

Alice walked out of her room and glanced at the cream envelope in her hand. Inside was a letter addressed to her husband, written on the hotel notepaper. She smiled. It hadn't been fun trying to get the pen from under the bed. She had a cat scratch to prove it. Once she had retrieved it, she had written Jeffrey a letter, telling him where she was and the reason she had gone there; to find out about Wendy, the lady he had been seeing years ago.

Alice wanted to know if they'd been having an affair. She didn't want to go home and discuss it in front of Freya, and she didn't wish to talk about it over the phone. Alice wanted Jeffrey to meet her at the guest house, where she suspected it had started all those years ago on their last visit there together. She wanted him to tell her everything.

She ended the letter with an ultimatum; if he wanted any hope of saving their marriage, then he had to travel to meet her face to face. Otherwise she would have to assume that he no longer wanted to be with her, and that their marriage was over.

Alice stared at the letter in her hands. Even if he did as she asked and met her, their marriage might still be over. But at least she would give him the benefit of the doubt in the meantime.

Perhaps things were not as she imagined – that he'd had an affair. Perhaps it was all innocent. Perhaps he and Wendy had crossed paths and for some reason, she had written to him.

And even if it hadn't been all innocent, as she hoped, then at least if he came to explain himself, there might be a chance she could forgive him. She knew why she might – because she had kept a secret from him all these years too; something she'd sworn she would never tell him. But perhaps now, finding out about Wendy might give her the opportunity to tell him – not out of spite, or tit-for-tat, but simply to get off her chest what she'd had to keep to herself all these years. A secret she wished she didn't have.

But what if he doesn't come? Alice didn't want to think about that. Jeffrey would come. She knew him – didn't she? Looking at the letter in her hands, she wasn't so sure. Not anymore. A part of her wished she'd never gone up in the loft, where she rarely ventured, and come across that old letter.

Alice slipped the room key into her pocket and made her way downstairs. She walked through the lounge, which was available for guests, with its cosy inglenook fireplace and wood-burning stove, floor-lamps, bookshelves full of novels adorning one wall, and sofas and armchairs in white cotton.

Alice stepped into the wooden conservatory off the lounge, where breakfast and dinner were served. The large structure was built onto the side of the property and had views over the gardens. They were mainly laid to lawn and had borders filled with plants that Alice guessed had been planted and grown over many years. The evergreen shrubs were so tall and dense in places that their foliage obscured some of the fencing surrounding the property boundary. She couldn't even begin to imagine what the garden would look like in a blaze of colour in summer when the rest of the trees weren't bare, and the potted plants and borders were in bloom. Alice took a seat at a table for two on the left by the window. Beyond the garden was a view of the cove and the sea.

The sea view was gorgeous in the morning, the sunrise beautiful on a clear day, even in winter. It was what she imagined some guests came here for.

Alice picked up the breakfast menu. She was just casting her eye over it when Joss walked in. She was about to say good morning when Emily stepped into the room with a small notepad and pen to hand and spotted Joss too.

He turned around and said, 'Good morning, Emily.'

Emily just about managed a reply. 'Yeah, morning,' before she walked over to Alice's table. 'What would you like for breakfast?'

Alice's gaze followed Joss as he took a seat at the table at the far end of the room. Alice was going to ask if he would like to join her. But the look on his face after Emily's perfunctory good morning had put him in a sullen mood. Alice could tell he wouldn't be interested in small talk. Neither was she.

Alice looked up at Emily and felt like saying something, but it wasn't the time or the place.

'Emily, can I ask you a quick question?'

'Of course, Alice. How can I help?'

Alice held up the letter. 'I have a letter to post. Can you tell me where the nearest post office is?' Alice guessed it was probably in Southwold.

Emily looked at the letter. 'We can post that for you?'

'You can?'

'Of course. Shall I take it?'

Alice hesitated.

Emily smiled. 'Honestly, it's no trouble. We pop into town most days for shopping or to run errands.'

Alice returned her smile. She didn't really want to get a taxi, which seemed such a waste for a stamp, and she expected that another lift with Joss was out of the question – he probably wouldn't be in the mood to do anyone a favour, now he'd found out he was still in Emily's bad books. She decided this was by far the better option. Besides, she wanted it to go out on Monday morning, first class. Which seemed a bit of an imposition to ask, but …

'Any chance it could be popped in the post today?' she asked.

'Not a problem. I'm nipping into town this afternoon. I'll do it personally.'

'That's so kind of you, Emily. Thank you.'

'You're welcome,' she said.

Alice watched Emily slip her letter into the front pocket of the little apron she was wearing. She caught Joss staring at Emily with a glum expression.

'So, what would you like for breakfast?' Emily asked.

Alice perused the menu. 'I'll have the porridge, then perhaps some scrambled egg and a couple of rashers of bacon. Oh, and some brown toast, please.'

'Coming right up.'

'And you'll remember to post my letter?'

Emily smiled. 'Of course.'

'Thank you.'

Alice called after her before she headed out of the room.

Emily walked back to her table. 'Was there something else?'

'You forgot to take Joss's order.' Alice registered the look on Emily's face. She had the feeling Emily hadn't forgotten at all. She glanced at her marching over to his table.

Alice sighed and turned in her seat. Poor Joss had really messed up. She hoped Joss would make amends and invite Emily to dinner that evening. He did no such thing. He just told her wanted he wanted for breakfast before turning to stare out of the window.

Emily stood a moment longer at the table after she'd taken his order, staring at the back of his head before turning on her heel and storming out of the conservatory.

Alice sighed and turned to look out of the window herself. The atmosphere was now decidedly frosty. She frowned when her husband came to mind. Had she done the right thing, writing that letter, telling him where she was, asking him to come for the sake of their marriage? She wasn't sure. But then she wasn't sure of anything. Finding the letters from Wendy had shocked her to the core – the prospect that Jeffrey, her dependable, steadfast husband, had actually had an affair just didn't seem possible.

Alice willed herself not to think about that.

Breakfast passed by without further incident, apart from Emily plonking Joss's plate down on the table hard when she took him his cooked breakfast. Alice finished her toast and left the conservatory. She was crossing the hallway when she spotted Emily sitting at the reception desk. She had an idea.

25

Alice sidled up to the desk. She had an agenda; she still wanted to get Joss and Emily back on speaking terms. 'Would you have any free time in the next few days? I'd like to go—'

The phone on reception rang, interrupting Alice.

Emily held up a finger. 'Hold on. Let me just get this.'

Alice stepped away from the desk and sat down in a high-backed easy chair under the stairs, where a little reading snug had been created. There was another high-backed easy chair, a small library of books on a bookshelf, and a large standard lamp that harked back to another era.

Alice scanned the bookshelves, listening to Emily's phone conversation.

'Yes, we have vacancies …'

For a split second she wondered if it was her husband. Her heart started to pound in her chest until she realised that it wasn't possible; the letter hadn't been posted yet. Jeffrey would have no idea where she was until he received the letter. Unless he'd guessed. Alice frowned at the thought. They had stayed there before, on their wedding anniversary, before they'd had Freya. But why would he think she'd returned there?

Alice brushed that thought aside and glanced at Emily as she scanned the computer screen. She had a plan to get Emily and Joss back on speaking terms, but it depended on Emily accompanying her to Aldeburgh. Alice wasn't just doing it for altruistic reasons. She was feeling lonely, staying in the hotel all on her own, and she liked Emily, who reminded her of her daughter – young, ready to embark on life's adventure. Alice fancied spending the afternoon in her company.

'Yes, I've booked you in. I can confirm your reservation is now on our system. See you tomorrow.'

Alice stood up as Emily put the phone down. She was about to walk over when Emily's mobile phone rang. 'Oh, hi. Yes, you're all booked in. The room will be ready, so you can turn up when you like, Clarissa. See you later. Bye.'

By the time she got off the phone, Alice was back again.

Emily glanced at Alice's letter on her desk.

So did Alice. 'I really hope you're not making a special trip just to post my letter.'

Emily smiled. 'Not at all. As I said before, I have some errands to run. There's some shopping to do, laundry to collect – that sort of thing.'

That made Alice feel better.

'Why don't you come along? I'm going into Aldeburgh.'

'Aldeburgh?' Just the place, thought Alice. 'Yes, please. Is it okay if I bring Hester? I'll have to leave my cat indoors, if that's okay.'

'That's fine, Alice. Shall we say midday? We could have some lunch together in town.'

Alice's smile widened. 'Oh, what a splendid idea. Are you sure it's okay if I tag along? You weren't intending to go with anyone else …?' She let the sentence hang without mentioning Joss's name.

'No.'

'Ok, great – I'll meet you in the foyer at midday.' Before she turned to the stairs, intending to pop back to her room and take Hester out for a morning walk, she looked at her letter. 'Shall I take that then, as I'm coming along?'

'Of course, as long as you don't forget to bring it with you,' Emily joked.

Alice was reaching for the letter when she stopped. 'On second thoughts, I think I will leave it with you.' Alice glanced at the computer 'So, there're other guests booked in? Sorry, I don't mean to be nosy. it's just … well, it's nice to meet other people.' *Specifically friendly people*, thought Alice, unlike Joss, who wouldn't be very chatty now he and Emily weren't on speaking terms.

Emily looked at her mobile. 'My best friend is coming to stay for a few days. She's having a break at the guest house while her ex has the kids for the half-term holidays.'

'I bet she's looking forward to it,' said Alice.

'She's always wanted to stay at the guest house. She won't have to shop, cook or run around after children for a whole week.'

Alice smiled. She could empathise, having been a working mother for years. 'Well, good for her.'

'And we have another gentleman booked in. He's come from abroad. It's turning out to be busier than it normally is this time of year.'

'From abroad?' Alice said with interest.

'Yes, Egypt, actually.'

'Egypt?'

'Uh-huh. That's where his address is – in Alexandria.' She stopped. 'Is something wrong, Alice?'

'Er, no,' Alice lied. 'Just curious.' That wasn't a lie. 'Is he, um, young, old …?'

Emily looked at Alice for a long moment.

Alice guessed she couldn't give out that information, but to her surprise Emily smiled, and said, 'I know what this is about!'

Alice stared at her, her heart pounding in her chest. She couldn't know about that night here at the guest house – could she? That was years earlier. Besides, it couldn't be the same person. That would just be too much of coincidence, if he turned up here the same time.

'You want to find out if there are any guests booked in that are your generation. Normally, our clientele are …'

'Old?'

'What I meant was that people who stay with us are quite mature. It's nice to meet people of your own generation, especially when travelling alone. I understand you must feel a bit outnumbered with Joss, and my best friend, Clarissa, turning up tomorrow. Well, you'll be pleased to know he's around your age.'

Alice's heart leapt in her chest. *It isn't him. It can't be. It's just a coincidence*, she thought. Her best friend, Jane, would say, *There's no such thing as a coincidence*, but Alice knew that what she really meant was, *Everything happens for a reason.*

Alice didn't believe in fate, or serendipity. At least she hadn't until that night when her whole world had changed. What had happened had certainly seemed like it was meant to be. The only person she'd confided in was Jane. She was dying to talk to her now, but she was abroad, and Alice didn't want to appear cheeky by asking to make an international phone call from the guest house. She was also loath to use the guest house's public network and send an email asking Jane what she thought. Could it be him? Although she'd know soon enough – he was arriving tomorrow.

26

'What's this?'

Emily put her mug of tea down and looked up at her mum, who was standing in front of her at the reception desk. She was holding up a letter.

Emily had been busy texting Clarissa and hadn't noticed her mum appear in front of her and pick up the letter Alice had left with her to post.

'Oh, it's from one of the guests. She just wants it posting. I was going to nip into Aldeburgh this afternoon, to run some errands, remember? So I'll take it with me to the post office.'

She turned the letter over in her hands. 'You don't have to do that.'

Emily put her phone down. 'It's fine, Mum, really.'

'No, it's okay, I'll do this one.' She fingered the letter in her hands. 'Look, since you returned home, you've been doing so much around here.'

Emily knew that was true. She was glad they had noticed how much she was doing.

'Why don't you take the day off and do something just for you, for a change?'

'Are you sure? I was going to collect the laundered bedsheets from the lady in town.'

'I'll do it.'

'And the letter …?'

'Don't you worry about that, either.'

'Okay. Are you sure I can take the whole day?'

'Of course you can. Your dad will manage reception while I get the two rooms made up for our new guests. Don't frown. He's perfectly capable – I think.'

Gerald had filled in before, here and there, mostly at the weekends when he wasn't at work. However, they both knew that using the booking system on the computer wasn't his strong suit.

'You'll make sure that if he takes any phone bookings, he just writes them down?' Emily asked. 'We can add them to the system later.'

A knowing smile passed between them. 'Of course I will, Emily.' She glanced at the computer. 'We don't normally have this many guests in February. It's lucky you're here.' Emily noticed her mum's smile fade as she added, 'I do want you to find a position as a vet.'

'I know.' Her mum usually managed all the bookings and cleaning and preparing the rooms for the guests this time of year, but she was right: it was unusual to have so many bookings in the low season. During the summer, they always took on a seasonal worker to help out. A student who wanted some summer work.

'How are the applications going?'

Emily frowned at her mum, wishing she hadn't asked. 'Not great.'

'I'm sure something will come up.'

Emily wasn't convinced. The closest she'd come to working

in a veterinary practice was being offered a position as an assistant. Although she could see her mum's point – it was a foot in the door – she turned it down. She hadn't gone to university and spent years studying veterinary medicine to assist a vet. She wanted to practice. Now she was wondering if her mum had been right. Maybe she should have accepted the position.

Emily didn't want to think about that. She wanted to think about her free day. 'I'll be off soon,' she called after her mum, watching her walk away with the letter in her hand.

'Okay, sweetheart.'

Emily locked the computer screen, gathered up her handbag, and stood up. She was just tucking the chair under her desk, intending to pop upstairs and ask Alice if she would like to come with her this morning, when she heard a creak on the stair. It was Alice with Hester.

'Are you okay if we leave now?'

'I was going to take Hester for a walk, but we could do that in Aldeburgh.'

Emily nodded. 'Great – come on.' She took her arm, almost pulling her out of the door, grabbing her coat from the coat rack on the way out. She glanced over her shoulder, hoping her mum didn't walk out of the kitchen and see her leaving with one of the guests. It was meant to be a free day, with no work-related chores. But Emily had promised Alice she'd take her out, and besides, she didn't see it as a chore. She liked Alice and didn't mind at all spending the time in her company. She got the feeling that Alice felt the same.

Emily shut the door behind her and took the steps two at a time down to the driveway. 'This is me,' Emily said, walking over and tapping the roof of her mini. It wasn't brand new. It was a second-hand one she'd saved up for and paid for outright. She loved the colour, a metallic blue.

'What about Hester?'

Emily opened the boot. She took out the shelf so that Hester could sit in the back and look out of the window. 'There you go. Do you need a hand?' Emily caught Alice trying to pick Hester up and put her in the car. 'Yes, please,' Alice said breathlessly. Together, they lifted Hester into the car. Emily considered advising Alice on portion control for Hester's meals, but thought better of it, for now. Alice was on holiday. The last thing she needed was criticism from the resident vet for letting her pet get overweight. Emily did plan to say something – for the sake of Hester's health – but not right now. Alice was looking forward to a trip out, she could tell.

'So, where shall we start?' Alice asked, rubbing her hands together and blowing on them.

Emily turned the heat up before she manoeuvred the car out of the drive. 'Cold – isn't it?'

'I'll say. Hope it doesn't snow.'

Although the winters in Suffolk weren't too harsh, they'd had their fair share of snow over the years. Emily remembered the Christmases as a child when she'd prayed for snow, but it had tended to arrive in the new year.

'Where would you like to start, Alice?'

'Aldeburgh.'

That suited Emily. There was a choice of cafés to have tea and scones. She was thinking of one in particular. She mentioned this to Alice.

'That sounds lovely. But first I'd like to visit a place called Cobblers Yard. Do you know it?'

Emily smiled. 'Oh, yes. Very well. My sister's best friend runs a flower shop there called The Potting Shed.' When she stopped the car at the junction to the main road at the top of the street, Emily glanced at Alice. 'Are you buying some flowers?'

'No, I'm not going there to visit the flower shop.'

'Oh, okay.' She was about to ask why Cobblers Yard in particular, when Alice said, 'Do you want me to post my letter while we're in Aldeburgh?'

'No, my mum's posting it.'

'How kind.'

'Don't mention it.' Emily concentrated on turning into the main road, finding a gap in the oncoming traffic. She sped down the main road. The rolling countryside around was so picturesque in spring and summer, with rolling acres of farmland full of bright yellow flowering rapeseed interspersed with green fields, and little villages nestled in between. Today, there were no views on either side of the road. Emily put her fog lights on.

'Is this unusual weather for Suffolk – the fog?'

'Yes, this time of year.'

Emily turned off the main road on to a country lane bordered by farmland, passing a farm shop and the odd cottage fronting the road. The fog was lifting. After a ten-minute drive through the rolling Suffolk countryside, the fog hovering a few feet above the fields, they arrived at a small roundabout on the fringes of Aldeburgh.

A left turn took them along a wide, winding road, passing detached houses that led to the seafront where there was parking on the street near the imposing Wentworth Hotel. Emily often parked there, in front of a stretch of grass bordering a wide path that ran alongside the shingle beach. There were black wooden huts on the beach where you could buy the fishermen's catch of the day. It was only a short walk from the sea front into town, but she couldn't find a parking space. However, she was in luck. There was a space just past the local supermarket in the high street. She backed her mini in between two parked cars, pulled the handbrake up and switched off the engine. She turned to Alice. 'Just along here is Cobblers Yard. Have you been to Aldeburgh before?'

Alice nodded. 'Yes, but it was years ago. I remember the sea front with the grand hotel overlooking the shingle beach and the odd fishing boat pulled up on the beach. From what I can remember, it hasn't changed. I saw one of the fishing boats as we drove past.'

Emily nodded. 'I'm going to buy some fresh fish for this evening.' Although Emily had been told to take the day off – no errands for the guest house – she couldn't help herself.

'I remember the wide high street, and the little boutique clothes shops, and of course the fish and chip shops.'

Hester woofed, making them both jump. They'd both forgotten Alice's dog was in the back. She was looking out of the window, furiously wagging her tail.

Alice looked about her as they got out of the car. 'I don't remember the ice-cream parlour over there.'

'That's relatively new,' commented Emily.

'Do you need a hand, Emily?'

'No, I've got this.' She opened the car boot and lifted Hester out of the car. 'Who needs to lose weight?' she said under her breath as she placed her on the pavement. She handed Alice the lead. Emily led the way along the high street. A few yards past the pet shop, she turned down a narrow, cobbled alleyway.

Alice followed.

'And here we are,' said Emily as they entered the small, cobbled courtyard with several little shops with old-fashioned bow-fronted windows. The yard had shops on three sides and was a dead end.

'Well, this is a surprise. I don't remember this place. I'm sure I never ventured in here on my last visit years ago.'

Emily turned around and looked at her. 'But I thought you said you wanted to visit some shops here?'

'Oh, I'm not here for me – I'm here for you.'

'Me?' She glanced at the flower shop across the way, the little music shop next door, with violins and guitars in the window, and the charity shop she knew well from her student days. It was a place she still visited, if for no other purpose than to have a natter and a catch-up with The Gossip Girls, as the two elderly sisters, both widows, who ran the charity shop were known. There was the old antique shop, and a bookshop that had been closed for years, spookily still displaying books from yesteryear in a window full of cobwebs. Emily glanced at the arts and crafts shop, which she had visited for stationery when she was a student. It was now closed, but unlike the bookshop, there was a sign in the window – it was up for sale.

Emily turned to Alice. 'There's nothing I really need in Cobblers Yard.' She glanced at The Potting Shed. Perhaps she'd pop back and buy some fresh flowers for the guest house before they left Aldeburgh.

Alice walked over to the arts and crafts shop and stood outside. Emily followed.

'Joss told me it had closed down,' commented Alice.

Emily frowned at the mention of his name.

'What a shame,' Alice continued. 'I wanted to buy a sketchpad and some pencils.'

'Are you interested in buying a shop?' Emily joked.

'Nope. But you might be.'

27

Emily and Alice were sitting in The Two Magpies Bakery on the high street, waiting for their lunch. It was a very popular place that also doubled as a café and sold homemade cakes and scones. They had been lucky to find a table.

'What is this all about?' asked Emily. Alice wouldn't tell her anything until they were seated in a cosy corner of the café, their lunch ordered and a large pot of tea sitting between them on the wooden table.

Alice glanced out of the window. The place where they were seated faced a side street which sloped gently uphill. There were pretty red-brick terraced cottages, some with holiday rental stickers in their windows, and a popular fish and chip shop on the corner with a queue snaking down the street. Even though it was the middle of winter, brave souls were going to sit on benches along the promenade, wrapped up in coats and scarves, to eat takeaway fish and chips.

Alice smiled. Perhaps the next time she was there, that was what she would do.

She turned from the window. 'It's about Joss.'

Emily looked at her quizzically. 'Pardon me?'

'Look, I wanted to come with you and show you the shop, to make amends.'

'I don't understand …'

Alice sighed. 'He mentioned he was taking you out the other evening.'

Emily frowned.

Alice could tell that it was still a sore point and that Emily didn't want to talk about it, although she was too polite to say so. Alice pressed on. 'He wanted to show you the vacant shop in Cobblers Yard. He thought it would make an ideal place to start a vet's practice.'

Emily looked at her in surprise. 'What makes Joss think I want to start my own vet's practice? And why would he be interested?'

'Not to state the obvious, Emily, but it's because he likes you.'

Emily blurted, 'Well, why didn't he take me out to dinner?' She shook her head. 'I was so embarrassed. I'd made an effort, thinking we were going out on a date.'

'I know.' Alice quickly added, 'Sorry, I wasn't being nosy, but I glanced out of the window and saw you and Joss having an argument, and then you stormed off. After what Joss had told me about where he was taking you, it was obvious that you realised you weren't having a romantic dinner date when you saw Joss in his ripped jeans and old jumper.'

Emily nodded. She dropped her eyes to the table, avoiding Alice's gaze. 'Now I feel embarrassed about the way I behaved.'

'That doesn't change the fact that he likes you, Emily.'

'So, why doesn't he ask me out on a *proper* date? Not to see some shop.'

'Why don't *you* ask him out?'

'On a date?'

Alice nodded. 'I imagine his reticence could be because he thinks he's too old for you.'

Emily had wondered that herself. She'd overheard her parents talking about Joss. Her dad enjoyed having their long-term houseguest around, but she got the vibe that her mum did not. She'd heard them talking, and her mum saying they knew nothing about him. Emily looked at Alice. 'I don't know anything about him.'

'Then why don't you find out?'

'How?'

'By asking him out. You got dressed up and were prepared to go out last night …'

Emily bit her lower lip. 'What if he says no?'

'What if he doesn't?'

Emily stared at her.

A young woman approached their table, interrupting their conversation. She set a tea-tray down and served up sandwiches with salad and crisps, and two slices of chocolate cake.

Alice picked up the teapot and poured them both a cup of tea, hoping that Emily would change her mind and ask Joss out. Apart from anything else, she was interested to find out more about the enigmatic other guest. He might be masquerading as a carefree surfer dude with his ripped jeans, tousled blonde hair, and faded tan that suggested it wasn't that long since he'd been bumming around somewhere like Thailand, but Alice wasn't fooled. There was a lot more to Joss than met the eye. Something had happened in his life; of that she was certain. Something that had thrown his life off course and led him there.

Alice was no stranger to that scenario. She was thinking of

her house move. But that wasn't why she was there. *We all have secrets*, she thought. *His can't be any worse than mine.* Was he there trying to escape something he'd done in his past? She could hardly say she was escaping her own past. The guest house was the last place she should have returned to. Where it happened, where it all began …

'Alice – the tea!' Emily exclaimed.

'Oh crumbs! Look what I've done!' The teacup was overflowing, the tea soaking the tablecloth. Alice put the teapot down.

The waitress, hearing the commotion at their table, came running over.

Alice said, 'I'm so sorry. I spilt the tea.'

'Don't worry.' The waitress mopped it up with a cloth. 'I'll bring you a fresh pot.'

Alice looked at the young woman apologetically. 'You're so kind.'

'Don't mention it.'

The waitress took the teapot and returned to the kitchen to collect a replacement.

Emily leaned forward in her seat. 'Are you all right, Alice?'

Alice fixed her gaze on Emily. She wanted to confide in her, tell someone what had happened at the guest house all those years earlier.

'What is it? What's wrong?' Emily asked, searching her face.

Alice took a deep breath. 'Years ago, when my husband and I stayed at the guest house—'

'Here's another pot of tea, ladies.'

Alice hadn't seen her coming. 'Oh, thanks.' She watched the young woman walk over to a couple who had just entered the café and were waiting to be seen to a table.

Turning back to Emily, she said, 'I think you'd better pour the tea this time.'

Emily smiled at her as she picked up the teapot. 'You were saying about the time you stayed at the guest house with your husband?'

You can't tell anyone.

Alice swallowed. *You can't tell anyone. It has to be our secret. We could go to prison for this.* Her husband's words always came back to haunt her. Even after all these years, could that still be the case? *Do you want to find out?* A little voice in her head said.

Emily set the teapot down and looked at her intently.

Alice looked sheepish. 'I've forgotten what I was going to say. How silly. Perhaps it will come back to me.' She spooned some sugar into her tea and added a splash of milk from a small jug. She sat staring at her cup, feeling Emily's eyes scrutinising her. She changed the subject. 'What about Joss? Will you ask him out?'

Emily sighed. 'I don't know.'

Alice took that as a no. What a shame.

'I think I'll start by apologising about last night and tell him why I was so upset.'

'I think that's a marvellous idea,' Alice replied. But she was disappointed by what Emily said next.

'I know it sounds silly, but I kind of believe things happen for a reason. Maybe what happened … between me and Joss, well perhaps we're not meant to be together.'

Alice's smile faded. Her thoughts wandered to the other guest who was due to arrive that day. The Egyptian. It couldn't be him – could it? She dismissed that idea entirely. Fate had thrown them together once, in that guest house. Surely not again. It was the night that had changed everything …

'Alice?'

'We should go back and look at the shop in Cobblers Yard.' Alice picked up her sandwich, avoiding eye contact, aware she had changed the subject.

'You think it might be suitable for a vet's practice?'

'I don't know anything about running one, but I do know that your talents are wasted helping your parents running their guest house – sitting on reception and serving breakfast. I'm sure your parents agree.' At least Alice hoped they did. Although she imagined that now Emily was back, they were going to have a hard time seeing her leave again.

Alice could empathise. She had missed Freya when she'd left home and moved in with Theo. Now she was used to having her home again, it would be hard to let her go. Empty nest syndrome all over again.

Alice enjoyed talking shop, as they called it, hearing all about Freya's day at the museum and progress with her PhD thesis. She got the impression that Freya enjoyed it too. Freya had mentioned that Theo wasn't interested – his eyes would glaze over every time she talked about it. Alice could empathise with that too; it had always been the same in her relationship with Jeffrey.

'I'd never thought of opening my own practice.' Emily stared into space, as though imagining it.

Alice looked at Emily. 'It's not a bad idea, you know. I had to go all the way to Southwold to see the vet.' Alice glanced at Hester, who was lying under the table, her head on her paws, her eyes closed. She wasn't fooling anybody. The moment a crumb dropped on the floor, she'd be there.

'But I haven't got any money to start a business.'

For some reason, Joss sprang to Alice's mind. She was thinking about how long Joss had been staying at the guest house and how much money that must be costing him. They might not know much about Joss, but something told her that he wasn't worried about money. She got the feeling he wasn't short of a bob or two. Perhaps he intended to invest in Emily's business. She looked at Emily. 'Perhaps something will come along …' *Or someone*, she thought, smiling. She still hoped Emily would change her mind about Joss and give him a second chance.

Emily smiled. 'I think I *will* return to Cobblers Yard.'

28

'There's something on your mind.' It wasn't a question.

Freya looked across the room at Jolene, working alone on a museum window display. Freya sighed, turning her attention to Tarek. She wasn't about to repeat the conversation she'd just had with Jolene while having their morning break.

'Tarek, there's nothing on my mind apart from sorting out this display case – all right?'

Tarek pursed his lips and muttered, 'All right, then.'

'What was that?'

'I said let's get on with it, then.'

'Fine.'

She gave him a sideways glance. He was helping her set up a new display case with some artefacts they had brought up from the storage vault. She had been paired with Tarek to work, even that day when they'd all come in to do overtime. She knew that it was her job, showing him how things were done at the museum. But there were people more qualified than her, who worked there full-time.

Freya glanced at the full-timers, who were talking amongst themselves as they worked. She was sure that her being paired up with Tarek for the next month hadn't been the dean's idea at all and had nothing to do with the fact that she had applied for that secondment. It was simply that the other women had nominated her because they didn't want to be stuck with the newbie.

Freya didn't want to be stuck with him either. On the other hand …

'There's definitely something on your mind.'

She rolled her eyes at Tarek. 'Why do you say that? Is it because I've been less talkative that usual?' Freya quipped. She was being sarcastic.

'No, that's not it.'

Tarek, Freya discovered, didn't get English humour. Perhaps it was the fact that English was his second language. Or perhaps he didn't get irony. Peculiarly, she found it rather endearing. She had discovered that with Tarek, what you saw was what you got.

She had barely been civil – in the beginning. He had been no different, acting like a sulky teenager who didn't want to be there. Although she kept up her frosty exterior most of the time, she'd shown a different side to herself at lunch. So had Tarek.

'You labelled the miniature statue incorrectly,' he said in a deadpan voice.

'What!' Freya looked at the little stone statue she'd just put in the display case with the wrong label. Her head still wasn't in the game. 'Oh, God.' It wasn't like her – and Tarek knew it.

Freya sighed. She was meant to be concentrating on work, but instead her attention kept wandering to Jolene. Tarek had caught her, not for the first time that day, staring Jolene's way. What was consuming Freya's thoughts was what her friend had said at coffee break. That Freya might have a half-sister. Could that really be true?

Was it possible that her dad had had an affair with a woman years ago, and they'd met regularly – not because they were still having an affair, but because they'd had a child together? Had bumping into this lady called Wendy in the park been a secretive way to meet, to see his other child, without raising suspicions?

She glanced at Tarek. His dark brown eyes were studying her intently. She frowned at him as she took the statue out of the display case. Why did he do that? Why did he make her come over all shy, like a teenager with a crush, every time she looked his way? Freya rewrote the label and replaced the statue in the display case. 'There – satisfied?' She didn't know why she was acting cross with him. She should be thankful that he'd noticed the error. But she knew she wasn't cross with him. It was what was on her mind.

'Ladies and gentleman!'

Freya turned her gaze to one of the older ladies, who was standing in the middle of the cavernous museum floor. Her voice echoed off the walls. 'It's lunchtime!'

Freya looked at her watch, wondering where the morning had gone.

'We'll all meet back here in an hour.'

Freya shut the display case and locked it. The lady who'd told them it was time for lunch had the keys to the museum. She would be the last to leave, locking the museum door behind them. Although there was the university cafeteria to get lunch in, Freya didn't fancy sitting in a noisy refectory with other students. Besides, Freya didn't think she could stomach a dinner. With things on her mind, she'd be lucky if she managed a sandwich.

'So, where shall we go for lunch today?' Tarek asked, smiling at her, brown eyes wide in anticipation.

'It's not a work day,' Freya reminded him. Meaning she wasn't obligated to go anywhere with him at lunchtime.

Jolene walked over.

Freya turned to her best friend. 'Where shall we go for lunch?'

'Oh, sorry, Freya, I can't.'

'What do you mean?'

'I'm meeting someone.'

Freya looked at her in surprise. 'You're meeting someone? You mean you've met someone?'

Jolene grinned and nodded. 'It's early days, but I'm hoping, you know, it might lead somewhere …' She trailed off. Her eyes flickered to Tarek, and back to Freya. Freya caught her look. She hoped her best friend didn't think there was anything going on between her and Tarek.

Freya cast that thought aside. 'Who is she?'

'A fellow student. She's kinda fun.'

Freya's smile faltered. *I'm fun too*, she thought. She knew she shouldn't be jealous and realised she could never be anything more than Jolene's best friend. But now she knew how it felt – competition for her best friend's affections. Perhaps she felt it more because she knew it was a woman rather than a man.

'Sorry, Freya.'

'Oh, don't be silly. Go have lunch with your girlfriend.'

'I'm not sure if she is yet.'

'Well, go and find out.' Freya gently pushed her toward the door.

Jolene turned around and said, 'What about you?'

Tarek, standing behind Freya, stepped in. 'She has me.'

Freya rolled her eyes.

'Great. Freya enjoys having lunch with you,' Jolene said, not helping matters, in Freya's view.

'She does?'

'Yes, she told me herself.'

'Jolene!'

'I'm only repeating what you told me,' she said with a naughty grin.

Freya slowly turned around to find Tarek staring at her. 'Ignore her. She's just playing around.'

Although Jolene was already heading to the door, she had overheard the comment. 'I'm not.'

Tarek said, 'Why don't I take you to lunch for a change?'

Freya looked at him in surprise. 'But you don't know Cambridge.'

Tarek smiled. 'Oh, but I do. How do you think I've been spending my evenings? Sitting in a room staring at four walls?'

Freya hadn't thought of that. 'All right.' It crossed her mind that, like Jolene, she could be meeting her significant other for lunch. That would be a way out of lunch with Tarek. So, why wasn't she texting Theo?

Freya's phone stayed in her back pocket. 'Okay – it's a date.'

Tarek raised his eyebrows.

Freya backtracked. 'What I meant to say was it's a lunch date.' She frowned. That hadn't come out right, either.

In front of her, one of the ladies who worked at the museum must have overheard. She turned around and looked at them. Freya said to her, 'It's a work day – isn't it? So I'm taking Tarek with me to lunch.'

Tarek intervened. 'Actually, I am taking Freya to lunch.'

Freya grabbed his arm and pulled him out of the door,

wishing he hadn't said that. As they stepped out of the museum, she caught the other women in a little huddle around the door, casting glances over their shoulders at them as they walked down the street.

Freya sighed and turned to Tarek. 'Well, where are we going?'

'It's a surprise.'

'I don't like surprises,' murmured Freya. Her dad and that woman called Wendy came to mind. And her mum. A question still on Freya's mind. Had her mum found out about Wendy? And was she going to tell her mum about those trips out with her dad at the weekends? That whenever he had taken her swimming, they had stopped off at the park on the way home, and that sometimes, perhaps once a month, she had met a girl her own age, and had played with her while her dad chatted to some woman? She hadn't thought about those Saturdays for years, but the memories were flooding back.

'Do you want to talk about it?' Tarek asked, shifting her mind back to the present.

Freya shook her head. 'There's nothing to talk about.' She changed the subject as they walked down the street. 'We've only got an hour. This place had better not be far.'

'It isn't,' he said, still not telling her the big surprise. But he quickened his pace.

29

They walked from the museum towards the canal, where rows of gondolas bobbed up and down on the water and young men and women touted for business, offering boat rides along the River Cam.

However, Tarek and Freya didn't continue to the river, but turned left, walking along a wide street with cafés and shops on the right and the impressive King's College on their left, where most tourists headed for a photo opportunity by the lawns in front of the stunning honey-coloured façade.

Freya weaved between the tourists as she walked along with Tarek. She glanced at him, taking in his tall slim frame, skinny blue jeans, trainers, blue sweatshirt and jacket that was too thin for the weather. His hands were thrust into his jean pockets and his shoulders were hunched as he walked. He wasn't dressed for the British weather, and was obviously cold. She doubted he even owned an overcoat, or a hat, scarf and gloves.

Freya, on the other hand, was wearing a long, quilted coat, a bobble hat, gloves and a long, cosy woollen scarf. She unwound the scarf from her neck, zipped her up coat to her chin, and turned to Tarek. 'Here.'

He looked at her, dropped his eyes to the scarf, and shook his head.

'I know it's pink, but it's better than nothing.'

'That's very kind of you,' he said, a bit taken aback but still refusing to take the scarf.

Freya rolled her eyes. *Men. They can be so dumb sometimes*, she thought. She glanced at him a couple more times before finally quickening her pace and turning around and stepping right in front of him. He stopped dead in front of her. 'We're not there yet.'

'I know.' She stood on tiptoes and wrapped the scarf around his neck.

He just stood there, staring at her.

Freya tied the scarf in a loop. 'There.' Her eyes caught his. 'What? I'm fed up with you looking so cold. It's stupid. I know the scarf is pink, but it's better than being cold.'

Freya expected him to take it off or protest that she would be cold without it. Instead, he just stood there staring at her, a look of bemusement on his face. She guessed why. Most of the time, she was distant and aloof. She wished she hadn't confessed to Jolene how much she enjoyed his company. But she'd kept it strictly professional – making sure Tarek never guessed how very fond of him she'd become in such a short space of time. Now showing concern by giving him the scarf might have given her away. She hoped not.

She found his silence a tad disconcerting. Sometimes she couldn't get a word in edgeways. 'What?'

Freya stared into his chocolate-brown eyes. And there it was again, that funny feeling in the pit of her stomach. One day soon, she'd never look into those eyes again. He would only be there for a short time, a matter of weeks, before he flew home.

'You have beautiful eyes.'

'Oh, right,' Freya said in a deadpan voice. That wasn't news to her. Everyone who knew her commented on the beautiful, and rather exotic, almond shape of her eyes.

'I think you have some Middle Eastern in your family tree.'

Freya laughed, falling in step with him as they walked. 'I don't think so.'

He glanced at her. 'But how do you know? Have you researched it?'

'My family tree?' Her first thought was, *why would I?* There would be nothing interesting to discover. But now she wasn't so sure. That woman and her child whom they used to meet in the park came to mind.

She looked at Tarek. 'No, I haven't.'

'You should. It might raise some interesting possibilities.'

Freya looked at him sharply. Had he been talking to Jolene? But his expression, one of polite inquiry, didn't indicate that he had a clue what she and her best friend had been talking about. Besides, she couldn't see Jolene getting into much of a conversation with Tarek.

'If you look, who knows? You might find something interesting in your past.'

'By interesting, you mean like a long-lost relative from some far-flung distant shore?'

'Yes.' Tarek came to a halt on the pavement. 'Here we are.'

'Where?' asked Freya, looking about her. They'd just passed a very nice café, which she had never ventured into because there was always a queue of people waiting to be seated. She had briefly hoped he might be taking her there, but she knew they wouldn't have time in their lunch hour to wait for a table. And it wasn't just that; the café was waiter service only, and she knew it was expensive.

'It's right here.' He pointed at some stone steps beside a church called St. Michaels.

'We're going into a church?'

He nodded and smiled before turning for the steps. She had walked past the church on Trinity Street countless times, but had taken no notice of the steps – or the small billboard outside encouraging people to go inside for refreshments.

She followed him down the stone steps and through a pair of double doors, then stopped in surprise. Inside, straight ahead of them, was a small counter with two people serving home-cooked meals and soups, along with the usual cakes and scones you'd find in most cafés. But what set this apart was the venue. It might have been the church crypt at one point. The soft yellow stone walls made it feel like the refectory of an old castle. And the room was quite cavernous. The place was packed, with hardly a spare seat at the small plastic tables.

'This place is called Michaelhouse Café. There's a mezzanine level up there.' Tarek pointed to a spiral staircase. She could see people sitting at tables, looking down over the room. 'It's got a marvellous view of the college if you get a table by the window.' They stopped in front of the counter. 'What would you like to eat, Freya?'

Freya saw the person ahead being handed a plate of lasagne. It looked delicious. She suddenly felt ravenous and realised that her bracing walk in the fresh air had built up at appetite. 'I'll have lasagne.'

He smiled. 'Perfect. Me too.'

Emily headed for the spiral staircase while Tarek waited in the queue. Up on the mezzanine level, there was a table by the window. But Freya fancied one that looked out over the impressive interior of the church. She pulled out the chair, took a seat, and marvelled at the stonemasonry.

A moment later, Tarek had joined her. 'This place is amazing,' she said. 'I can't believe in all the years I've lived in Cambridge, I've never discovered this place.'

Tarek smiled. 'I think perhaps it is a best-kept secret among a certain generation.' He nodded toward the other diners.

Freya noticed they were mostly retirement age. She returned his smiled. 'I see what you mean. How did you find this place?'

'I was just walking around at the weekend, and I thought I'd pop in and see this church. Like you, I didn't take much notice of the sign, so imagine my surprise when I discovered it was a café.' Tarek set a plate of lasagne down in front of her, along with some cutlery. 'I'll just return the tray.'

She turned in her seat and watched him walk down the staircase and leave the tray by a counter with cutlery and sauces. When he took a seat opposite her, he said, 'Do you like it? Was it a nice surprise?'

'Oh, yes. I like it very much.' Freya tried the lasagne. 'This is amazing.'

'I know.'

She looked at him curiously.

'What?'

'I think you've been in here a lot.'

He nodded. 'It beats the university food in the halls.'

'Oh, yes – I forgot that's where you were.'

'Yes. I haven't lived in halls of residence since, well, since I was a student in Alexandria.'

Freya smiled. She loved to hear stories of Tarek's life in Egypt. Inevitably, the conversation led back to Alexandria. This time, though, he got on to the subject of his accommodation in Cambridge.

'I'm in halls in Christ College. It's okay, I guess. Not what I would have chosen, though.'

'I wouldn't have thought they'd have given you accommodation at a college.' She'd expected he'd have to rent somewhere privately.

'It wasn't my choice. It was my father's because this is the college he came to years ago, before I was born, when he taught here for a while.'

'Your father was here in Cambridge?'

'No – he *is* here.'

'You mean – your father came too?' Freya looked at him wide-eyed. It was little wonder that the college accommodated them. Tarek's father was a world-renowned professor of archaeology at Alexandria University and an eminent Egyptologist. He had been involved in many archaeological digs in and around the Nile and had written many books and articles in his field. Any a student of archaeology and antiquities would have loved to meet him. That was one of the reasons she had wanted the secondment to Alexandria. Of course, she could go there on holiday, but that wouldn't come with a behind the scenes look at the archaeology department at the university or the famous library. And she wasn't about to go there on holiday – not with her partner. Theo had made his views clear; he wasn't interested in that sort of thing.

Freya sighed as she put her knife and fork down on her

empty plate. How was it that she ended up with a guy who had absolutely no interested in Ancient Egypt? So many people found the pyramids and Giza and The Valley of the Kings fascinating. But not Theo.

Staring at Tarek, she was still taken aback that his father was there in England. 'You are joking – right?'

'Nope. No joke.'

Freya guessed that was why he hadn't appeared happy to be there in England when she'd first met him.

'At first I wasn't happy that he'd insisted I come.'

'And now?'

Tarek eyed her thoughtfully. 'I think you know the answer to that question.'

Freya could feel those butterflies in her tummy again as she there under his gaze.

'So, that's the reason we're staying at that college. It's his old stomping ground—' He paused, catching Freya grinning. 'What is it?'

'Stomping ground – you sound so …'

'English?'

She nodded.

'Blame that on my father.'

Tarek had a cut-glass English accent. He'd been to boarding school in England, but it wasn't that which surprised her; it was the very English idioms that he suddenly came out with that she didn't expect.

'Oh, how he loves England, and his old college.'

'Sounds as though he really enjoyed his time here. He must have fallen in love with the place.'

Tarek regarded her thoughtfully.

'What?' Freya put an elbow on the table, her chin in her hand, studying his dark eyes. She wondered what his father looked like. Did Tarek take after him?

Freya steered the conversation back to his father. 'So, was there something in particular he loved about England?'

'Someone,' said Tarek, surprising her. 'Once, he said he met the love of his life here.'

'Your mother was a student here too? They met at Cambridge?'

Tarek shook his head. 'No. My mother never ventured out of Egypt. Theirs was an arranged marriage.'

'Was?' repeated Freya.

'She passed away a few months ago. My mother was much younger than my father. He didn't marry until his thirties, so he didn't expect to lose her so young.'

'I'm so sorry.' Now she understood why his father had wanted to accompany him to England.

'My father talked of his wish to visit England many times, but my mother wouldn't come, so he put off the trip.' He lowered his voice. 'I think it's just as well. Something tells me it isn't Cambridge he's returned to see after all these years.'

'You think there was someone before your mother?'

'They'd been betrothed since my mother was twelve, but …'

Freya leaned towards him, staring at him with rapt attention. 'What happened?'

'It was the eve of his wedding, when he was due to fly home, so mother told me, and he'd missed his flight. It was all because his Cambridge friends had found out about his wedding and taken him on a stag night.'

'Oh, dear. I imagine that wasn't something he intended to do.'

'No, it wasn't.'

She imagined it wasn't something he'd forget in a hurry, either.

'My father was open to all new English cultural experiences.'

Freya frowned. 'I wouldn't exactly call that cultural.' Although she imagined not all stag parties involved getting drunk and doing really dumb things, but she guessed most fell into that category. 'What happened?'

'I think he met someone that night and fell in love.'

'In one night? Are you serious? That's crazy.'

Tarek disagreed. 'It happens – love at first sight.'

There followed a very uncomfortable moment in which they both sat staring at one another across the table. One of the diners interrupted them, asking, 'Is this chair free?'

'Yes,' they both said in unison, neither one of them turning to look at the man standing there with a hand on the chair.

'Er … thanks.'

Freya finally tore her eyes away. *What is going on here?* she wondered. *What am I even doing here with Tarek rather than meeting Theo for lunch?* She knew the answer. It's *because I prefer Tarek's company.*

Freya pursed her lips, feeling terribly guilty. For the first time, this innocent thing between them wasn't feeling innocent at all – not for her, at any rate. Without thinking, Freya asked, 'Have you got a girlfriend?' She regretted asking as soon as those words were out of her mouth.

He was still staring at her, she could tell, although her eyes were firmly fixed on her fingernails, embarrassed that she'd asked the question.

'No, I haven't.'

Not quite sure why she felt relieved by his answer, Freya changed the subject. 'Anyway, about your dad …' She looked up to find Tarek with a look of amusement on his face. 'What happened on his stag night?'

'He missed his flight and had to get another one. Almost missed his own wedding.'

'Er, no – I meant what happened *during* the stag do. Where did they go? Who did he meet?'

Tarek sighed. 'Your guess is as good as mine.'

'So, he didn't tell you anything more about this woman he'd met – the love of his life?'

Tarek shook his head. 'I brought it up once, what he'd said about meeting the love of his life here, but he waved it away, saying I must have misheard.'

'But you didn't – did you?'

'No.'

They fell silent again until Freya asked another question. 'Do you think that's why he came back after your mother died?'

Tarek frowned. 'I don't understand …'

Freya pursed her lips, realising that in light of his mother's death, it was a delicate question. 'Do you think he's returned to find someone – his lost love?'

Tarek shook his head. 'I don't see how that's possible. He'd have to find her first.'

'Do you think he met her on the stag do?'

He nodded. 'It's possible.'

'Where do you think they had the stag do – here in Cambridge?'

Tarek shrugged. 'I imagine he wouldn't remember.'

Don't be so sure, thought Freya, looking around the café,

thinking that she'd remember this – their lunch dates together. Her thoughts returned to Tarek's father. To meet and fall in love with someone just before you were going to marry someone else. That was … well, that was just not possible – was it? Her gaze shifted to Tarek once again, but this time she was thinking about Theo. They were engaged and yet here she was – with someone else.

'I'd love to meet your dad,' she said.

'Why?'

'Well, any aspiring archaeologist would.'

'All right.'

Freya's eyes went wide. 'Did you just say *yes*?'

He nodded. 'Of course – why not?'

'When? Can we meet him today, after work?'

Tarek's eyes dropped to his cup of coffee. He shook his head. He picked up a spoon and slowly stirred his black coffee.

Freya sat back in her chair, disappointed. 'Oh – another time then?'

'It's not that I don't want you to meet him. The problem is, he isn't in Cambridge at the moment. He skipped town.'

'Huh?'

'He left me a note to say he's gone away for a few days. Something about a guest house and wanting to return to somewhere called Suffolk, for old times' sake.' Tarek had a thought. 'Do you think it's got something to do with—'

'Did you just say a guest house in Suffolk?'

Tarek nodded. 'The Guest House at Shingle Cove.'

Freya stared at him. 'Run that by me again.'

Tarek put the spoon down and reached inside his coat pocket. 'Look, this is the note.' He slid it across the table.

Freya didn't know why he was showing her the note. She couldn't speak Arabic, let alone read it, although it was something she'd very much love to learn.

Tarek caught her expression. 'It's in English.'

'What is it?' he asked, seeing the look of surprise on her face when she'd read it.

Freya bit her bottom lip, an idea forming in her mind. 'How would you like to go on a road trip? See a different county in England?'

He looked at her quizzically. 'Are you talking about going *there*?' His finger stabbed the piece of paper in front of her.

She nodded.

'You can't wait to meet him – can you?'

Freya pursed her lips. Wasn't this the perfect excuse to get away and visit that guest house? Of all the places – what a coincidence! What was really on Freya's mind was finding that woman called Wendy. She gave Tarek a sideways glance. Of course, it had nothing to do with also finding an excuse to spend more time with Tarek.

30

'You know you're going to have to lie to your boyfriend, don't you?'

Freya frowned at Jolene. 'What do you mean?'

'You can't very well turn round and say, *by the way, I'm going to stay in a guest house on the Suffolk Coast with Tarek.*'

Freya and Tarek had returned from their lunch break – late. But Freya hadn't cared about that. She couldn't wait to tell Jolene what she'd discovered at lunch – that Tarek's father was staying in the very guest house from where the woman called Wendy had phoned her dad – and that she was going there with Tarek to meet his father.

She knew very well she could wait until Tarek's father returned to Cambridge to meet him, but it was a perfect excuse to go there and find out about Wendy.

'Too perfect,' commented Jolene after she'd told her all this. 'What if Theo finds out?'

'How can he? I'm going to tell him I'm going with you.'

Jolene scratched her head. 'What if he sees me in Cambridge?'

Freya cocked her head to one side. 'Last time I checked,

Theo doesn't visit any museums, and certainly doesn't frequent gay bars.'

Jolene grinned. 'I should hope not. He's the last person I'd want to see on a night out.'

Freya bit her lip.

Jolene offered her a sly grin. 'I bet he'd say the same thing about me.'

Freya looked sheepish. It was so true. Her best friend and her boyfriend had nothing in common. They barely tolerated one another. It made Freya wonder what she had in common with Theo herself, apart from the fact that they'd met at a wedding and had fancied each other, and had then moved in together. Was that a solid basis for a long-term relationship? Why was she even wondering that? It had never crossed her mind before. *Not until I met Tarek*, she thought.

Her parents came to mind, and the woman called Wendy with whom her father might, or might not, have had an affair. It made her wonder about relationships. She'd heard it said that there was someone out there for everyone, that each person has a soulmate. But that didn't mean your soulmate would be the person you ended up marrying. What if you didn't even realise the person you were with wasn't *the one* until that person came along?

Jolene eyed her friend. 'What are you thinking about?' She caught Freya casting a furtive glance in Tarek's direction. Jolene rolled her eyes. 'Okay, I guess I should say, *who* are you thinking about?'

Freya nudged her arm. 'Oh, stop it.'

Jolene sighed. 'What are you going to do?'

'I'm going to arrange the trip. Tarek wants to come.'

'I bet he does.'

Freya ignored that remark.

'What I meant,' said Jolene, leaning towards her and lowering her voice, 'is what are you going to do about Tarek?'

Freya creased her brow. 'What do you mean?'

'You like him – I can tell. I'm not talking about as a friend.'

Freya stared at her. She was about to tell Jolene not to be silly, but if she couldn't be honest with her best friend, who could she talk candidly with?

'Honestly, I don't know,' she said.

'He'll leave at the end of the month. Your life is here in Cambridge …'

'With Theo,' Freya added. 'Is that what you're saying?'

'I didn't say that, but the fact remains, he won't be here forever. Then what? I don't want to be the one to say it, but I'm just giving you a reality check. If you go to this guest house together, just don't—'

'Don't *what?*'

'Don't do anything you'll regret.'

They both knew what she was saying.

'Besides, how long have you known Tarek? You know nothing about him.'

I know I'm falling in love. Freya bit her bottom lip. The thought had come out of nowhere.

'He might have a girlfriend back in Alexandria.'

'He hasn't – I asked him.'

Jolene stared at her.

Freya looked away. She wished she hadn't said that.

'Theo is a good guy. You've got plans together. Don't throw that away on, well, on a crush.'

It's not a crush, thought Freya. She frowned. 'I never thought I'd hear you side with Theo,' she said.

Jolene stood there shaking her head. 'It's not about sides, Freya. I'm thinking about you. And your future, here in Cambridge – which you love – with a guy who'd do anything for you.'

'Are you saying I shouldn't take this trip?'

'No, but I'd prefer it if you were going with me or on your own.'

Freya stared at her. Both were possibilities, but she wanted to go with Tarek, and besides, he could introduce her to his father. 'I want to meet his father, so I need to go with Tarek.'

'You tell yourself that,' Jolene scoffed.

'Oh, don't be like that, Jolene.'

'Look, you're my best friend, you know that, right? I'm not being mean, I just … I don't think you should get involved with him.'

'I won't. It's purely a business trip, as far as he is concerned. He doesn't know I've got some personal reasons for going to that guest house.'

The look on Jolene's face said she believed her. 'All right. Talking of your personal reasons, you want to find that lady called Wendy, don't you?'

Freya nodded. She looked at her phone.

Jolene sighed. 'You know, that's like the tenth time you've checked your phone in the last twenty minutes.'

Freya looked up. 'Sorry.'

'Has your Mum been in contact yet?'

Freya shook her head.

'Look, this is only the second day she's been gone. She's

probably just away for the weekend to have a break from packing for the house move.'

'But what if it's more than that? What if she found out about Wendy?'

Jolene rolled her eyes. 'You don't even know if your dad and this Wendy had an affair.'

'Or if the girl I used to meet over the park, Wendy's daughter, is my half-sister.'

'Exactly.' Jolene studied her intently. 'There is one way to find out if you've got a half-sister out there, apart from having an awkward conversation with your dad.'

'I know. Find Wendy and ask her.'

'Well, that's a possibility. But even if you do find her at this guest house, do you think she's just going to come out with it and tell you the truth?'

Freya hadn't thought of that.

Jolene smiled. 'I've got an idea. There's something I think you should do before you go …'

31

'I had a wonderful time,' said Alice.

Emily pulled the car up outside the guest house. She unclipped her seatbelt and turned to Alice. 'Me too.' But she wasn't thinking about The Two Magpies Bakery, where they'd just had lunch together, or the stroll up and down the high street, nipping in and out of some of the little boutique shops where she'd bought a sketchbook and a lovely set of pencils. Or the visit to the pet shop to buy a dog treat for Hester and a toy for Marley, who sounded from what Alice had said like he was feeling much better. Emily had laughed when Alice had told her about Marley's antics with her pen, when he'd stolen it and disappeared under the bed.

Instead, Emily was still thinking about the decision to return to Cobblers Yard afterwards to have another look at the shop that was up for sale. The thought had her on cloud nine.

'Are you thinking about the shop in Cobblers Yard?' asked Alice, reading her mind.

'Yes. It never crossed my mind to open my own practice. I love Cobblers Yard. I know the two old ladies, Mabel and Marjorie, sisters who volunteer in the charity shop, and the lady who took over The Potting Shed. Then there's Reggie, who I don't think will ever retire. He's run the little music shop for years and years. It's where I bought my first recorder, and my parents bought me an electric guitar for my twelfth birthday. I went through a phase when I decided I wanted to be a rock star when I grew up.'

Alice nodded. How many children went through similar phases? Probably a lot. Not Freya, though. All she'd ever wanted to be was an archaeologist and join digs in Egypt. 'Cobblers Yard would be a lovely little place to work,' she said.

Emily's smile faded.

Alice noticed. 'So, what's the problem?'

Emily sighed. 'I don't think I'm experienced enough to run my own practice.'

'Pah! You've got your qualification. I'm sure there will be people who can give you advice. I imagine an established vet's practice would be more than happy to talk to you about their experiences of starting their own practice. Or perhaps someone from your university might point you towards a short business course you could do to learn the ropes.' Alice glanced out of the window at the guest house. 'Perhaps your parents could advise you on some of the nuances of running your own business.'

Emily nodded. 'Maybe. But then there's the issue of money. Where does it come from?' She frowned. 'I haven't got the means to buy the shop.'

'Are you still going to speak to Joss, and apologise about last night?'

Emily heaved a sigh. There was that too. She'd promised Alice she would. It didn't change the fact that she'd thought it was a date, and she still felt embarrassed for assuming it was.

And the suggestion Alice had made when they were sitting having lunch in The Two Magpies Bakery, that she should ask him out, was playing on her mind. What if she did, and he said no? Alice had said, *what if he doesn't?* But she didn't want to dig herself an even bigger pit of embarrassment if, despite Alice's assurances that he was interested in her, it turned out he wasn't. And it wasn't as though she'd see the back of him any time soon. He'd asked for the room booking to be open-ended. Who knew how long he'd be staying? *Until his savings run out,* she thought. But how long would that be?

'Are you going to ask him out?'

Emily had been staring at the guest house, wishing he'd leave. Today. Now. She rolled her eyes. Of course she wouldn't ask him out. But she didn't want Alice on her case either. She cast a sheepish look her way, and replied, 'Maybe.' She took the key out of the ignition. 'Shall we go in?'

Alice hesitated. 'Do you think your other guest might have arrived?'

Emily caught something in her voice; a note of hesitation. She stared at Alice for a long moment. What was she doing here, with her pets and with umpteen suitcases? And without her husband? She had a feeling that something had happened and that Alice had left him. She had noticed that Alice's letter was addressed to her husband. Were they splitting up? Did he even know she was there, or had she just left, skipping town without telling him? It was all rather strange. She wondered what Clarissa would make of it.

Clarissa! Emily stared wide-eyed at Alice. Talking of new arrivals – her best friend was due to arrive. 'Come on, let's find out!'

Emily was already out of the car before Alice had even opened the car door.

Emily ran around the car and opened the door for her.

'Oh, thanks.'

Emily opened the passenger car door behind Alice. Because she'd been well-behaved, Emily had let Hester travel home sitting on the back seat. Out jumped an excited beagle. 'Well, at least someone is pleased to be back,' she said under her breath.

'Do you think my letter will be posted today?'

'Oh, yes. I think she must have some stamps after all. I imagine my mum walked up to the post box and posted it herself. But I will ask her for you, as soon as I see her, and check.'

'All right.'

Emily bounded up the guest house steps, hoping Clarissa was there already. They'd be no tell-tale car parked outside to herald her arrival, although she imagined her friend's dad had helped her down the road with her suitcases.

As she stepped inside the guest house, Emily saw her dad. There was no one else in sight, but someone *had* arrived; her dad was picking up a suitcase. The new guest must have already taken their room key and gone upstairs.

Alice stepped into the guest house with Hester and noticed the suitcase too. 'Is it the Egyptian?' she asked Gerald.

Gerald looked at his daughter. 'An Egyptian?'

'Yes, Dad. The guest that was meant to arrive a couple of days ago – remember? I've tried contacting him by email. We didn't have a mobile phone number. I have kept his reservation open, although I'm not sure if he is still coming.'

'We're getting quite booked up,' Gerald commented.

'I know. Crazy, isn't it? This time of year we are normally so quiet. I will have to let his room go if we have any more guests.'

'I think something pinged on the computer,' Gerald added. 'Perhaps another booking?'

'Sounds like it,' said Emily. She was about to have a look when she heard a familiar voice and footsteps running down the stairs.

'Emily! I thought I heard your voice. I've arrived!'

'So, I see.' Emily grinned and ran into her arms.

'Oh, my god. I am so excited. How stupid is that!'

'Not at all stupid!' Emily replied.

Clarissa cast a gaze at the other guest. 'As you can see, I'm not the Egyptian!' She'd overheard the conversation in the hall on the way down the stairs.

Emily turned to Alice. 'This is my best friend, Clarissa.' She turned to her friend. 'This is Alice, one of our guests.'

Clarissa stepped forward. 'Pleased to meet you.'

'Oh, god!' exclaimed Emily when she saw Donut bounding down the stairs behind Clarissa. She'd forgotten all about Clarissa bringing her rather large, and very playful, St. Bernard dog. One small, well-behaved pet was allowed in the guest house. That rule had already gone out of the window when Alice had arrived, although at least her three pets were well-behaved.

'Oh, you brought a dog too!' said Alice.

Donut seemed to sense a dog lover in his sights, and made straight for Alice, bouncing in front of her, looking like he was fit to burst with excitement. 'Well, aren't you a lovely boy?' She looked at Clarissa. 'Boy or girl?'

'Oh, he's a boy.'

'And what is your name, you lovely boy?'

Emily smiled at the crazy dog. 'Alice, meet Donut.'

Donut calmed down just long enough for Alice to reach out and stroke his head.

Emily looked over at her dad. When she'd booked Clarissa a room, she had failed to mention that Clarissa's dog would be coming too. Her dad didn't seem to mind. But it wasn't her dad she was worried about. If her mum walked in … well, Emily didn't want to think about that as she watched Donut run up to Gerald and get a fuss.

Donut then sniffed the air and darted back to Alice. Hester was hiding behind her legs – or trying to.

The large dog skirted around Alice, playfully crouching on his front paws, his behind in the air, tail wagging furiously. He barked at Hester.

Emily winced. Bloody hell, his bark's loud, she thought. She looked over at her dad. 'Where's Mum?'

'She's out. Said she had some errands to run.'

Emily was just breathing a sigh of relief when the guest house door opened. *Oh, god. Is that Mum?*

Clarissa had a ball in her hand. Before Emily could stop her, she threw the tennis ball across the hall.

Two dogs darted after it. They all arrived in an excited heap, skidding on the wooden floor just as the front door opened.

Emily's mum nearly dropped her shopping bag in surprise. 'What the …!?' Her eyes drifted to Emily. 'Emily – a word please.'

'I'm just showing Clarissa to her room.'

'Now!'

Emily frowned. Perhaps Clarissa staying there hadn't been the best idea.

An awkward silence followed, interrupted by Gerald. 'Ahem. Well, I think I'll take these cases upstairs.'

'Emily – I still want a word.'

Emily frowned at her mum as she followed her down the hall.

When she returned to the reception desk, after a grilling from her mum, Clarissa was sitting on the bottom stair waiting for her. 'I'm guessing you didn't tell your mum Donut was staying too.'

Emily shook her head. 'Talking of which – where is your dog?'

'He followed Gerald upstairs.' Clarissa stood up. 'I want to see my room.'

Emily followed her up the stairs.

'You know, I signed the guestbook, and I saw Joss's name above your other guest's. I didn't realise how long he'd been here.'

'Yeah, it's been a while,' Emily replied. She was pretty sure she had told Clarissa.

'Well, there's someone with a story to tell. I mean who stays in a guest house for weeks on end, and obviously has the means to do it?'

Emily rolled her eyes. 'Clarissa, you are not on a busman's holiday.' Her best friend was still in journalist mode, looking for a story. 'You are here to have a break and not think about work.'

'I can't help it.'

'Well – try. Besides, you won't get anything out of him. As you noticed, he's not very approachable.'

'Or talkative,' added Clarissa. She glanced at Emily. 'I might try to change that.'

'And how do you propose to do that?'

'Oh, a sweet dog called Donut.'

'How do you know Joss likes animals?' In all the time he'd been there, Emily hadn't thought to ask.

'I'll find out,' Clarissa replied.

Emily sighed. 'You never give up, do you?' She guessed that it was a trait you needed as an aspiring investigative journalist.

'Never! Not when there's a cute guy involved.'

Emily frowned at her back as they continued up the stairs. She'd rather Clarissa hadn't called Joss cute. She suddenly felt a surprising pang of jealousy that her best friend might fancy him.

Clarissa glanced over her shoulder, adding, 'And he sounds quite mysterious. I want to find out his secret.'

'A secret? What are you on about?'

'He's hiding something – can't you tell?'

Now Emily thought about it, she did wonder why Joss was there, at a remote, out-of-the-way guest house on the sleepy Suffolk Coast.

'If I had to hazard a guess,' said Clarissa, pausing on the stairs, 'I'd say that he's running away from something.'

'Or someone.'

Clarissa said, 'Don't you worry. I'll get to the bottom of it.'

That was what Emily was afraid of. Did their guests want their pasts and their secrets unravelled by a journalist who would stop at nothing to further her career? Emily was looking at her friend in a whole new light – and it wasn't a favourable one.

'So, what do we know about the other guest, Alice?'

'You mean, what do *I* know?'

Clarissa grinned.

'I shouldn't be discussing the guests.'

'Oh, Emily, don't be a spoil sport. Besides, it's just between you and me.'

Emily raised her eyebrows.

'Cross my heart,' said Clarissa, a bit too flippantly.

Emily sighed. What harm would it do? 'She's here on her own, arrived with a menagerie of pets, well, three – a cat, a dog, and a parrot.'

'A parrot? You're joking with me.'

'Nope.'

They continued up the stairs while Emily talked in a hushed voice behind her. 'She wrote a letter to her husband and asked us to post it.'

Clarissa glanced at Emily over her shoulder. 'A letter to her husband?'

Emily nodded. 'It was addressed to a man with the same surname, so I'm guessing that's him.' Emily frowned, thinking about that very letter. She'd found it in the kitchen when she was being told off about Donut. Her mum hadn't posted it. There wasn't even a stamp on it ready for posting.

'Why do you want to invite her to our little party?'

'She's nice. I like her. And she's got the room right next door.' Emily pointed as she opened the door to Clarissa's room.

'Ah. You think she's a light sleeper?'

Emily shrugged. 'I don't know.'

Clarissa walked in, taking in the white, airy room with wooden floors, a large double bed with a colourful patchwork quilt, and gorgeous light oak furnishings. She whirled around full circle. 'Oh, I love it. This is just perfect.'

Emily smiled at her reaction.

'Have you asked Alice yet whether she wants to come to our little soiree?'

'No, but I will. It's only fair to let her know, as she might hear us next door. Although I doubt she'll accept.'

32

'Oh, that's so kind of you to invite me – I'd love to come.'

'Really?'

'Oh yes. A party sounds such fun.' Emily had knocked on Alice's door while she was preparing to go down and sit in the lounge set aside for guests. She had planned to have a pleasant afternoon reading while she waited for dinner. On her own. She had her pets – she glanced at Marley, who was in her arms, purring – but she missed human company. A little party would be something to look forward to.

Although she'd only been gone a day, and she'd spent a lovely afternoon with Emily, it had been the night before that she'd felt very lonely. Going out with Emily had made her realise how much she missed her family; especially Freya.

Emily turned to go.

'Tell me about your friend,' Alice asked, keen for her to stay for a chat. 'Are you childhood friends?'

Emily shook her head. 'My sister, my older half-sister, married her brother. That's how we got to know one another. Clarissa has split up from her husband. He's got the children for a few days, so she fancied a break in a hotel.'

Alice nodded. She remembered Emily mentioning her best friend coming to stay while her ex-husband looked after the children. 'Has she come far?'

Emily chuckled. 'Actually, she lives just up the street.'

Alice stared at her. 'Shingle Street? And she's come to stay here?'

'I know it sounds crazy. She wanted somewhere where she could bring her dog too. Her husband didn't want to look after Donut as well. He lives in a flat in London, said it wouldn't be practical.'

Alice could understand that.

'So, Gerald suggested she could stay here.' Emily's smile faded somewhat.

Alice noticed. 'What is it?'

'I would have loved her to have grown up here so that I'd have had a friend who could just pop round. We would have been like sisters. I would have loved that.'

'But didn't you say that you have a half-sister?

'Yes, she's older than me. We were never really close growing up, not like I imagine siblings ought to be.'

Alice understood. She often thought of Freya growing up an only child and how she had missed out on having siblings. She thought of Theo. He was like a son to them, especially to Jeffrey, whom she knew would have loved more children. Of course, their shared interest in writing, talking about plots and characters, Theo passing his work to Jeffrey to cast his eye over, was something they both enjoyed. And from what Jeffrey had said, it sounded as though Theo was on his way to writing his first novel. Jeffrey was so proud. Alice's mind had wandered. She looked at Emily. 'So, does Clarissa work?'

'Oh, yes. I'm so happy for her. She's always wanted to be a journalist.'

'A journalist?'

'Yes, she did an evening course. She used to work in admin, typing up news stories, but now the local paper has taken her on in a new position. She's a reporter now and starting her new role next week. I think they want her to find a local story that might interest their readers.'

'Do they?' Alice stared at Emily. 'You know what? It's really kind of you to invite me, but I think it would be better if you two girls didn't have an oldie intruding on your party.'

'Oh, no, don't be silly. We'd love you to come. Clarissa especially. She wants to meet the other guests.'

I bet she does, Alice thought. It made her wonder if there was more to Clarissa staying in the guest house than merely a bit of pampering and a catch-up with her best friend. Maybe she was looking for a news story. Alice suddenly had a marvellous idea. 'But if you do want to invite someone else, why don't you invite Joss?'

'Joss?'

She could tell that the idea hadn't crossed Emily's mind. 'It might be a way to break the ice over what happened last night.'

Emily stood there, biting her lip. 'That isn't a bad idea.'

Alice wondered if Emily was thinking what she was thinking. She imagined there would be alcohol. She was sure she'd heard the faint chink of bottles when Clarissa had walked up the stairs to her room with her bag. Perhaps a few drinks would loosen his tongue, and Emily would find out about more about him. Maybe there would be something in his past worthy of a news story.

Alice watched Emily as she headed to her friend's room. She

was thinking of what had taken place in the guest house twenty-five years earlier. That event was worthy of a news story all right – and a police investigation. Alice shuddered. She would much rather Clarissa focused her attention on Joss – or on anybody else, for that matter.

Alice had seen the way Clarissa looked at Joss. She wasn't surprised. He was good-looking even with his grim expression, which made him look as though he was carrying the weight of the world on his shoulders. She hoped that Clarissa would focus on the more interesting, better-looking, younger guest rather than her; that she wouldn't ask what Alice was doing there with a menagerie of pets and without her husband.

Of course, there was one way of avoiding any potential scrutiny from a budding journalist. And that was to leave. But she wasn't ready to leave – not yet, anyway. Now she regretted asking Emily about the other guest they were still expecting. She didn't want to appear to be showing an interest; it might get back to Clarissa.

Alice smiled as she shut the door. It occurred to her that she was worrying out of hand. She imagined that the two young women had other things on their minds – young men, for instance, like Joss. She decided she had nothing to worry about.

33

'So, you're saying that as soon as you mentioned I was a journalist, she changed her mind about coming to the party?'

Emily nodded. 'She was really enthusiastic, and said yes immediately when I invited her. She didn't hesitate until I mentioned your job. You should have seen her face. I mean, she almost went ashen.'

'Really?'

They were sitting cross-legged on Clarissa's king-sized bed, facing each other, waiting for the other invite to arrive. Emily wondered if she was doing the right thing, telling her all this about Alice. And the wine was making her embellish the story. Alice hadn't gone ashen, but Emily could have sworn she had seen something cross her face, as though she had something to hide. Emily downed another glass of wine and added that too.

'Really?'

Emily nodded. 'Yeah – pretty sure that's the look I caught on her face.' She glanced at the bottle in Clarissa's hand. 'May I have another?'

Clarissa hesitated. 'Are you sure? I mean, you've only been here like twenty minutes.' She studied her friend intently. 'You don't want to be off your head when Joss arrives.'

Emily held up her glass, thinking, *yes I do*.

She was also feeling self-conscious in the nightwear she was wearing. It was ten o'clock at night, and they'd chosen this time for a get-together with wine and nibbles when her parents were tucked up in bed. They'd already had takeout together in her room earlier, Clarissa choosing to have dinner with Emily rather than the other guests. Earlier in the evening, they'd gone for a walk along the beach together, taking Donut for his evening constitutional, and spotted Alice doing the same with Hester. Although they'd both waved their arms, they'd failed to attract her attention further up the beach – either that or she was avoiding them. Much later, when all was quiet in the guest house, Emily had stolen into Clarissa's room wearing her comfy pink pyjamas with hearts and 'I love my sleep' emblazoned on the top.

The moment Clarissa saw her pyjamas, she'd said, 'Considering the company, I don't think that will do at all.'

Emily had looked down at her pyjamas and wished she hadn't insisted on sticking to the original plan of a slumber party, considering it was no longer just her and Clarissa. 'You know what? This feels weird, now it's not just the two of us,' she'd said. 'I'm going to go back to my room and get dressed.'

'Oh, Emily. Don't be a prude. What's the harm?' She'd eyed Emily's pyjamas. 'I've got a better idea.'

They'd swapped. Clarissa was now wearing Emily's pink, albeit slightly small for her tall frame, cotton pyjamas, and Emily had changed into her much more sophisticated purple silk pyjama set that seemed to follow her contours. When she'd objected, at first, to changing, Clarissa had said, 'Why do you think I brought these along?'

'You were hoping you might meet someone here at the guest house?'

'You never know.'

Emily shook her head, thinking of the age range of the guests who normally booked into her mum's quiet guest house.

As Clarissa poured her another glass, she said, 'Do you know what you're doing?'

Emily's thoughts switched to Joss. 'Oh, yes. I'm building up the nerve to ask him out.'

Clarissa frowned. 'But you don't know anything about him. You said so yourself.'

'I'm hoping tonight will change that. You can change that.'

'Ah, I get it. Two against one. I like it. We'll get to the bottom of what he is doing here, or I will,' said Clarissa. 'If for no other reason than I want to find out if he's good enough for my best friend.'

Emily held up her glass, hoping she really meant that and wasn't thinking about whether he was good enough for herself. 'To being good enough.'

They both giggled. Clarissa said, 'I'm looking forward to the guest arriving.'

'Guest?'

'Joss – who did you think I was talking about? He's a guest here, too, isn't he?'

'Well, yes, but …' What Emily was trying to put across was that Joss didn't feel like a guest anymore, not after the length of time he'd been here. He felt more like family.

Clarissa said, 'So, here's the plan. You can chat to Joss, ply him with a bit of wine, see what you can find out.'

Emily nodded.

'Then we can swap.'

'Swap?' said Emily in alarm, wondering what she'd got herself into.

'Swap notes, when he goes, about what we've discovered.'

'Oh, I see,' Emily said, relieved. She had wondered whether Clarissa had more on her mind than just talking.

'I was hoping to take him to one side, perhaps while you go and powder your nose, and see what I could glean.' She looked at Emily. 'What did you think I meant?'

'Oh, never mind.' She was relieved for all of two seconds until a thought occurred to her. 'But … what if Joss doesn't come?' She had written him a note on his napkin and placed it on his table during dinner, hoping he read it. The napkin was gone when she went to clear his dinner plate, but so was Joss. She hadn't seen him since dinner, so she had no idea whether he'd even read her note, let alone decided to come.

'Well, let's cross that bridge when we come to it,' replied Clarissa.

Emily felt mean for thinking it, but perhaps she'd rather he didn't. Then she could have what she'd originally intended, which was just a girly night in. Things were just getting too complicated by half.

'So, while we wait, tell me more about Alice.'

Emily joined her on the bed, after Clarissa had ordered Donut off the bed so they had some room. They sat on the bed next to each other, legs outstretched. Emily put her wine glass down and turned to one side, staring at her friend's profile. 'Why are you so interested?'

'I don't know. It just strikes me as a little strange. She's come here with a load of luggage and all her pets. I mean, it's as though she's moved out, left her husband.'

'Yeah – so? It happens. You of all people should know that.' Emily's eyes went wide. 'God, that's the wine talking, no filter from my brain to my mouth – sorry.'

Clarissa turned to her. 'There's no need to be sorry. You're just stating a fact. Yes, I was in the same boat. I left him, it's true.'

'Sorry,' Emily said again. 'You deserve to meet someone.'

'And so do you.'

They both turned to look at the door.

'Do you think he'll come?' Clarissa asked.

Emily yawned. 'I imagine so.' She was still wondering if Clarissa had her eye on Joss.

Clarissa yawned, too. 'It's so warm and cosy at your parents' guest house – and quiet. Perhaps it's the fact that it is detached and there are no neighbours either side. Although I can hear the waves lapping on the shore. So soothing …'

'Do you want me to put some music on?' Emily asked. They might not have television or Wi-Fi in the bedrooms, but Emily had brought her mp3 player to cast her playlist too.

'In a bit,' said Clarissa. She finished her glass of wine and lay down. Emily lay down too. They turned to face one another. Emily imagined this was just what sleepovers would have been like if she'd had any when she was a child. She decided to enjoy it while it lasted.

'So, you were going to tell me more about Alice?'

Emily looked at Clarissa thoughtfully. 'I don't think there's much else to tell.' She paused. 'Apart from one thing.'

'Do tell …'

'Well, it's a bit odd.'

Clarissa grinned. 'I like odd. It means there might be a little interesting kernel of a story in there.'

'Well, it's not much. It's just when I mentioned the other guest who's due to arrive. An Egyptian. She looked really surprised. She started asking questions about him. Of course, I don't know anything much about him. That was yesterday, when she overheard me talking about the new guests coming. Then she asked today if he would be arriving soon.'

'Do you think they know each other?'

'I'm not sure. I mean, it could be anybody from Egypt – right?'

'Yes, but how many Egyptians have you had to stay in the guest house over the years?'

'One – I think.'

'Are you sure?'

'Yes, I joked about it with my mum, and she said they have had an Egyptian stay here before.'

'Do you think it's the same person?'

'I don't know.'

'Well, can you find out?'

'Sure. All I have to do is go through the ledgers. We have them going right back to when Mum first bought the house and turned it into a guest house. It was way before she had a computer, and she's kept the paper ledgers going. Sort of old-fashioned if you ask me, but she likes to keep some of the old hotel traditions alive.'

'So, you could see if it's the same guest.'

'That's right.'

'And while you're at it, how's this for an idea? You can find out if Alice stayed in the guest house at the same time as this Egyptian.' It made her wonder if they might be old friends. It piqued her interest as to whether they had both stayed there, years earlier, before Alice married. Perhaps they had been lovers before they'd had to part ways; maybe she'd returned to her life and he'd returned to his, in Egypt.

'How romantic,' gushed Emily after Clarissa had shared her thoughts.

'Assuming it's the same person,' commented Clarissa.

Emily nodded and yawned. 'It will be a bit of a task. The books date back to before I was born.'

'Then we'll need help.' Clarissa grinned. 'Are you thinking what I'm thinking?'

'What are you thinking?'

'With three of us going through the ledgers, we'll do it in double-quick time.'

Emily looked at her. 'You can't be serious.' She yawned in Clarissa's face. 'Sorry. But I thought we wanted to find out more about Joss, not Alice.'

Clarissa shrugged. 'Why can't it be a fact-finding mission about both of them? He can help us go through the ledgers while we chat.'

Emily wasn't convinced. It was meant to be a party, some fun, a few drinks, perhaps a snog with Joss when Clarissa was out of the way. Emily winced. Where had that thought come from? She said, 'We'd have to bring the ledgers up to your room, and my mum might notice them missing.'

'What – at this time of night?'

Emily sighed. Clarissa had a point. She still couldn't imagine going through them all. Not just then, anyway.

'Well, if you don't want to do it with Joss …' Clarissa smirked. '… I meant looking through the ledgers, we should go downstairs, when he leaves, and check them out ourselves.'

'Okay.'

'It is odd though, what you said about her interest in the Egyptian.'

'To be honest, all our guests are a little odd at the moment.'

'Does that go for me too?'

'Oh, that definitely goes for you.'

Clarissa slapped her arm affectionately.

They fell about laughing until they were interrupted by a knock on the door.

'I'll get it.' Emily got up, hoping it was Joss. She checked her pyjamas and her hair in the mirror before answering the door.

'I thought I'd find you here.'

Emily stared at her mum. 'What do you want?' Her eyes darted down the hall. She prayed that Joss didn't choose that moment to take them up on the invite to Clarissa's room.

Her mum smiled. 'I was passing your bedroom, so I knocked to say goodnight, but you didn't answer. I thought you'd be here. Just don't have the music on too loud, and make sure you get to bed at a reasonable hour – remember we have another guest turning up tomorrow.'

'Oh, okay.' Emily was about to close the door, wanting her mum to go, when she said, 'And Emily. I'm sorry I didn't let you have sleepovers when you were young.'

Emily was surprised by the comment. It was a sore point. 'You always put the hotel first before your family, before me …' she blurted, aware the wine was talking again. She'd never have said that to her mum's face if she hadn't been drunk, and she was aware that she sounded like a spoilt brat, which, as the youngest, no doubt she was.

She stood there in the doorway, feeling uncomfortable under her mother's scrutiny. She expected to be told off for being rude and ungrateful, but her mother said nothing. It was not like her to be so quiet, and she looked as though something was on her mind.

Emily stared at her. 'Mum – what is it?'

Her mum's gaze drifted to Clarissa, who was lying in bed in Emily's pyjamas. 'I made a mistake, Emily. Years ago.'

Even though she'd drunk too much, Emily focused on what her mum was saying. 'What do you mean? What mistake?'

'Oh, there you are, Wendy. Another booking came through on the computer earlier.'

Emily looked at her dad. 'Do you want me to sort that out?' she asked, remembering that he'd mentioned it earlier but that with the excitement of her friend's arrival, she'd forgotten all about it.

'No, honey, you enjoy yourself with Clarissa.'

'Ok, Dad. Goodnight.'

'Goodnight, sweetheart.' Gerald walked down the stairs.

'Mum – what were you going to say?'

'Nothing. I'll see you in the morning. Goodnight, Emily.'

'Goodnight, Mum.'

'Who's Wendy?' Clarissa asked, when Emily lay back down in bed next to her.

'Oh, that's my mum's name.'

Clarissa turned on her side to face her. 'I thought your mum's name was Anthea.'

'That's her middle name, the name she likes to be known by. Says she prefers it. Mum always gets cross when dad forgets and calls her Wendy.'

'There isn't any other reason she might not want to use her first name, is there?'

'Like what?'

Clarissa stared at her. 'Oh, ignore me, I haven't got a clue.'

But Emily couldn't ignore her. She was thinking about what her mum had said about a mistake she'd made. Had that mistake happened when she was Wendy?

'I overheard what your mum said. It seemed like she was trying to confess something. She said she'd made a mistake. What do you think she meant by that?'

'Maybe she was talking about the sleepovers I could never have when I was a child.'

Clarissa shook her head. 'I get the feeling it wasn't about that.'

Something occurred to Emily. 'I think I know what it's about.'

'You do?' whispered Clarissa.

'It's about my mum and her estrangement from her sister in America. Thank god I didn't tell her what I thought about that too,' said Emily. She'd always wanted her mum to mend bridges with her sister, but for some reason her mum said it just wasn't possible.

'I didn't know you had an aunt in America.'

'Yes, the black sheep of the family, apparently. She's married to an American. I might have American cousins that I never see.'

'Do you want to find your relatives in America?' Clarissa asked.

'I've thought about it a lot over the years, but I don't know where to start.'

'I do. Have you heard of AncestryDNA?'

'Is it that website where you post your DNA and see if there's a match?'

'Do you want to do it? I don't see what you've got to lose, apart from the joining fee, if nothing comes out of it. What do you think?'

'I think it's an excellent idea.' Emily could feel her eyelids growing heavy. It didn't help that she was staring at her best friend, who was looking drowsy too.

'Good. Let's do that tomorrow.'

'Tomorrow?'

'Yes – why not? You want to find them, don't you?'

'Yes, of course.'

'So, let's do it.'

'Okay.'

'Do you think we should close our eyes just for a moment?'

Emily nodded. 'Just for a moment.'

34

Alice put her book down. She was bored. She cast her gaze down the bed and was surprised to find Hester and Marley curled up together at the end of the bed, both asleep. 'Well, I never!' Alice said under her breath. It was a Kodak moment, if ever she'd seen one. She frowned when she remembered that she didn't have her mobile phone to take a photo and send it to Freya.

Alice inched her way off the bed so as not to disturb them. She never let them sleep in her bedroom at home, not because she didn't want to but because Jeffrey had allergies and he didn't want them in the bedroom. She stood for a moment, staring at them, Hester with her muzzle resting on her two front paws, and Marley curled in a furry ball, snuggled next to her. She hadn't pulled her curtains closed yet. The full moon bathed her room in a monochrome light.

Alice walked over to the desk and picked up her wristwatch; it was later than she'd thought. She hadn't undressed and changed into her nightwear, but had sat there on her bed reading, expecting to be disturbed by the two girls next door having their slumber party. Earlier in the evening, she'd heard them talking, although their voices were deadened by the thick party walls, so she couldn't make out what they were saying. But she could imagine. They were probably chatting about relationships.

Alice slipped on a cosy jumper and stared out of the window, the full moon casting an ethereal, otherworldly light over the deserted beach and the gently lapping water on the shore. She was thinking about that night twenty-five years earlier when her world had changed forever. She closed her eyes for a moment, wondering what her life would have looked like if she hadn't …

Her thoughts suddenly turned to Jeffrey and that letter she'd found from someone called Wendy, the headed paper from here in this guest house. She didn't know anybody called Wendy. She remembered those courses her husband had gone on over the years. He'd said they were in London, and she'd believed him. But had they been in London? Had he even been on any courses? Or – she cast her gaze around the room – had he been here, at the guest house, with someone called Wendy?

Alice frowned. If she said it out loud, it would sound ludicrous. She knew her husband – he wouldn't have an affair, would he? Although she'd sent the letter, asking him to come to the guest house, intending to confront him over the possibility he'd had an affair, Alice had a thought. There was another way to find out.

The ledgers.

Alice turned from the window. If Jeffrey and Wendy had stayed there at the same time, their names would be in one of those books – she was sure of it. Unless they had stayed under false names and paid in cash.

Alice frowned, but she still thought it was worth a try. She tiptoed across the room and glanced at her two sweet pets, still fast asleep, before she opened the door.

'Alice?'

Alice jumped at the sound of a voice right behind her. She whirled around to find Joss standing there. She said, 'I was about to knock on Clarissa's door.'

Alice had been standing there for some time, debating whether to knock or not. She had been adamant that she wasn't going to go to Clarissa and Emily's little party after she's discovered that Clarissa was a journalist, but she'd been sitting in her room, reading a book and hearing them talking next door, when on the spur of the moment she'd had a change of heart. She'd bottled out of the idea of looking at the ledgers, afraid of what she might discover about Jeffrey and the woman called Wendy.

'Emily invited me to join them for drinks,' Alice said, knocking on the door. She looked at Joss. 'What are *you* doing here?'

Joss held up a napkin. 'Emily invited me to a little party.'

'Oh, really?' Alice suppressed a smile.

They both stood awkwardly in front of the door, waiting. Nobody was answering. 'I don't hear any music, or the girls chatting,' commented Joss. He turned to Alice. 'Do you?'

Alice shook his head. 'I thought I heard them from my room a little while ago. Do you think they went out, like to a bar or something, and forgot to tell us?'

'Or they decided they didn't want to spend the evening with us after all.' Joss sighed. He wouldn't be surprised if Emily's friend had convinced her he was too old for her, and they'd gone clubbing instead. He knew there were clubs up the road in the large seaside resort of Lowestoft. Joss turned on his heel to leave.

'You're leaving?' Alice said in surprise.

'Well, they're not here, are they?'

'Either that or they've fallen asleep.'

They both stared at each other a moment, and said in unison, 'No, they went out.'

'I left it too late,' said Alice, disappointed. 'I was in two minds whether to come.'

Joss heaved a sigh. 'Me too.' Joss was thinking of the previous evening and of Emily dressed up, expecting an evening out, thinking he was taking her on a date.

He groaned inwardly. Alice had suggested taking Emily for a meal afterwards. Why hadn't he listened to her? He knew why; he wasn't sure she was interested in him in that way. She was in her twenties, and he was in his mid-thirties. He wasn't afraid to ask her out and wasn't afraid of rejection. But he was afraid of what she'd think of him when she found out about his past. So, what was he doing, accepting her invitation? Joss scrunched up the napkin in his hand as he turned from the door. Perhaps this was for the best.

'Where are you going?'

Joss turned around, staring at Alice. 'I'm going back to my room.'

'Wait – I think I can hear something.' Alice put her ear to the door. 'Do you hear that?'

Joss stepped forward and did the same. He stared at Alice. He could just hear the faint sound of someone snoring.

'Unbelievable!' said Joss, although he was smiling. Alice smiled too, although her smile quickly dissipated. She was thinking that perhaps it was just as well. They were young, and she couldn't imagine they would have wanted her there, although it had been very nice of Emily to ask. But it wasn't just that.

Alice was still having second thoughts over Clarissa and what she might wheedle out of her after a few drinks. She was disappointed for Joss, though.

Joss turned to go.

'Are you disappointed – about the party?' Alice asked.

'Kinda. I mean, I like Emily a lot. I'm guessing she likes me, but I picked up a vibe that her mum doesn't want me dating her daughter. I know what she's thinking – I'm too old for her.'

'What do you mean? You're only around thirty, aren't you?'

'I'm thirty-five.'

'So?'

'And I've done things I'm not proud of. I've screwed up.'

'You're not the only one,' Alice said with a heavy sigh.

They stared at each other.

Joss said, 'I don't want to go back to my room and stare at four walls.'

'Me neither.'

'Shall we see if we can find a drink? There's bound to be some wine or something in the kitchen.'

Alice thought about it for all of two seconds. 'Yes, let's do that.'

35

In the hallway, a standard lamp illuminated the desk, casting the rest of the reception hall, with its oak furniture, wooden flooring, rugs, and the snug under the stairs, cloaked in shadow. She couldn't imagine anyone else would be up at that time of night.

She stepped up to the reception desk, feeling her heart pounding in her chest, and looked about her before walking around the desk. She sat down in the comfortable office chair and swivelled in her seat, turning to face the cupboard behind her, which had glass-fronted cupboard doors. Inside was a row of leather-bound books similar to the one she had signed on her arrival. The ledgers. She reached for the cupboard doors, expecting them to be locked. They weren't.

And the best part was that the ledgers were dated, with the years and the months written on the spine. 'Perfect.' She put the torch down, her hand moving along the row, her mind full of indecision over which year to start with.

'The beginning would be the obvious place to start,' Alice said to herself. She frowned at the thought of finding out that her husband and Wendy had met here so soon after she'd married him. With a shaky hand, Alice reached for the first ledger.

She swivelled around in her chair, placed the ledger on the desk, glanced at the time and realised that the task could take her all night. She opened the book. Although the pages were yellowed with age, the handwriting was still legible. It didn't take long to find the entry that she and Jeffrey had made. She shook her head. Young love. She remembered now that she'd written their names and drawn a heart shape around them, adding *Just Married.* They hadn't been young newlyweds, like Freya would be if she married Theo this year, which everyone anticipated they would. Alice and Jeffrey had been in their mid-thirties; they had both been dedicated to their careers, eventually finding *the one* later in life. Alice hadn't cared. She'd still had plenty of child-bearing years ahead of her to start a family – or so she'd thought.

She flicked through the rest of the ledger, wondering if this Wendy character had been someone from before the time they were married. But Jeffrey had never mentioned her.

There hadn't many guests that year. She recalled that the guest house had just opened and still needed a lot of work; she shook her head, recalling that she'd thought it seemed a lot to take on for a young widow with two small children. In the intervening years, she'd obviously made a success of it, and had remarried and had another child – Emily.

Emily reminded her of Freya in so many ways. She knew why; they were both young, full of life. *Oh, to be twenty-odd again*, mused Alice, staring into space and forgetting what she was doing there.

She snapped back to reality and closed the ledger. There was no mention of Wendy or Jeffrey returning that year. The other guests had not only given their names, but they had provided their addresses. Some had been there with friends, others were couples with children; there were no single people who might be meeting up here. Nothing suggesting that her husband had visited the guest house again that year.

Alice sighed in relief. She looked at the long row of ledgers, twenty-five in all. Alice felt like skipping the next two years' ledgers because she and Jeffrey had returned there two more years in a row, and she still couldn't imagine he would have met someone while she was here with him. Apart from anything else, what opportunity would he have had?

But I had an opportunity …

Alice frowned. 'This isn't about me,' she said under her breath, ignoring the voice of conscience that kept popping up at the most inopportune time. Alice pursed her lips, replaced the first ledger, and took down the second one from the bookshelf. She swivelled in her chair and sat staring at it, almost afraid to open it. It wasn't the thought that this woman Wendy might be in it. That wasn't it. It was something else entirely.

'What are you doing?'

Alice jumped at the sound of a voice behind her. She swivelled around in the chair, still holding one of the books.

Joss offered her a lop-sided grin. 'Look what I found.' He held up two bottles. 'I thought we were having a drink together?'

❖

Alice took a seat in the lounge, thankful that Joss hadn't mentioned finding her nosing through the ledgers at the reception desk. She caught the whiff of drink on his breath as he leaned towards her to hand her a glass of wine. He'd obviously had a glass or two immediately before he found her.

Joss poured himself another large glass and took a seat on

the sofa opposite. He downed the contents of his glass.

Alice followed suit, downing her glass and helping herself to another.

They drank in silence for some time, both lost in thoughts of past misdeeds. Alice went to pour herself another glass and discovered that the second bottle was empty. 'Oh, dear,' she said, surprised that her speech sounded slurred.

'Do we need another bottle?' Joss asked. He attempted to stand up.

Alice watched him sway and then back down abruptly. 'Perhaps I should let the ten or so glasses go down first.' He laughed. 'Ten or so glasses. That's funny.'

'Before you get another bottle,' said Alice, surprised that the ground was moving beneath her feet; it was the most peculiar floaty sensation, as though she was sitting in a boat. Alice knew that all this had been a bad idea. The fact was, she didn't drink. She looked at Joss and said in surprise, 'Am I drunk?'

Joss laughed again. 'Probably.'

'I want to get something off my chest, Joss. I get the feeling that whatever it was that you used to do; you can keep a confidence.'

'I can do that, yes.'

'I did something years ago, and it's haunted me ever since …'

Joss leaned towards her and attempted to put his empty glass on the coffee table. He missed. It fell on the carpet. 'Oh, bother.'

'Never mind that,' said Alice. 'I want to tell you my secret.'

❖

Clarissa crept out of her room. It was late, well past midnight, and she was thirsty. She wanted a glass of water. Unsure whether the water from the tap in the en suite bathroom was drinking water, she decided to go downstairs and find the kitchen. She'd had the impulse to wake Emily and ask, but her friend was fast asleep and she didn't want to disturb her.

Clarissa crept past Joss's room, aware that despite her saying otherwise, Emily had been disappointed that he hadn't taken her up on the invitation.

She walked down the stairs, her mobile phone to hand, thinking she'd need a light, but the stairs and reception hall downstairs were lit quite adequately. As she stepped off the bottom stair, she thought she heard voices.

Clarissa followed the voices to the lounge. She hovered in the doorway, staring at Joss and Alice and the empty bottles of wine on the coffee table in front of them. She frowned, hoping Emily didn't find out that Joss would rather spend the evening with Alice than with her. *Well, I'm not going to tell her*, thought Clarissa as she backed out of the room before they saw her. She was just turning on her heel when she thought she heard Alice say, 'I want to tell you my secret.'

Clarissa stopped dead and turned around.

'But first I need to ask: can you help me?'

'Whatever with, Alice?'

'To stop my daughter taking a DNA test and finding out the truth.'

Clarissa knew she'd had a bit too much to drink herself that evening. She rubbed her face, thinking, *I didn't hear what I thought I just heard.* She even felt she must be imagining Alice and Joss sitting there drinking together.

Clarissa walked back to her room, forgetting why she had ventured downstairs.

'Where were you?' Emily asked, catching Clarissa creeping back into the room.

'I went to get a glass of water.'

Emily rubbed her eyes. 'Well, where is it?'

Clarissa looked at her empty hands. She burst out laughing, then clamped a hand to her mouth.

Emily shook her head. 'You're still drunk.' She rolled over in bed.

Clarissa got in beside her. She whispered in her ear, 'I think I know Alice's secret.'

'Okay, good. Tell me in the morning.'

36

'Did you come down here drunk last night and disturb my ledgers?'

'What do you mean?' Emily asked. She'd opened her door to find her mum standing outside, arms folded across her chest, looking at her, unamused. 'We've both been in bed the whole night – haven't we, Clarissa?'

Clarissa stared at Emily. 'Oh, yeah right. I'm pretty sure … er, yes, we were both here all night.' She frowned, thinking about her dream during the night – that she'd ventured downstairs and discovered Joss and Alice talking together in the lounge, drinking wine, and that Alice had said something about her daughter. Then she'd returned to bed and Emily had seen her and asked her what she was doing.

Clearly it hadn't actually happened, otherwise Emily would have remembered – wouldn't she? Unless she was telling her mum a fib so they didn't get into trouble. One look at Emily's mum's face said that was a definite possibility.

She ushered them both downstairs, even though they were still in their pyjamas, to show them where she'd found it.

'I found this on the desk.'

Emily didn't get what the problem was. 'Yeah – so? Perhaps I left it out ready for the next guest to turn up?'

'This is from the second year we opened. So, I want to ask you again – did you take this ledger out of the cabinet?'

Emily exchanged a glance with Clarissa and shook her head vehemently. But as soon as her mother's back was turned, she mimed at Clarissa, *Did we?*

Clarissa shrugged.

'Well, put it back for me.'

They both watched Emily's mum walk off. Clarissa whispered, 'To be honest, I can't remember. I know we were talking about it …'

'I remember that,' said Emily. 'The thing is, I was so drunk.'

'Me too. I mean it's not as though I drank a lot last night, but with the kids, and my new career, I haven't had time for the simple pleasure of just putting my feet up and chilling with a glass of wine – or several.'

Emily could only imagine.

'We fell asleep.'

'Did we do anything before we fell asleep?'

'Maybe,' said Clarissa. They both turned to look at the ledger. 'I want to take a look.'

'So do I.'

'Let's take it up to my room,' suggested Clarissa.

'Good idea. I don't want my mum catching us nosing through this. We obviously found something, but for the life of me, I can't remember.'

'Me neither.'

Tucking the journal under her dressing gown, Emily took the stairs, two at a time, followed by Clarissa. Their timing was a bit unfortunate. As they reached the top of the stairs, Joss walked out of his bedroom. He looked like he was nursing a headache. He stepped back in surprise when they rushed up towards him. 'Where's the fire?' he joked.

Emily looked at him. 'Pardon me?' she said coldly, unhappy that she'd been snubbed for the second time. He hadn't come to her get-together. In fact, he looked as though he'd had a party of his own. 'Excuse me,' Emily said, barging past him.

'What's with her?' said Joss, following her with his gaze.

Clarissa rolled her eyes at the daft question. 'I think she might be cheesed off that you didn't take her up on her invite last night.'

'But I did. We both did.'

'You and Alice?'

'Uh-huh.'

Two doors down, Emily had stopped outside the bedroom door. She turned around to look at Joss, overhearing what he'd just said.

'We arrived outside your door about the same time.'

'Then why didn't you knock?' Clarissa asked in exasperation.

'We did.' At first we thought you'd got tired of waiting and had gone out. Then we realised you'd turned in for the night.'

'What makes you say that?' Emily asked.

'We heard snoring coming from behind the door.'

'Oh.' Emily looked away, embarrassed.

Joss said, 'Raincheck?'

Emily smiled. 'Yes please.'

'Well, you two love birds have made up,' Clarissa said, with a cheeky grin.

Her smile faltered when Alice stepped out of her room also

looking as though she was feeling the effects of the night before.

'I thought I heard voices outside my door,' said Alice. 'I'm just taking Hester for a walk before breakfast.'

Clarissa caught Alice giving Joss a sideways glance as she headed for the stairs. Was it her imagination, or was Alice looking anxious as she sidled past him? There was no mistaking her cheeks flushing red. Clarissa watched her heading for the stairs wondering what that was all about.

'What's that?' Joss spotted the ledger in Emily's hand.

'It's one of the ledgers from years ago,' Emily replied. 'Mum found it had been taken out of the cupboard and blamed it on me and Clarissa.'

'Alice was sitting at the reception desk downstairs looking through a book just like it last night,' Joss mused.

Clarissa raised her eyebrows. 'She was – how do you know?'

Emily stared at Clarissa.

There followed an awkward silence.

Emily eyed Joss. 'Is it my imagination or do you two look like you've got a hangover?' She glanced over at Alice who was making her way down the stairs with Hester, oblivious to their conversation.

Joss scratched his head. 'Is it that obvious?' He sighed. 'Well, after we knocked, I think we were kind of looking forward to seeing you guys …' his eyes drifted to Emily. 'We were really disappointed, so we kind of decided to go for a drink.'

'You drove into town?'

'Er, no, we found a bottle or two in the fridge in the kitchen.' Joss winced and cast a sheepish gaze at Emily. 'Sorry. I'll pay for the booze.'

Emily shook her head. 'Don't worry about it. But I'd better

replace it. I don't think my mum was too happy with me and Clarissa having a few drinks in our room, so I think it will be a good idea if she doesn't find out about you guys getting drunk last night.' She mimicked her mum. 'We run a respectable guest house.'

Joss smiled.

'I think she's looking for any excuse to get shot of you.' Emily pursed her lips, wishing she hadn't blurted that. Like Joss and Alice, she was nursing a hangover and still wasn't exactly thinking straight or filtering what came out of her mouth. 'Sorry, it's just that you've been here weeks, and she doesn't know anything about you. Come to think of it, neither do I.'

This time it was Clarissa who stepped into the awkward silence. 'I don't know what you're complaining about, Emily. At least you and Joss are going to be friends again, so you can soon solve that.' She stared at Joss. 'Just what were you and Alice talking about downstairs in the lounge last night?'

Emily stepped forward. 'Clarissa, that's none of your—'

Clarissa ignored Emily and stared at Joss.

'Client privilege. I'm afraid I can't say.'

Clarissa stared at him. 'What do you mean she's your client?'

Joss looked over at Emily. 'I'm a lawyer.'

Clarissa's eyes went wide. 'Does your new client need a lawyer?'

As far as Clarissa was concerned, his silence was answer enough.

37

'Why does she need a lawyer?'

'A lawyer.' Emily lay down on the bed. 'Of all things, I never imagined that.' She smiled. 'My mum is going to be so pleased when she finds out I'm dating a lawyer.'

Clarissa groaned loudly. 'For one thing, you are not dating him.'

'But I might be, very soon.'

Clarissa sat down on the stool by the dressing table. She looked at Emily. 'Well, if he's some hotshot lawyer, what is he doing in a backwater Suffolk village, spending his days in ripped jeans, living in a guest house and helping your dad cut firewood and mend fences?'

'I think something happened.'

'What happened is he came here to help out his uncle, who lives in the next town, after he suffered a bereavement. That's what I found out from my sister Abigail. Except they didn't exactly hit it off, with Joss living under his roof, so he came to live here instead.'

'Yeah – you tell yourself that. But what if something happened, in London, where he used to work, and he had to leave? And it just happened to coincide with his uncle's bereavement?'

'Like what?'

'I don't know.'

'Oh, Clarissa. I don't know whether it's because you're a journalist, but you always look at the worst-case scenario.'

'Never mind that, back to my question – why do you think Alice needs a lawyer?'

Emily shrugged. 'How do I know?' She sat up in bed. 'Perhaps Alice is divorcing her husband and needs a lawyer to sort out the finances and make sure she gets a good deal.'

Clarissa looked at her thoughtfully. 'That is a possibility. I just think there's more to it than that.'

'Why?'

'Call it intuition.'

Emily sighed. 'You're just looking for a good news story.'

'I think I may have found one, now I know Joss is a lawyer.'

'What are you talking about?'

Although she had been very drunk the previous night, and had wondered if she'd dreamed her trip downstairs, she now knew it hadn't been a dream. She looked at Emily. 'Don't you remember me waking you up when I returned to our room last night, saying I went to get a glass of water, and telling you I had overheard something?'

Emily shook her head from side to side. 'Sorry, Clarissa, but I don't remember what you said, just that you woke me up.'

'Well, when I went downstairs, it was around midnight, I guess, and I thought I heard voices,' Clarissa said. She remembered seeing the bottle of wine on the coffee table in front of them, and wondering why Joss preferred to spend the evening with Alice rather than Emily. Now that little mystery was solved, she didn't mind telling Emily what happened.

'I overheard them talking …'

'About?'

'It's the strangest thing …'

'Oh, for goodness' sake, don't keep me in suspense.'

'It sounds as though she's been carrying a secret around for years, decades, and she needs help.'

'What sort of help?'

'I guess the legal sort.'

'How come? What did she say?'

'She said something about her daughter …'

'Her daughter? Can you remember exactly what she said?'

Clarissa heaved a sigh. 'I really wish I hadn't drunk so much last night.'

Emily rubbed her forehead. 'I know what you mean. Perhaps if I hadn't been so drunk either I would remember what you said to me last night.'

Clarissa stood up and walked over. 'I think a clue is in this ledger she was looking at last night.'

'You think she was looking at this ledger?'

'Yes, you heard what Joss said.'

They both turned to the ledger. 'Let's see who was visiting in …' she turned the ledger on its side to look at the year.

Clarissa sat next to Emily on the bed. They both turned the pages looking for an entry with Alice's name. 'Here, look!'

'Let me see.'

Clarissa passed the ledger over.

Emily put it on her lap. 'That's Alice and her husband.'

'But look here …' Clarissa leaned over and pointed to an

entry further down. A chap had turned up late at night. 'Look, at the name.'

'It looks foreign,' commented Emily.

'Egyptian – maybe?'

'Hold on just one sec.' Emily rushed out of the door. She was back a moment later with her phone. 'I've got an app on my phone, so I have access to our bookings.'

'Is it the same name, the Egyptian that Alice is so interested in? This is going to sound insane, or maybe not, but what if she was here with her husband, but she ended up having a one-night stand with the Egyptian? She's got a daughter around your age – right?'

'Yeah, I mentioned that. So, you're saying she might have slept with this guy and her husband never knew he was bringing up someone else's child?' Emily frowned. 'But wouldn't her daughter look, you know, a bit Middle Eastern?'

'Depends on which side of the family she takes after. Look on your phone, see if it's the same guy.'

Emily said, 'We might not be able to tell. I mean, the handwriting in this ledger isn't very legible, is it? And it's not like I can check on our database of past guests because my parents didn't use a computer back then.'

Emily switched on her phone. Clarissa saw her expression. 'What is it?'

'Oh, my god. I think you have your news story.'

'So, it's him – the same guy?' Clarissa frowned. She really wasn't thinking straight that morning. She heaved a sigh, looking at Emily staring at her phone. 'Emily, I don't think someone having an affair, and having a child out of wedlock is going to be particularly newsworthy or be my big break.'

'I agree.' Emily thrust her phone in Clarissa's face, 'But what about this?'

Clarissa stared at the live news feed of a press conference in London. They were waiting for their star guest, by the name of Omar Youssef. 'Is that the same guy, the one staying here at your guest house, the eminent archaeologist who discovered that new tomb in the Valley of the Kings?'

Emily grinned. 'I think so.'

'Oh, my god,' exclaimed Clarissa. 'He's like practically famous.'

'I know – right!'

'It says here,' Emily started reading the news feed below the press conference, 'that he was due at the conference to speak about the new exhibition of artefacts from the tomb. They'll be displayed in a museum at Cambridge University before the new exhibition moves to London.'

'So, where is he?' Clarissa asked, watching the news conference live.

'According to the newsfeed, they're not sure where their star guest is, and why he hasn't turned up. So the curators at the British Museum are pressing on without him to talk about the new find and the exhibits that will be coming to London soon.'

Emily paused. 'It sounds as though it's caused quite a stir – there's a lot of press there hoping to be the first to get an interview with him.'

Clarissa said, 'Check the name of your new guest. Are you sure it's—'

'I'm positive.'

Clarissa and Emily turned to look at one another as a car drew up outside the guest house.

They both rushed to the window. 'Is it … is it him? The Egyptian?' asked Clarissa.

They both watched a tall, older man, who had to be in his sixties, get out of the taxi. He was wearing a Panama hat and a cream-coloured suit. 'I think it's Hercules Poirot without the pot belly,' Emily joked. He suddenly looked up.

'Oh, god – I think he spotted us.'

They both quickly withdrew from the window. Clarissa looked at Emily, wide-eyed. 'It's him, isn't it?'

Emily grinned and nodded. 'It's the famous archaeologist. Oh, my god. I'm so excited. You know what this means, don't you? You could be the first to secure an exclusive interview and get the inside scoop about the new exhibition.'

Clarissa stared at Emily without comment.

Emily looked at her. 'That's what you want – don't you? Your big news story?'

Clarissa looked at her thoughtfully. 'What I'm more interested in is what he is doing here instead of at that press conference in London.'

Emily glanced at the book in her hands. 'I better take this back to reception.'

'I'm coming too,' Clarissa stood up. 'I want to meet the Egyptian.' She grinned mischievously. 'Shall we knock on Alice's door and see if she is back from her walk and let her know he's arrived?'

'Absolutely not.'

'Oh, Emily, you're no fun.'

'I tell you what we better do before we go downstairs.'

'What?'

'Change out of our pyjamas!'

38

Alice glanced at her watch as she walked down the stairs. She'd just make it for breakfast after taking Hester for a walk and changing out of her wet clothes. Unfortunately, she'd been caught out in a rather heavy shower with no umbrella. But she didn't think going downstairs just in time to catch breakfast was a bad thing. It would be quieter with no one around but herself. Joss, probably nursing a hangover like her, perhaps wouldn't be down at all. That left the other guest – Clarissa.

Alice frowned. She'd much rather she didn't bump into the budding journalist, not after what she'd told Joss last night. What had she told Joss? Alice's frown deepened. She still couldn't remember. She wished she hadn't drunk so much wine. What if she'd told Joss everything? And he'd told Clarissa?

Alice swallowed. Perhaps it was time to pack her bags, and her pets, and get out of Dodge. She rolled her eyes at the cowboy analogy. She'd sat through far too many old westerns with her husband in her youth. But maybe she really should leave. She knew she shouldn't have gone there in the first place.

What about Wendy? a little voice in her head said as she stepped from the stairs into the reception hall. She glanced at the bookshelves containing those bound ledgers. She'd been interrupted by Joss before she'd had a chance to look at them all. Emily's mum was sitting at reception that morning. Alice stole a glance, hoping Joss hadn't remembered anything from the previous night and hadn't told Emily's mum.

Alice doubted it. Even so, she gave her a wide berth and dismissed any thoughts of finding Wendy. Now she wished she hadn't sent that note demanding that Jeffrey came here. This was the last place she wanted to be. Alice decided it was time to cut her losses and head home. She imagined with snail mail he probably hadn't even received her letter yet. She decided she could have breakfast, and head home, before the letter had even arrived.

Alice walked into breakfast with a plan for the day, little realising it was about to be thrown into complete disarray when she saw who was sitting at breakfast. Alice blinked in surprise when she saw she wasn't the only one in the conservatory. It wasn't Joss, or even Clarissa, but a new arrival.

The Egyptian. She came to an abrupt halt in the doorway, watching him lift his eyes from the newspaper he was reading. He slowly rose from the table. They stood staring at each other across the room.

'Oh, I thought everyone had had breakfast,' said Emily approaching Alice standing in the doorway. 'You'll be our last one this morning. You'll have the place to yourself, then.'

'I don't think so.'

Emily looked over Alice's shoulder. 'Oh, I see what you mean. Mr Youssef arrived earlier, so he's having breakfast too. I didn't realise you were still here, Mr Youssef.'

'Apologies, I will leave now.'

'Oh, don't go. Have another cup of coffee. Alice? Would you like to take a seat?'

Alice caught Emily throwing her a look, as if to say *why are you still standing in the doorway?* Alice knew it must look odd. She stepped into the room, but only just.

They were still staring at one another.

Alice found her voice, still shocked that he was here. After all these years, he'd come back.

'Omar?'

'Alice?'

'What are you doing here?' they both said in unison.

Emily said, 'Is it the gentleman you've been asking after?'

'You've been asking after me?'

Alice could feel her face growing hot with embarrassment. 'Well, no, not exactly. I found out a guest from Egypt was coming here to stay, but I couldn't imagine in my wildest dreams it would be you.'

'And I couldn't have imagined in my wildest dreams you'd be here too – again.' He motioned at his table. 'Come, join me.'

Emily raised her eyebrows, thinking that Clarissa would have a field day if she had been there, listening to them. It made her wonder where her friend was.

'I'll lay an extra place setting,' she said. She headed for the kitchen to get more cutlery and crockery.

Alice pulled out a chair and tentatively sat down, her eyes never leaving his. She could hear footsteps behind her. She picked up the breakfast menu, imagining Emily was walking over to take her order.

'Good morning, Alice.'

Alice looked up to discover she wasn't the last one who had

come down for breakfast after all. Clarissa was standing in front of their table.

'Morning.' Alice noted her eyes roving to the gentleman sitting opposite her.

'Morning,' she said to him. 'I'm Clarissa.'

He shifted his attention from Alice. 'Good morning, Clarissa.'

Clarissa grinned. 'You two know each other?'

Alice nodded. She pursed her lips, silently berating herself for being late for breakfast. If she hadn't been, she would have avoided the budding journalist, who was no doubt looking for a story. Alice nodded. 'We're old acquaintances.'

'Old acquaintances,' repeated Clarissa, eyeing Alice. 'Well, isn't that a coincidence, you two turning up here? Or were you planning to meet up at the guest house?'

'Clarissa, your table is over here.'

Alice breathed a sigh of relief when Emily stepped in and saved them from any more awkward questions. Alice wasn't the only one frowning at Clarissa's back as she took a seat at a table. Emily didn't look pleased either. Fortunately, Emily seated her friend on the other side of the room so they wouldn't be disturbed again.

Omar leaned across the small table for two, and in barely a whisper said, 'The other guest is rather inquisitive – is she not?'

Alice picked up her napkin and placed it on her lap. 'That's a polite way of putting it. She's being nosy. She's a journalist, apparently.'

'Ah, and here I was hoping to go somewhere where I wouldn't be hounded by the press.'

Alice looked at him in surprise. 'I'm pretty sure she didn't follow you here.' Alice knew Clarissa was staying at the hotel as a break from her children, and to catch up with Emily. Even so, she whispered back, 'Why would a journalist follow you here?'

'Oh, perhaps to get a story on the artefacts that we've brought over from Alexandria. There will be temporary exhibits in museums around the country before they're moved to the British Museum.'

Alice smiled. 'So, you're still an archaeologist?'

He smiled. 'You remembered.'

'Of course.' She lowered her voice. 'How could I forget that night?'

He stared at her. 'Of all the places in all the world, you walk in here.'

'You sound like Humphrey Bogart in Casablanca. Except I'm pretty sure the famous quote involved something to do with gin joints.'

He laughed. 'You British and your sense of humour.'

'No, I'm being serious.'

He smiled nevertheless. 'I've never forgotten you, you know.'

Alice glanced at Clarissa, who quickly looked away. Alice sighed. She had a feeling that Clarissa was trying to listen in on their conversation. Alice returned her attention to Omar. In a hushed voice, she said, 'We could go for a walk after breakfast, catch up properly?' She moved her eyes to the left and nodded in Clarissa's direction. 'If you know what I mean?'

He nodded, glancing across the room at the inquisitive guest. 'Yes, of course. I understand.'

Emily appeared at that table. 'What can I get you this morning, Alice?'

'I'll just have some porridge and toast, thank you.'

'Of course.'

'How was the party?' Alice asked out of politeness. She guessed there hadn't been much of a party. She already knew they'd fallen asleep.

Emily sighed. 'It was lucky you didn't come after all. We're both not used to drinking too much. We ended up falling asleep.'

Alice acted surprised. 'Oh, well. There's always another night.'

'Not really. I'm afraid Clarissa will be gone for a day or so; something cropped up and she has to do something for work, so she'll be leaving straight after breakfast.'

'Oh dear, that is a shame.' Alice tried hard to sound sincere. 'Will she be returning to the guest house?'

'I don't know. She booked the room for the week.' Emily was confident she'd be back – she had her big news story. She just hoped she would still stay for her week's holiday, and her big scoop didn't encourage her to return to work earlier. 'I hope she decides to stay on.'

I hope she doesn't, thought Alice, feeling a bit guilty for being so selfish. Not that it should bother her – wasn't she meant to be going home today? But that was before she discovered Omar was there.

Alice turned in her seat, smiling. Even if Clarissa did come back tonight, the fact that she wouldn't be around for the rest of the day was music to Alice's ears. Apart from Joss, she and Omar would have the guest house practically to themselves. Which was just as well. Alice's idea to go for a bracing walk along the deserted beach after breakfast was already looking less likely. The early morning sunshine, which she'd woken up to in her room, before turning over and having another hour in bed, had already given way to thick storm clouds. And now she heard the patter of raindrops on the conservatory roof. Outside in the garden, tree branches swayed in the wind. Alice was still mystified as to how she and Omar had both come to be there at the same time. She said as much.

'I'm just as mystified as you, Alice.'

She kept her voice barely above a whisper when she asked, 'Have you visited here since that night?'

He shook his head. 'No. I have not. And you?'

'No. Why did you come?'

'Nostalgia. Perhaps I wanted to recapture my youth, the best time of my life.' His voice dropped to a whisper. 'The best *night* of my life,' he said, raising his eyebrows as if to say, *you know what I'm talking about*. 'The last thing I expected was for you to be here too. Although going back to that night, I'm not sure it was for you, to begin with, the best night of your life.'

Alice frowned. How could he think that?

'I'm talking about you being out walking alone in the dark, looking lost.. Do you remember?'

'Oh, yes.' Alice remembered a whole lot more besides. She looked sheepishly at Omar. The trouble was that he didn't know the whole story. She wasn't about to put him in the picture now, all these years later. Why should she? And what would he think of her if he knew what had really gone on that night before he and his friends came across a young lady, late at night, walking aimlessly on her own?

'Did I say something wrong, Alice?'

'No, not at all.' They had been staying at the guest house at the time for a nostalgic break two years after their honeymoon, for their second wedding anniversary – except that it had felt as though the honeymoon period was well and truly over. They'd had a massive row and Jeffrey had gone to bed, giving her the silent treatment. Alice had left the guest house, taking a long walk even though it was dark and she had no idea where she was heading.

If it hadn't been for Omar and his college friends happening along, out on a pub crawl, she might have been wandering aimlessly for hours. It was late and Alice had got lost. They had been looking for a place with vacancies, so she'd suggested the guest house, not letting on that she was already booked in there with her husband. That had been Omar's fault. She remembered getting into the back of the car with him. She hadn't been able to take her eyes off him. It hadn't helped that he was an archaeologist on an exchange to his alma mater, Cambridge University. It was her alma mater too. And she had studied the same subjects, although they had attended at different times, as Omar had already finished his degree when she'd started.

Alice heaved a sigh, remembering all this. Like Omar, she would never forget that night. Fortunately, despite the very late hour, someone had been around – a live-in cleaner, who had booked them all rooms. She hadn't recognised Alice, who had kept in the background during the check-in process. They were all only staying for one night. The trouble was that at the height of summer, there was a shortage of rooms. They would have to share.

Alice had known that she should creep back to her own room, where her husband was sleeping. But she had not. Not straight away. She had decided she would rather talk to Omar about the subject she loved and his life in Alexandria. It sounded so exciting, so exotic. She'd decided that as soon as he fell asleep, she'd creep back to her room. She knew the group were checking out the next day and would have to leave by ten. She'd feign a headache so she didn't have to go down to breakfast, and that way she'd avoid them. It had all been very innocent – to begin with. Omar had insisted on sleeping on the floor, on a throw. She'd tossed him a pillow. But the wooden floor was very uncomfortable. She'd invited him into bed. They'd lain there as far apart as possible, feeling awkward …

'What are you thinking?'

'About that night.' Alice kept her voice low.

He took a sip of coffee and wiped his moustache with a handkerchief.

They both sat there, staring at each other, remembering. He said, 'Where did you go … afterwards? I woke up in the morning and you were gone.'

Alice thought of Jeffrey. She hadn't mentioned the young man she'd met, Omar, and what had really transpired that night before she snuck back to her own room and gingerly got back into bed beside her sleeping husband, who must have had no idea how long she'd been gone.

'Is that why you came back? Nostalgia for what might have been?'

Nostalgia had been the last thing on Alice's mind when she'd returned. What was nostalgic about finding out your husband might have had an affair? And there was the other thing … Alice glanced around, wondering if Joss would also appear at breakfast. She was still worried about what she might have told him last night in an alcoholic haze.

'If … if you hadn't disappeared,' continued Omar, 'I thought … I know it was just one night, but I felt we had something, a connection.' He ventured, 'For me, it was love at first sight.'

Alice breathed a sigh. She glanced at Clarissa, who was eating toast and scrolling through her phone; she appeared to have lost interest in them. Alice buttered some toast and left it on her plate. She looked at Omar. After all these years, he still wanted to know if she'd felt the same way. 'It was a mistake, Omar.'

He slowly nodded his head and sat back in his seat. 'I thought as much.'

'When we met, Omar. The timing.'

'Oh.'

'You see …' Alice took a deep breath. 'It wasn't you. It was me. I was … I was already married …'

'Oh. I … I had no idea.'

'I know.'

'But you … we … slept together.'

'I know that too.' She dropped her eyes to the table, embarrassed that he now knew the truth. When she raised her eyes, she saw the way Omar was looking at her. 'You must think I'm a terrible person.'

'No, I'm just surprised – that's all. I didn't think … I couldn't imagine you would, well …' He stopped. 'This is very forward of me to say, but if things weren't going well in your marriage, why didn't you tell me? You could have left him – for me.'

Alice bit her lower lip. Of course it had crossed her mind at the time. In that one night, just like Omar, she'd felt she had met her soulmate. After only a short time as a married couple, things hadn't been going well between her and Jeffrey. It hadn't been Jeffrey's fault. But then again, it hadn't been her fault either. It was the hand they had both been dealt – or *she* had been dealt.

'Alice?'

But there was something else, something Omar had said to

her, that had sounded the death knell for any future with him, and it had had nothing to do with already being married – that could be undone; it was what Omar saw in his future that she knew he could never have with her. She had realised they were not meant to be together – not back then, at any rate.

'Did you get married, Omar? Did you have children?'

He nodded and smiled. 'I have a son.'

Alice nodded. It was what he'd always wanted. 'And your wife?' Alice looked around, suddenly aware that Mrs Youssef might be coming down to breakfast to join her husband. Why hadn't that occurred to her?

'I'm a widower.'

'Oh, Omar, I'm so sorry.'

'But we had some very good times. I have fond memories of Fatima. You know, I never told you this, but when we first met, I was engaged.'

Alice looked at him in surprise. 'You were getting married?'

'Yes. It was an arranged marriage. It had been arranged between our families since we were twelve.'

'You had an arranged marriage?'

'Oh, it wasn't what you imagine. We'd met each other, got to know one another, and we always had the choice to back out.'

'But you didn't.'

'The thought never crossed my mind – until I met you.'

Alice's eyes dropped to her uneaten toast.

'So, my English friends found out, and took me on a stag trip.'

Alice smiled. 'You mean, a stag *do*.'

'Yes – that. We were doing a pub crawl that night and aiming to book into a hotel along the way.' He paused. 'Who would have thought I'd fall in love that night, here in The Guest House at Shingle Cove.' He stared at her thoughtfully.

Alice avoided his gaze. She knew what he was thinking; if she'd felt the same way, why hadn't she left her husband for him?

'So, how are things with you, with your … family?'

Alice breathed a sigh. 'Obviously, I'm on my own.' She quickly added, 'I meant I'm here alone. My husband and I …'

'Another rocky patch?'

Alice thought of the letter from the woman called Wendy. She nodded. 'I've come away to sort my head out, so to speak.' *And find Wendy*, she thought, although she knew it probably wouldn't happen. She'd have to confront Jeffrey to find out about that. But now Omar was there, she couldn't imagine confronting him at the guest house. Alice stared at Omar.

'How long are you here for, Alice?'

Until my husband turns up. And if he doesn't, I'll know that he doesn't want to attempt to save our marriage.

'A few days, perhaps longer,' Alice said. She knew it sounded vague, but it all depended on Jeffrey.

'And you?'

'It was going to be just for a night or two, but now I'm thinking I'd like to stay longer …'

Their eyes locked in silent understanding; they both wanted to spend more time together.

Omar broke the silence. 'You know, this was a spur of the moment thing. I was due to arrive here yesterday, but I called in to see some old friends, and ended up staying with them overnight.' He took a sip of coffee. 'The friends I dropped in to see were the ones I was out with that night when we came across you. And now here we are – again.'

'Yes.' Alice glanced outside. The storm clouds were clearing. The sun was breaking out. 'Oh, look! I think it's going to turn out a lovely day after all.'

Omar smiled. 'I second that.'

Alice caught him staring at her and smiling. 'I am talking about the weather.'

'Of course. Of course. Would you like to take a walk together in the sunshine after breakfast?'

'Yes, as long as you don't mind that I'll have to bring my dog.'

'You brought your dog?'

Alice nodded, deciding not to mention her other pets.

'We could go down to the cove and walk along the beach,' Alice suggested. 'It's going to be chilly, though.'

'I don't mind.'

'Me neither.'

'Can I take these plates?' Emily asked as she approached their table.

'Yes, thank you,' said Omar handing her a plate.

'Afterwards we could go into Aldeburgh for lunch,' suggested Alice. 'We'll have to take a taxi.'

'That's not a problem,' said Emily overhearing their plans. 'I could arrange one.'

'Thank you, Emily.' She smiled at her before turning to Omar, and adding, 'I know a lovely little café called The Two Magpies Bakery.'

Emily paused with the plates balanced in her hands and asked, 'Would you like to sit together for dinner this evening? I could lay the table for two?'

Alice looked at Omar. 'It seems silly to sit apart.'

'I agree.'

'Yes, please,' Alice said.

She didn't notice Clarissa looking their way and exchanging a smile with Emily as she carried the plates out of the room.

39

'So, have you heard from your mum?' Jolene asked.

Freya turned around and frowned at Jolene for bringing that up. 'No.'

Jolene had followed her into the ladies' toilets and was standing there, arms folded across her chest, watching Freya wash her hands.

Freya gave her a sideways glance. 'Did you follow me into the loo?'

Jolene stepped to one side so Freya could dry her hands. 'Well, this is the only time I get to talk to my best friend.'

'I don't know what you're on about.'

'You're always with Tarek.'

Freya threw a paper towel in the bin and turned to face her, her expression one of exasperation. 'Well, of course I'm always with him. We work together.'

'That's not what I mean.'

'Then what do you mean?'

'Have you heard from your mum? Because it's been like over a week, y'know.'

Freya looked at her, surprised she had randomly changed the

subject. 'Yes, I do know, thank you very much for reminding me. No, I haven't heard from her.' Although she had brought up her concerns with her dad as the days had passed by with no sign of her mum, he didn't seem unduly worried. In fact he had insisted there was nothing to worry about; he'd said that Alice had just needed to get away for a few days and have some time to herself. Freya knew it wasn't Jolene's fault her mum had gone AWOL, but despite her dad's reassurances, she still felt guilty over the fact that the days had passed in a blur and she hadn't bothered to try and contact her – not that she could, given that her mum had left her mobile phone at home. It occurred to her that she might have done that on purpose.

'I've been busy with the exhibition.' Freya walked out of the toilets, Jolene following close behind.

'Oh, really,' commented Jolene to her back. 'Busy with Tarek, don't you mean?'

Freya whirled around to face her before they both stepped inside the gallery. Were they back to that again? She repeated, through clenched teeth, 'We work together.'

'And play together.'

'Pardon me?'

'I overheard Tarek talking about the things you two have been doing in Cambridge.'

'Yeah – so I'm showing him the sights – what's your problem?'

'My problem?' Jolene cocked her head to one side. 'I haven't got a problem, Freya. I think you're the one with the problem.'

'Oh yeah – do tell,' said Freya sarcastically, 'what do you think my problem is?'

Jolene lowered her voice and whispered. 'You're falling for him.'

She took one look at Freya's expression, and said, 'Crap, you *have* fallen for him. It's not going to end well, Freya. Does he know you're engaged?'

Freya clamped her mouth shut. She was going to tell her all about the previous day and the place Tarek had taken her to. She'd really enjoyed lunch with Tarek at the Michaelhouse Café – it was such a surprise, having lived in Cambridge all her life, she didn't know it existed although she guessed that she must have walked past St Michael's a hundred times and never realised it was there.

Freya recalled telling Tarek she had a surprise for him – she was taking him to a peaceful place for lunch not far from the hustle and bustle of the city centre, and this time it was her treat. Freya avoided Jolene's gaze. She opened the door to the gallery. 'I've got a lot to do before lunch.'

'Lunch with Tarek – again?'

As the week drew to a close, Freya had something special planned. She avoided eye contact, refusing to answer the question. Instead she walked into the gallery, straight up to Tarek, who was organising a display case. 'Now, where were we?'

❖

It was a bright but cold afternoon and, having worked tirelessly on the exhibition for most of the morning, Freya was looking forward to a brisk walk and a stop for lunch at the Botanic Gardens. The beautiful landscaped gardens were now a public park. She'd listened to Tarek telling her all about Alexandria and the stunning gardens around the Montazah Palace, which had once been the grounds of a royal palace and hunting lodge. She was eager to show him what Cambridge had to offer.

Freya turned at the sound of footsteps behind her and spotted Tarek walking through the exit. Freya smiled when she thought about how well things had turned out, working with Tarek. They had agreed on many aspects of the setting-up of the exhibition – the labelling and presentation of the artefacts – and it was all turning out to be a stunning revival of the era.

Freya grinned as he fell in step with her. They walked down Trumpington Street, which led to the main entrance to the gardens. On the way, she gave Tarek a potted history of what he was about to see.

'The first Botanic Gardens were founded in 1762 to educate students from the colleges in the use of plants for medicinal purposes. And later, during the 1800s – with more overseas explorations taking place – more exciting species of plants were discovered.'

Freya glanced up at Tarek as she was speaking. Freya had printed off a map of the gardens. She stopped and handed him the map. 'What would you like to see first?'

Tarek looked at the map, grabbed her hand and said, 'Let's just walk.'

'Ouch!' Freya pulled away. 'You're holding my hand too hard.'

Tarek released his grip. 'Sorry – but let's go. I'm busy and have no time to waste on frivolous outings.' He strode off through the gardens with Freya almost running to keep up with him. That wasn't what he'd said all week when they'd had lunch together and found time for what he now called frivolous outings, like browsing a second-hand bookshop down a cobbled side street or wandering into the Cambridge Arts Centre to pick up a programme on forthcoming plays. Freya had thought it would be a great idea to take Tarek to the English theatre – for cultural reasons. But it was more than that; she wanted an excuse to spend more time with him.

She caught up with him. 'Where are we heading?' said Freya, realising he was not taking in the beautiful surroundings.

Tarek stopped and glanced at the map. 'Let's head for the café, and then you can tell me what this all means,' he replied.

Freya looked at him, puzzled. What was he talking about? She followed him along Main Walk until they reached the café.

Freya was so disappointed Tarek was not enjoying all this. She'd thought it would be the perfect surprise. As they strode along the path, up ahead she could see the café, which was in a beautiful landscape setting; she should be looking forward to lunch, but Tarek's mood had spoiled her surprise.

Tarek stopped for a moment to look at some plants clustered amongst the trees.

'They're snowdrops,' Freya offered as they stopped to admire the flowers which were exquisitely displayed amongst the evergreens and trees. A wisp of a smile crossed Tarek's face.

'Look there's the sign to the café.' Freya pointed, stealing a glance at him, noticing his sour expression had softened. They walked along in companionable silence until they reached the café.

Once inside, Tarek chose a table in a secluded corner while Freya went to collect a menu.

Tarek looked at the menu and ordered a cheese and tomato baguette with an Americano while Freya settled on a bowl of soup followed by a fruit scone with a pot of English Breakfast tea. Once they had placed their order, Tarek turned to Freya. His mood had changed, she could tell. 'So, why weren't you honest with me?'

Freya furrowed her brow, confused. Had something happened when Tarek was on his way out of the museum? 'I don't know what you mean,' she said.

'Oh, come on! What is this between you and me? Are you just playing around with my feelings?'

Freya stared at him. She knew how she felt about him, and unfortunately, so did Jolene, but she hadn't thought those feelings were reciprocated – at first. Freya avoided eye contact. When, over the course of the past week, had these innocent lunch dates become something more … not just for her, but for him?

'When were you going to tell me?'

'Tell you what?' Freya was taken aback. It wasn't like Tarek to be argumentative and confrontational. She'd thought they were getting along. Although she did recall that he'd been like that in the beginning when they'd first met – but so had she. They had patched up their differences. Working alongside Tarek, she'd thought they were getting on really well – too well. She dismissed the thought, along with the words she'd had with Jolene that morning. She didn't want to think about it. She knew what her best friend was saying – she was getting in too deep.

'That you're engaged.'

Freya looked into those deep brown eyes and frowned at the thought that Jolene, her best friend, had told him.

Tarek regarded her a long moment. 'So, it's true.'

She narrowed her eyes. She bet it wasn't Jolene. She knew her best friend. She wouldn't betray a confidence. Freya was convinced she knew what had happened. Some of the other staff members were gossiping about her, and Tarek had overheard. Freya felt angry that they were talking about her behind her back when all she had done was make Tarek feel part of the team by being friendly and helpful. But, of course, there was more to it than that, and Jolene obviously wasn't the only one who had realised.

'So, why aren't you wearing your engagement ring?' Tarek asked, interrupting her thoughts.

Freya was about to tell him when a friendly older woman came over to their table with their lunch. Placing the baguette and coffee in front of Tarek and the scone and tea in front of Freya, she wished them both a relaxing lunch.

'Thank you,' Tarek replied in a dismissive tone.

The woman got the message and abruptly walked away – leaving the two miserable youngsters to get on with it.

'Well?' Tarek demanded. 'What have you got to say?'

Freya poured herself a cup of tea. She looked across the table at Tarek's pained expression.

'I am sorry I've upset you, but it wasn't intentional, Tarek. When we first met in the dean's office and she asked me to support you in setting up the exhibition, I was really angry that you had been sent to Cambridge. I thought I was being seconded to Alexandria. So I was not in a good place and am aware I was downright unfriendly.'

Tarek stirred his coffee.

'But as we worked together and chatted about your life in Egypt things changed between us,' Freya admitted. 'Yes, I am engaged – it's true. But before you say anything more on the matter, no I did not keep this from you to purposely deceive you."

Freya glanced at her hands. 'The reason I am not wearing my engagement ring is that I'd have to take it off anyway so I don't damage the artefacts when I'm handling them. It seemed better just not to wear it when I am at work.' Freya took a deep breath. He listened as she told him how she had met Theo, believing she was in love with him, that he was the one.

Tarek leaned forward in his seat. 'And now?'

Freya stared across the table at him. 'I'm confused. I should have told you, but I … I didn't think it mattered.'

'Well – it does!'

Freya looked at Tarek and saw the hurt and distrust in his eyes. She told him she was deeply sorry for not being honest with him. 'How could I, when I wasn't sure myself what was happening between us?' she asked. Jolene had told her it was just a *crush* – but over the past week with Tarek, it had dawned on her that this was no mere crush.

Without speaking, Tarek rose from his seat and went to settle the bill, even though they had hardly touched their food. She stared after him. Why was he treating her like this? She had been honest about her feelings – couldn't he at least acknowledge that?

Tarek returned to the table. 'I have to go. There are some posters I have ordered for the exhibition that need collecting from the printers.'

Freya looked at him. His expression was cold and professional. 'Is that it? After all I've said, you're just going to walk away?' said Freya.

He tipped his head in response, turned and walked out of the café, leaving Freya staring after him.

Freya walked out of the café. She didn't feel like rushing back to the museum. Instead, she made her way along the path towards the rock gardens. The afternoon sun was low in the sky and she felt a chill run through her. Freya spotted the glasshouse in the distance and hurried towards it. Stepping inside, she found herself alone. She burst into tears. Jolene had been right – she should never have got involved with Tarek. *But you couldn't help yourself*, a little voice in her head responded.

She stamped her foot angrily. Everything had been just fine until he'd turned up. She turned when she heard people walking into the glasshouse and hurried outside, wiping the tears from her face. Jolene's words came back to haunt her. *It's not going to end well, Freya.*

40

Freya made her way through the entrance and headed to the area where they were setting up the exhibition. She was hoping to find Jolene. She strode past some of the other members of the team, giving them a sour look. She wondered which of them had been gossiping about her.

She imagined Jolene was down in the basement area, sorting out the final exhibits to be displayed. She hurried downstairs and entered the vast basement room that held the artefacts. It was dimly lit, but she spotted a bright light further down the aisles.

'Jolene!' Freya called out when she saw her friend bending over a crate and examining the label with a small hand torch.

Jolene rose and looked at her friend. 'Where have you been? I thought you were meeting up with Tarek for lunch, but he returned a short time ago with some posters, and when I asked where you were he told me to mind my own business.'

'Oh, Jolene, I've been such a fool. I should have listened to you and not got involved,' said Freya as she burst into tears.

Jolene rushed over and put her arms around Freya, leading her to a bench that ran alongside a trestle table in the middle of the room. Fortunately, there was no one else in the room to hear them. 'Just take a seat, Freya. I'm going to grab a couple of drinks and will be straight back. Nothing is insurmountable. We will sort this out.'

Freya sobbed. 'It's all his fault! Everything was perfect until he came along.' Even as she was saying the words to the empty room, she knew they weren't exactly true.

Jolene was gone only a few moments. She returned with two steaming paper cups from the vending machine.

Freya looked at Jolene in surprise. 'We're not allowed food and drink down here – you know that.'

Jolene took her hand and placed one of the cups between her fingers. 'I think today we're just going to have to make an exception, don't you?' Jolene found a clean tissue and gently wiped the tears from Freya's cheeks. 'Now, drink. It's hot chocolate.'

Freya eyed her friend as she took some sips of the soothing, velvety hot chocolate.

Jolene said, 'Theo loves you, and you can't have done something that bad that you'd want to break off your engagement.'

'Break off my engagement?' Freya stopped drinking and looked at her best friend. 'I'm not talking about Theo …'

'Oh, I thought you and Theo had had a falling-out, and that's what this was about.'

'It's about Tarek,' blurted Freya.

Jolene sighed heavily. 'Of course it is.' She rolled her eyes. 'So that's why Tarek was so rude and abrupt when he came back from the printer's. He's been biting everyone's head off ever since he returned. Nothing's right with the exhibition, according to him, and we've all got to come in early tomorrow morning to deal with it. He has a list of what has to be put right – and he's expecting the whole team – and he emphasised *whole* team – to sort out their differences and deliver his list of requirements, or the exhibition won't take place.'

Freya looked up – horrified. 'Can he do that?'

'Evidently, he can.' Jolene stared at her. 'What on earth did you say to him over lunch?'

Freya bit her bottom lip. 'He found out I was engaged.'

'He found out. How?'

Freya looked at Jolene, relieved to discover it definitely wasn't her. 'He was angry when he found out. I think he has feelings for me.'

'Oh, y'think?' Jolene said sarcastically. 'Of course he has feelings for you. Anyone with two eyes can see the way he looks at you, hangs on your every word. Everyone apart from you, obviously.'

'I didn't think … didn't realise …' Freya trailed off. Perhaps she'd been afraid to acknowledge his feelings for her because she hadn't told him the truth – that she was with someone else. But now that didn't matter. He'd made his feelings known – she'd betrayed his trust.

Jolene said, 'Look, I don't know what you're going to do about Tarek and Theo, but right now – and excuse me for being blunt – but we've got an urgent problem: what if the exhibition doesn't go ahead? I get the feeling Tarek is going to put a real spanner in the works.'

Freya stared at Jolene. 'This is all my fault. What will the dean say if Tarek refuses to open the exhibition? The museum has acquired such a global reputation for its displays of rare and wonderful artefacts. It could be damaged if they cancel a once-in-a-lifetime event and people found it was all because …'

'Two people met and fell in love?'

Freya frowned.

Jolene shook her head, looked at Freya and thought – *what a bloody mess*. Jolene rose from her seat. 'Leave this with me, Freya.'

'What are you going to do?'

'I'm off to have a word with the team before they leave to-night. We'll get done exactly what he's asked of us. Then what can he do? There will be no reason for the exhibition opening not to go ahead.' Jolene picked up her drink and studied her friend. 'Promise me one thing,' she said.

Freya had been staring at her hot chocolate. She looked up.

'You must put things right with Theo – you have to explain what's happened. If you really have such strong feelings for Tarek then you must be honest with Theo. He deserves the truth. I think you should break off the engagement.'

'I wished I'd never met Tarek.'

Jolene smiled. 'I'll bet.' Who had once said the course of true love never did run smooth? Was that Shakespeare? Jolene couldn't remember. But what she did know was that her best friend was all at sea over these unexpected – and right now, unwanted – feelings for another man. And some time soon, she would have to make a choice between the man she was engaged to and the man she had obviously fallen in love with.

❖

The team assembled in the cordoned-off area of the new exhibition room, waiting for Tarek to arrive. Jolene stood with a comforting arm around Freya – she could feel her trembling at the thought of seeing him again. Jolene squeezed her hand and whispered, 'Everything will be all right – just you wait and see. I had a word with the team last night and emphasised the importance of working together on this. Nobody but you and I know where his sudden sullen, rude attitude has come from.'

Footsteps could be heard marching down the outer corridor, and then Tarek appeared carrying various poster tubes. After saying a cursory good morning and getting a lukewarm response in return, he placed the tubes on a spare exhibit bench and opened his briefcase. Turning to the team, he looked around.

Freya wished the ground would open and swallow her up as he spotted her and gave her a surly nod.

'Asshole,' said Jolene under her breath.

'Did you have something to say, Jolene?' Tarek asked. 'If so, please could you speak up as I am sure the whole team would value your input. If not, then let's get down to business.'

Jolene remained quiet.

'As you can see, I have had various posters made which highlight the artefacts on display. Please can you start by looking through these and deciding amongst yourselves which area of the exhibition you would like to work on, then you can take the relevant posters. I find working together is really beneficial in these matters and brings out the best results.'

'Oh really!' Jolene remarked.

Tarek glared at Jolene, who was obviously upsetting his equilibrium. 'Jolene, perhaps you can hand out this list of requirements to each team member. It's a plan for where I would like to see the exhibits displayed.'

Freya could hear some of the team members tittering as Jolene made her way to the front. Even Freya tried to suppress a smile as Tarek handed out the sheets of paper to Jolene. It was like being at school. Freya felt sorry for Tarek. He was acting like a pompous git. She knew what was really going on here; he was trying to hide his discomfort behind a mask of authority. She was just hiding, doing her best to melt into the background and avoiding his gaze.

'I will be out of the museum for a while and leave it in your very capable hands, Jolene, to oversee my requests.'

Jolene looked across at Freya apologetically, aware that she was the one who was meant to be working with Tarek to co-ordinate and complete the exhibition. It was Freya who should be overseeing matters.

'I'll be back around lunchtime and expect all the work to be completed by then. If it meets with my approval then you can all have a free afternoon.' Tarek turned on his heel, glanced at Freya, and walked out of the room, leaving the team in shocked silence.

'Right,' said Jolene once she had been left in charge. 'I think we need to regroup over a coffee, look at the new plan for the exhibits and choose amongst ourselves who wants to deal with a particular aspect of the exhibition. Once that's decided, we can all set to work. We have just four hours to re-arrange the location of the exhibits, put up these new posters and sort out the hands-on exhibits for the children. Everyone in agreement?'

The small group standing in front of her all nodded their heads and then filed out to the coffee machine. Freya watched them go, thinking Tarek would have a fit if he returned just then and found them all on a coffee break.

'Hold up, everyone!' Jolene's voice boomed out, stopping everyone in their tracks.

'Before we get the drinks, can we agree that Freya takes charge once I have handed these lists around? After all, she's the expert here, and it will be in all our interests to get this right.

What do you think?'

A round of applause went up, and Freya was ushered to the front – all happily volunteering her for the role – and presumably for the blame if things didn't work out.

Despite – or perhaps because of – being aware that the buck stopped with her if Tarek wasn't happy with the final results, Freya was determined to make it work and turn out the best exhibition the museum had ever put on.

❖

Freya stood in front of the team as they sipped their drinks. They each had the plan in front of them. Reading it had depleted their enthusiasm. As one team member had pointed out, it seemed overwhelming to be asked to achieve all this in just four hours.

Freya looked at the list and then folded it and placed it on the table. 'Yes, there is a lot to do – but we can simplify the process if we fall back on the range of experience you've all already acquired over many years. I'm sure we will get this done. It's just a matter of coordinating moving the exhibits between display cases. But first things first. Do you remember when the dean gave her talk to us about why people love coming to a museum and what draws them in?'

'To get out of the rain,' Jolene quipped.

'Step in somewhere warm for a few moments, when it's blooming chilly out,' another quipped, following Jolene's lead.

There was a ripple of laughter. 'Yes and no,' replied Freya, smiling at her friend, who had managed to lighten the atmosphere.

'People love coming to museums because right here, we tell

stories about the past – about peoples' lives, the places they inhabited, and in some cases, their loves, hopes and dreams. And we do that by creating powerful and inspiring exhibits.'

Freya continued. 'You've already decided amongst yourselves where your strengths lie. So, once you've completed the changes to your area of the exhibit, those working on interactive displays and the children's area will be given the opportunity to showcase their work as the rest of us will pretend to be the younger visitors.'

There were smiles all round. That was the fun part. 'Let's see if you can grab our attention and interest!'

Freya clapped her hands together. 'Now, off you go. Oh, and let me just finish by saying that whatever the outcome – give it your best. You are a great team and don't let anyone – *and I mean anyone*,' she was thinking of one person in particular, 'tell you otherwise.'

When Freya finished talking, the room was distinctly quiet – and then a round of applause went up before the team rose from their seats and shuffled off to get on with the task ahead.

Jolene walked up to her. 'You know, have you ever thought of going into teaching when you finish your PhD?'

Freya shook her head. 'No – why?'

'I think you'd make the most amazing, inspiring teacher – just like your dad.'

❖

Freya wrapped the blanket around her legs and looked at Tarek, who was standing awkwardly in the punt and trying to guide it down the River Cam using one of the super-long oars that she thought was probably called a quant. He wasn't doing a good job of it. They kept bumping into the riverbank or into other punts. It was all very embarrassing.

Freya was trying her best not to laugh, and Tarek was getting annoyed. She pulled her scarf tightly around her neck as wisps of hair escaped from her bobble hat. She noticed that Tarek was wearing his own scarf this time – she guessed he wasn't keen on pink after all. The river and riverbank were peaceful at this time of the year. She knew there were stunning views of the backs of the colleges along the river, which added to the serenity of the place – if they ever got that far down river.

Unfortunately, Tarek had decided to take the punt out himself, thinking it would be easy.

Tarek had arranged the punting tour when he'd left them all to complete the exhibition. He'd bought them all tickets as a surprise treat, along with dinner afterwards, as a reward for completing the exhibition to his exacting standards. Everyone knew what it really was; an apology for the way he had behaved.

The others, sensibly, had hired boats with punters who took them down the river, so they didn't have to do what Tarek was doing. They had left Tarek and Freya way behind.

Although it was cold, it was a perfect excuse to enjoy each other's company and take in all the sights – or so Freya thought. They'd only made it a few hundred yards along the river. But she didn't care about that. She was enjoying it, nonetheless.

The way the team had set up the exhibition had been a complete success – and now it would open to the public. But first, it had to have Tarek's father's approval when he made it back to Cambridge.

After congratulating the team on all their hard work, Tarek had turned to Freya and invited her on the tour. She had guessed he hadn't expected her to accept. 'Only if you behave like a gentleman this time,' Freya had replied in a stern voice, alluding to the argument they'd had a lunch yesterday and the way he'd treated her.

In hindsight, although she'd been upset, she knew Tarek was very upset too – it wasn't like him to act that way. It was her own fault for not telling him about Theo and her engagement. Although Tarek had apologised profusely for his behaviour, Freya had insisted that she was the one who should apologise. They'd both accepted they had feelings for one another. She guessed that Tarek realised she had some big decisions to make about her future, and she wouldn't be able to untangle her feelings overnight.

Freya was relieved they were back on speaking terms. They were both honest enough to admit that they didn't know where to go next, but the one thing they did want to do was this – have some fun together on the river and enjoy the rest of the afternoon.

She smiled at him. It had been obvious that Tarek was overjoyed when they'd apologised to one another and she'd accepted his invitation. The trouble was, Tarek's happy mood had dissipated. Fortunately, it was not her fault this time.

'Oh, I give up!' Tarek put the oar down and carefully took a seat beside her, the boat listing slightly as he did so.

'Don't beat yourself up, Tarek. It's a lot harder than it looks.'

'Tell me about it!' He grinned at her.

His face dropped at what she said next. 'Remember that you were talking about your dad last weekend when we had lunch together. You said he'd gone to the Suffolk Coast to stay in a guest house?'

Tarek frowned. 'He was meant to help us with the exhibition.'

'Oh, I didn't know that.'

'Well, you know now.' He paused. 'You still want to meet him, don't you?'

Freya nodded. 'I do. He's not back from the guest house, then?'

'Nope.'

Freya looked at him thoughtfully. Now the exhibition was completed, she was back to thinking about her mum – and that woman called Wendy.

'This conversation feels a bit déjà vu,' commented Tarek.

Freya nodded, thinking back to the previous week at lunch. The time had flown by. 'Yes, I know.'

'What are you thinking?'

She looked at Tarek sheepishly. Once again, she was thinking that as his father was still away at the guest house, wasn't this the perfect excuse to go there?

41

'Go over the story again, so I'm clear, because I'm just worried if Theo asks anything …'

Freya glanced at her watch. She didn't have time for this. If she got a move on, she'd be there by around eleven.

She rolled her eyes. 'Theo is not going to ask anything, Jolene. When is he going to get the opportunity? You hardly ever meet, and it's not as though you're going to bump into each other while I'm gone.' Freya didn't mean to, but she was getting a little irritated with Jolene. They'd been over this before.

'Oh, crap!' Freya said as she dropped her phone. She'd had it balanced in the crook of her neck while she packed a suitcase. Fortunately, it just fell on top of some clothes in her case. She picked it up. 'Look, I'm a bit busy just packing some things, Jolene. I don't see what you're worried about.'

'I don't like, you know, lying.'

'Who says you have to? I told you, you won't bump into Theo. And besides, it's *me* telling a fib – not you.' Freya's eyes darted to the bedroom door. She could have sworn she'd heard someone outside the door. 'Jolene, I've got to go.'

'Is it worth it? I mean why don't you just confront your dad?

It will be a darn sight easier than making the trip.'

Freya had thought about that. But who was to say he wouldn't deny that he knew anyone called Wendy, or that her mum had gone AWOL because she'd found out about a possible affair? Freya still couldn't believe it, the idea that her dad had cheated on her mum. But there was something going on, some reason her mum had just upped and left.

'It's all speculation, you know.'

'That's why I'm going to this guest house, to find Wendy.'

'What if she's not there?'

'Well, she rang from that number.'

'She might have checked out by the time you get there.'

Freya sighed. That was true.

'You know the other, better way I mentioned, trying to find out if you've got a half-sister. Did you do it? Did you join AncestryDNA and send off a sample?'

'I did, yes. It was handy getting those DNA testing kits and a trial of AncestryDNA – they were handed out as presents at a party Theo and I went to. I wasn't going to bother with mine, but now I'm pleased I kept it. When will the results feed through, do you think?'

'Quite soon, I expect.'

'I gave my details, like my mobile phone number.'

'Good. It will be just a case of waiting to see if there's someone on the database you are related to.'

'Okay.'

'I take it you haven't changed your mind about going?'

Freya vehemently shook her head. 'Nice try, but no, I'm going anyway.'

'Is it something to do with the fact that you're going with

Tarek? You could wait until Tarek's father returns to Cambridge.'

Freya fell silent. She'd run out of excuses.

'I hope you know what you're doing, Freya.'

Freya sighed. They'd had this conversation already too. She knew Jolene's attitude. Despite there being no particular affection between her best friend and Theo, Jolene had reminded her that she was engaged and had implied she shouldn't be off gallivanting with Tarek.

For someone who on the surface appeared to have no scruples with bending the rules, or flouting conventions, Jolene was all smoke and mirrors; she was, in fact, quite conservative when it came to relationships and norms. For her, if you committed to someone, if you were engaged and had accepted a marriage proposal, then you didn't go back on your word. Freya knew that she used to be like that herself. She still was, really. It was just that Tarek had confused her.

She whirled around at the sound of a creaky floorboard outside her bedroom door. 'Dad, is that you?'

There was a pause. 'No, it's me, Theo.'

Freya walked over to the door and opened it. He was standing the other side with a cup of tea and a plate of biscuits. 'Elevenses.' He caught an expression on her face. 'What?'

Her eyes dropped to his tea. She could still see a whirl of steam that suggested he'd just made it and hadn't been standing outside her door, listening. She hoped not.

His eyes drifted to her case. 'Going soon?'

'Yes. I'm nearly packed.' She felt a pang of guilt. *But nothing is going on, you're just making the trip with a guy you fancy, that's all.* Freya swept that thought aside, focusing on his plate of biscuits. He liked the same biscuits her dad did. They were like two peas in a pod. She didn't know how far Theo had got with the novel he was writing in his spare time under her dad's tutelage, and she felt guilty that she couldn't be bothered to ask. Perhaps she was ever so slightly jealous. Theo was like the son her dad had never had. She suddenly wondered, in passing, why her parents hadn't had more children.

'Are you sure you don't want me to come? I could bring my laptop and work in the hotel.'

Freya swallowed. There had been an awkward moment the previous night when she'd told him she was going on a work trip, and he'd invited himself along, saying that he could work in the hotel room while she attended an archaeological dig she'd told him was going on in Suffolk. Thinking on her feet, Freya had admitted the reason she was really going – one of the reasons, at least – she had told him about the conversation she'd overheard between her dad and a woman, and about finding out the phone number of the last caller and tracing it to a guest house in Suffolk. A row had ensued, their first one ever, when Theo discovered she'd lied to him. Freya thought back to that conversation.

'Why didn't you tell me this in the first place?' he'd said.

'There is a guy staying there, an eminent archaeologist apparently, so it is kinda work-related,' she'd replied.

'But that's not the main reason you're going.'

'No,' she'd admitted.

She'd then told him about the days out with her dad as a child where they'd inevitably met up with a woman and her child – a girl that Freya believed had been around the same age as herself. 'We played together while my dad chatted to her mum,' she'd told Theo.

Theo had shrugged, and said, 'So? People meet and chat in parks all the time.'

'But it was the same parent, the same child, the same park – *every* time. Don't you think that's a bit of a coincidence?' she'd said. Then she'd shared her theory that her dad might have had a brief fling, and this other girl was the result.

Theo had appeared quite defensive and upset. Anyone would have thought it was his own dad she was accusing of having an affair. He'd said exactly what Jolene had said: 'Why don't you confront your dad?' On top of which, he'd voiced her own sentiments, 'Personally, I just don't think your dad is the type to have an affair, or a fling, or a one-night stand, or whatever you think it was.'

Perhaps that was the reason she didn't want to confront her dad. Because if it wasn't true, then what would he think of her accusing him of something he hadn't done, and listening in on his phone conversations? She'd told Theo that too.

'Then I think you should go,' Theo had said. 'If for no other reason than to put your mind at rest that nothing was going on.'

So here she was, packing her case. She paused to look at Theo. After that conversation the previous night, she knew he was convinced there was nothing going on with her dad and another woman.

'Why do you think my mum just walked out?'

'I think she doesn't want to move house.'

That didn't surprise Freya. 'But why not sit down and talk about it?' Something was off, and she knew it.

He added. 'You know, it's not unusual when a child leaves home, for good, that relationships, even long ones, fall apart.'

Freya knew what he was talking about – empty nest

syndrome. But why now? She'd left home and moved in with Theo ages ago, and now she'd returned. She didn't think that was the problem.

'You don't think it's that, do you?' Theo said, reading her mind.

'Freya shook her head. All I know is that something is going on, with Mum and Dad.'

'If that's how you feel, then you should go.'

'Promise me, you won't say anything about this to Dad.' She knew how thick as thieves the two of them were.

'Of course, I won't.'

She looked at him a long moment, satisfied he was being earnest. She put a hand on his shoulder, leaned in and gave him a kiss. 'Goodbye, Theo.'

'God that sounds a bit final,' he joked, smiling at her.

She frowned. *It did, didn't it?* she thought. 'Thanks for letting me do this on my own.'

'I understand completely.'

Unfortunately, he didn't. Freya took a deep breath. 'We must talk when I get back from my trip,' she said.

Theo's smile faded. 'What about?' he quizzed her as she walked towards the door.

She stopped in the doorway and turned around. 'Us.'

He didn't appear surprised. In fact, the look on his face suggested to Freya that he already knew something was up. Perhaps it hadn't escaped his notice how she had changed towards him, especially since Tarek had arrived.

Freya averted her gaze. She felt another guilty pang at the thought that before starting on the two-hour journey to the Suffolk Coast, she was making a detour to pick up Tarek without telling Theo her plans. It crossed her mind that perhaps she should forget the detour and go on her own.

42

'For goodness' sake, why does this have to happen now?' Freya rubbed her hands together and stamped her feet, trying to keep warm. She stared angrily at her car, which was at a standstill with the bonnet up. 'She's normally so reliable. I've never broken down once!'

'Perhaps your little car doesn't like long distances?'

'You think?' Freya shot back, annoyed. She knew it wasn't Tarek's fault, but they would be there by now if it wasn't for this. An hour into their journey along the A14, and her car had suddenly shuddered and started to lose power. Fortunately, they'd managed to make it to the layby a hundred yards down the road, where her car had spluttered to a halt. Freya stared at her phone. She'd called the AA, so they were on their way. She really hoped that whatever the problem was, it could be fixed it at the roadside and they'd be on their way. She didn't know what they were going to do if her car had to be towed to a garage.

'God!' Freya kicked the tyre with her boot. It wasn't like she could ring her dad or Theo and ask them to come and pick her up. She eyed Tarek. This was her own fault. This was karma for not telling her boyfriend who she was making the trip with.

'Karma,' said Freya, nodding her head.

Tarek's head popped up from under the bonnet. 'Pardon?'

'Nothing!' She glared at him. 'And what are you doing anyway – are you a mechanic?'

'No. I was just having a look.'

'Well – don't! It's annoying me.'

Tarek walked over and stood beside her. They both stared in the direction of the oncoming traffic, looking for the yellow AA truck.

'What are we going to do if they can't fix it roadside?'

'Then it gets towed to the nearest garage and we hire a car for a day and carry on with our journey.'

'Oh, right. Of course.' Freya hadn't thought of that. The AA man would take them to the garage, where there would be hire cars.' She brightened. 'Then we can still stay over for one night and pick the car up on the journey home.'

The AA had turned up in good time, but as she suspected, her car couldn't be fixed at the roadside. Then they'd arrived at the nearest garage to find a grumpy, unhelpful young man on his tea break who told Freya that all the hire cars were booked out.

'What? Now what are we supposed to do?'

'Get a taxi to your destination?'

'But that's at least an hour and a half up the road. It will cost a small fortune. Then we'd have to take a taxi back.'

The young man shrugged as if to say, *not my problem*.

'I can try and get this fixed today for you if you're prepared to wait?'

Freya folded her arms. 'How long?'

He pointed at the row of cars in front of hers. 'Might be a while.'

'Oh, that's just great! What are we going to do in the meantime?'

Tarek said, 'You know, it's only half an hour back to Cambridge. We could get a taxi back. My father will be coming home soon anyway. We don't have to make the journey if—'

'No, I'm still going.' She looked at Tarek. 'You can call a taxi and go back, if you want. In fact, why don't you?'

He eyed her. 'You don't want me to come anymore?'

Freya sighed. The trouble was that she didn't want him to leave. 'Come if you want.'

Tarek smiled. 'Of course I want to, if it means spending more time with you.'

A heavy sigh interrupted their conversation. 'I'll phone you when the car's fixed. There's a truck stop just down the road. You can't miss it; it's got the word *Diner* emblazoned on the roof. If you two lovebirds want some lunch.'

Freya frowned at the mechanic.

Tarek grinned. 'Yep, sounds good. Be a bit different to our usual lunchtime haunts.'

Freya agreed. 'I'll say.'

'There's a big shopping outlet next door if you need to kill some time afterwards.'

Freya realised they were going to be there for quite a while. She wasn't surprised about the shopping outlet. The garage was located on a big industrial retail park. She didn't plan on clothes shopping, but she guessed it wouldn't hurt to browse. If they had to kill a couple of hours, there were worse places they could find themselves. She looked at the row of cars in front of hers and smiled sweetly at the mechanic. 'Any way you could bump my little car up the list, so she gets seen a bit quicker?'

The young mechanic started to shake his head until Tarek stepped in. 'It would be a huge favour for the lady – and for me.' He flashed a big grin at the mechanic, large, dark soulful eyes staring at him.

Freya looked from the mechanic to Tarek and back again. She realised why when she had tried to turn on the charm it hadn't worked. For some reason, she was annoyed with Tarek.

'I'll see what I can do,' the mechanic said, smiling at him.

Tarek turned around and caught the expression on her face. 'What?'

'Nothing.'

'Shall we have lunch?'

Freya looked at her watch, surprised that it was midday already. Two wasted hours waiting for the AA man to arrive. She frowned at her car. Who knew how long it would take to fix – if it could be fixed at all? She didn't want to think of the worst-case scenario. 'Yeah, let's get out of here.'

They walked out of the garage, heading down the road that skirted the big retail outlets on the way to the diner.

'We could go shopping afterwards,' suggested Tarek. 'I haven't been to one of these retail parks before.'

Freya frowned. 'You're not missing much.' She preferred shopping in Cambridge city centre, rather than driving to soulless places like this. But she was there, and there was nothing else to do. 'Okay.'

'Do you need to buy anything?' he asked.

A wedding dress. Freya would rather not think about Theo or her upcoming nuptials. It wasn't as though anything had been planned, or booked, but wasn't that the expectation once someone proposed, and you got engaged? She still hadn't committed to even looking for a dress, let alone starting the ball rolling with planning a wedding.

She knew that the conversation she'd promised Theo before she left was long overdue. It had been festering for some time now, before she'd even set eyes on Tarek; a feeling that she was not ready to take the final step with Theo, and probably never would be. But she was only just starting to acknowledge that.

'Freya?'

She glanced at Tarek, realising that she hadn't answered his question. She shook her head.

'I would like to look at the English clothes,' said Tarek.

Freya gave him a sideways glance. 'They're not much different to what you're wearing, really.'

'Still, I would like to see inside the big retail shops.'

'Okay, then it's decided. That's the plan after lunch – unless the mechanic calls us.' Freya looked at her phone and sighed as she put it in her bag. She could look at it until the cows came home, but that wouldn't make the mechanic work any faster. In fact, she wouldn't be surprised if right now he was on another tea break.

43

'Look at it this way,' said Tarek, sitting beside her in the car, 'It could have been worse.'

'How so?' Freya barked back as she put the key in the ignition. 'It's almost eight in the evening. I was hoping to arrive at the guest house for dinner.'

'At least we haven't had to stay the night at the hotel over there.' He pointed at a Holiday Inn. 'It looks nice, though.' He shifted his gaze to Freya. 'The mechanic was very good to work late in the evening.'

'Well, he didn't do it out of the kindness of his heart.' The mechanic had phoned her to say he might have to finish the repairs tomorrow, unless …

That *unless* had cost her an extra hundred quid, on top of the cost of repairing the car.

Tarek had immediately paid the mechanic by card over the phone, before she had a chance to object.

'I'll pay you back,' Freya had insisted.

He'd just smiled, infuriating her even more.

As she drove the car down the slip road to join the dual carriageway leading to Suffolk, Freya had a thought. 'Do you think they've kept our rooms for us?'

She'd forgotten to phone ahead to let the guest house know they were on their way and to check that they hadn't booked out their rooms to other guests.

'I don't know. I wouldn't expect they'd be busy this time of year.'

Freya nodded. Tarek had a point. Even so, she thought it may be an idea to ring ahead and say they were running late.

❖

'Have they turned up yet?'

Emily shook her head. She'd taken the booking over the phone and mentioned a young lady was due to arrive, but her mum hadn't asked for any details. That wasn't like her, not to inquire after new guests, but Emily knew why she hadn't bothered this time: her mum looked exhausted. 'Mum, why don't you go to bed. I'll wait up and see if they arrive.'

Her mum rubbed her eyes. 'I'm too old for this.'

'When are you going to retire?' Emily asked. She'd had this conversation with her mum before. The place was too big for her to run single-handedly. She hired a student who did a few hours a week, mainly cleaning in the evenings and a Saturday spent helping serve meals. But that was in the peak summer holiday season and the other busy periods like Christmas and Easter.

'I've told you before, Emily, it's costly running a house this size. We need the guests to pay for running the place.'

Emily was aware of that.

'You could sell …' she ventured.

'Yes, I have thought of that. I wonder who would buy a place like this?'

'There might be someone out there who'd take it on as a guest house.'

'Or buy it as a family home.'

Emily didn't voice her thoughts. She would have loved to take on her childhood home as her own home in adulthood and bring up children there, but she couldn't afford to buy her parents out. Even if she could, she had two half-siblings who would be entitled to a share. She would have to keep it as a going concern and still run it as a guest house as a means to buy them out. But who would do all the work? She didn't want to serve breakfasts, cook meals, and make up beds. She wanted to practice veterinary medicine. She shook her head. It wasn't as though she'd ever face that conundrum. She'd never find the money to buy it anyway.

Her thoughts were interrupted by the house phone. She answered it. 'Hello? Yes, this is The Guest House at Shingle Cove. Oh, sorry to hear your car broke down.' Emily glanced at her mum. 'We haven't cancelled your booking. Don't worry, there will be someone on reception when you arrive … How long? Not a problem. See you then.' Emily put the phone down and looked at her mum. 'They'll arrive around ten.'

'Can I leave you to it, then?'

'Of course, Mum. Goodnight.'

'Goodnight, sweetheart. Oh, before I forget, are you cancelling Clarissa's week and refunding her?'

Emily shook her head and smiled. 'Nope, she's staying on. You were out when she arrived back from Cambridge.'

'Cambridge? What was she doing there?'

Emily pursed her lips. She knew that Clarissa had decided to catch a train to Cambridge to talk to the museum staff. She had wanted to see what she could find out about the eminent professor from the staff at the museum before she asked him for an interview, in case he declined. She had also thought it wouldn't hurt to see the new exhibition for herself, so that she had a starting point for the interview, even though that wasn't the reason she wanted to speak with him.

Emily hadn't told her mum that Clarissa was after an interview with one of the guests. She thought perhaps it was best not to mention that, especially as Clarissa was after finding out what exactly he was doing there instead of at that press conference in London. She was convinced it had something to do with their other guest, Alice.

'So, are we full?'

'Yes, the lady who just phoned had booked the last room.'

'The single?'

'I know we don't normally rent out that room because it's quite small. I did warn her it was just a single, but she said she was fine with that. Perhaps she didn't realise we are only a small guest house with five guest bedrooms, and obviously the four doubles are already booked.'

'Well, night night.'

'Night night, Mum.'

Emily watched her mum make her way along the hall and downstairs to the basement level where their family suite was, comprising their lounge, two bedrooms, the house kitchen, and their own private bathroom. Although all the rooms had windows to let in natural light, Emily preferred sleeping upstairs on the top floor in Clarissa's room; it was lovely having views. Now she was back in the servant's quarters, as she called them, downstairs in the bowels of the house.

Emily didn't see the point of waiting at the reception desk for the next hour. She had a rough idea of when their next guest would be arriving. She decided to check that the lights were turned off in the reception rooms. No one was around – or so she thought. She was about to switch off the lights in the lounge when she spotted Alice and Omar. She'd made them coffee and biscuits a couple of hours earlier, but didn't expect them to still be sitting together talking. 'Oh, sorry, I thought you had retired for the evening.'

Alice glanced at her watch and stood up. 'I'd better turn in.'

'Me too,' said Omar.

Emily stood to one side as they left the lounge. She went in to collect their coffee cups and came back out just in time to see them reach the top of the stairs. She knew Alice's room was on one side of the landing, Omar's on the other. Feeling terribly nosy, she lingered a moment to see which way they were headed. They seemed to hesitate. 'Well, I'm this way,' she heard Alice say.

'And I'm that way.'

She watched them part ways. Each evening for the past week, she'd seen and overheard the same shenanigans; Omar inviting her to his room for a nightcap and Alice declining. They'd been spending a lot of time in one another's company. She thought it was inevitable that one evening, Alice would accept his invitation. She raised her eyebrows. Alice must have changed her mind because she walked back past the head of the stairs in Omar's direction.

Emily grinned. 'How romantic,' she commented under her breath. She shook her head at the incredible timing, at the fact that they should both find themselves back here at the same time – a chance to rekindle lost love, perhaps?

Emily's smile faded. Perhaps it wasn't fate or serendipity that had brought Alice and Omar back here after all. Perhaps they had planned it.

Emily shrugged. *Who knows*? she thought. She took the cups down to the kitchen, popped them in the dishwasher, put the kettle on and took a seat at the kitchen table. She scrolled through her phone; she wanted to find out whether the vacant shop in Cobblers Yard was listed on a property website, and how much it might be.

Sometime later, after getting side-tracked in a fruitless search for a profile of Joss Harper, lawyer, on places like LinkedIn, Emily logged on to her account at AncestryDNA. She'd only posted her details a few days earlier. She didn't want to get her hopes up, but she was rather hoping to find her cousins in America and her aunt.

Emily heard a ping. Something appeared in her inbox and she scrolled down to look. She stared at her phone for a long moment as the enormity sunk in. 'Oh. My. God. I've got a hit on the Ancestry site!'

She felt slightly afraid of what it might mean. Her mum was estranged from her sister, for reasons she wouldn't talk about. Now, someone's DNA had matched Emily's. It wasn't her half-brother or sister, because they hadn't used the site. She'd texted them and checked before she signed up. Her dad was an only child. That meant it had to be from her mum's side of the family.

Emily clutched her phone. She still couldn't believe it. She wanted to run upstairs and tell Clarissa. She was about to click on the contact information of the DNA match when she heard a car draw up on the driveway outside. She slipped her phone in her back pocket and made her way upstairs, just in time to hear a knock at the door. She opened it to find, to her dismay, a young, good-looking couple walking in, wheeling a suitcase each. Had there been some miscommunication? The young lady she'd spoken to had said she only needed a single room.

'Hi, I'm Freya, and this is Tarek. We've got two rooms booked for tonight.'

Emily offered them a weak smile and walked over to the reception desk. Perhaps it was she who had made the mistake. She sat down and in front of the computer.

'We're so sorry we're late. Thank goodness you hadn't given away our rooms.'

Emily looked up at the couple. 'Well, um, the thing is, when I spoke with you on the phone, you said a single room was fine.'

'Yes.' Freya paused. 'Oh, crumbs, I get it. You think we're a couple. We're not. This is a business trip. There should be two rooms.'

'But you only booked one – a single.'

'That's right.' She was still smiling. 'Tarek, my colleague here, booked the other room.'

'I did?' He looked at her, surprised.

'You knew we were going on this trip.'

'You asked me to come, Freya, so I thought you'd taken care of everything.'

'I didn't book you a room. I thought you were booking your own room.'

Emily looked from one to the other. She could see this was going to be awkward. 'I'm afraid all we have is the single room you booked.'

'Really – this time of year?'

Emily nodded at the young woman. 'I'm afraid so. We're not

normally this busy …' she said apologetically, trailing off.

'Actually, that's okay. I can share with my father.' He turned to Emily. 'Do the doubles have couches?'

'Well, yes.' Emily frowned. 'What do you mean, you'll share with your father?'

'He's here, in the hotel. The name is Omar Youssef.'

Emily stared at him. This was about to get really awkward. It was obvious that Omar's son had no idea his father was here with a woman. 'Look, I don't think you can share with him.'

'Why not?' asked Freya. 'You can't have any objections to him using the couch – surely?'

'I'll still pay a room rate,' Tarek added.

'Um, it's not either of those things. You see, the thing is, he has company.'

'Company – in his room?'

'Yes, a lady friend.'

Tarek stared at her. 'A what?'

'A friend. A woman.'

'Pardon me? That can't be right.'

Emily pursed her lips. 'Sorry, but I saw them go up together.'

❖

'I can sleep on that, if you want.'

'No. It's fine.'

Freya had tried to get to sleep on the single bed, but all she could hear was the *creak, creak* of Tarek's folding bed as he tossed and turned. She sat up and gazed at him. 'I don't mind, really I don't.'

'I said it's fine!' Tarek turned over with his back to her.

Freya decided to leave him to think. Since he'd found out

that his father was not there alone, Tarek hadn't exactly been talkative. In fact, he'd been sullen and withdrawn and had clearly found it hard to believe that his father had met someone. For Tarek, it must have almost felt like a betrayal.

Freya thought of her dad and the possibility that he'd had an affair. She knew how it felt to discover something like that. Except that Tarek's mother was gone, and his father, a widower, was free to move on with his life, if he wished. Freya had made the mistake of sharing that thought with Tarek. And now they were barely speaking.

Freya sighed. *Trust me to open my big mouth*, she thought. 'Goodnight, Tarek.'

'Good. Night.'

Freya stared at him for a full minute before she turned over in bed and stared at the wall. She wished she hadn't come. If she hadn't, then Tarek wouldn't be here and he'd be none the wiser as to what was going on with his father and a woman. No wonder he wanted to get away to a hotel for a few days.

Before she drifted off to sleep, Freya's last thought was whom they would meet at breakfast in the morning. Would Tarek's father and the woman he was with be there? Would Wendy?

Freya's eyes shot open. 'I'm not looking forward to meeting her if she is here.'

'Did you say something?' Tarek asked.

'No – go back to sleep.'

44

Alice woke up, yawned, and sat up slowly. Marley was snuggled next to Hester at the end of her bed. The cat raised his head. Alice whispered, 'Marley,' so as not to wake Hester. She watched her cat stand up and stretch. He came over, curled in a ball on her lap, and settled in for another snooze. Alice sat for a moment and stroked him, but she had to shift him so she could nip out of bed and pop the kettle on.

She chose an English Breakfast tea bag from the little wooden box and then opened the curtains while she waited for the kettle to boil. The sun appeared on the horizon and the morning light bathed the shingle beach in a soft hazy glow. 'The Sunrise Coast,' she whispered as she recalled that this particular stretch of coastline in Suffolk was sometimes called by that name because the sunrises were so beautiful.

The sea was calm, and she spotted a single, solitary fishing boat bobbing on the water. She wondered if Gerald was already out there at work.

The kettle boiled. Alice poured the hot water, dunked her tea bag a few times, added sugar and milk, and sipped her tea. She stared out towards the horizon. The scene was so tranquil. She wondered what today would bring. It had been lovely to catch up with Omar over the last few days. She thought back to the previous night. After coffee in the lounge, Omar had asked if she'd go to his room for a nightcap. He'd asked every evening, and every evening she'd declined. But on her way upstairs the night before, she'd changed her mind, turned on her heel and headed to his room.

She was surprised she'd woken up this early. They'd talked into the early hours, and it had reminded them of the night they had stayed together in this guest house years earlier when they'd chatted until the early hours about their passion for archaeology.

Their shared interest was still just as strong. Omar's work was fascinating, and Alice wished that she hadn't given it up and become a teacher. But that was all in the past now. They'd had a wonderful evening together, and she had sensed that Omar wanted her to stay. Perhaps she wanted to stay too. But Alice's situation was more complicated than Omar's. She was still married. And despite the fact that Jeffrey may have had – or maybe was still having – an affair, an older, wiser Alice couldn't spend the night with Omar because she knew, this time, that there would be no going back.

Very soon, the postman would arrive at home with her letter on headed paper from the guest house. She'd thought about that all week. Perhaps the post had been delayed or Emily's mum had forgotten to post it. Or Jeffrey had the letter already and he didn't care that she was there, in the very place from where someone called Wendy had written to him.

Despite still anticipating that her husband might turn up at any moment, she had agreed to meet Omar and have breakfast with him. She had her own decisions to make about her future.

Alice shifted her gaze from the horizon to the beach. Although it was early, she could see someone taking their dog for a walk. She took another sip of tea and lowered the mug. She recognised the dog; it was Donut. And she recognised the young woman. It was Clarissa. Alice frowned. She had done her best to steer clear of Clarissa since she'd returned to the guest house the previous day – although there had been one disconcerting moment when she'd discovered Clarissa sitting with Omar, a pad and pen in her hands.

She raised her eyebrows. What had they talked about? It hadn't crossed her mind to ask Omar last night. She'd assumed Clarissa had interviewed him about his work. She hoped her named hadn't cropped up in the conversation. Perhaps if she'd gone straight to bed and not joined Omar for a nightcap in his room last night, which had only consisted of a cup of tea, then she wouldn't be so worried. She couldn't see how that would get back to Clarissa, though.

Alice's thoughts were interrupted by Marley, who had jumped up on to the windowsill in front of her. She smiled at him and stroked the top of his head. Marley purred. Her thoughts returned to her husband and Wendy.

She sighed. 'I wonder what today will bring,' she murmured to Marley.

❖

'At least come down for breakfast before we leave.'

As soon as he had woken up, Tarek had decided he was leaving. 'Why would I want to go down for breakfast and see them together?'

He had a point. Even so, selfishly, Freya didn't want to sit at breakfast on her own. And she wanted to build up the courage to confront Wendy, if she was here.

'I don't think now is the time for you to meet my father,' Tarek said.

Freya was inclined to agree, but for a different reason. It didn't seem appropriate to intrude on a romantic liaison. Freya gave Tarek a sideways glance. She decided to keep that thought to herself.

She made them both a cup of tea. They sat in their beds and drank their tea while they decided on how they would play the day. Freya had opened the curtains while she was making the tea. She'd spied a young woman walking her dog on the beach, and she felt like at least having breakfast and exploring the little cove before they set off back to Cambridge.

It was a beautiful morning, and it was going to turn out to be a lovely, bright winter's day. Despite Tarek's foul mood, she didn't feel inclined to drive straight home. And she had unfinished business of her own. Freya shifted her gaze from the window and looked at Tarek, who was drinking his tea in silence. She decided that perhaps she should come clean about what she was really doing there; about the fact that he wasn't the only one who'd discovered his parent had a secret.

'Tarek.'

He looked up.

'I've got something to tell you.' She took a deep breath. 'Look, I haven't been completely honest about my reasons for coming here.' Freya launched into her story, starting with her mum walking out, and then the conversation she'd overheard between her dad and a woman called Wendy, who had phoned from this hotel.

'So, you're here to find her?'

'I am, yes.'

Tarek looked at her thoughtfully.

'There's something else.' Freya told him about those days out with her dad, when she was a child, and the visits to the park where she'd played with a girl around her own age while her dad had sat and talked with a woman. Tarek listened intently. 'Do you think this woman he used to meet may have been Wendy?'

'I'm not sure. Jolene had a theory that my dad had had an affair years ago with this Wendy, and that the girl I used to play with was … is … my half-sister.'

'I suppose that is one possibility. Perhaps you'll find the answers you're looking for here, at the guest house.'

'I hope so.'

'Then we must stay, at least for today.'

Freya put her tea down, got out of bed, sat on the edge of the folding bed and flung her arms around him to give him a hug. It wasn't that she needed his permission to stay, or that they both had to return to Cambridge together. He could leave straight away in a taxi and she could make her own way home. But Freya wanted him there, as moral support, as someone she could talk to. She drew back, her nose almost touching his. She could tell that she'd caught him by surprise, this sudden display of affection. But what followed, their first kiss, was inevitable. She knew that now. And as she kissed him deeply, she realised why she was here with Tarek. For the first time in her life, she knew what it meant to be in love.

Freya's heart sank. Very soon he would leave and return to Alexandria. She drew back before this went any further, her heart pounding in her chest at the awful thought of him leaving. How would she survive without him? She had never felt that way about being apart from Theo.

'I, er, I'd better get ready. Breakfast is at eight.'

Tarek glanced at his watch. 'But it's only seven.'

Freya grabbed her clothes and her overnight bag and rushed into the bathroom. She stopped in front of the bathroom mirror and tried to put the thought of Tarek leaving out of her mind. She focused on her parents, the woman called Wendy, and the young girl she used to meet in the park.

'I wonder what today will bring,' she said to her reflection.

45

The first thing Emily did after waking was to log on to the AncestryDNA website to check she hadn't imagined things the previous night; to make sure there really was someone on there she was related to. It *was* true. She hadn't imagined it. She was so excited. She'd contact the person later that day.

Emily got out of bed and opened her curtains, smiling. The sun was shining, and there wasn't a cloud in the sky. The beautiful morning mirrored her mood. She glanced at the website on her phone and wondered what the day would bring.

She couldn't wait to tell Clarissa. Was it too early to knock on her friend's door and tell her the news? Emily knew she had to lay out the breakfast buffet in the conservatory. She decided to do it straight away so that by the time she finished, Clarissa might be up and about.

Emily could hear her parents moving about in the room next door. Her dad was due to go to work. Normally, he'd be gone well before now, but the other fishing trawler crew member had come down with the flu; her dad couldn't go out on the trawler alone. As she got dressed she could hear their voices, indistinctly, although from the tone she got the impression they were having words. Emily stopped and frowned. She wondered what was going on.

She brightened when she realised what it might be. Her dad didn't like missing work, and her mum wouldn't like him moping around, under her feet all day. She smiled. Perhaps it was for the best that he was at home today. They were so booked up this morning. An extra pair of hands to help out with the breakfasts wouldn't be a bad thing.

❖

'Why did you open her mail?'

Wendy pulled a face, admonishing herself for forgetting to bin the letter. Worse still, she'd left it in plain sight on the mantel shelf, intending to dispose of it, but it had completely slipped her mind. Gerald, who had been looking for things to do, and a reason to get out of the house, had spotted the letter and offered to post it.

Before she'd reached it, he'd taken it down from the mantel shelf, realised it was not his wife's handwriting, and discovered the envelope had been opened.

'You read a guest's private letter?'

'Give it here.' Wendy snatched it out of his hand.

'I don't understand …'

Wendy started to tear it up into tiny pieces.

He stared at her, wide-eyed.

'It's from Alice to her husband, Jeffrey. Sounds as though she's discovered something..'

Gerald frowned. 'Discovered something? Discovered what?'

'I don't know. He's aware she's here, though.'

'How?'

'I phoned him.'

'You did *what*? I thought the understanding was that you wouldn't contact each other ever again.'

Wendy dropped her gaze. 'It was. But I had to tell him she was here. Now she's written this letter asking him to come.'

'Why?'

'I don't know.'

He sighed heavily. 'Do you think … she knows?'

'I haven't a clue.'

'There was nothing written in the letter about …?'

'No. But I do know one thing – he can't come. Things might get … awkward.'

'Awkward!' Gerald threw his arms in the air in exasperation. 'That's a bit of an understatement, don't you think?'

Wendy eyed him coldly. 'It's not my fault.'

Gerald fell silent. 'Did we make the right decision, all those years ago?'

'God, are we back to that again?'

Gerald slumped down on the end of the bed. What they'd done – what she'd done – was unfortunately never far from his mind. 'What do we do now?'

'Nothing. When he doesn't turn up – and I very much doubt he will – let's hope she just leaves and doesn't extend her stay again.'

'You could tell her that the room is booked, and we've got no more vacancies. We are pretty booked up.'

'You mean lie?'

Gerald nodded. 'It's something we've become accustomed to over the years, don't you think?'

Wendy frowned at him.

He shrugged. 'What else can we do? She can't stay here any longer.'

'I agree.'

'That's settled then.' Gerald sighed. 'I'd much rather be at work,' he mumbled as an afterthought.

She shot him a look. 'What was that?'

'Nothing. Look, as I'm at home today, I might as well be useful. What can I do to help? I expect it will be busy at breakfast. We're nearly full.'

'We *are* full. Emily booked another guest into the single room. I wasn't involved with that booking. Apparently, the lady was due to arrive late last night. I've got to assume she's arrived. I heard Emily leave her room, so I expect she's started to lay out the breakfast. You could help with that.'

'Great. I'll do that, Wendy.'

'For god's sake, Gerald. Don't call me Wendy!'

❖

Emily was in the middle of laying out some of the breakfast things in the conservatory. She'd set each table with cutlery, plates, teacups and saucers. She made her way down the hall, intending to go downstairs to the kitchen for the little pots of jam and marmalade, the pats of butter and the breakfast cereals, when she heard the front door open. She turned around to find a huge dog bounding towards her. 'Donut!' Emily gave him a fuss and looked up. Clarissa shut the front door.

'I didn't realise you were up already.'

Clarissa smiled. 'I had to walk the dog. Didn't want him to have an accident in the room.'

Emily looked at Donut. 'You wouldn't do that, would you?'

She was aware he was still a young dog, and accidents did sometimes happen.

'Clarissa, I've got some news.' Emily got out her mobile phone.

'What is it? Have you and Joss …?'

'Oh, no nothing like that.' Although she was hoping they might go out on a date very soon and that he would tell her more about his life back in London, working as a lawyer. Would he go back to London, and his career in law? That she had yet to find out.

'Look.' Emily showed her the AncestryDNA website. 'I've found a relation.'

Clarissa stared at her. 'Wow, that was fast.'

'I know!'

'To be honest, I didn't think you would. I mean who knows when or even if someone from your aunt's side of the family in America would join that site – if it is a cousin, that is.'

'What do you mean *if it is a cousin*? Who else would it be?'

'I don't know.'

Emily thought of the disclaimer she'd seen when she'd joined the website; it almost read as a warning about what you might unearth in pursuit of long-lost relatives or researching family trees. In other words, you might not like what you found.

'So, are you going to ring the number and find out who is on the other end?' Clarissa asked.

Emily had been surprised that the person had given out their contact phone number, although she had been feeling a little reticent as there was no profile photo or details of who she would be calling. Despite that, Emily had still been mostly enthusiastic about making that call, until she'd spoken to Clarissa.

She thought of her mum's estrangement from her sister and wondered again what it had all been about. It was something her mother refused to talk about. She did want to find her aunt. However, she looked at the phone number, thought of the AncestryDNA's disclaimer, and began to have second thoughts.

'Those questions you have about your aunt in America, and cousins that you might have over there, could all be answered by that one phone call.'

Emily bit her lower lip and frowned.

'What's the matter?'

'But what if this … this person isn't—'

'Who you thought they were, namely your aunt, or a relative in America?'

Emily nodded. 'I've always felt that my parents have harboured a secret. As though there was something they've kept from me all these years.'

'What do you mean?'

Emily scratched her head. 'I don't know.'

'Then why don't you phone that number and find out who they are?'

'But what if, well, I don't like what I find out?'

Clarissa sighed heavily. 'I can't answer that, Emily. All I know is that you've opened Pandora's Box, and try as you might, you're going to find it very hard not to look inside.'

Emily looked at her phone. 'It's only going to be about two or three in the morning in America.'

Clarissa stared at her. 'You're not phoning someone in America. Look, the area code is +44. That's a British mobile phone.'

Emily bit her bottom lip and stared at her phone. 'I'll phone later.' She glanced at Clarissa. 'You think I should contact them now, don't you?'

Clarissa shrugged. 'Why leave it until later? Once the other guests come down for breakfast, I imagine you won't have time. Make the call, if for no other reason than I'm dying to know who it is.' Clarissa grinned. 'You know what I'm like – nosy as hell.'

Emily smiled. 'Yeah, I know that.'

'Please, do it for me.'

Emily was just about to dial the number when she heard a door close upstairs and footsteps heading along the landing. 'Damn,' she said under her breath.

'What is it?' Clarissa asked.

'I think someone is coming down for breakfast. I'll have to do it when I've got a spare moment.'

Clarissa looked disappointed. 'Okay.'

Emily watched Clarissa walk up the stairs, just as the couple who had arrived late last night made their way down. She heard her friend say, 'Morning!' to them as they passed on the stairs. 'Donut – no! Sorry.'

'Oh, don't worry, he's lovely.' Freya stopped to pet the dog. 'Isn't he sweet,' she said to Tarek.

'Er, yeah, sure.'

'He's too friendly by half,' said Clarissa, taking him by the collar and pulling him up the stairs.

'Morning,' Emily said to the couple when they reached the bottom stair. She noticed the young woman's expression change. Emily felt uncomfortable under her gaze. 'Breakfast is this way.'

'What's your name?'

Emily looked at her, surprised by the abrupt question.

'I'm Emily.'

'Emily?'

'Yes.' Emily had a strange feeling that she had met her before. Maybe the new guest felt the same. 'Do I know you?' she asked.

The guest peered at her. 'I don't think so. I just had the feeling we'd met before, that's all.'

Emily shrugged. If they had, she couldn't recall. 'Let me show you to the dining room. It's actually the conservatory overlooking the garden. You're the first down, so you've got it to yourselves. At least for the moment.'

As Emily showed them to a table, she still couldn't shake the feeling that she'd met their new guest, Freya, somewhere before.

❖

Freya waited until she was seated at a table before she said to Tarek, 'I wonder when the other guests will arrive for breakfast.'

'You're thinking of that woman, aren't you? You still think your father was having an affair with a woman called Wendy?'

'I don't know, but there was something going on, I know that.'

'So, you think she's here?'

'I hope so. I know the call was made from here.'

'But how will you know who it is?'

'It will be someone of my parents' generation.'

Tarek leaned across the table. 'Can we at least have breakfast and not confront someone in the middle of the dining room with all the guests here?'

'Don't worry, Tarek, I wouldn't dream of it.'

Tarek breathed a sigh of relief.

'But …'

'But what?'

'I don't want to bring it up, but your father is bound to come down to breakfast with his lady friend. What are you going to do when he does?'

'I haven't thought of that.'

'Will you try and not lift off? I mean, I know it hasn't been long since your mum … passed away. But doesn't he deserve to find someone else?'

Tarek sighed. 'I agree.'

'You do?'

'Of course. But what has thrown me is that it's so soon, you know?'

Freya looked at him sympathetically. 'I understand.'

She looked up as Emily, who was approaching the table. 'What can I get you for breakfast?'

Freya smiled at her, and she and Tarek both ordered a veggie cooked breakfast. She intended to enjoy her breakfast, although she would be keeping an eye out for the other guests. It meant she'd have to glance over her shoulder to look; they were sitting at the far end of the conservatory.

Freya heard footsteps and Emily wishing someone a good morning.

She was about to ask Tarek if he could see who had arrived, but although he'd already ordered breakfast, he had the menu up in front of his face and was still looking at the choices. She sighed and turned in her seat to look.

'Christ!' she said under her breath as the couple took their seats, eyes only for each other.

Freya knew she hadn't been spotted. She quickly turned in her seat to face Tarek.

He lowered the menu and caught her surprised expression. 'What is it?' He leaned to one side so he could see behind her and spotted his father. The lady sitting with him had her back to them. 'That's my father,' he whispered. 'I'm going over to say good morning. Hopefully, I won't give him a heart attack when he finds out I'm here.'

Freya grabbed his sleeve. 'Don't!' She stole a glance behind her. *What was her mum doing here? How did she know Tarek's father?*

Freya could not get her head around this turn of events. She'd come here to find out if her father had been having an affair, and instead she'd discovered her mum was having a secret liaison with Tarek's father. *Oh, my god.* She stared at Tarek. How was she going to tell him that his father's companion was her mum?

'You would rather we just let them enjoy breakfast together.'

Freya was thinking nothing of the sort. But she nodded, nonetheless.

Emily brought over their breakfast. Freya took one look at it and thought she was going to be sick. Thankfully she wasn't, but she had lost her appetite. While Tarek tucked in, Freya moved the food around on her plate.

'Do you want that sausage?' Tarek asked, eyeing her plate. 'These veggie sausages are amazing.' He'd already polished off his breakfast.

'No, I'm not that hungry.' Emily pushed the plate towards him. She picked up a slice of toast instead. She kept finding herself turning in her chair to stare at the couple.

'You can't wait to meet him, can you?' Tarek commented.

Freya frowned at them before turning in her chair. 'Oh, you have no idea.'

46

'How's breakfast going?'

Emily looked up at her mum, who was coming down the stairs carrying some towels for the laundry. She'd been upstairs making up beds and putting out fresh towels.

'Busy.'

'Did the guest arrive last night? I haven't been to the single room yet to change the towels and make up the bed.'

'Beds,' Emily corrected her.

Her mum raised her eyebrows.

'I had to sort out a folding bed. I'm not sure what happened but a couple arrived, not a single person as I expected.'

'Did you book them into the wrong room?'

'Of course not.' Emily hated that the guest was always right and that her mum assumed it was she who had made a mistake. 'I reiterated over the phone that it was the only room left, and it was a single. Freya was fine with that.'

'I'm sorry, what did you just say?'

'I said I reiterated that it was—'

'No, not that. You said *Freya*?''

'Yes, Freya. That's the name of the guest.'

Her mum dropped the towels in surprise.

Emily stared at her mum. 'What is it?'

Her mum raced around the reception desk to the computer. 'What is her home address? Show me the booking.'

'What's the matter?'

'Just show me the booking!'

Emily punched some keys and brought up the booking. 'She lives in Cambridge.'

'Oh my god.'

Emily picked up the towels and put them on the reception desk. She stared at her mum. 'What's going on?'

She heard her mum mumble, 'She can't be here,' before racing to the conservatory.

Emily followed her. They both stopped in the doorway. 'Where is she?'

'Over there.' Emily pointed, keeping her voice down. 'Do you know her?'

'Where's Alice?'

'She's there.' Emily pointed at Alice seated with her back to Freya. 'Hey, that's odd, they've both got the same surname.' Emily had been so busy that it hadn't registered until now. 'Is she Alice's daughter? I don't think she realises Freya is here, and Freya hasn't noticed her either.' Emily had a thought. 'It can't be a coincidence that they're both here.'

'How long is she staying?'

'Oh, just the night. They'll check out later this morning.'

'Good.'

Emily caught Clarissa looking her way. She'd come down to breakfast, leaving Donut upstairs. Alice had left her dog in her room too.

Emily followed her mum back to reception and watched her pick up the towels. She asked again, 'What's this all about? Do you know her?'

'Emily, just go back and serve the breakfasts please.'

'But Mum …' Emily frowned at her mum's back. Her mum had recognised Freya's name. She knew Alice too, Emily was sure of it. Emily's frown deepened. Freya did seem familiar somehow, although she still couldn't put her finger on where they might have met before.

'See to our guests, Emily,' her mum said. She'd cast a glance over her shoulder before making her way down the stairs and had caught Emily standing there staring into space.

'All right!' Emily turned on her heel and walked back to the dining room. She'd already cleared some plates. There wasn't much left to do. She went from table to table, offering tea and coffee refills. She walked over to Clarissa's table.

'Is something going on?' Clarissa asked.

'I don't know. My mum is being weird.'

'Really – what about?'

Emily glanced at Freya. She might overhear their conversation. 'I'll tell you later. Want a refill?'

'I'm fine, thanks.'

'Have you made that call yet?'

Emily shook her head. 'I haven't had a chance.'

'What about now?'

Emily cast her gaze around the room. The cooked breakfasts had been served, and toast, tea and coffee had been provided, so she really didn't have much to do right now until the guests had eaten, and she could clear some plates and dishes, and offer more toast or refills of tea and coffee.

'Go on, Emily. Ring the number.'

'Oh, all right.' Emily got out her mobile phone from the back pocket of her jeans as she walked to the door. She rang the number on the way out. She did an about-turn in the doorway when she heard a mobile phone ring tone in the conservatory. Coincidence? Emily ended the call. The other mobile phone belonging to one of the guests at breakfast immediately stopped ringing.

Emily's eyes locked with Clarissa's. Her friend was gesticulating with her phone for Emily to ring the number again.

Emily pressed the icon on her phone to call the number again. This time she stood in the doorway, waiting for someone to answer their phone.

She could see Clarissa looking around the conservatory. Joss was sitting at another table. He looked about him too. Omar and Alice just exchanged glances and shrugged; it clearly wasn't their mobile phones. Emily shifted her attention to the young couple. Freya took out her mobile phone and put it to her ear. Emily heard her voice down the phone. 'Hello?'

Emily was about to step forward when she spotted Alice turning around, looking in Freya's direction.

'Hello?' Freya said again.

Alice said, 'Freya, what on earth are you doing here?'

Freya turned in her seat.

Emily didn't reply. She caught Clarissa staring at her, holding her hands up as if to say, *What are you doing? Answer her!*

But Emily could see that Clarissa's attention was quickly being drawn back to Freya, who still had the mobile phone in her hand. Emily overhead Freya say, 'Mum, what are you doing here – with him?'

The young man with Freya said, 'Wait – that's your mother?'

Omar looked just as shocked as Alice, as he exclaimed, 'Tarek, what are *you* doing here?'

'We came to see you. Freya is doing a PhD in archaeology. She wanted to meet you. So, I thought I'd surprise you. It seems I'm the one who got the surprise.'

Emily could hear all this down her phone, although no one, apart from Clarissa, had spotted Emily standing in the doorway holding her mobile to her ear.

'It is not what you think, Tarek.'

Tarek asked Freya, 'Did you know?'

'Of course I didn't. I had no idea my mum was here. I came to find Wendy.'

Emily froze. So it *was* true – her mum did know Freya. But from where? And how come, according to the AncestryDNA website, they were related? Her relations were in America – weren't they?

Alice asked, 'What are you talking about, Freya?'

'Wendy, the woman who phoned my dad the other night. I think I used to meet Wendy and her daughter who was around my age, when Dad took me to London on day trips at the weekend.'

Emily stared at Freya. So that was why she seemed familiar. She remembered those trips to London with her mum, just the two of them. And she recalled playing with a girl – a dark-haired, dark-eyed girl in the swing-park. She'd had such fun on those trips. Her two half-siblings had never been there; it had always been just the two of them, their special time together. Now she knew where she'd seen Freya before. She had been a young girl then, but she was just as strikingly beautiful today.

Emily wasn't the only one staring at them. Clarissa and Joss looked their way.

Alice put her serviette on the table.

Freya still had her phone in her hand, forgetting she was on a call. Emily watched her pull up a chair to her table.

'I don't know how to tell you this, but I think Dad and a woman called Wendy, had an affair years ago and they had a daughter around my age. When Dad used to take me on trips with him to London, I think it was a ruse to meet Wendy and see her daughter – *their* daughter.'

Emily stared at them, her heart pounding in her chest. *Was it true?*

'Is it true?' asked Freya.

Alice stared at her. 'You used to meet a woman called Wendy?'

'Well, Dad did.'

Alice said, 'Give me your phone!'

'Why?'

'I haven't got mine and I want to speak to your father – right now!'

'So, you think it's true?'

Emily was still listening to all this, shocked at what she was hearing.

Tarek interrupted. 'Freya, who called your phone?'

She held it up. 'Oh, I don't know.' She put her phone to her ear again. 'Hello?'

Emily ended the call and ran from the doorway.

47

Emily came to an abrupt stop in the hallway and turned around when she heard her mum speaking to someone at the front door. 'What are you doing here? I told you not to come!'

Emily saw two men – an older guy around her parents' age and a young man – barge into the hallway. 'Where are they?'

'They're having breakfast. Look, Alice doesn't know yet that Freya is here. Go now before she sees you here.'

'But Freya …'

'I'll deal with that, Jeffrey.'

'How?'

'I don't know. I swear no one is going to find out. If you go. Now!'

'Find out what?'

Everyone turned around and looked at Emily.

'Emily, sweetheart, these people called in on the off-chance there was a room vacant.'

Emily folded her arms and frowned at her mum for telling her an outright lie. She ignored her and turned to the older man. 'Are you Alice's husband?'

Before he answered her question, his mobile phone rang.

Emily watched him answer his mobile. 'Alice?'

And that answered Emily's question. She stared at him, thinking, *Oh my god, are you my father?*

'Yes, okay. I'm, er. right here, in the guest house.'

A moment later, Alice, Freya, Tarek and Omar walked out of the conservatory, heading their way. The young man with Alice's husband immediately launched into an apology about telling Freya's dad where she was, before his eyes shifted to Tarek. 'What's he doing here?'

Freya appeared to avoid the question.

'Did you get my letter?' asked Alice.

'What letter?'

'So, you didn't get *my* letter, but I found the letter addressed to you from a woman called Wendy …'

Emily noticed that she'd let the sentence hang, obviously waiting for an explanation.

When it wasn't forthcoming, she added, 'Freya told me that you used to meet her years ago in London. Were you having an affair? Are you still having an affair?'

Emily looked from her mum to Jeffrey. When were they going to tell Alice that Wendy was standing right there, in front of them? She had already realised Alice wouldn't know that because her mum went by her middle name, Anthea. Only people who knew her mum well were aware that her first name was really Wendy. Emily stared hard at Jeffrey.

Jeffrey still hadn't answered Alice's question. Instead, his eyes drifted to Omar. 'Who is this?'

Freya stepped in. 'What is going on? Dad, did you have an affair with a woman called Wendy?'

He turned to Freya.

'I heard you on the phone talking to her.'

Jeffrey heaved a sigh. 'Look, let's talk about this privately.'

'We can go into the lounge,' suggested Alice.

'I'm coming too,' said Emily.

Everyone turned around to look at Emily. Just as she expected, her mum said, 'Emily, this has got nothing to do with you.'

'Is that a fact?' Emily said. She had it on the tip of her tongue to tell Alice who her mum was, but first she chose that moment to take out her mobile phone and ring Freya's number again.

Freya answered. 'Hello.'

'Hello.'

Freya lowered her mobile phone and looked at Emily. 'What's going on? Why are you phoning my mobile?'

'Don't you recognise me from those trips to London?'

Freya stared at her. 'I thought you seemed familiar. You're the girl I used to play with.'

'I got your number from AncestryDNA,' Emily said to Freya. 'Have you checked the site since you signed up?'

Freya shook her head.

Alice and Jeffrey said in unison, 'You used AncestryDNA?'

Freya nodded. 'Jolene suggested it. It's all the rage in America.'

Wendy turned to Emily. 'What were you doing on AncestryDNA?'

'I wanted to find my auntie, and my cousins if I have any, in America. But I found Freya instead.'

Emily caught sight of Gerald. He must have walked up the stairs from the basement kitchen and seen them all standing in the hall by the front door. She wondered how long he'd been listening to all this, unnoticed behind the group. Gerald stepped forward. 'Wendy, what's going on?'

'Wendy?' Alice turned to her in surprise.

Emily looked at her mum and held her breath, waiting for her response.

'I'm Anthea.'

Alice looked confused. 'But Gerald just called you—'

'That's my first name, but I prefer to go by the name you know me as – Anthea.'

Alice turned to Jeffrey. 'So, you two were meeting up behind my back when the girls were young?'

Jeffrey looked at her sheepishly.

She frowned at him. 'But that was never agreed, Jeffrey. Why would you do that?'

Gerald let out a tremendous groan as he turned to his wife, and said, 'I told you your decision would come back to haunt us.'

Wendy whirled around. 'Oh, so it was *my* decision, was it?'

Alice stepped in. 'Excuse me, Gerald, but how was it just *her* decision? We were all involved, you, me, Wendy, and Jeffrey.'

Freya and Emily exchanged glances. Emily didn't know what they were on about, but one thing she did want to clear up was what exactly had been going on between her mum and Freya's dad. 'Mum, were you having an affair with Freya's dad? Am I Jeffrey's daughter?'

Wendy turned to her daughter. 'Of course not. Whatever gave you that idea?'

'The trips to London, just you and me, to meet Jeffrey and—
'

'Excuse me.' Omar, who had been standing apart from the

group, stepped forward, interrupting. He peered at Freya. 'Tarek – you haven't had relations with this girl, have you?'

'Dad! That is none of your business.'

Emily caught the young man who had arrived with Alice's husband staring at Freya.

Tarek frowned. 'Well, you're one to talk, aren't you, Dad? You are carrying on with Alice!'

'Whatever you think, Tarek, nothing happened!'

'I saw you.'

Alice turned to Emily. 'Excuse me?'

'You were going to your room, then you changed your mind. I saw you heading along the hall towards Omar's room last night.'

'We had a cup of tea. That was all.'

'Is that true – Dad?'

Omar nodded at Tarek. 'We are just old friends. Nothing happened.'

Jeffrey looked at his wife. 'Old friends? How long has this been going on?'

Alice sighed, 'Nothing has been going on, Jeffrey.'

'But he said—'

'That was a long time ago.'

Omar said, 'Is she … is Freya my daughter?'

Jeffrey looked at him sharply. 'Why would you think that?'

Alice and Omar exchanged a look.

'Oh, my god! You slept together?'

48

'Can we talk about this privately?' said Alice. They were all still standing in the hallway by the front door. This wasn't a conversation she wanted to have in front of an audience.

Jeffrey didn't budge.

Neither did anybody else.

He shook his head. 'I don't understand … How? When? We never spent a night apart after we were married!'

Alice heaved a sigh and looked about her. This wasn't how she pictured telling Jeffrey about Omar, but then perhaps this was just what she deserved for cheating on her husband. Her face went bright crimson as she said, 'Remember when we came here for our wedding anniversary?'

'How could I forget?'

'We rowed. I took off and went for a walk alone. I have no idea how far I'd walked or for how long. In hindsight, it was a stupid thing to do, go out alone walking in the dark, but Omar and his friends happened along. They brought me back to the guest house, where I stayed the night.

'With Omar?'

She nodded.

'Then you slipped back to our room before I woke up. You thought I hadn't noticed.'

Alice wasn't proud of that. She'd made it appear to Omar that she was staying at the guest house on her own and told him she didn't want to spend the night alone.

Jeffrey said, 'That explains why you didn't want to go down to breakfast that morning, in case we bumped into Omar.'

'You remember that?' She bit her lip. 'He left after breakfast, and we never saw each other again, until a few days ago when I spotted him in Cambridge.'

'So, you agreed to meet up here, have another affair?'

'It wasn't an affair.'

'A one-night stand then.'

Alice looked at the floor. 'I had no idea he'd be here.'

'Would you have left me for him, back then, if it wasn't for …' He trailed off.

Alice said in a small voice, 'Maybe. I don't know.'

'If it wasn't for *what*?' said Omar, looking from Alice to Jeffrey. Neither of them answered his question. He fixed his attention on Freya. 'Is she mine?'

Everyone turned to look at Freya.

Jeffrey shook his head, and said matter-of-factly, 'She isn't, Omar.'

'Well, you would say that, wouldn't you?' Omar shot back.

'Say it isn't true,' Freya pleaded.

'He's right, Freya. You're not his child,' said Alice. 'You can't be.'

'After what you've just revealed,' Freya said, biting back tears as she eyed Omar, 'how can you be so sure without a DNA test?'

Emily nodded her head, agreeing with that argument.

'I don't need one to know.' Alice continued, 'Remember that night, Omar, you said what you wanted more than anything was to have a son?' Alice glanced at Tarek. 'I knew I couldn't give you that.'

Omar shook his head from side to side. 'There are no certainties in life, I understand that. But we could have tried, if we'd stayed together.'

Alice breathed a heavy sigh. 'I'm afraid no amount of trying would have given us a son. You see, our marriage problems …' her eyes flickered to Jeffrey, 'were stemming from *my* problem. I'm infertile. I can't have children.'

Jeffrey took her hand, surprising her by his gentle touch as she added, 'I didn't know until after I was married and we started trying for a family.'

Freya said, 'But that's just not true – you had me!'

Alice cast a gaze at Jeffrey, Wendy and Gerald, her eyes finally settling on Freya. 'I am *so* sorry. We should have told you.'

49

'Am I adopted?' asked Freya.

'Not officially.'

'What does that mean?' She looked around the room. Everyone was seated in the lounge. Tarek had joined her because she needed him to be there, and Omar was seated next to his son.

'And what do you mean *we* should have told you?' She turned from her parents and eyed Wendy and Gerald. They stared at the floor, heads bowed, avoiding eye-contact. 'You *all* knew?'

There were nods of heads, but no one said anything.

'I don't understand.' She turned to her parents. 'I don't know these people. What's it got to do with them?

'It's got everything to do with them – isn't that right, Jeffrey?'

Freya caught him glance sheepishly at her before answering, 'Er, yes.'

Freya's breath caught in her throat. 'Wait, are you trying to tell me that Wendy and Gerald are my *real* parents?'

Alice and Jeffrey furiously shook their heads. 'No, of course not,' Alice replied. 'Look, let me explain.'

Freya folded her arms and eyed her suspiciously, the look in her face clearly suggesting she didn't know what to think.

Alice continued, 'We'd returned to the guest house on our second wedding anniversary. We'd honeymooned here. But this time we weren't in a good place. I wasn't in a good place. It was the night we rowed and I … took off.' she glanced at Omar. She'd already told them what had happened that night. 'Well, in the morning …'

'In the morning …?' Freya prompted her.

'It was a miracle. *You* were a miracle, Freya.'

'What are you talking about?'

'I heard a baby crying. That wasn't unusual in this household at that time. Anthea had a baby girl.' Alice paused, glancing at her. 'Or should I call you Wendy?'

Wendy stole a glance at her and shrugged.

Alice continued. 'I thought she had twins.'

Emily looked at her mum. 'Twins? What made you think that, Alice?'

'There were *two* babies. At first, I wasn't aware one of the babies wasn't hers. It was the summer when we were there, and that week I enjoyed sitting on the lawn in the summer with the babies lying on blankets, and I often accompanied Anthea – I mean Wendy – to the beach, pushing them down there in their strollers. I became very attached to one of them – it was very wrong of me. Then I discovered the baby, another girl, had been left with Wendy by a relative.'

Alice turned to Wendy. 'You weren't coping but couldn't face the thought of putting the baby up for adoption to go to strangers.' Alice turned to Emily. 'She had a baby of her own – you, Emily, and two other children, and a guest house she was still in the throes of doing up. She couldn't cope with another baby too, so…'

Freya stared at her mother, wide-eyed. 'Oh. My. God. So you took me?'

'Wendy had got to know us, me. We could offer you a wonderful home, a good upbringing, loving parents.'

'Loving parents? What about my own parents? Did you even bother to try and contact them?'

Alice gave Jeffrey a sideways glance. He looked at his hands.

Freya got out of her seat. 'Oh. My. God. You stole a baby!' She looked at Gerald and Wendy. 'And you were all in it together?'

Alice swallowed. 'It wasn't like that. I just explained. Your mother abandoned you, left you with a relative.'

'But who was she?' Freya looked at Wendy. When she got no response, she turned to Alice. 'What if she was a teenage mother, and was frightened and alone? Didn't you want to find out who she was, why she had abandoned me and left me with her?' Freya pointed at Wendy.

Alice sighed. 'When I took you home, I was holding a baby in my arms that I didn't want to let go, but I realised there was someone out there who wasn't holding their child. I …. I knew I must return to the guest house and try and find her, the mother, and … and hand you back if that's what she wanted. But …'

'But …?'

Alice looked at Jeffrey. 'He convinced me not to.'

Freya turned to him. 'Why would you do that?'

❖

Emily stared wide-eyed at Freya. She tried to get her head round all this. She couldn't. Something didn't add up. She looked at her mum. 'Sorry, but I just need to clear one thing up. So, you didn't have an affair with Alice's husband?'

Wendy scoffed, 'Of course not. And before you ask, *you* are *our* daughter, Gerald's and mine.'

'But Freya is related to me and to you guys then. You said she was … is … a relative's child.'

There was a long silence. 'Mum? If she's not my half-sister, then what relation is she to me – to us?'

When she didn't answer the question, Emily got out her phone. She'd just realised there was something she'd forgotten to do that could answer all this. In her haste to get in contact with this new relative she'd discovered, who'd turned out to be Freya, she'd failed to check the details of the DNA match. Hopefully, it would tell her just what relation Freya was to her. 'I'm logging back on to AncestryDNA.'

'Why?' Jeffrey shot back.

'Because I can find out for myself, for ourselves.' She pointedly looked at Freya.

Wendy leaned forward in her seat. 'How accurate is this DNA stuff anyway?'

Jeffrey said, 'You know, there's always room for error, surely. What if DNA tests get mixed up? That wouldn't be beyond the realms of possibility. You hear about it all the time.'

'Do you?' Alice said flatly. She stared at her husband, catching him surreptitiously looking Wendy's way. She shifted her gaze to Gerald, who looked decidedly nervous. He stared around the room and looked anywhere but at her. 'You didn't answer Emily's question.' Alice narrowed her eyes. 'What is it you're not telling us?'

Jeffrey smiled nervously, glancing at Wendy and Gerald. 'I'm sorry – who are you asking?'

'All three of you.'

Freya, Emily, Tarek, Omar and Theo were looking at them and had caught those nervous glances too. Everyone in the room knew they were hiding something.

Wendy said, 'Jeffrey, I think *you* should tell her. Come on, Gerald, we must go. We've got guests to see to.'

Gerald looked at her in surprise. 'But Wendy, it wasn't just Jeffrey's decision.'

Emily exchanged a glance with Freya. 'Nobody leaves the room. I think we all need to hear this.'

Theo stood up. 'I'll leave, as this is a family thing.'

'Sit down, Theo,' said Jeffrey. 'You're as good as family.'

Freya closed her eyes. 'Actually, I'm breaking off the engagement.' Freya slowly slid the ring off her finger. She crossed the room, and handed it to Theo. 'I am *so* sorry to do this to you.'

Theo took the ring. He didn't appear surprised by this revelation. 'I thought there was something going on. I didn't mean to tell your dad about where you were going, but then when he set off, I wanted to come too. I had a feeling what you wanted to talk to me about had something to do with this trip.' He glanced at Tarek knowingly.

Freya bowed her head. 'Sorry.'

'You know what, Freya? There's nothing to be sorry about. I knew this was coming. I mean, we got on really well, there's no denying that, but sometimes I looked at our married friends and … well ...' Theo stared at the ring. 'I don't know how to explain it, but I didn't feel we were …' He appeared to be searching for the right word.

'Soulmates?'

Theo's eyes drifted to Tarek again. 'Yes, soulmates.' Theo

slipped the ring into his trouser pocket. 'I think I'll leave now.'

'No, Theo.' Jeffrey reached for his arm. 'And you won't be packing your things and leaving either on our return.'

'But we're not getting married anymore.'

Jeffrey shrugged. 'So?'

Freya smiled at Theo. 'You don't get it – do you? You're like a son to him.'

'But I'm not going to be his son-in-law.'

'That doesn't matter.'

Jeffrey said, 'No, it doesn't. I want you to stay as long as you like. I've got to see how that novel you're writing pans out.'

Freya frowned. 'You might as well stay, Theo. Look at me, I'm not related to them either, so they might as well adopt you too while they're at it. Oh sorry, not officially, I should add.'

'Now Freya, that's not fair,' admonished Jeffrey.

'Isn't it?'

'No, because Emily is correct.' He took a breath and looked from Gerald to Wendy. 'You are related to them, but also to … to me. You're my biological daughter.'

Emily stared at him. How was that possible? She was the same age as Freya. Her mum and Freya's dad couldn't have—

'I slept with Wendy's sister.'

50

'You did *what?*' Alice was on her feet. 'And who in heaven's name is Wendy's sister?'

Before Jeffrey could get a word in, she whirled around to Wendy. 'You knew! That's why, for the first ten years of her life, you met up with Jeffrey in London so that you could see your niece – so you could see Freya!'

Emily stared at her cousin.

Jeffrey bit his fingernail.

Alice said, 'This all makes sense now, why you persuaded me not to look for the mother – because you *knew* her. Because you, you …' Alice couldn't say it. She then had a thought. She turned to Wendy. 'So, that's why you were vague when it came to which relative had left the baby with you. You knew Jeffrey was the father too!'

Jeffrey took a deep breath. 'Look, we couldn't tell you. You would have left me if you'd found out.'

'But all these years I thought you'd falsified the birth certificate, putting your name as the father, and I was complicit, going along with it.'

'Wait! You falsified my birth certificate?' Freya blurted.

'No, of course I didn't,' said Jeffrey.

'But I didn't know that!' Alice seethed. She'd lived all these years with that hanging over her head, afraid someone in authority would find out. She'd colluded in what she thought was a lie as she foresaw problems down the road bringing up Freya because they hadn't officially adopted her. She knew her name wasn't on the birth certificate; it was Freya's birth mother who was named there. What she had believed, though, was that Jeffrey had falsely added his own name on the birth certificate as the baby's father. All those times she'd been beside herself with worry that someone would find out when they'd needed to use her birth certificate to register her for nursery and school, and apply for a passport, when in fact the birth certificate hadn't been falsified at all. There had been no wrongdoing – not officially, anyway. Simply, Freya's father had decided to bring her up and it was an understanding between the two parents which wouldn't have needed to go through the courts unless there was a dispute over this arrangement, which there was not.

But all these years, Alice had not been privy to this information. It was never about the fact that he had falsified his name on the birth certificate, it was the fact that he hadn't! She glared at her husband. But there was still one thing she couldn't understand. 'But when … how?' Alice realised she sounded just like her husband a short time earlier when he'd discovered she'd slept with Omar.

Jeffrey stole a glance at his daughter, before turning to face Alice. 'Remember that time we came here, and we'd rowed over the fact that we couldn't start a family, even though I swore to you that I was okay with that. You got in the car and left, returning home on your own.'

Alice hadn't thought about that in a long time. Apart from their honeymoon, the other trip here that had always stuck in her mind was their wedding anniversary two years later when she'd met Omar at the guest house – and of course baby Freya. But now she recalled that short break in between, when Jeffrey had ended up staying a night at the guest house alone – or so she'd thought. He'd returned the next day by train to Cambridge.

They'd never talked about that episode. And now she knew why. The dates tallied. Nine months later, Freya had been born, and not long afterwards they'd returned to the guest house for that holiday on their wedding anniversary.

'I got a bit drunk that night.' Jeffrey lowered his gaze. 'A young woman was staying in the guest house. I swear I didn't know it was Wendy's sister. We slept together. It was a stupid mistake – on the one hand.'

'On the one hand?'

'When we'd returned here months later for our anniversary, I realised that morning at the guest house could either be the breaking of us – or the making of us. There was a baby. It was what you'd always wanted. It was your dream come true.'

'But she wasn't mine.'

'I know, but she was mine. And I wanted to keep her, bring her up – with you. I just don't think that would have happened if you'd known she was the result of my one-night stand with Wendy's sister.'

'So, did you know about the baby, *your* baby, when we booked to return and spend our anniversary here?'

She took Jeffrey's silence as a yes.

Freya stood there with her mouth open. 'Oh, my god, this all makes sense now. I've never seen my birth certificate. There's been no need. You applied for my first adult passport nearly ten years ago. I always knew I was born in Suffolk – it's written in black and white on my passport. But you two told me when I brought it up once that you were on holiday there, I mean here, when you were heavily pregnant and I came early. That's why I was born in a Suffolk hospital instead of Cambridge. But that was a lie!'

The room was deathly silent. Alice stole a glance at her.

'How long did you think you could keep this from me?'

Still silence.

'This is crazy! How could you all be so stupid. Didn't either of you think that one day I might need my birth certificate?'

Jeffrey shook his head. 'Once you've held a passport, you can simply renew it.'

Freya threw her arms in the air. 'I'm not just talking about passport renewal! I might need it for a job or … or …'

'Getting married,' offered Tarek.

Freya turned to him. 'Yes, I'd need a copy of my birth certificate.'

'No, you wouldn't,' said Gerald, 'you can just provide your passport.'

Wendy nudged him to shut his mouth.

Freya stared at them. 'Didn't it ever occur to you all that the truth would out, at some point, about my real mother?'

Alice swallowed. This was just what she had dreaded all these years. They should have told her. She shouldn't have listened to Jeffrey. She knew what he'd been doing all these years – protecting her from the truth, that he'd had a one-night stand with Freya's mother. But now all the lies and deceit on all their parts had finally come home to roost.

Freya wasn't the only one who wanted to know everything.

Alice stared at her husband. 'What about Freya's mother?' She turned to Wendy.

'My little sister was in love with an American from a local air base.'

Freya interrupted. 'What's that got to do with anything?'

Jeffrey said, 'Let her explain.'

'Our parents didn't want them seeing each other. They made her break it off. He wanted her to return to the States with him. She was very young. He was older …' Wendy's eyes drifted to Emily. 'His regiment left the UK the next day, and she was beside herself. She came to live with me at the guest house, but that night she got drunk, and I found out she'd slept with a guest. There was only one guest that night – well, two, but they'd had a blazing row and his wife, Alice, had left. Months later, the love of my sister's life, the American, got in touch. He asked her again to go to America. But there was a problem.'

'Me,' said Freya.

Wendy continued. 'She stayed to have you here, at the guest house, and asked me to take care of you. She said she'd be back for you when she'd plucked up the courage to tell him. I knew my sister, and I knew him. He was a staunch Catholic, and his family would never accept my sister if they'd found out she'd had a child out of wedlock. She'd made her choice when she got on that flight and left you behind.'

Wendy fell silent for a moment.

Emily looked at her mother. 'Is that why you've been estranged from your sister, because she'd left her baby?'

'I want to say that is all there is to it, Emily, but there are always two sides to every story. She asked me to raise Freya, with

Gerald, but I already had two young children, a guest house to run, and a baby of my own. How would I cope with another child? But she didn't care about that.'

Wendy focused her attention on Jeffrey. 'I told my sister what I had intended to do – contact the father and tell him about the baby.' Wendy exchanged a glance with Gerald. 'We knew they were good sorts, decent, hard-working, and they had a lovely home in Cambridge they'd worked hard for. And his wife desperately wanted a child. Although my sister gave her blessing, she did so grudgingly, and things were never the same between us again. I knew she felt I had let her down, but Gerald and I talked things through. Freya might not grow up knowing her mother, but that didn't mean she had to be deprived of her other parent too. It just seemed the right thing to do, for Freya to have an opportunity to grow up with one of her parents.'

Wendy shifted her attention to Alice. 'When we contacted Jeffrey and told him about the baby, we weren't sure how he would react. Of course, Jeffrey was shocked. There was a baby that was his, right here in the guest house. But he so wanted a child. I'm so sorry, Alice, that we had to hatch a plan and deceive you to take the baby. Gerald never did agree with it. He wanted us to tell you the truth.'

Emily smiled affectionately at her dad. That was him all over. She wouldn't have expected anything less.

'I'm sorry, Alice. We played you. We played on your innermost desire to have a baby. And we delivered you one on a plate, along with a side order of lies.'

Wendy fell silent.

Jeffrey spoke up. 'We took the baby on the understanding that we would sever all ties with the guest house. I knew Alice couldn't take this baby home and then have the mother appear, a week, a month, a year, even ten years later to take her back.' He turned to Alice. 'I couldn't do that to you.'

'But you met Wendy in London.'

'Yes. She wrote to me. She couldn't sever all ties with her niece. So we agreed to meet.'

'Why did it stop?' Freya asked.

'You got too old for swing parks. That was the only way we could meet up without arousing suspicion.'

'It wasn't just that, Jeffrey, was it?'

Jeffrey glanced at Wendy. 'No, it wasn't.'

Wendy frowned. 'I made a mistake. On your tenth birthday, my sister got in contact out of the blue. She'd told her husband about Freya. She said she couldn't stand it any longer, she had to tell him the truth.'

Freya blinked. 'What happened?'

'Of course he was stunned by this revelation. My sister wanted to visit me, and he came too. They wanted to meet Freya.'

Alice stared at her. 'I never knew this.'

Jeffrey sat there, shaking his head. 'Neither did I until I met Wendy in London that summer, and she had brought along her sister and husband. I was shocked and angry that you didn't forewarn me, Wendy. I would never have agreed to it.'

'You wouldn't have come.'

'Damn right!' said Jeffrey.

'I thought I owed my sister. I imagined all she wanted to do was get a glimpse of her daughter in the flesh, rather than the photos.'

'You sent her photos?' said Jeffrey in surprise. 'They were for you.'

'Sorry.'

Alice stared at Wendy. 'She wanted to take her – didn't she?'

'Wendy turned to Alice. 'To begin with, I wasn't sure what her intentions were. In hindsight, I realised she could see the beautiful woman she was going to be, and she wanted her back.'

'After all those years?' said Freya. 'How selfish.'

'Yes, I thought so too. Especially when I found out that she couldn't have any more children.'

Emily said, 'There are no American cousins?'

Wendy smiled at her daughter, shaking her head. 'No, honey. The only cousin you have is Freya.'

'I wish I'd known about her.'

'I am so sorry, Emily.'

Emily said, 'What happened. Did she try and take her?'

'No. It was her husband who stepped in. He said that if had been his daughter, he wouldn't want anybody to take her away from him. He'd put himself in Jeffrey's shoes and told his wife that what is done, is done. There was no going back. Freya was a happy, thriving child, and his wife had no right to turn Freya's life upside down on a whim, just because it suited her now to have her back in her life.'

They all fell silent.

Wendy said, 'I'm so sorry, Freya. If you'd like to meet her sometime, I can arrange …' She trailed off when she saw Freya shaking her head.

'I'd understand, sweetheart,' Alice added softly. 'You must have questions that only she can answer.'

'Is that why my maternal grandparents, your parents, didn't want anything to do with me – because they knew I was no relation?'

'It wasn't you, Freya, it was me. They knew I couldn't have children. They anticipated I might think of adoption. Then a baby appears without going through an adoption process. I made the mistake of confiding in my mother what had happened at the guest house, and they virtually disowned me, said it was wrong, and I should give you back to the lady at the guest house. But I couldn't do it. I wouldn't. I loved you so much, Freya. My heart would have broken if I'd had to give you up.'

Freya stared at the woman who had brought her up as her own. She was thinking about how her life had turned out. If she'd grown up in America, perhaps she wouldn't be the person she was today. In fact, she was pretty sure she wouldn't be. Her love of archaeology stemmed from Alice and all those wonderful books she'd grown up around. And of course, Cambridge, her home.

And she would never have met Tarek, the love of her life. And she probably would never have known her biological father, who most likely would never write that novel and be the great published writer he aspired to be – but that didn't matter to her one bit. He was a great teacher, and he'd taught her how to live her best life. They both had.

By leaving her behind, her real mother had given her the most stupendous gift; the life she'd had right here in England, growing up with the two people she loved most in the world. Of course, Freya wasn't going to tell them all this right now. She was still angry and upset about the secret they'd kept from her. But in time, she knew she could forgive them – how could she not? They were her parents.

Alice and Jeffrey said in unison, 'Can you ever forgive us, Freya?'

'Can you ever forgive *us*?' said Gerald, taking Wendy's hand in his.

Freya looked at Gerald and Wendy. 'I understand why you did it. And I'm glad.'

Wendy sighed in relief. Gerald slapped his thigh. 'That's fantastic.'

'As for you.' She turned in her seat to face her parents. She could feel Tarek's hand close around hers, giving it a gentle squeeze, an unspoken suggestion to go easy on them. *They are your parents, after all.* Freya's whole body seemed to tingle at his touch. How could she be away from him when he left for Alexandria? There was a simple solution to that. She looked at her parents. 'Mum.'

Alice's eyes went wide at Freya still calling her Mum. 'Yes?'

'I don't know what this thing is between you and Omar.' She had it on the tip of her tongue to say that she wanted it to stop. But how could she? They were all adults. If her mum still loved Omar, how could she stand in her way? 'I want you to go home with Dad and have some marriage counselling, or at least talk to one another before you … you …' Her eyes drifted to Omar.

Jeffrey grinned at this suggestion. For a moment, he thought he'd lost her – both of them. But now, although he knew it was possible she'd still leave him for Omar, or perhaps leave him anyway after she'd found out the truth, at least Freya had given him a chance to put things right. Oh, how he loved his daughter. He grinned at her.

Freya kept her face straight. 'As for you, Dad.'

His smile faltered. 'Yes?'

'You're not selling the house.'

'Excuse me? But I'm doing it for you.'

'I know you are, and that's the problem. I think you've put me first all my life. What about what Mum wants?'

Alice stared at her.

Jeffrey shook his head. 'But you need money, a deposit for a house.'

'Theo and I aren't getting married. But that's beside the point. I'm not settling in Cambridge. At least not right now.'

Alice said, 'What do you mean?'

Freya squeezed Tarek's hand. Before they went down to breakfast she'd told him how she felt about him. He couldn't live without her either. Right now, the plan was for her to return to Alexandria with him and try to get a job in the famous library while she finished her PhD. She told her parents the news.

'That's wonderful news,' gushed Alice. She looked over at Theo, 'Sorry, Theo.'

He shook his head, staring at Tarek. 'I could never give her that life.'

'But you're going to be a writer,' said Freya. 'I know you are.' She looked at her dad. 'And that brings me to the other thing. You'll let Theo stay on with you, living in your house until he gets on his feet with work?'

Jeff smiled. 'Of course he can. As I said before, he's like a son to me.'

'I'm right here, guys.'

Jeff turned to him. 'If that's okay with you.'

'Of course it is, if that's okay with you, Mrs B?'

Alice shook her head, although she couldn't help smiling. Oh, how she'd missed Theo helping himself to snacks and calling her Mrs B An old saying came to mind – when your son gets married, you lose a son but gain a daughter. With Freya moving to Egypt, it felt as though she was losing a daughter but gaining a son. And soon she would gain another one – Omar's son, Tarek. But then their lives, although conventional in appearance, had actually been anything but. 'Will you be back?' Alice asked Freya.

'Of course. Cambridge is my home. It always will be.'

'And the guest house?' ventured Emily. 'Will you visit us too?'

Wendy said, 'You know I have photos of you two together before I … before you started your new life in Cambridge. Would you like to see them?'

Freya and Emily nodded. Freya said, 'I would love to come back and visit you both, if you would like me too?'

Emily and Wendy smiled. 'Of course we would.'

'Perhaps next time we could book a room with a double bed?' She gazed at Tarek.

'Ahem.' Tarek looked embarrassed.

Freya saw Omar's gaze settle on Alice.

Alice wasn't looking at Omar, but at her husband. She stood up and held out her hand. 'Come on, let's go home.'

Jeffrey smiled. That was music to his ears.

'And book those marriage counselling sessions.'

'Of course.' He winked at Freya, mouthing, *Thank you.* As Omar had said, there were no certainties in life, but at least this was a start, a chance to find out if they had a future together. He glanced at her hand in his and thought that it boded well – very well indeed – as they walked hand-in-hand out the door. He glanced over his shoulder. 'Theo – are you coming?'

'Yes, be with you in a sec.'

Theo stood up too. He walked over to Tarek and held out his hand. Tarek tentatively took it, and they shook hands.

'I just want you to know there are no hard feelings, Tarek.'

Freya heard Tarek breath an audible sigh of relief. 'Thank you, Theo.'

Theo turned to Freya. 'I love your parents.'

'I know.'

'You will come home if things don't work out, won't you? They're *your* parents. Just because I'm there—'

Freya put a finger to his lips. 'Shush. It's fine. I'm sure you don't want me to say this, but you feel like a brother to me.'

Theo smiled. 'Actually, I feel the same way – I mean about you being like a sister to me. I've felt like that for a while.'

'Why didn't you tell me sooner?'

'I'd proposed. I felt things had carried us along and there was the expectation from our friends, from your parents …' He trailed off. He didn't have to say any more. They both understood.

Theo followed her parents out of the room. She could hear them trooping upstairs to collect her mum's luggage and her pets to take home.

'Well, we'd better get on,' said Wendy. 'We've got guests to see to.'

Wendy and Gerald stood up and both hugged Freya before leaving the room.

Emily lingered. She stared at her cousin. 'I wish we'd grown up together. I do. It would have been such fun having someone my own age. You would have been like a sister.'

'I know. I grew up an only child, but you've got two older half-siblings.'

'Yes, they're your cousins too. Next time you visit you must meet them.'

'I'll be sure to do that,' said Freya, smiling.

Tarek took Freya's hand. They walked towards the door. Tarek turned around to his father. 'Will you return with us to Cambridge today? We have to be back at the museum for the opening of the exhibition tomorrow.'

Omar shook his head. 'I think I'll stay on a couple of days.'

But what about the opening, and the press conference in Cambridge? You already missed the one in London.'

Omar smiled. 'I think it's time I handed over the reins to the next generation of talented archaeologists.'

Tarek frowned. 'I don't understand …'

Freya stared at Omar and turned to look at Tarek.

Tarek said, 'You want me to officially open the exhibition and speak at the press conference?' He looked taken aback.

'Of course. I notice it is my name that is in all the papers and on social media, but I wasn't the only one on the dig. In fact, it was you, Tarek, that was instrumental in locating the new tomb.'

'You were?' said Freya in surprise. 'You never told me that.'

Omar shook his head. 'Tarek has diligently worked hard in my shadow, refusing to take any credit away from the great, eminent archaeologist and Egyptologist, Omar Youssef. But it is high time the world discovered your talent. I think it's time you stepped up and took credit where credit is due, Tarek. Besides, I want to retire.'

'Retire? You said you'd never do that!'

'Well, from the limelight at least.'

Tarek cast a gaze around the guest house. 'I don't think Alice will be back.'

Omar surprised him by smiling. 'I know. I don't think I will be either. It was never meant to be – Alice and me. I realise that now. That's why I had such a wonderful marriage to your mother.

And I had you, my dear son. It was meant to be.'

Freya saw tears in Tarek's eyes.

Omar walked up to them. 'But you and Freya. You *are* meant to be. You won't change your mind. You will you return with us to Alexandria, Freya?'

She smiled. 'Oh, yes.'

'Then it's settled.' He leaned in and kissed her on both cheeks. 'Welcome to my family.'

51

Emily watched Freya and Tarek head out to the garden. Although it was freezing outside, the sun was shining and the views down to the cove in the winter sunlight were very romantic. She was disappointed they couldn't stay beyond today, but she understood they had to leave; they had an important exhibition to open in Cambridge.

She walked into the dining room to find Joss still eating breakfast. He smiled her way. She smiled shyly back. She caught Clarissa waving at her.

Emily walked over.

'God, you were gone ages. What happened?'

'She's my cousin.'

'Your cousin? From America?'

'No, from Cambridge.'

'Cambridge?' Clarissa looked at her.

Emily grinned. 'It's a very long story.' She caught Joss glancing her way and threw him a smile. She was looking forward to the evening meal he'd booked for them at a little restaurant in Southwold.

She turned to her best friend. 'I saw you talking with Omar.

Did you get your story, Clarissa?'

Clarissa frowned. 'Not exactly.'

Emily assumed Clarissa was after Omar's personal story. She thought of Alice and the conversation she'd been privy to a few moments earlier. Emily didn't feel inclined to share with her best friend just what she'd heard about that night years earlier which Alice had spent here at the guest house with Omar. That was their affair, and certainly not something either of them would want to make its way into a national or international newspaper.

Emily remained tight-lipped. 'Oh, that's a shame. So there was no scoop, no article you could publish?'

'Well yes and no. Omar is stepping down. He said he will continue his work as a professor at Alexandria University, and publish books and articles, but he won't do interviews, press conferences or open exhibitions. He said it is time for the world to be introduced to a new and very talented Egyptologist.' Clarissa shrugged. 'And that was it! So much for getting my exclusive.'

Emily grinned.

Clarissa frowned. 'Why are you looking so pleased? I just told you that I didn't get a thing.'

'Oh, but you did. You got your exclusive.'

Clarissa shook her head. 'I don't understand …'

'He's told you that he's retiring from the limelight, and there's a new kid on the block.'

'Yeah – so?'

'Well, that's your story.'

'But it's not much of a story if I don't know who—' Clarissa stopped abruptly. She stared at Emily. 'You know who he's talking about, don't you?'

Emily shifted her gaze to the young couple she'd spied through the conservatory window taking a romantic stroll, hand-in-hand, in the gardens.

Clarissa followed her gaze.

'When they come in, I'll ask Tarek if wouldn't mind giving an interview before they leave.'

❖

Freya glanced at her watch and looked at Tarek. 'We should go.'

Gerald and Wendy had just joined them in the hall. Wendy gave Freya a hug. Emily looked over at Clarissa, who winked at her before she rushed up the stairs with her notepad. Emily smiled. She knew what she was up to. Clarissa was returning to her room to write her article. Tarek had agreed to the interview. She'd got her inside scoop, her exclusive and that meant, to Emily's relief, that Clarissa had quickly lost interest in her family affairs and had decided to return to Cambridge to cover the opening of the exhibition. She wasn't the only one. They'd all decided to be there. Emily and Clarissa would travel to Cambridge tomorrow morning with her parents.

Emily turned to Freya. 'You will come back though, won't you, to stay at the guest house?'

Freya hugged Emily. 'You know I will.'

Emily watched Freya pick up her bags and leave with Tarek. She heard her say, 'I hope the car doesn't break down again on the way home.'

Jeffrey said, 'You can follow us home, just in case.'

'Good idea.'

Alice and Jeffrey paused at the front door. 'Bye Wendy, Gerald, Emily.'

'Bye!' they all said in unison. Gerald and Wendy stepped outside, waving. The sound of car doors clunking shut and car engines switching on heralded the guests' departure.

Emily lingered by the front door with her mum and dad as the cars turned out of the driveway. 'Do you think we might go to Egypt one day?'

Wendy said, 'It's always been on my bucket list.'

Gerald grinned. 'Mine too.'

'What's on your bucket lists?' Joss asked, overhearing their conversation as he walked up behind them.

Emily smiled. 'Egypt. We all want to go someday.'

'Well, you can count me in,' said Joss, draping an arm affectionately around Emily's shoulders.

This time Wendy didn't object to Joss's display of affection towards her daughter – not at all. In fact, Wendy and Gerald had talked to Joss, and they'd had a little heart-to-heart about their future and the future of the guest house. There was just one thing – they had yet to tell Emily their plans, and it all hinged on Emily's agreement.

Epilogue

'So, I hear there have been big changes at the guest house in the last six months,' commented Jeffrey, fixing his gaze on Emily across the glass-topped wicker table. He wiped his sweaty brow with a handkerchief, reached for the glass in front of him and downed the refreshing lemonade with ice and a slice. He'd known the weather would be hot, but he hadn't thought it would be *this* hot.

He caught Alice giving him a look. He'd apologised for complaining about the heat when they were changing in their cabin after dinner. He'd thought that with the sun setting, it would cool down. He'd been wrong.

Emily shifted her attention from the stunning views of the River Nile to Jeffrey, who was sitting across from her. Joss sat holding her hand and gave it an affectionate squeeze as she said, 'Yes, the last six months have been crazy busy.'

'Indeed they have,' added Wendy, eyeing Gerald as he crossed the wooden deck with two tall glasses of something cool and bubbly. He looked very relaxed and quite dapper in his cream trouser suit. He'd taken off the matching waistcoat after dinner and rolled up his white shirt sleeves to sit out on the deck.

He wore a Panama hat that he'd bought in a souk on one of the excursions in Cairo.

Wendy smiled. Retirement suited him. It suited Wendy too. They were no longer woken by the sound of an alarm clock set to go off at an unearthly hour for Gerald to get up and go out on the trawler. There were no more early rises for Wendy either, unless she chose them. There were no beds to make or breakfasts to prepare or new arrivals at the guest house – unless they were of the four-legged variety.

Alice said, 'You must tell us all about it. I heard that the guest house has changed hands …' She smiled knowingly. They had all kept in touch. That was how they had come to be on this cruise together.

It had taken a quite bit of planning to book the holiday when they were all free to go, but eventually everything had come together, and here they all were – even Omar. He'd been on cruises down the Nile countless times before, but everyone had insisted that he still joined them. He was having an after-dinner nap in his cabin.

Freya and Tarek were taking a romantic walk around the deck. Alice waved at them again. The boat was quite small, intimate even, with just a few cabins and not many tourists aboard. The pair had already completed several circuits, passing their table a few times. They were now heading upstairs to the top deck to watch the sunset together. Alice knew that something rather special would happen up there as the sun set over the Nile.

A wisp of a smile crossed her face when she recalled what Tarek had confided before they'd set sail. He had shown her the engagement ring.

Alice thoughts turned to Theo. He was the only one who

hadn't been able to make the trip. He was at a book signing in London.

Freya and Tarek weren't the only ones who'd moved on with their lives. Theo had moved out of their house in Cambridge. They were so sad to see him go, but his writing career had taken off; he'd got an advance for his first book to be published. And he'd met his soulmate; he'd fallen in love with an editor at the publishing house that had given him his big break.

Jeffrey was beside himself with pride that Theo's book was being published. Theo had used his advance wisely, putting a sizeable chunk of it down as a deposit on a new home. He had purchased a modern penthouse apartment, just outside Cambridge, which didn't surprise anyone – least of all Alice and Freya. He never had liked old houses.

When Alice told Freya, she didn't sense any regrets – just relief that Theo was moving on with his life. Alice had been especially pleased when Theo had had an interview with a magazine and cited Jeffrey as the person who'd taught him all there was to know about writing, had been his inspiration, and had encouraged him to finish his book. He was, in Theo's words, a truly great teacher and deserving of high praise.

At first, Alice hadn't been best pleased when she'd found out the title he'd eventually settled on for the book – *The Secret of the Guest House*. Thankfully his book was entirely a work of fiction. The book was a dark thriller about the disappearance of a child.

Alice sipped her cool drink and thought about the book, and about Freya. In interviews, Theo had been asked time and again where the idea for his bestselling book had come from. Everybody seated around the table knew the answer to that question. However, Theo had never revealed any details about

The Guest House at Shingle Cove or what he knew had happened there. But it had given him a spark of an idea which had led to a different story altogether than the real story of her family and her good friends seated around this table. Perhaps that was what all great writers did, she mused.

She smiled at the thought that after the Nile cruise they were all looking forward to a stopover in Alexandria before they flew home – Alice especially. She was dying to visit the famous library and museum and pay a visit to Alexandria University where Freya, Tarek and Omar worked.

She was so proud of her daughter. Freya had completed her PhD and, to everyone's surprise, had taken up a teaching position at the university; she was now a lecturer in the Department of Archaeology and doing what she'd always dreamed of, joining Tarek on archaeological digs in Egypt.

Alice turned her attention to Emily. Freya wasn't the only one leading her dream life. She knew a lot had changed for Emily in the last six months. She was dying for Emily to tell her all about it. Alice put her glass down. 'So, Emily, I want to hear all about the guest house.' She glanced at Wendy. 'I hear there's been some big changes.'

'Well, do you remember Joss had an idea that I should start my own veterinary practice? And you showed me that vacant shop in Cobblers Yard, in Aldeburgh, that used to be the arts and crafts store?'

Alice smiled. Of course she remembered. It was a lovely afternoon she'd spent with Emily visiting Cobblers Yard and the café at The Two Magpies Bakery for lunch. Although Emily had returned to take another look at the shop to consider changing the premises to a veterinary practice, that hadn't materialised.

What had, was something that had taken Alice by surprise – but in a good way.

Emily smiled, recalling her parents and Joss sitting down to share with her the plan for the guest house, and to explain what that would mean for all of them – most especially for her and Joss – if she agreed.

Emily was so pleased she had agreed. The plan for the guest house had changed all their lives.

'You know it's still a guest house – kind of.'

Alice grinned. 'I heard.'

'But it's got a different clientele now.'

'More discerning?'

'More … furry.' She grinned.

So did Alice, sharing the joke. Wendy had told her that Joss had bought them out, enabling them to retire to a cottage that had come on the market in Shingle Street, and that Joss and Emily intended to keep it running as a guest house, but that the new guests would be a little…. different.

'I've renamed it The Four Paws Guest House.'

'That's very apt,' Alice replied.

'I thought so too.'

'Me too,' said Gerald, guffawing.

'I think it's very clever of you to combine your veterinary practice with a hotel for cats and dogs.'

'And parrots, if need be.'

Everyone up the table laughed at the reference to Alice's parrot, Percy.

'It was Joss's idea for me to run my veterinary practice from the house and offer a boarding kennel service too. There's the room, and it's just the best, working from a home I love, and doing what I adore all day. Emily smiled. 'I run my veterinary practice from there, but first and foremost I always wanted it to be a family home. My clients enjoy coming to my home with the ambience and gardens instead of the cold, clinical, modern practices they were used to.'

'And if they are going away on holiday, they can also leave their pets with you to board.' Alice knew that was one of the reasons organising this get-together in Egypt hadn't been easy. Emily couldn't just leave her business without considerable planning. She had animals in her care most of the time. But she had recently taken on another newly qualified vet, as her practice had expanded rapidly. Word had soon spread of her expertise as a vet, and the rather unique setting in a beautiful house overlooking the sea.

Alice imagined that the news spreading was in no small part down to Emily's best friend, Clarissa, and the wonderful article she'd written in the local paper about the old guest house and its new owner. Despite Joss buying out the guest house, he had put it all in Emily's name, even though they were soon to be married.

Emily smiled and nodded. 'Yes, it made perfect sense to combine the two, working as a vet and running a hotel for pets. It's a lot of work, but I enjoy it. And of course I have Joss to help me, when he's not at his practice.'

'That's right,' interjected Jeffrey. 'I heard about that. You took on the shop in Cobblers Yard.'

Joss nodded. 'I did. I run a drop-in centre offering legal advice pro bono and helping start-ups. It's also where I manage some of my charitable investments in overseas projects.'

All of them at the table were now aware of Joss's background. He had been a self-made millionaire by the time he was thirty, running his own legal firm in the city, his wealth accrued from his involvement in private equity firms whose sole purpose was to buy out companies, asset-strip them, and then sell them on for a huge profit, mostly to the detriment of the company. Some employees who'd worked for those companies had lost their livelihoods in their wake.

Nobody sitting around the table really understood the ins and outs of the work he used to do, apart from some snippets they'd heard about the guilt Joss felt over the lives destroyed, financially and otherwise, by firms like his who helped broker these deals.

Now, Joss was a changed man. He had his work, helping others set up businesses and investing in them to help them grow and prosper, and he had Emily and their beautiful home at Shingle Cove. Emily smiled affectionately at Joss, her engagement ring glinting in the last rays of sunshine as the sun set over the Nile.

'And how are things in Cambridge?' Emily asked.

Alice exchanged a glance with Jeffrey as Freya and Tarek walked over to their table. Jeffrey got up to fetch two more chairs and everyone made room for them at the table.

Freya had overheard the question. She looked at her mum and dad. 'Shall I tell them, or shall you guys?'

Alice smiled at her daughter. 'Why don't you?'

Alice's hand closed around Jeffrey's. When he'd heard Omar was coming on the Nile cruise too, he hadn't been happy. Alice realised it was the first argument they'd had since they returned to Cambridge. She'd called him a silly man for thinking there was anything other than friendship between them. But she knew why he felt that way. After all, she had practically spent a week with

Omar, at the guest house, getting to know him all over again.

However, what Jeffrey had come round to understand was that although in that week a great friendship was borne out of their shared passion for Egypt, that was all it would ever be. Unlike Freya and Tarek, who had found love, that was not where Alice and Omar's relationship would ever lead. For there was more to love than a shared passion for something. It was something indefinable, that special something Omar had found with Fatima and Alice had found with Jeffrey.

And besides, she hadn't just spent that week with Omar. She had taken wonderful walks along the cove with Hester. She had bought some paints and a canvas and had sat in her room for hours, trying to paint, often interrupted by Marley stealing her little paint tubes and her brushes. She'd even woken up one morning and found a paint paw print on her canvas. Alice could laugh about it now, but she was so happy to return home and step into another room, away from Marley's mischievous antics.

Thinking of home, her life hadn't changed so radically in the last six months like Wendy and Gerald's had. They hadn't sold their house in Cambridge. Their buyers had been disappointed by their decision to withdraw from the sale of their house, but they'd both come to the realisation that selling their home wasn't going to change anything. Freya had a life now in Egypt, and they strongly suspected she would not return to Cambridge. As for them, they had decided to focus on themselves and their relationship before they made any big decisions – like moving house.

They'd been to marriage counselling, just like they'd promised Freya, and had been open and honest about what had happened in their marriage. Although they'd both had to work through each other's infidelity, and the fallout that was Jeffrey's child, Freya, there was a huge upside to going through all that together. It was the realisation that they were, and always had been, very deeply in love. It was just that they'd never put aside the baggage they'd carried around in their marriage – baggage about children and the family they thought they were meant to have – and it had stopped them from figuring that out. But they had now, and it had made their lives all the richer for knowing they were, like Tarek and Freya, Emily and Joss, and Gerald and Wendy, meant to be together. For Alice, and for Jeffrey, it was the best feeling in the world; knowing that despite all the mistakes and setbacks in life, their marriage wasn't one of them.

Freya smiled affectionately at her parents. 'Mum formally adopted me.'

Alice reached across the table and squeezed her hand. Freya's biological mother had given her permission years ago for Alice to legally become Freya's mother, but there had been a complication – Jeffrey. For this to happen, he would have had to tell Alice the truth. But now that was all behind them, and to Alice's utmost relief, Freya had agreed.

Although it seemed so silly now that Freya was an adult, it meant so much to her, and Freya, that she was now officially her mother. It was what Alice had dreamed of for so many years. Nothing could make her happier – or so she thought.

'Shall I tell them the other piece of news?' Freya asked.

Alice smiled affectionately at her daughter. 'Oh go on, then. I know you're dying to.'

Freya grinned as she looked around the table. 'Mum and Dad renewed their wedding vows at the church where they got married in Cambridge.'

'Oh, that's wonderful news.' Emily clapped her hands. 'It's like a double celebration!'

'Congratulations,' Wendy said, smiling happily.

Gerald held up his hand, ushering over a waiter. 'I think this calls for a round of drinks.'

'We're thinking of this trip as our second honeymoon,' said Jeffrey, smiling at his wife.

'That we are,' agreed Alice. 'And soon, someone else will be on their honeymoon too.' Alice wasn't looking at Emily, whom she knew was engaged, but at Freya.

Freya held up her ring. She had tears in her eyes. 'Tarek proposed.'

Everyone was suddenly talking at once, congratulating the happy couple. Alice, Emily and Wendy each gave Freya a hug.

As they all took their seats, and the waiter appeared with a large bottle of bubbly in an ice bucket, Freya turned to Emily. 'I know this might be a lot to ask, so I won't be offended if it's just not possible but …' she took a breath, 'I was thinking of having our honeymoon at the guest house. I know it's not a guest house anymore, but I wondered if you could make an exception, just for us?'

'Oh, my goodness. Of course you can. You can come and stay any time. There's plenty of spare bedrooms. In fact, I've got a brilliant idea. Have you considered having your wedding reception there? I don't know where you intend to marry. I bet you don't either right now, but you must consider it. There's plenty of room, and wouldn't it be a great excuse for us all to get together again at Shingle Cove? I'd love that.'

'So would I,' Freya agreed.

Gerald poured everyone around the table a glass of bubbly,

just as Omar appeared, looking a little bleary-eyed. 'Omar,' Gerald called out. 'Come and join us.'

Omar walked over. Gerald thrust a glass of champagne in his hand.

Omar looked at the glass and cast a glance at everyone around the table. 'Are we celebrating something?'

'Oh, yes,' said Jeffrey. He stood up. 'Let's raise a glass.'

They all raised their glasses.

He turned to his daughter and Tarek. 'To the happy couple. Congratulations on your engagement, sweetheart.'

Freya said, 'Thank you, Dad.'

Omar grinned and slapped his son on the back.

'To the happy couple,' everyone said in unison.

They sat for a moment watching the sun disappear beyond the horizon, bathing the banks of the Nile in a beautiful, almost otherworldly golden glow before the sun set, casting the banks in shadow.

Freya said, 'I would like to make another toast.'

Everyone turned to look at her.

'Let's raise a glass to the place that will always have, for me, a special place in my heart, and I'm sure for everyone seated around this table.'

They all raised their glasses

'To The Guest House at Shingle Cove.'

'The Guest House!' they said, smiling at one another, each thinking of their own lives and how friendships, loves, and futures had been forged in that little guest house on the beautiful Suffolk Coast.

And how one day soon, they would all meet up there again, to toast the start of another young couple's journey and the future they would forge for their own children, perhaps in Cambridge, perhaps here in Egypt.

Who knew where life would take them? But as they all sat around the table, sharing this special moment together, Alice knew that although there were no certainties in life, right here, right now, everything was quite all right, and that was the most joyous thing any of them could ever hope for.

The Sunrise Coast Series continues in

The Houseboat by the Quay

Paperback and Kindle eBook available from Amazon

If you enjoyed *The Guest House at Shingle Cove* I would be grateful if you would leave a review on Amazon.

For further details about the author and her novels visit the author's website.

www.elisedarcy.com

Printed in Dunstable, United Kingdom

80328698R00224